Georgia Raye is the pseudonym for two New York-based editors who have travelled in the glamorous fast-paced circles about which they write. *Born Rich* is the first novel they have written together.

D0681915

GEORGIA RAYE

Born Rich

This edition published 1995 for
Parrallel Books
Units 13–17 Avonbridge Industrial Estate
Atlantic Road
Avonmouth, Bristol BS11 9QD
by Diamond Books
77–85 Fulham Palace Road
Hammersmith, London W6 8JB

Published by Diamond Books 1993, 1994

Copyright © Deborah Chiel and George Coleman 1989

The Authors assert the moral right
to be identified as the authors of this work

ISBN 0 261 66696 7

Set in Times
Printed in Great Britain

All rights reserved. No part of this publication may be
reproduced, stored in a retrieval system, or transmitted,
in any form, or by any means, electronic, mechanical,
photocopying, recording or otherwise, without the prior
permission of the publishers.

CONDITIONS OF SALE
This book is sold subject to the condition
that it shall not, by way of trade or otherwise,
be lent, re-sold, hired out or otherwise circulated
without the publisher's prior consent in any form of
binding or cover other than that in which it is
published and without a similar condition
including this condition being imposed
on the subsequent purchaser.

For
Mark Lameier
and
Henry Dreher

Acknowledgments

The author wishes to thank the following people who so generously gave their advice, inspiration, and support:

Millin Andrews, Daniel Chiel, Kinneret Chiel, Carrie Coleman, Diane Dreher, Henry Dreher, Barbara Gess, John Hawkins, David Hooks, Shelley Katsh, Mark Lameier, Irving Lazar, Robert Lombardo, Esq., Thomas Ward Miller, Geoffrey Paul, Michael Renn, Linda Shacknow, Judith Stern, Louis Wolfe, and all the others, both on Seventh Avenue and off, who told perhaps more than they should have and who wish to remain anonymous.

Prologue

New York, 1984

Tonight was a true star-studded media event. Everyone had turned out for Countess Dani diPortanova.

The crème de la crème of New York society – the glitterati from the charity ball circuit, the movers and shakers from Central Park West to Madison Avenue, the Old Guard and the Eurotrash from the Upper East Side, SoHo, and Tribeca – had all put on their party clothes for the evening's festivities at the Fashion Institute of Technology.

Oscar de la Renta was there, the sand still clinging to his toes, just back from his home in the Dominican Republic. Calvin, of course, looking trim and handsome. Ralph Lauren and his wife, Rickie. Diane Von Furstenberg, shorn of her shoulder-length waves for the first time in years, sporting a freshly bobbed haircut. Norma Kamali, flipping through her 'life book' as she walked past the photographers' strobes, double-checking what party she'd be attending afterward. Halston, as usual dressed from head to toe in black.

Escorted by a famous photographer, an equally famous model mugged impishly for the reporters and photographers from *People*, the New York *Post*, the *Daily News*, *Interview*, *Women's Wear Daily*, and the tabloids. Close behind was Andy Warhol and, behind him, the leaders of the fashion industry, writers, and retailers, as well as a flurry of titled Europeans.

Everyone who tracked fashion trends and the A list

crowd was also present on this gloriously balmy September evening for the 42nd Annual Coty American Fashion Critics Awards. Usually the Coty was a lesser happening, rated a faint second-best by the men and women whose names filled the gossip columns. Indeed, the event had never before pulled down a full court press. But tonight the Beautiful People and the chroniclers were all in attendance.

Tonight Countess Dani diPortanova was being inducted into the Coty Hall of Fame. The thirty-year-old fashion *wunderkind* was being awarded the ultimate fashion accolade. The woman who had turned the industry upside down was proving once again that she was no ordinary star designer.

And she was late, of course.

She was as famous for being late as she was for her dresses and cosmetics, her fragrances and accessories, her headline-grabbing lifestyle, and her audacious ads. 'Born three weeks late,' Liz Smith had once written about her in the *Daily News*. 'Dani diPortanova has been in a hurry to catch up ever since.'

Years before, racing from one social event to another as she and Nino were taking New York's social circuit by storm, she had perfected the art of applying makeup in a moving limousine. Now, as her chauffeur maneuvered her midnight blue stretch through traffic, heading down Seventh Avenue through Chelsea, Dani effortlessly highlighted her enormous gray eyes with Hot Flash Dusky Gray eye shadow and moistened her full, pouty lips with Hot Flash Fatally Red lip gloss. Both were licensed, of course, by Countess Dani, Inc. She adjusted the top of her red silk strapless evening gown just as the limousine eased up to the curb of the driveway.

The paparazzi were waiting.

Her driver jumped out to get the back door open before

8

Dani did. She was never one to wait for the usual formalities, but on nights like this, she let him do his job.

Dani stepped out of the car into a blaze of lights.

'Hey, Dani!' shouted a photographer. 'Where's your main man?'

Dani blushed and grinned happily. 'I thought you fellows knew where *everyone* was. I'm not about to reveal any secrets.'

Cameras clicking, the paparazzi focused for the umpteenth time on Countess Dani diPortanova's tall, slender figure. The reporters scribbled notes about her show-stopping outfit, which showed off to perfection her broad shoulders, full breasts, and long legs.

She was about to step forward when she was suddenly hit by the reality of concrete beneath her feet.

'Damn,' she said under her breath. Her shoes were in the limo.

She wondered whether she should retrieve the shoes from the car. *What the hell*, she thought with a giggle. She had an award to accept.

Halting at the top of the steps, she turned, extended a foot, and winked at the crowd of press people, autograph hounds, and fans. 'I guess they'll have to introduce me as the barefoot contessa,' she quipped.

Their appreciative laughter followed her all the way into the building.

Forty-five blocks uptown at Central Park West and Seventy-second Street, on the fifth floor of the Dakota – an apartment building known for its fortresslike facade, its round-the-clock security guards, and its electronic gates – someone carefully extracted a Fichet key identical to the one that lay at the bottom of Dani's purse. The intruder, whose admiration for Dani diPortanova was heavily colored by other, darker emotions, unlocked the carved mahogany door to Dani's apartment and stepped inside, listening for sounds.

The intruder checked the living room, then walked back across the foyer where a Rodin dancer, cast especially for Dani by the Musée Rodin, posed gracefully atop a gleaming glass table. Moving stealthily past the dining room, the first-floor library, and the guest rooms, the trespasser reached the dimly lit master bedroom, then stopped in the doorway and listened for signs of life in the apartment.

The bedroom spoke of Dani diPortanova. Her specially created Hot Flash perfume lingered in the air. A pair of underpants, a bra, and a thick purple Countess Dani terry-cloth robe were strewn messily across her four-poster bed.

The light shone in her dressing room. Open doors revealed row upon double-tiered row of dresses, gowns, pants, shirts, hats, and jackets, hundreds of pairs of shoes and boots. A jumbo crayon box of colors, the clothes were a fabric artist's fantasy. Without question, this was the closet of a woman who loved to dress and who knew fashion. Created fashion.

On her antique dressing table a blue porcelain lamp cast a narrow beam of light on a diamond necklace, earrings, and bracelet, a matched set, the value of which was roughly equivalent to the price of a small Manhattan town house. One couldn't help but gasp in admiration and wonder at the intricate settings of the fifteen-carat diamonds. One couldn't help but pick up and touch the glittering stones, hold them up to the light, as the intruder did now, speculating on their value. This unwanted guest stared into the luminous depths at the heart of the prism.

Diamonds, warm and glowing. But so cold at the core.

* * *

As soon as the awards ceremony was over, Dani made a fast exit, blowing one last kiss at the army of well-wishers and journalists. Then she ducked into her car and sank back against the dark blue velvet seat.

'Where to, Dani?' asked Joe.

'Straight home, Joe.'

'No party? I thought this was your big night.'

Dani uncorked a chilled bottle of champagne from the bar, poured herself a glass, and raised it to the rearview mirror. 'Who says I can't celebrate at home, Joe?'

'Just as long as you're not alone.' Joe winked.

'Don't worry,' Dani said with a laugh. 'I won't be.'

'Then I guess I gotta drive like hell,' he said, stepping on the accelerator. He was glad she had someone to celebrate with. Not that she was one of those women who always had to have a guy at her side. Dani knew how to make her own way in the world. But she hadn't looked this happy in a long, long time.

During his years of service, Joe had seen a hell of a lot from his driver's seat, but her new man seemed like a good guy, pretty regular. He'd even phoned Joe to remind him to put champagne in the limo bar.

The car sped uptown on Sixth Avenue and cut through a moonlit Central Park. Dani made a quick stop at the Häagen-Dazs store on Columbus and Seventy-fifth, where she loaded up on ice cream, and moments later the limo pulled up in front of the imposing nineteenth-century building that had been her home for almost thirteen years.

''Night, Joe,' Dani said, grabbing the bag of ice cream. 'See you in the morning.'

The Dakota guard helped her out of the limo. Dani didn't notice his perplexed look. 'Hello, Harry. Oh, the gentleman I put on the guest list earlier in the week will

11

be coming by soon. Don't bother calling. Just send him right up.'

'Will . . . do,' Harry said slowly, trying to hide his surprise at seeing her. Hadn't she . . . No, of course not. He really had to lay off the booze on his breaks.

Dani passed through the dark courtyard and rode the mahogany-paneled elevator up to her apartment in the building's northwest section. Unlocking the door, she thought, *What a night*. And the best was yet to come.

The ice cream went into the freezer. The servants were off tonight, so they would have the whole place to themselves. She debated whether to take a bath now or wait until he arrived. A shower, she decided. Then later they could drink champagne in the Jacuzzi.

Even before she walked into the bedroom, she was pulling her gown up over her head. Her mind was filled with thoughts of her lover. He was everything she had hoped to find. Marvelous in bed. Tender, passionate, imaginative, uninhibited. Alert to her slightest signal or response. Her breath quickened at the thought of him lying next to her in bed.

She laughed aloud in the silent room as she contemplated herself in the full-length oak-framed mirror that stood beside her dresser. Might as well admit it. She was horny. Her nipples stood erect and turned dark pink at the mere thought of his hands and lips.

Closing her eyes, she lightly stroked her upper thighs.

'Hurry up . . . please,' she whispered, almost moaning with awakened desire.

Touching her fingers to her lips, she opened her eyes.

And saw, reflected in the mirror, a figure standing in the shadowy darkness behind her. A figure slowly drawing closer, moving into the circle of light cast by the lamp.

Frozen with fear, Dani forced herself to catch her

breath, to swallow the scream in her throat. For an instant she thought she might be imagining this apparition.

The figure took a step forward.

And then Dani saw the gun.

Part One

Part One

Chapter One

New York, 1974

Dani stepped down from the curb, delicately placed two fingers between her lips, and produced a whistle shrill enough to rate a thumbs-up from the cop at the gridlocked corner of Fifty-second Street and Fifth Avenue.

'Hey, lady!' the cop yelled. 'I like your style.'

Lots of people liked Dani diPortanova's style – the mostly admiring columnists who reported on her antics and outfits, their gossip-hungry readers who followed her breathless comings and goings, and her friends who applauded her trend-setting spontaneity.

Eunice Lieberman, however, frowned noticeably as Dani waved to the cop and threw him a kiss for pointing a cab in their direction. But they were already late, and if Dani had left it to her stepmother, they'd still be standing here tomorrow.

She'd been late getting to her ten o'clock ballet class and late meeting Eunice for lunch. Now, unless the cabbie screeching to a halt in front of them drove like a genius, she and Eunice would be late for the show. Though she had yet to attend a fashion show that actually began when it was supposed to, Dani knew that the best seats went quickly. Especially when the show was Mr Reggie's.

The inside of the cab felt like a furnace on this unseasonably hot October day. There was no air-conditioning, and the breeze from the windows, stuck halfway down, provided little relief.

'Thirty-eighth and Seventh, please – and hurry.' She

17

leaned back against the sticky vinyl and fanned her face with her hand.

'Relax,' Eunice said, composed as ever in her beige linen short-sleeved suit. 'We're not going to a fire.'

'You never know with Mr Reggie. I wouldn't put it past him to have an engine company spraying down the models as part of the show. Actually,' Dani said, laughing and pushing her hair off the back of her neck, 'that sounds pretty good to me right now.'

'Something wrong?' As usual, Eunice's voice was slightly hoarse from smoking too many cigarettes.

'Just hot, that's all.'

Since returning to New York as the wife of Count Nino diPortanova, Dani had tried to make friends with the woman who had taken her mother's place in Maurice Lieberman's heart and home. But even now, when Dani easily fit into a size six and was one of society's darlings, she only had to spend a couple of hours with Eunice to feel fat, awkward, and seventeen again. Perhaps it was because she knew how Maurice doted on his much younger second wife. Eunice was small and delicate. Her hair never frizzed, she never blushed, and she could always be counted on to say the right thing.

Dani wondered what Eunice would say if she confided to her that despite her fairy-tale life, she felt an itch of dissatisfaction that she couldn't cure.

Maybe it was just a case of post-anniversary blues. She still hadn't quite recovered from the anniversary party a week ago. It was expected of Countess Danielle diPortanova that she throw the most fun, most original social event of the season. She'd spent months planning every detail with the caterer, the florist, her interior designer.

In keeping with the traditional third-anniversary motif, the theme had been leather. 'Whip yourself into a frenzy,' read the message on the gold-stamped black suede invitations that had gone out to one hundred fifty of their closest friends.

Traffic had snarled to a standstill on Central Park West between Sixty-fifth and Seventy-second streets as one limo after another deposited the leather-clad invitees in front of the Dakota. Many of the guests had worn Ultrasuede, Halston's newly created fabric. Others had opted for tight leather pants and skirts that advertised every curve and bulge.

One group showed up with a woman in a fierce-looking leather mask that covered everything but her eyes and lips. Tugging at the leash around her neck, they explained that they'd picked her up at a downtown pierside S&M club and thought she'd fit right in. She certainly had.

The wife of one of New York's most conservative politicians had gotten stoned on Thai stick and belly danced naked on the Louis XVI marble table in the foyer.

'Do it, baby, do it,' urged a conceptual artist, snapping pictures of her with his Asahi Pentax.

The diPortanovas' upstairs neighbor, a world-famous rock star, brought his former drummer and their instruments and jammed until dawn.

The next day a syndicated columnist proclaimed that 'It was the party of the year by the couple of the year.'

More like the mess of a lifetime, Dani thought when she woke up at dusk and surveyed the wreckage in her bedroom.

The cleaning crew had managed to tidy up most of the other rooms, and her housekeeper reported that the damage had been minimal. Only a few items had been stolen: a pair of Baccarat candlesticks, some Limoges china, a couple of sterling silver picture frames, and a porcelain lamp. How the lamp had been smuggled out, Dani couldn't begin to imagine.

Nothing priceless, nothing irreplaceable.

Just like our lives, Dani had thought with a pang of melancholy.

Their party had kicked off the New York season, and she and Nino were booked through Christmas. Another fall of openings, benefits, late-night parties, all-night dancing, and endless champagne. Like chocolate truffles, such a diet was sinfully rich and delicious, but lacking in nourishment.

During the summer, bored with basking in the Mediterranean sun, she had picked up a sketch pad for the first time in years and tried her hand at designing a new wardrobe. Everything she'd seen in the stores and in the couturier houses had left her decidedly unimpressed.

She liked her sketches well enough and had decided to turn a few of the designs into reality. Long ago she'd dreamed of being a dress designer. Fate – and lack of confidence – had intervened. But to create a few of her own pieces, as a lark . . . She thought, *What the hell?*

Besides, she needed a project, something to keep her busy, so she wouldn't start brooding about Nino. She loved him dearly and never doubted his love for her. But Nino was in a hurry to do everything but grow up. He drove too fast, spent too much money, and probably drank more than he should. His wild, high-spirited ways made headlines, and the tabloids ate it all up.

His father, the aristocratic, conservative Roberto diPortanova, who had made such a fuss about his son marrying a Jew, was no doubt having regular fits. There were days like today when Dani didn't know whether she owed Roberto any thanks for finally consenting to the marriage. She and Nino had been out for five nights in a row, and last night they'd been scheduled to attend yet another party. They hardly knew the hostess, but Nino wanted action.

Too tired to argue, Dani had suggested he go by himself. Off he'd gone – and he still hadn't made it home when she'd left for her dance class this morning. That was typically Nino. Irrepressible. Inexhaustible. Irresponsible. The very reasons she had fallen madly in love with him.

The blond dancer moaned with pleasure under Nino diPortanova's sure touch.

'Such a body,' Nino murmured. 'Such a beautiful, beautiful body.'

He stroked the dancer's nipples, then continued downward across the taut belly to play with the thicket of silky blond hair.

'Turn over. Show me your gorgeous ass,' he whispered.

Slowly he caressed the downy hair, barely visible between the dancer's perfectly shaped cheeks, and groaned with contentment.

He had never before slept with a dancer. So lean and sinewy, without an ounce of fat, yet soft and sensuous. And limber enough to assume the most acrobatic positions.

Even by Nino's jaded standards, it had been quite a party. He'd bumped into a former girlfriend from the University of Grenoble. She'd since married an international financier who was obsessed with mergers. Unfortunately, she'd confided to Nino, not mergers with her.

'Nino, *mon chéri*, how I remember the good old days,' she'd said with a sigh and boldly licked her lips with her long, pointy tongue.

Nino remembered her tongue with much fondness. It still promised greatness. But the rest of her hadn't aged as well.

Someone had handed him an aquavit and introduced him to one of the most stunning blonds he'd seen this side of the Riviera. He'd said yes to a second round, and the rest of the night was a blank, including how he'd ended up in this apartment. From the looks of the view beyond the bedroom window, he was somewhere on the Upper West Side. Probably not too far from his own apartment.

A thought flashed through the recesses of his sleep-deprived, alcohol-soaked brain. He'd promised Dani he would be home by sunrise.

Ah . . . but the blond – sweet, ripe, and lovely – demanded his attention.

Nino believed that fucking was an art. Like an artist, he had perfected his strokes, his texture, and the quality of the canvases on which he worked as the years passed. Now, as his cock began to harden again (he'd come twice since dawn), he buried his head of black curls between the blond's legs and breathed in the scent of sex.

'Please,' the dancer pleaded, 'don't make me wait. Fuck me now.'

'Oh, yes,' Nino agreed. He prided himself on his timing. He eased himself inside, then withdrew slightly, gently teasing the welcoming muscles, so hot and ready for him. 'You want me, *si*?' he asked tenderly.

'Yes! Yes, I want you!'

Nino entered again, this time more forcefully. As his movements quickened, the dancer matched his rhythm. Perspiration lubricated their bodies. They rocked in a wave of frenzy that climaxed in a moment of violent explosion.

Finally sated, they collapsed in each other's arms, gasping for breath. Nino closed his eyes and stroked the dancer's beautifully sculpted body.

'Sant'archangelo!' Nino sighed. 'You have such a marvelous cock!'

Reggie Bolt hurried down the corridor toward the dressing room, chewing on what was left of his usually well-manicured fingernails. He was a total wreck. He couldn't eat. Sleep was out of the question. He couldn't get it up no matter who fell into his bed.

It had been six years since his first show had proven him to be one of the top talents of American fashion. Ever since, the industry and fashion critics had been singing his praises. But twice a year, every year, Reggie lived in terror that *this* show would be different. This time there would be no applause, no standing ovations, no big orders. This time there would be scornful laughter, hisses, and boos. The critics would walk out, signifying that Reggie Bolt, America's hottest designer, was washed up. A has-been.

But if the price he had to pay for success was loss of sleep, food, and sex, so be it. Not that he hadn't already paid his dues, of course. He had, and then some . . .

During the two years Reggie Bolt had put in at the Parsons School of Design, he commuted from the dingy apartment in Queens that he shared with his mother, aunt, and older sister. He had earned money for his tuition by working as a gofer on Seventh Avenue. And he had longed for Paris, the city where style had originated.

One night at a leather bar in Greenwich Village, Reggie met a man who begged him to come home with him and whip his bare buttocks. Reggie had been asked to perform much weirder acts since coming out of the closet. They fell into a relationship. Reggie was the master to his friend's slave.

'Take me to Paris,' Reggie eventually told his lover, stroking the man's hugely erect penis with the tip of his whip.

'Of course, whatever you want,' the man said, his brown eyes filling with tears of pleasure.

In Paris, Reggie discovered that the secret of success was equal parts inspiration, perspiration, and a willingness to take advantage of any opportunity. He got as much as he could from the leather freak, then found someone else who wanted to play games with an American kid who was open to new experiences.

When he returned to New York eight years later, he'd lost his Queens accent and his last name. He'd learned to wear silk dressing robes and cravats. He'd been re-created as 'Mr Reggie.' But his sense of style was distinctly American.

Armed with letters of recommendation from two of Paris's most renowned couturiers, he got himself hired by Claire McCardell, the legendary American sportswear designer. She liked his portfolio and appreciated his willingness to turn his back on European conventions now that he had returned to American soil. Seven years after that he had his own line, complete with a small showroom, a pair of assistants, several skilled seamstresses, and a credit line large enough to cover salaries, overhead, and the wildly expensive fabrics that became his trademark.

'The rest is history,' he was fond of saying to his adoring entourage who vied for invitations to his dinner parties, where the conversation was as rich as the food.

Pre-show, of course, there were no dinner parties. Mr Reggie dined alone late at night on Valium, Maalox, and strong shots of one-hundred-proof vodka. Telephone at his elbow, he sought constant reassurance from his friends that he would not fail, that the show would be a success, and that the magic formula would still work for him.

Not until the agonizing moment when the first model sauntered down the runway and the audience responded with a comforting burst of applause could Mr Reggie relax. Then he was himself again – America's favorite designer, the name every fashion-conscious woman coveted and paid dearly to have in her closet.

Through the years Mr Reggie had told interviewers that he wasn't interested in dressing women who were over-weight and underfunded. His remarks always drew letters of protest, but Mr Reggie couldn't have cared less. His clothes were cut for that fortunate group of wealthy women who were naturally thin or had the time and money to maintain themselves properly.

Now he paused in the doorway of the dressing room and surveyed his domain. Tall, thin, half-naked girls with sharp cheekbones stood about, chewing gum and gossiping. Assistants and dressers swarmed around them like worker bees, making last-minute adjustments.

Reggie's second-in-command, Magee Sullivan, was on her knees in the middle of the room, redoing the hem on one of the models.

'Hurry up and get out there,' she said, spitting straight pins. 'They're about to begin.'

'I can't,' Reggie whimpered. 'My stomach's all in knots. I feel like I'm going to throw up.'

'Not in here, you don't,' Magee said unsympathetically.

Reggie stepped into the bathroom and checked his face. Just as he'd suspected – a mask of horror. He fished his cosmetic case out of his leather clutch bag and with four quick brush strokes, added a lustrous glow of blush to his silicone-perfected cheekbones. A dab of lip gloss, a light flick of the hairbrush through his professionally high-lighted brown hair, a spritz of Binaca, and he was ready to face the firing squad.

He presented himself to Magee for inspection.

'You'll knock 'em dead,' she promised, dragging him to his appointed vantage point backstage. 'Break a leg, baby.'

Through his nervous haze, Reggie picked out familiar faces on the other side of the curtain – the key members of the fashion press corps, the department store and

25

specialty shop buyers who were his most faithful customers. Behind them was the usual assortment of moneyed patrons. A Belgian princess who was rumored to be sleeping with her maid. Two rows behind her, the princess's husband's mistress. And just behind her, seated next to her stepmother, Countess Dani diPortanova.

The stage manager tapped him on the shoulder. Reggie jumped three feet.

'We're ready to start, sir.'

The awful, sickening moment of truth.

The hard-driving rhythms of the Rolling Stones' hit, 'Jumpin' Jack Flash,' pounded out of the enormous speakers set in the four corners of the room. The curtain rose, the stage lights went bright. Reggie's first piece, a red silk evening gown that was split up the back and could have passed for a thousand-dollar-a-night whore's nightgown, was paraded insolently across the stage.

The audience gasped with surprise and delight. Reggie let out a long sigh of relief. He'd been right to lead off with the Stones and the whore's nightie. He could tell already. He was safe for another season.

The show would be a smash.

Nino vigorously toweled himself off and gazed at the young man lying spent on the bed. It had been ages since he'd slept with a boy. Actually, not since that night in Rome three years earlier. He chuckled quietly. Papa would kill him if he knew. But Papa would never find out. Nor would anyone else, for that matter. He would make a grateful exit and – *finito*!

Of course, he would send his traditional case of champagne, along with his standard note: 'Always, Nino.' Though they all knew it wouldn't be for always, if ever again. After all, he *was* a married man.

One last kiss good-bye. 'Such lovely lips. Like rose

petals,' he told the dancer, forgetting that he had used those precise words with his wife a scant twenty-four hours earlier.

The dancer placed his fingers to his lips. 'Do you really think so? Nobody's ever told me that before. Cock and ass, yes. But lips . . .'

Nino grinned happily as the boy rattled on. Another conquest. He could never understand why people had trouble getting laid.

'Will you come see me dance? I'd love to get together again,' the boy said hopefully as he zipped himself into a pair of faded bell-bottoms that looked as if they'd been sprayed on.

Nino eyed the boy's crotch and almost said yes. But it was impossible. He loved his wife and respected the institution of marriage, no matter whom he slept with. Boys were too dangerous.

'I travel a lot,' he said vaguely. 'It would be very difficult.'

'Well, why don't we at least have lunch?' said the dancer. 'I'm starving. Aren't you?'

'That,' said Nino, pulling the boy up to meet his lips, 'is a wonderful idea.'

The magic never failed to overtake Dani the moment a model strutted down the runway, pausing to swirl and mug, to show off a brand-new design. She had adored the drama of the shows ever since she'd gone to them as a little girl with her mother. Back then she had stared wide-eyed with excitement as the tall, beautiful women in brightly colored clothes made of the soft, pretty fabrics danced – or so it seemed – to the wonderful music.

When she was ten, her parents had taken her to Disneyland, but she'd been disappointed. The phony cartoon characters, even Snow White and Cinderella,

27

were no match for her memories of the Pauline Trigère fashion show she'd seen earlier in the spring.

'You can get lots of satisfaction,' the emcee now promised, 'in this silk-cashmere fantasy. The strapless, wrapped bodice, the full-cut pants, the oversize scarf, will see you through a season's worth of elegant evenings . . .'

Dani tuned out the rest of the commentary to concentrate on the details – the cleverly cut top that looked as if at any moment it might slip and reveal the model's almost nonexistent breasts; the accessory scarf, also smartly cut to complement rather than overwhelm; the subtleties that only a very few would notice and applaud out of respect for the artist who had conceived them.

A discomforting sense of déjà vu pricked her. The pants were different – fuller, less clingy – but the other two pieces were uncannily similar to an outfit she herself had designed. A design that had finally pleased even her critical eye after months of having nothing to show for her hours of sketching but a pile of crumpled papers beneath her desk.

Eunice whispered, 'What's wrong? You have the most dreadful expression on your face.'

'Eunice, what do you think of that outfit?'

As if on cue, the model turned toward them, winked, and twirled the plum-colored silk scarf in a slow, mocking striptease.

'Interesting. Not for me, of course, but I certainly could see it on you. Reggie's very talented, isn't he?'

Dani nodded miserably. At least she'd learned one lesson today. She had a far better design sense than she gave herself credit for.

Maybe she even had talent.

Who would believe it?

Certainly not her father . . .

* * *

Danielle Lieberman was that rare breed, a native New York. She was born on a muggy day in June 1954 to Maurice and Sophie Lieberman. The Liebermans were European immigrants, the sole survivors of two upper-class Viennese Jewish families who had been wiped out in Hitler's death camps. Danielle was the long-awaited answer to Sophie's prayers, a miraculous blessing from God, who had kept her safe in hiding during the war while Maurice had fought with the French Resistance.

Maurice had had his heart set on a boy to carry on the Lieberman name, but he swallowed his disappointment at the news of a daughter. As long as Sophie was happy . . . His wife had never been quite herself after the difficult war years, but little Dani's arrival seemed to restore some of her spirit.

Growing up, Dani saw little of her father. Papa was an art dealer who sold lots of paintings like the ones that hung in their Upper West Side apartment, across the street from Central Park, where she loved to play on the swings and the slide. He was usually too busy with his meetings and phone calls to play with Dani. Sometimes it seemed as if he only noticed her when he caught her doing something bad or dumb. Dani often wished he could love her as much as he loved Mama.

The Lieberman Gallery across Central Park on Madison Avenue and Sixty-fourth Street felt like a shrine, a museum created by Maurice. Whenever Mama took her to visit, Dani tried to memorize the paintings and remember the names of the artists who had painted them, in case Papa asked her which was her favorite. But he never asked. More often, he got angry.

Like the time he caught her fingering the brush strokes on one of the oil paintings. 'How many times have I told you not to touch the paintings, dammit?' he shouted. 'Will you never learn?'

29

She held in her tears. At least she had Mama and Helene, her French nanny, to love her and teach her things. And not just about art, either. Sophie told wonderful stories about her life with Papa in Vienna and Paris before the war, about the rich people who came to buy clothes at the House of Balenciaga where Mama had been an assistant to an assistant, while Papa had sold paintings from his gallery in Montparnasse.

In the afternoons after school, while Mama sewed on her machine and talked to her and Helene baked lovely cakes and cookies and tarts, the apartment would feel cozy and full of laughter.

But Dani never stopped trying to please her father. Knowing how much value Papa placed on hard work and excellence, she slaved over her schoolwork, hoping he would notice. And he did. In fifth grade, having already mastered the basics of basting and hemming and following a pattern, Dani was given a special project by her sewing teacher to create an outfit of her own design. She spent weeks working on the skirt and matching top, refusing help from her mother or Helene, agonizing over every detail. It had to be absolutely perfect. Finally she was satisfied. She put on the two pieces to model for her parents.

'Beautiful, darling,' said her mother. 'Don't you think so, Maurice?'

'Yes, it's quite pretty. Is it the right length?'

'I think so, Papa.'

'Of course it is, Maurice,' Sophie said sharply.

'Ah, well, very good, then,' said Maurice, not really paying attention.

Dani was halfway out of the library when she overheard her father say to the young artist who'd been invited for dinner, 'She'll never be a Coco Chanel, will she?'

In tenth grade Dani decided she would be an artist. Next to her mother, art was what her father loved best. Fantasies

30

filled her head of critical and financial success, of being represented by her father and the Lieberman Gallery. Her art teacher encouraged her, and she progressed from pastels and watercolors to oils. By the end of the year, she had earned an A and the confidence to show her work to her father.

'Very interesting,' Maurice said, studying her oil painting of the New York skyline, which she had had framed with money saved from her allowance. 'Not bad, but I wouldn't plan to make a career out of this.'

Soon after, Dani had neither the time nor the heart to dream of ways to win Maurice's approval. Her mother was very ill. At first the doctors blamed the symptoms on Sophie's chronic depression. Too late they discovered that the real cause of her headaches, amnesia, and sudden fits of anger was a malignant brain tumor. Sophie underwent brain surgery, followed by harrowing rounds of chemotherapy.

When she died, Dani's world all but disintegrated. Maurice had promised Sophie he would pay more attention to their daughter, but his pain was too great. He retreated further into his work. Dani turned to Helene for comfort, and Helene lavished her with love and consoled her with food. Maurice sat at the head of the dinner table and watched with disgust as his daughter stuffed herself with Helene's excellent French cooking. He bit his tongue, determined to keep his promise to Sophie to be less critical of Dani.

The first five pounds didn't make much difference. But then Dani gained another five, and then ten, and then twenty more. The streets of New York became her food paradise, an oasis of coffee shops and restaurants, one-slice pizza parlors, hot dog stands, and gourmet shops, which she took in through haunted, hungry eyes. She blew up to 165 pounds and dreaded going to school where the boys taunted her with cruel nicknames: porker, thunder thighs, beached whale, watermelon tits.

Periodically she vowed to lose weight, but none of the diets had any lasting effect. Helene thought she was beautiful and kept offering her second helpings of the heavily sauced roasts and rich pastries. Maurice was no help. He was preoccupied with his gallery – and with Eunice Collins, his longtime assistant, whom he'd begun to date barely six months after Sophie's death.

Maurice even invited Eunice to dinner with them to celebrate Dani's graduation from high school. Dani's misery was complete. She hated everyone – her father, Eunice, who was gorgeous and skinny, and most of all herself. When Eunice suggested a famous weight-loss clinic in Switzerland, Dani wanted to wring her scrawny neck.

Later she decided the clinic was worth a try. Anything to get away from home.

It was a decision that was to change her life.

No ordinary fat farm, the Clinique Etiole was famous throughout Europe for producing results. Located in the mountains north of Lausanne, it was luxuriously housed in a nineteenth-century chalet that was decorated in baroque revival – all gold and marble and ornately framed portraits of long-deceased European royalty. The facilities included an Olympic-size swimming pool, tennis courts, stables, and a fully equipped gym. The skimpy meals were in direct contrast to the elegant decor. And the exercise regimen rivaled boot-camp training.

From the moment she checked in, Dani knew she had made a dreadful mistake. She worried that they were starving her to death, was horrified by the rigorous daily schedule, and lived in terror of the every-other-day weigh-ins. Worst of all was her roommate, a beautiful Austrian girl (Maurice would have been furious if he'd known about the girl's nationality) named Monika von Reich who hardly gave her a second glance. But Monika was not only stuck-up, she was also thin!

What the hell was she doing at the clinic? Dani wondered.

She quickly discovered that Monika was also running away from a horrible parent. Monika's mother was the wicked witch of Salzburg. Their common bond helped bridge the gap between the two girls and made them friends. Beneath Monika's protective icy mask was a warm and mischievous soul mate who traded her encyclopedic knowledge of sex for Dani's store of information about clothes, New York, and American rock music. Monika especially loved soul – the Temptations, Al Green, James Brown, and Marvin Gaye.

'"Let's Get It On"?' said Dani.

'Oooh, my favorite,' Monika squealed.

One night, desperate for real food, Dani 'borrowed' her weight counselor's Renault and took off with Monika for Lausanne. They did a tour of the city's cafés, where they stuffed themselves with tortes, strudels, and chocolate fondue. Long after midnight, they headed back to the clinic.

The steep mountain road was dark and foggy. The abundant quantities of sugar-laden food had made them sleepy. Dani lost the struggle to keep her eyes open and woke up too late. The Renault went flying into a ditch, then smashed sideways into a tree. Miraculously, neither of the girls suffered more than a few bruises and scrapes. They trudged up the hill, sneaked back into the clinic without getting caught, and gratefully sank into their beds.

Just as they were nodding off, Monika whispered, 'Liebchen, we were very lucky, ja?'

'Ja,' said Dani, 'very lucky.'

The accident was a turning point. Together they decided to beat the clinic at its own game. They got up earlier, pushed themselves harder, ran extra miles, did double reps of the exercises.

Six weeks later, Dani had lost almost forty pounds. Her prominent cheekbones, formerly hidden under mounds of flesh, underscored her large gray almond-shaped eyes. She had bones she had forgotten, curves she had never seen, and skin that glowed with health. A beautiful young woman had emerged from the cocoon of fat. For the first time in her life, she felt good about herself.

But she wasn't ready to go home yet. Thanks to Monika's credit cards and the von Reich family's unlimited line of credit, she didn't have to.

'Come to Cannes,' Monika said. 'Mother thinks I need a tan. She won't be there, so she won't care if I bring a friend.'

They spent the mornings on the sun deck of the von Reich yacht, hit the boutiques on the rue d'Antibes and the Croisette in the afternoons, and danced all night at the discos. The men whistled and nipped at their heels like dogs chasing bitches in heat.

One afternoon they stepped off the sidewalk on rue Meynadier into the speeding path of a shiny red Lamborghini Miura. Their startled screams were as loud as the screech of the Lamborghini's brakes.

A young man leapt out of the car.

'Madonna mia! Scusi, I'm so sorry,' he exclaimed. 'I didn't even see you. The sun was in my eyes. State bene? Are you girls all right?'

The girls looked at each other and laughed shakily. 'Liebchen, we were very lucky, ja?'

'Ja, but do you get the feeling that cars don't like us?'

They laughed again, their high spirits restored.

'Permit me to introduce myself,' said the driver. 'Nino diPortanova.'

Dani had never met such an extraordinary-looking man.

34

Nino diPortanova had a perfect deep tan, black curly hair, chocolate brown eyes, and a dazzling white smile. And he was older – at least twenty-four or twenty-five. She couldn't stop staring at him, and then she blushed and couldn't meet his gaze.

His eyes were as warm and inviting as the first soft day of spring.

'Permit me to buy you both a drink. Please, I insist, as an apology. I probably was driving too fast. My weakness. I love cars almost as much as I love . . . well,' he said with a grin and shrugged his broad shoulders like a hapless child, 'you can imagine.'

By dinnertime, Dani was in love.

They stayed on in Cannes. While Monika amused herself at the discos and casinos, Dani and Nino drank champagne on the yacht, danced barefoot in the moonlight, made love to the sound of the waves lapping gently against the side of the boat. Her happiness was complete.

Three weeks later, when Nino proposed, she didn't hesitate to say yes for a second. Together they flew to Asolo, the town in northern Italy where the diPortanovas summered, to tell Nino's family. But instead of making her welcome, Nino's father, Roberto, let it be known that he would never consent to the match. Nino vowed he would force his father to reconsider, but gently suggested that in the meantime Dani return to New York.

Maurice, too, was opposed to the marriage. Dani was too young to get married, he ranted. Never mind that Sophie had been exactly Dani's age when she married Maurice. He wanted her to go to college, date men who were more suitable. More appropriate. Jewish, was what he meant.

But Dani ignored his objections when Roberto diPortanova inexplicably changed his mind and telephoned Dani to give her his blessing. In October 1971, she and

Nino were married in one of Italy's most publicized weddings. Dani's white silk gown, custom-designed for her by Givenchy, had a twenty-foot train. The matching Alexandre headdress made of silk lilies of the valley looked like a sunburst around her head. Their six-month honeymoon began in Rome and ended in Ireland, and they covered much of Europe in between.

They decided to make New York their home base because, they agreed, it was unlikely they'd ever get bored there. Nino bought a fifteen-room duplex apartment at the Dakota on Central Park West, not far from where Dani had grown up. They hired one of America's preeminent interior designers to create a space that was both livable and elegant.

The first two years of their marriage was a blur of parties and openings and balls. Lots of champagne and very little sleep. The young diPortanovas were the darlings of the social set. They dined at the trendiest restaurants, danced at the best clubs, and rushed from gallery openings to benefit fund-raisers to cultural events.

In the beginning, they were good copy, but still too new to warrant more than peripheral coverage. Ink was something they had to earn.

As the press got to know them, the coverage became more frequent.

And then, inevitably, they were elevated to celebrity status. A day didn't pass that someone somewhere wasn't writing something about the diPortanovas.

One night Maurice came to dinner. 'Dani,' he said approvingly, 'you've finally discovered your true talent – marriage.'

But now, here before Dani on the runway, was evidence that she could dream up a design that was all but identical to one created by the acknowledged king of American fashion. Perhaps Maurice had been wrong. Perhaps she did, in fact, have a talent for something other than marriage . . .

The show continued. Sportswear. Day wear. Styles that were sexy and provocative. A couple of military-style pants suits, Mr Reggie's nod to the war raging in southeast Asia.

'Go for broke this year,' urged the emcee.

A burst of applause all but drowned out the blaring disco version of the theme from *2001: A Space Odyssey*, as the model unbuttoned the jacket of an audacious linen suit to reveal a black silk-and-satin quilted bra. The linen skirt hugged her narrow hips and ended just above her knees.

'With a flick of the jacket button,' the emcee purred, 'a suit that takes you from a romantic lunch for two to an evening out on the town.'

Another Mr Reggie triumph.

The applause crescendoed.

The outfit was the kind of masterful design for which Mr Reggie was famous. A daring one-of-a-kind suit that said, 'I'm a lady, but you can fuck me.'

Dani was the only member of the audience who didn't applaud. She sat gaping with astonishment, stunned by the certainty that this was *not* a Mr Reggie original. She recognized the cut of the lapels, the cunning dip of the waist just below the belly button, the way the bra was ever so discreetly hidden when the jacket was buttoned. She knew this suit intimately, down to its smallest detail.

She had designed it.

The model vamped past them and turned at the end of the runway.

'Breathtaking,' murmured a woman to Dani's right. 'A stunning creation.'

Dani's creation. But she had no way to prove it.

37

Chapter Two

London

On her way downstairs to the dining room, Monika Bletz scooped the mail off the antique ormolu Regency table in the foyer of her suite at the Connaught Hotel. She paused a moment to check herself in the gilt-framed mirror. As always, her jade green eyes were perfectly outlined with extremely expensive shadow and liner. Her pale-as-porcelain cheeks were highlighted with equally expensive custom-blended powder. Her long hair hung like a silky buttercup-yellow curtain around her face, softening features that otherwise could have been read as arrogant.

Her new dress, a ballerina-length silk vision in precisely the same shade of green as her eyes, had been designed for her by Yves Saint Laurent. She wore it to perfection on her trim model-like figure.

She looked sensational and she knew it. She also knew that her appearance was utterly wasted.

'Are you dining alone this evening, Mrs Bletz?' the maître d' asked sympathetically.

Ja, she thought and nodded. *As usual*.

Her husband was tied up at yet another meeting with some Arabs who wanted to invade yet another country and needed Helmut's assistance for whatever it was they used these days to kill people. That was Helmut – always thinking of mankind and how to destroy it. The heir to Bletz Chemicals, he was a business autotron whose greatest pleasure came from maneuvering his way through a complicated business deal and coming out on top.

38

Dining alone in the hotel was not much fun, but it beat joining Helmut and the boys. They were impeccably mannered, but behind Helmut's back, one of them would invariably pinch her ass and whisper that he wanted to screw her blond pussy. Which was a better offer than anything Helmut had ever proposed.

Monika ordered a chateaubriand and the most expensive red wine on the Connaught's wine list. Then she turned her attention to her mail. Dani's familiar scrawl jumped out at her from a thick monogrammed envelope. Tearing it open, she hungrily read Dani's letter.

'London? For a month???' she had written.

Typical Dani. No time to bother with a convenient greeting. Straight to whatever was on her mind.

'Couldn't you have managed to spare just a week in New York for your best friend's anniversary bash?'

Business meetings in Rome had conflicted with Dani's party. Correction. Helmut had conflicted with Dani's party.

'You are needed at my side,' he had reminded her. 'It is essential that I am recognized not only as an outstanding businessman but also as an outstanding husband.'

'Darling,' Dani wrote, 'can you believe we've both been married almost *three years*?! Come visit! Bring Helmut, and we can celebrate our anniversaries together. Nino can persuade even Helmut to unbutton his tie and boogie. Call me anytime day or night and tell me when you're coming. Love and a million hugs, Dani.'

Fat chance, thought Monika. Helmut was allergic to fun. In his vocabulary, 'passion' was a dirty word. Sex was what a man did to relieve the tension of a successfully negotiated business deal.

And, for Monika, each new deal for Bletz Chemicals meant yet another hideous session in bed with Helmut. They had the drill down pat. Helmut would straddle

Monika's face and have her suck him until he got hard. Then he would shove his cock inside her and come almost instantly. Sometimes it wasn't even that interesting.

Monika had two weapons to relieve her frustration. She made good use of the ivory-handled vibrator she'd bought at a back-street sex shop behind the Kempinski Hotel in Berlin. And she spent huge sums of Helmut's money shopping. Helmut didn't care. It was good for his image. His bank accounts, he said proudly, were limitless.

Monika's most recent purchases included a full-length natural golden sable coat encrusted with semiprecious stones ($150,000); a set of diamond and emerald earrings and a matching necklace from Chaumet in Paris ($650,000); a new Audemars Piguet sport watch ($45,000); a strand of pearls from Mikimoto ($200,000); and a ruby and diamond dinner ring especially designed for her by Bulgari ($240,000).

Monika stared at her long, slender fingers. The other day she had spotted a beautiful 21.75-carat emerald-cut diamond at Graff's on Brompton Road. The price tag was a cool million. Perhaps she'd stop by there tomorrow and buy it.

Or perhaps she'd have a manicure instead. What difference did it make, as long as she managed to kill a few more long, lonely hours?

New York

Dani mumbled to Eunice, 'I have to get out of here,' and bolted out of Reggie's showroom. En route to her apartment, she tried to remember what she could have done with her sketches of the suit. She had a vague recollection of tucking them away on the day of her party in the midst of all the chaos. Once or twice since then she had rummaged through her desk drawers, racking her brains trying to figure out where she might have stashed them.

She had never suspected for even a second that someone might have taken them.

Admittedly, it was a ridiculous idea. Preposterous. Reggie Bolt was a star. She was nothing more than a wealthy socialite who wore his clothes and gave great parties.

Parties to which Reggie Bolt was invited.

'Thanks for coming,' she remembered saying to him, kissing his cheek. 'Sorry you have to leave so early.'

'Thank *you*,' he'd trilled.

Now she understood just how much he had to thank her for.

The son of a bitch had stolen her design, called it his own, and flaunted it under her nose. But why? Certainly he wasn't that desperate . . . or was she that good?

'*Merde, merde, merde!*' she swore between gritted teeth.

After all these years, the French still came easily. 'In French, "shit" sounds less vulgar,' Sophie used to say.

Suddenly she remembered something else Sophie used to say: 'Don't get mad. Get even.'

Get ready, Reggie, Dani thought. *Because goddammit, you bastard, I'm going to get even*.

Elvira, the diPortanovas' housekeeper, pointed Nino toward the bedroom.

'Shhh,' he said, grinning at her conspiratorially.

'She's been in there since she got home,' whispered Elvira. 'Told me to take messages. Rather in a snit, I think.'

Nino nodded and gave himself credit for thinking to buy Dani the diamond and emerald Breguet watch she'd admired. He had, after all, stayed out all night, and it was

41

wise to come prepared. This might be the rare occasion when his charm wasn't sufficient to ease him out of a tight spot. Rare because, after his trust fund, charm was his greatest asset. Few people, male or female, were able to resist the potent blend of Nino's winning personality and his angelic smile.

He didn't have to turn on his charm. He exuded it . . .

Nino's family had been winegrowers since the days of the Renaissance in the province of Veneto. His father was a descendant of the doge of Venice. His mother was a Montecchio, more familiar to readers of Shakespeare as Montague, Romeo's Anglicized surname.

Like the fine wines their vineyards produced, the family's fortune had increased in value through the centuries. In the twentieth century, Nino's grandfather had thought to go into the business of manufacturing electric heaters to warm castles and condos all across Europe. The diPortanovas' worth had quadrupled. Besides the estate on Lake Garda where Nino was born and christened Gianni Fioretti, his family also owned a sixteenth-century summer villa in Asolo, as well as homes in Venice, Paris, and London.

The long-awaited male and heir, Nino was adored and spoiled from the moment of his birth by his mother and three older sisters. He had inherited his mother's dimples and sunny disposition, his father's dark brown eyes, jet black hair, and trim build.

Unfortunately, he hadn't inherited his father's self-discipline and sense of responsibility.

Briefly he attended the University of Bologna, where he majored in women . . .

'. . . but I know the child isn't mine,' he had insisted to his father.

'That's what you said the last time!' his father had bellowed, writing out a settlement check . . .

. . . and cars.

On his eighteenth birthday, he picked out a suitable gift for himself.

'How much is the Maserati?' he asked the dealer.

'Nineteen million lire.'

'I'll take it. Send the bill to my father.'

Nino dreamed someday of racing in the Grand Prix, Turin, Le Mans, Buenos Aires. His heroes were Andrea di Adamici, Reine Wisell, and Jackie Stewart. Nothing, not even a beautiful woman or champagne, was more intoxicating than the thrill of high speed in a sleek car on the open road.

The summer he met Dani he was living near Antibes, where the mountain roads were an endless challenge to his racing skills. He'd been on his way to a picnic date with a French actress when he all but ran over his future wife.

Immediately he liked the way her plum-colored minidress showed off her ass and long legs and her perfect full breasts. He liked how her thick, wavy hair tumbled halfway down her back. He even liked her hot pink patent leather flats and the bright yellow cotton sweater she wore flung over one shoulder. This was a girl who deserved to be noticed, and knew it.

He promptly forgot about the French actress and spent the rest of the afternoon staring at Dani across a café table . . . falling in love with her gray eyes, the sprinkling of freckles on her nose, her slender hands, which she clapped like a child listening to his tales of mischief. And her lips – ah, her full, pouty lips that glistened with a hint of pale pink gloss.

She told him this was her first visit to the Riviera. He was astounded. She was meant for Cannes and Saint Tropez, he said. And she had never heard of the diPortanova family, though her pretty blond friend recognized the name and gave him a knowing wink.

Nino was totally smitten by the sweet American girl, so beautiful and sexy, but so innocent and unpretentious. He'd never met anyone like her.

But the biggest and best surprise was yet to come. Dani Lieberman was a virgin. He was her first lover. In a moment of rare introspection, Nino realized that for all his playboy ways, at heart he was an old-fashioned romantic. And here was the girl whose long list of impressive virtues met his high standards.

He couldn't wait to introduce her to his parents and sisters.

The diPortanova women welcomed the pretty American girl with nervous smiles. This time Nino really had gone too far. They shuddered at the thought of his father's reaction when he met the girl Nino was calling his fiancée.

'Your surname is German,' noted Roberto diPortanova when Nino introduced him to Dani.

'My family was originally from Vienna,' Dani replied.

'Yes? And why did they leave?'

'They wanted to live in Paris . . . and then the war, and all of that. You know, because we're Jewish.'

'I see,' said Roberto. 'How interesting. Please, let me pour you a glass of the Bardolino. It's from our estate. Gianni, may I see you a moment in my study?'

Quietly he shut the door and turned to face his errant son.

'A Jew?' he asked icily. 'In all the centuries of our family's history, there's never been a drop of Jewish blood to sully our lineage. Gianni, you are nothing but a spoiled playboy! I'll put up with no more of your foolishness. I've waited far too long for you to take your place in the business and marry someone whose background does credit to the diPortanova name. Someone who will provide us with an heir. How dare you even think of marrying an immigrant Jew?'

Nino pleaded, protested, threatened.

'Save your breath,' Roberto growled.

'And what if I marry her without your approval?' Nino asked boldly.

Roberto's eyes bored into his son's. 'If you do, I will cut you out of my will and see that you get not one more lira from me or anyone else in the family.'

'Papa!'

'Finito!'

Dani and Nino parted tearfully at Leonardo da Vinci Airport. Afterward, Nino went on a tear in Rome, trying to blot out his sorrow by drinking and screwing.

And then, inexplicably, Roberto changed his mind and permitted him to marry his beloved Dani. The wedding, held in Asolo at Roberto's insistence, was laced with a dash of scandal. Dani's father sent his regrets that 'he could not attend.' Roberto declined to give the wedding toast. But Nino couldn't have cared less. He walked down the aisle feeling as if all the gods were smiling down upon him.

Now Nino found Dani seated cross-legged on their bed amid a jumble of sheets, sketch pads, and colored pens and pencils. Her cheeks and nose were smudged with charcoal pencil, her hair was a tangle of waves, and still she looked beautiful.

'*Cara,*' he cooed.

'Nino, you bastard! I suppose I should be grateful you're still alive. Where the hell have you been? Passed out on somebody's floor?' She looked at him sharply. 'Or was it somebody's bed?'

'I brought you a present,' he said, bending to kiss her.

She twisted out of his reach. 'Screw your present. And screw you! Where've you been all afternoon when I needed to talk to you?'

He discreetly checked his watch. Six o'clock. He'd had

no idea it was so late. 'I'm sorry. You must have worried,' he said contritely.

'Worried? Why the hell should I be worried? Just because for all I knew you could have been dead . . .'

'Well, perhaps some champagne, then, to celebrate that I'm still alive.'

Her voice shrilled with anger. 'Forget the damn champagne and for once in your life be serious. I've been robbed, goddammit!'

'Robbed? Of what, your purse? Did you call the police? Dani, are you all right?' he asked, genuinely concerned.

'Yes, I'm fine – as if you really cared.'

Even unhappy, she was lovely. Dark, fierce, and passionate. He felt the stirrings of an erection.

'Of course I care. You're the most important person in the world to me. Tell me who robbed you,' he said heatedly. 'If he hurt you in any way, I swear by the Virgin Mary I'll kill the bastard.'

Dani laughed shortly. 'Nice of you to offer, but Mr Reggie doesn't play by the rules. I'm sure he doesn't fight clean, either.'

'Mr Reggie?' Nino laughed. 'Your designer friend?'

She burst into tears.

If there was one thing Nino diPortanova couldn't bear, it was the sight of a woman he loved crying. He hated seeing Dani like this, so sad and angry. '*Cara*, I beg you, talk to me.'

Tears wet her long lashes and streamed down her cheeks.

He sat down next to her and folded her into his arms. He moved his hands beneath her shirt and lightly cupped her breasts.

'Don't you dare!' She pushed him away. 'Don't you ever think of anything but sex?'

'Yes, of course I do!' he defended himself, imagining

46

his fingers playing over her nipples until they stiffened into pale pink rosebuds. 'Now, please, I insist you tell me why you're so upset.'

Dani grabbed a tissue, blotted her eyes, and blew her nose. 'Not that I believe for one single second that this will mean anything to you, or that you could possibly understand how pissed off and upset I am, but . . .'

She began to talk, filling him in on her afternoon. The shock of discovering that Reggie Bolt had ripped off her designs. The frustration of realizing that, though she had underestimated her abilities, Reggie hadn't. Her rage that she couldn't prove the designs belonged to her.

'You should feel complimented, Dani. Getting ripped off by such a star. Take it as a signal that you have the talent. Now all you have to do is come up with other designs.'

'Screw that shit!' she snapped. 'That suit is *mine*! Besides,' she said dolefully, 'I'll never do anything as good. I tried all afternoon. Nothing worked.'

'You were upset. What did you expect?'

Dani frowned. Nino meant well, but he didn't get it. Reggie had stolen what was hers and presented it as his own, without so much as a nod or an acknowledgment to her. The fashion world was applauding him, and she was powerless, because Reggie was hot, and being hot meant being powerful.

Of course, as his long-valued customer, she could confront him and ask him for an explanation. But what good would it do her? He could probably perjure himself with one hand on the Bible and not even have the grace to blush.

It would be her word against his. On the society pages, hers was a name to be reckoned with, but that meant zilch on Seventh Avenue. Dani diPortanova, socialite, versus Reggie Bolt, star designer.

47

What a ballsy son of a bitch he was! He had to have known she would be at the show, had to have figured she would recognize her own design. She shook her head at his arrogance. She almost had to admire a guy with that much moxie.

Her only consolation was the knowledge that her father had been wrong, after all. She did indeed have talent. But the fact remained that Reggie Bolt had paraded her designs down the runway and called them his own. And *that* pissed the countess off royally.

Mr Reggie sailed into the Four Seasons, a portrait of triumph and glory. Whatever doubts he'd had earlier in the day about his new collection had long since evaporated. His renewed confidence showed in his regal posture and on his face. This was a glorious moment, second only to the finale of his show. People waved from every direction, showering him with congratulatory words and kisses.

'Bravo, Mr Reggie, bravo,' enthused a society grande dame who ruled the matrons of the East Side from her Fifth Avenue penthouse.

'So good to see you, Mr Reggie,' her companion twittered self-consciously. She had defected from his camp last year and hadn't attended this afternoon's show.

A distinguished-looking white-haired man who owned the controlling share of a New York sports team walked by. 'Hello, Reggie,' he said, stealthily slipping a card with his home phone number on it into Reggie's jacket pocket.

'Mr Reggie!' The maître d' hurried over to shake his hand. 'Congratulations! You're the talk of the town.'

Reggie modestly lowered his eyelashes. 'Thank you, thank you.'

'Your party is already seated. Follow me, if you please.'

Magee and his design staff were waiting for him at a

large round table in the middle of the Grill room. Magee stood up, champagne glass in hand, and proposed a toast. The glasses clinked lightly, music to his ears.

'Thank you, one and all,' he said, beaming. 'Now, if you'll excuse me, I need to freshen up.'

The mirror in the men's room told him he was looking every bit as wonderful as he was feeling. But a little pick-me-up never hurt. Out came his vial of coke and a tiny sterling silver spoon. Two quick snorts and Reggie was soaring.

Two more snorts and he was ready to take on Givenchy and Yves Saint Laurent.

The door to the bathroom swung open. In walked a blond young hunk. Their eyes met, and a pleasant recollection teased at the edges of Reggie's memory. He'd met this god before. Pretending to comb his hair, he stole glances at the boy, trying to place him.

Then it came back: Dani diPortanova's anniversary party.

Reggie had been smashed and he'd flirted shamelessly with the boy, who'd also had a lot to drink. Inhibitions completely shot to hell, he'd grabbed the boy by the hand, led him into one of the bedrooms, and locked the door. Then he had yanked down his pants and begged the boy to fuck him fast and hard.

But before anything could happen, Reggie had changed his mind about getting laid. For there before him, spread out on the top of the desk, was a set of sketches that made some of his new designs look like last year's markdowns. He'd pulled up his pants, murmured, 'Let's try it again another time,' and shoved the boy out of the room. Riffling through the rest of the sketches, he had picked out the two he liked best and stuffed them under his shirt.

One of them had been the crowning glory of his new collection. And no one could ever prove they weren't his.

Now he spritzed his mouth with Binaca and turned to the boy, who was zipping up his pants. 'Didn't I meet you at Dani diPortanova's party?'

The boy smiled coolly. 'Oh? Was that whose place it was? Yes. I seem to remember some unfinished business.'

'Well,' Reggie simpered, emboldened by the coke, 'here we are again. Why not seize the opportunity?'

'Actually,' the boy said, 'I don't usually give it away for free. But for you, tonight, I'd make an exception.'

He beckoned Reggie into the nearest stall and firmly latched the door.

Success was wonderful.

London

From close-range observation of her mother and her husband, Monika had learned that money carried weight. One simply had to be careful about how one threw it around. Securing an immediate appointment at the exclusive Neville Daniel Limited beauty salon, no matter how busy they might be, fell well within the limits of her prerogatives.

The day stretched ahead of her. Monika decided on the full treatment – manicure, pedicure, facial, and massage. The salon manager, sniffing the unmistakable scent of a wealthy, potentially loyal customer, smiled obsequiously and ushered Monika into the inner sanctum.

In the hushed darkness of the carpeted private room, her face wrapped in warm, lightly scented cloths to maximize the effects of the pore-cleansing herbal mask, Monika drifted in and out of sleep. She dreamed of Dani and the snow-peaked mountains of Switzerland and, just across the border, Austria.

Home . . .

Monika had grown up in the largest, most imposing schloss in Salzburg. Her father, Friedrich, had inherited from his father von Reich Industries, a huge industrial corporation, the cornerstone of which was a thriving munitions company. During World War II, the von Reichs had patriotically supplied the Nazis with close to 30 percent of their arms. Friedrich had banked much of the firm's profits in Switzerland, so that despite the defeat of the Fatherland, von Reich Industries marched into the postwar era stronger and more solvent than ever.

Karola, Monika's mother, had a blond, baby-faced prettiness that belied her intelligence and ambitions. After a well-planned campaign to win Friedrich's heart, she showed great courage and fortitude when her husband began to act . . . strange.

'She's driving him crazy,' whispered the servants.

Whatever the cause of Herr von Reich's erratic behavior, by Monika's fifth birthday her father was spending more time at an expensive Swiss mental hospital than he was at home. Karola was running von Reich Industries. She entrusted the upbringing of her two children, Monika and her older brother, Dieter, to the same nanny who had brought her up.

Karola unquestioningly agreed with Fräulein's disciplinary methods. After all, the beatings and deprivations she had endured as a child had done her no harm. Fräulein didn't hesitate to dole out punishments for the slightest show of misbehavior.

But Monika liked to tempt fate and take chances, because acting naughty was worth the risk. Playing 'Herr

51

Doktor' with Dieter after Fräulein *had turned off the nursery lights at night was being very naughty.*

'Herr Doktor,' *Monika would giggle, crawling into her brother's bed, 'I'm sick. I need an examination.'*

She knew that Fräulein *would spank her with a paddle if ever she got caught touching Dieter's peepee. Just as she would be punished if* Fräulein *found her peeking at the books in her mother's library. The ones with all the dirty pictures. A tiny shiver went through her. Scary was also exciting.*

Monika had a hard time making friends at the nearby private school she attended. The other girls mistook her shyness for snobbishness and made fun of her because she got picked up after school by a man in a uniform who drove a big car, rather than by a mother or a nanny. After a while, Monika stopped caring whether or not she had friends or did well in school. She knew her mother would probably tell Fräulein *to spank her and take away her privileges. But so what? Waiting to see what would happen was all part of the fun.*

Karola inspected her daughter's report card and looked at Fräulein *for an explanation.*

Fräulein *cleared her throat. 'Her teacher suggests that perhaps Monika is not . . . very bright.'*

Karola's nostrils flared. 'Perhaps her teacher is not very bright. Monika is my daughter. There is no reason she should have difficulty with her schoolwork. She will study at home with Dieter and his tutor. Soon we will see where the problem lies.'

Happy that her obstinacy had paid off, Monika plunged into her private lessons. She loved studying side by side with Dieter. Her brother never teased her, and he always had so many interesting stories, some of them naughty, some of them not. But by the time he went off to university in England, Monika was sick of being stuck at home and wanted adventure. For once Karola agreed and sent her off for two years to a finishing school near Zurich.

Though still a virgin, Monika knew more about sex than most girls her age. She had pored over Karola's collection of technical manuals, treatises on sex – normal and perverse – her trashy novels, and the illustrated editions of Oriental erotica.

When she turned sixteen, she lost her virginity to an English teacher whose idea of foreplay was to kiss her roughly and twist her nipples as if they were radio knobs. Her seduction was quickly the talk of the school; but instead of suffering from a tarnished reputation, Monika was branded a sophisticated woman of the world.

She enjoyed the attention and the friendships it brought her, but the experience left her suspicious of quick, groping sex. She diplomatically rebuffed her teacher's further advances and concentrated on her studies. Her goal was to follow Dieter to the London School of Economics, where she would learn the intricacies of business and finance, how to wheel and deal. She would make her own fortune and be free forever of Karola and the von Reich billions.

Home for Christmas of her senior year, she announced her decision to Karola.

Her mother had other plans for Monika's future.

They would be having a guest for dinner, Helmut Bletz, the head of a major chemical company in Zurich. Herr Bletz, Karola told Monika, was intelligent, hardworking, and wealthy. He was also in the market for a wife. Karola approved of him as suitor for Monika's hand. The merger between the two families was not only socially acceptable but also financially profitable for von Reich Industries.

Monika's protests went ignored by her mother, and Helmut was everything she had feared he would be. Predictably, he was a flabby-faced blond with pale blue eyes behind his wire-rimmed glasses, and a mouthful of gleaming white teeth. He held himself as stiffly as a ventriloquist's dummy. His shirt was so heavily starched it could have sliced cake.

He wooed her assiduously, though he was so proper that he never gave her more than a kiss on the hand or the cheek. Helmut thought Monika would make an excellent wife, but he told Karola, 'I would prefer that she lose ten pounds.'

'Absolutely,' Karola declared. 'I'll see to it. It's all that starchy food she's served at school.'

As appalled as she was by the prospect of marrying Helmut, Monika knew she had no choice. At least marriage would release her from Karola's clutches. And once she had escaped to her new home in Zurich, she would figure out how to ditch Helmut.

Her last summer of unwedded bliss was spent at the Clinique Etiole, followed by a last fling in Cannes with Dani. In October, coincidentally on the same day as Dani's wedding, Monika and Helmut were married in the Salzburg Cathedral. It was just as well Dani couldn't attend. Karola wouldn't hear of inviting Dani to the ceremony. She didn't care who the girl had trapped into marrying her. Dani Lieberman would never fit in at a von Reich affair.

On her wedding night, Monika discovered that Helmut's approach to lovemaking was as crude as her English teacher's had been. He undressed, carefully hung his clothes on the wooden valet, then joined her in bed.

'Get me hard,' he ordered her, shoving his penis into her mouth.

Moments later, he pushed apart her legs, shoved himself inside her without so much as touching her, and quickly came. Afterward, he didn't say a word, simply pulled out of her and wiped himself clean with a handful of tissues.

'Danke schön, Monika,' he said politely as he put on his

pajama bottoms. Within minutes he was fast asleep and snoring in the other bed.

Monika was stunned into silence with rage and frustration. She would teach that stupid idiot, she vowed as she silently fingered herself to an orgasm.

Little did she know that with a few minor variations, Helmut's wedding-night performance would set the pattern for the rest of their married days.

The Neville Daniel masseuse had strong, gentle fingers that kneaded Monika's anger-tightened muscles and worked out the knots of tension. Monika floated out of the massage room feeling relaxed . . . and very horny. Her body was aching with three years of pent-up frustration and lust. How she longed for a lover who knew how to make love! Who enjoyed the soft curves and moist hidden places of a woman's body.

Absentmindedly, she stared at the young Russian manicurist who was polishing her nails with Icy Pink Glaze – so appropriate for the wife of the Icicle Cock! The girl had dark hair and huge dark eyes that sparkled with intelligence.

'What's your name?' she asked her.

'Anya.' She smiled prettily.

'Is everything satisfactory?' asked the manager, coming by to check on Monika's progress. 'Can we offer you anything else today?'

'Actually, you can,' Monika said. She studied her long pink fingernails. 'I'd like to have my legs waxed. But I don't have time now. This afternoon would be better. At two o'clock. Send this girl to my room at the Connaught, *ja*? I'll be happy to pay extra for the personal service, of course.'

'Of course.' The manager bobbed her head happily.

Promptly at two o'clock Anya arrived with her waxing

paraphernalia. She shyly asked Monika to remove her skirt and panties and to make herself comfortable on the portable massage table provided by the hotel. She inspected Monika's legs. Holding up a flat, wooden spatula dripping with golden brown honey wax, she smiled at Monika. 'Relax, please. You have legs waxed before? I do very good job.'

Monika breathed deeply and gave herself up to the sensation of the warm wax being smoothed onto her legs, followed by the momentary flash of pain as the girl swiftly removed the hardened wax with strips of white linen. Anya worked quickly and efficiently. When she was finished, she held up a bottle of clear lotion.

'Will soothe you,' she said. 'It tingles. Very nice, you'll see.'

Her deft touch was better than nice.

Monika quivered with desire at Anya's ministrations. She almost cried out in disappointment when the girl stopped and wiped the lotion off her hands with a clean towel. But then, without a change of expression, Anya said, 'You want me to do something here, too, yes?' She gently fondled the triangle of Monika's pubic hair.

Monika's heart was pounding. '*Ja, ja*, I do,' she whispered.

The girl slowly bent down and kissed her between the legs, at first softly, then more passionately.

Monika groaned and thrust her hips forward to capture Anya's face. Moments later, she came in wrenching waves. After she caught her breath, she pulled Anya's face up to hers and hungrily kissed her.

The girl was both willing and imaginative.

They spent the rest of the afternoon in bed.

Monika's face was buried in Anya's crotch when she heard Helmut's cold, cold voice.

'Good afternoon,' he said. 'Please, Monika, introduce me to your friend.'

Then, for the first time since they had met, Monika saw her husband lose his iron control. 'Get the fuck out of here,' he snarled, and hurled Anya, still naked, into the hotel corridor.

Wrapped in the sheet that reeked of their lovemaking, Monika cowered on the bed.

'You slut!' Helmut raged. 'I've given you everything you could possibly want, but I see that my money and my cock aren't enough for you. You're nothing but a pig and a whore!'

He slapped her across the face, then slapped her again, so hard that her head snapped back. Then he dropped his trousers, yanked her beneath him, and shoved himself inside her, pounding at her until he came, mercifully quickly.

His icy calm regained, he cleaned himself off and cleared his throat. He said, 'I never want to see you again. You have precisely thirty minutes to clear out of here, you dyke.'

Numb with shock and pain, Monika knew only that she couldn't let herself cry or break down until she was safely away from Helmut. With shaky hands she grabbed her golden sable coat, threw a few things into a shoulder bag, thought to retrieve her jewels and a wad of cash from the hotel safe, and hailed a cab. She wept all the way to Heathrow.

'You all right, ma'am?' asked the cabbie.

'*Nein*,' she said, sobbing. 'I mean, *ja, ja*, I am.' Or she would be, now that her marriage was over. Even Karola would certainly understand that her husband was too cruel and abusive to live with.

From a phone booth at the airport she placed a call to Salzburg.

57

But Helmut had already spoken to Karola.

Her mother's voice was thin and distant. 'Monika,' she said, 'your husband has described how you betrayed him and our honor. Consider yourself no longer a member of the von Reich family. You cannot be my daughter. No daughter of mine would act in such a depraved, filthy manner.' She hung up without saying good-bye.

Monika sank down in the nearest chair and huddled inside her fur coat. If only she could call Dieter. But he was somewhere in Africa on a photography safari. He hadn't made any contact with his family in months except for a couple of postcards. She laughed weakly. Her brother would have appreciated the humor of her situation. Three years of terrible sex . . . three years of being a faithful wife . . . only to get caught in the act with another woman! So much for taking chances.

New York

Reggie Bolt had spared no expense in designing his offices and showroom in the style befitting his adopted persona of English country gentleman. He had called in an interior designer who owed him a favor and had told him to give the place a look that reeked of old money. The designer knew that the money was new and that Reggie hailed from Queens. Nevertheless, he obliged with paintings from the English School, specially designed upholstery fabrics, antique rugs, hardwood floors, and masses of English furniture.

The result was a genteel shabbiness that made the office of Mr Reggie, Inc., look more like a hundred-year-old Boston law firm than a couturier house. It was a haven high above the dirt and grime of Seventh Avenue. Reggie's customers felt so at home there that they often forgot how much money they were spending on his clothes. Friends bumped into friends, lunch and dinner dates were arranged, charity functions were planned, as all the while the ladies were being fitted for tens of thousands of dollars' worth of merchandise.

Today Reggie was feeling like a million dollars. The morning papers had proclaimed his new collection a triumph, and last night's trick had been the best sex he'd had in months. He was holding court with his friends by speakerphone and having his hair streaked when his secretary announced that Countess diPortanova wanted to see him.

The countess really should have called ahead to make an appointment. She was an important client, but not *that* important. After all, time was money, and his time was worth a *lot* of money. And its value was increasing daily. Nevertheless . . . He sighed. 'All right. Show the countess in.'

'Danielle!' he greeted her enthusiastically, not daring to rise. One false move and the streaking could be ruined. 'How are you? I still haven't recovered from that marvelous party.'

'We need to talk, Reggie,' Dani said tersely. 'I have something very serious to discuss with you. I want to do it in private.'

Reggie rolled his eyes upward in the direction of the stylist and said, 'He's French. Doesn't speak a word of English. What's the matter? You look upset.'

'Reggie, I was at your show yesterday. I liked some of the designs very much. Especially the bra-suit combination. Maybe the reason I liked it so much, Reggie, was because I designed it. As well as at least one other that you passed off as your own. You stole them from my desk during the party, didn't you?' She glared at him, daring him to contradict her.

Reggie smiled a thin, tight smile. 'Dani, dear heart, what are you saying? Are you feeling unwell? Certainly you're not implying that I or anyone on my staff would ever need to use someone else's designs . . . especially the designs of someone who isn't even a designer.' He laughed out loud.

She had expected him to deny her charge, but still, the gall of the man! 'Listen, you son of a bitch, those are *my* designs! You stole them, and you know it.'

Reggie looked at her evenly. He said, 'My dear, those outfits have been in this house for six months. Really, you flatter yourself to think you could ever create a design I would covet. The only design you ever executed that was worth anything was the one that landed you that titled wop.'

'You pretentious queen!' Dani shouted, past caring what she was saying. 'You call yourself a designer, but you're nothing but a thief! And you'd better believe that I'm going to make sure everyone in this city knows it!'

Reggie's eyes glittered. 'I may be a queen, but I'm a true queen. You,' he said, pointing a high-glossed index finger at her, 'are nothing more than a bogus Jewish countess.'

Dani stormed out of his office, slamming the door behind her hard enough to rattle the glass. The hair stylist was so unnerved that his hand slipped, and the streaking brush left a thick, jagged mark across one side of Reggie's head.

'Cunt!' Reggie screamed.

'Oh, here she is now,' Elvira said into the phone in the front foyer. She held her hand over the receiver. 'Countess, you have a collect call from – '

Dani shook her head. 'No, not now. Take a message. I don't want to speak to anyone.'

60

'Yes, ma'am.' She turned back to the phone. 'I'm sorry, operator, but the countess is not available. Could you please tell Frau Bletz – '

That was all Dani needed to hear.

She grabbed the phone. 'Operator, I'll accept. Monika? Monika, your timing is uncanny. But why are you calling collect? Have you bankrupted Helmut? . . . He did? But why . . . With a woman? . . . He didn't! Oh, Monika, you poor darling! But do you have any money? . . . Good. Now, listen, how soon can you get here? . . . Terrific! I'll meet you outside customs. And don't worry about a thing. I can't wait to see you! *Ciao, ciao.*'

And she thought *she* had problems!

Chapter Three

New York

The International Arrivals building at Kennedy Airport was a teeming madhouse. Skinny, pimply-faced teenagers toting overstuffed backpacks competed for standing room with exhausted parents and crying children. Anxious tour guides wearing polyester pants suits shepherded their charges through the bedlam, screaming, 'Coming through . . . coming through . . . excuse us, please. We're a group.' Foreigners, looking awed and bewildered, clutched at their Fodor's guides and their cameras.

'Monika!' Dani called out. 'Over here! . . . Monika! Monika, look over here!'

Heads turned, but Dani ignored the disapproving stares.

It was purely a miracle, Dani thought, that she had managed to spot Monika among the hordes of passengers fighting their way through customs. Poor kid, having to cope with all this noise and confusion as well as her own problems.

'Monika!' Dani yelled again and waved frantically to get her attention. More scowls from the people to her right and left, but Countess diPortanova was used to being stared at.

Dani raised her voice another notch. 'Monika, I'm over here, by the pillar.'

Finally!

Monika looked up and waved back. Then she pointed to a dark-haired, handsome man standing next to her and mouthed some words Dani couldn't hear. But she could see, even at this distance, that her best friend appeared none the worse for her ordeal. The shit-eating grin on her baby face spoke volumes. And the man she was talking to, whoever he might be, had his arm draped comfortably around Monika's shoulder.

Monika elbowed her way through the crowds with the deftness of an experienced international traveler. Dani sighed with relief. She should have known that it would take more than a bad fight with Helmut to knock the wind out of Monika von Reich.

The good-looking man still in tow, Monika fell into Dani's arms, talking a mile a minute.

'*Liebchen*, you look beautiful. And I love your dress. You must take me shopping tomorrow and tell me where to get my hair cut. Where is Nino? Just look at you, so skinny and beautiful! *Ach*, it's heaven to be in New York. I'm dying to stay up all night and go dancing!'

'Anything you want, darling, just say the word. But let's get the hell out of here before we get assaulted by one of those backpacks. Monika, you look indecently gorgeous.'

'*Ach*, I feel like a dowdy Swiss *hausfrau* in this boring dress. And would you look at all this hair! I'm like Rapunzel, trapped in the tower, waiting to be rescued. But I'm definitely going to make up for lost time. Speaking of which, I want you to meet a new friend of mine. I've told him all about you.'

Dani appreciatively eyed the tall, broad-shouldered man at Monika's side. He was grinning from ear to ear.

In a Texas-dipped accent, he said, 'Countess, pleased to meet you. I'm David Hooks. I wish I could stay and chat, but I've got to catch a plane to Dallas.'

'David and I met on the plane,' Monika explained. 'He helped me celebrate my flight to freedom.'

Dani could only imagine *how* they'd celebrated.

Hooks blushed and shifted his expensively clad feet. 'I'll give you a call in a day or two to see how you're doing, Monika. And if you feel like exploring Dallas, you're always welcome.' He bid them farewell, giving Monika a warm hug, shaking Dani's hand, then disappeared into the crowd.

Monika handed Dani her sable coat. 'You carry this, and I'll manage the rest of the stuff. Is New York always this hot in September?'

'Where's all your luggage?'

Monika patted the huge Vuitton bag slung over one shoulder and picked up her matching Vuitton suitcase. 'I'm traveling light this trip. I made a quick getaway with only the essentials and the jewels and cash we had in the hotel safe. So, *liebchen*, unfortunately, I don't have much of a wardrobe.'

'No problem,' Dani said reassuringly. 'We're still the same size, aren't we? You can wear my clothes until you have time to go shopping.'

'Just like the good old days on the Riviera.' Monika sighed happily as they made their way through the crowds to the exit. 'Well, what did you think of Herr Hooks?'

'He's a hunk.'

'*Ja . . . ja*,' Monika said wistfully.

'You didn't – '

'*Ja*, we did. We were the only ones in first class. I wasn't going to let all that space go to waste! I must write British Airways to thank them for their extra-wide seats. A good fuck and good riddance to Helmut, just what I needed.'

'Whatever happened to fucking in the lavatories?' teased Dani.

'Passé,' Monika declared. 'Besides, we wouldn't have

64

fit. You know how they say, "Everything's bigger in Texas"? *Liebchen*, it's *true!*'

Horns honked in protest as they ignored the traffic light and dashed across the road that separated the terminal from the short-term parking lot.

'Where's Nino?'

'He had a meeting, but he said he'll catch up with us at the restaurant.' Dani fished in her bag for her car keys. 'For somebody who's just been kicked out by her husband, you're handling the situation pretty well. You sounded so miserable when you called from Heathrow that I thought I'd have to carry you home in a basket.'

'I *was* a wreck,' Monika agreed cheerfully. 'But after I talked to you, I realized that Helmut did me a favor. Life with him was like one long funeral – my own. And if Karola wants me out of her life, well, there's certainly no point in crying over that.' She climbed into Dani's fire-engine-red Jaguar convertible. 'Nice car. Birthday present from Nino?'

Dani shrugged. 'To tell you the truth, I can't remember what the occasion was. I think it was to make up after one of our fights.' Dani quickly changed the subject. 'Are you hungry?'

'*Ja*, but not just for food. Seeing you, seeing the New York skyline, made me realize just how hungry I am for everything – my own car, my own place to live, lots of men – and clothes. Ooh,' she moaned, 'do I need new clothes. I want leather pants and boots and minis. And *jeans*! Everything I couldn't have as Helmut's wife. But in the meantime, a huge dinner sounds wonderful.'

'Good.' Dani glanced out her rearview mirror, shifted into third, and snaked onto the Van Wyck Expressway. 'Maybe for once Nino will even be on time.'

'That rascal, how is he?'

'Oh, you know Nino. Never a dull moment.'

* * *

Chez Antoinette, a lace-curtained gem of a restaurant on Bleecker Street just off Hudson, was the kind of place people kept a secret, even from their best friends. The tiny two-room bistro held no more than twelve tables, discreetly distanced one from the next for maximum privacy. The service was excellent, the food superb, the ambience conducive to intimate tête-à-têtes. The owner, Antoinette Martine, had grown up in Nice, the daughter of a restauranteur, and the menu was heavily accented with the flavors of Provence.

Chez Antoinette was where Dani and Nino ate when they wanted a relaxed, romantic meal, free of interruptions by photographers or fawning gossip columnists. Madame Antoinette treated them like family and always made sure to seat them in the quieter back room, near, but not too near, the fireplace.

Now, noticing that Nino had finished his scotch and was glancing impatiently at his watch, she bustled over to soothe his temper.

'Would you care for another aperitif, *monsieur le comte*?' she asked placatingly.

Nino mulled it over.

His meeting with the vice president and chief operating officer of diPortanova USA – the American branch of his family's company – had ended earlier than anticipated. Nino had returned a few phone calls, then hurried out of the office, claiming urgent business elsewhere.

He had fooled no one. The staff knew that Nino's 'urgent business' was usually conducted between a pair of sheets. And not necessarily with his beautiful wife. This afternoon had been no exception. He hadn't seen Magda since the house party on her husband's Caribbean island last February.

Fortunately, she was staying just across the street from his office, at the Plaza.

Fortunately, her husband was in Paris.

Fortunately, she and Nino had similar interests – hot sex and expensive champagne.

It wasn't that Dani didn't satisfy him. She did, and he loved her for it. But sometimes a man needed a change of pace. A steady diet of anything – no matter how delicious – would quickly lose its appeal.

Magda had been ripe for another round. But the hour was late, so he'd rushed downtown. And now here he sat, cooling his heels, as the restaurant filled up around him.

'*Oui*, Antoinette, another Glenfiddich, please.'

No doubt there was heavy traffic coming in from Kennedy. Pity, he thought, remembering Magda's sweet quivering breasts and eager mouth. Her moist, succulent pussy . . .

Elise, Antoinette's seventeen-year-old daughter, brought Nino his scotch.

'Alone, Monsieur Nino?' she said, licking her lips suggestively.

A student at the Lycée Français, Elise helped out at her mother's restaurant at dinner and on weekends. She and Nino had been sleeping together off and on for almost two years, and she was one of his most dependable sources for high-grade hashish. She was also a superb pastry chef, and her hazelnut tortes were almost as memorable as her blow jobs.

Casting a careful sideways glance at her mother, Elise sidled up to Nino, bent low so that he got a stunning view of her enormous breasts, and whispered, 'I recommend my hot pussy for dinner.'

'Is that one of the house specialties?' Nino grinned. 'I don't see it on the menu.'

'Only for you.'

'*Cara*, it's been too long,' Nino murmured earnestly.

'I've been visiting my family in France,' Elise explained.

'And,' she added sotto voce, 'I smuggled in some stuff that will blow your mind.'

'How about lunch tomorrow? At the usual place?'

'Can't wait,' Elise purred. She picked up the half-filled bread basket and said loudly, 'Certainly, *monsieur*, more bread, immediately!'

Monika had forgotten about Dani's driving. She clutched at the dashboard for extra protection and closed her eyes as Dani took turns at breakneck speeds. Suddenly she remembered in all too vivid detail that terrible night in the Swiss Alps when they had almost been killed.

'Relax,' Dani kept telling her now. 'You ought to try driving with Nino sometime.'

Danke, nein, thought Monika.

They yakked all the way into Manhattan. Dani was aghast at Monika's stories about life with Helmut.

'But, Monika,' she said, screeching to a halt right in front of Chez Antoinette and squeezing the Jag into a minuscule parking space, 'you never said a word! How could you stand it?'

'I didn't think I had a choice.' Monika shrugged. 'But tell me about you and Nino. Three years of marriage when the press wasn't predicting more than six months. How is it? Are you happy?'

'Depends on the day. Nino is the most generous man in the world. A wonderful lover, a great friend. He's also irresponsible, spoiled, and, I suspect, unfaithful. A child who'll probably never, ever grow up.'

She paused for a moment before walking into the restaurant and said casually, 'Check out the waitress with the big boobs. I think Nino's sleeping with her. And the worst of it is, I'm not even sure I care. I have a lot to tell you, Monika.'

And talk they did, all through dinner. The interruptions

68

were frequent, the contradictions many, the laughter continuous. The champagne flowed. Nino proposed a toast. He lifted his glass and cleared his throat.

'To the three of us and a lifetime of nothing but fun and adventure. May we never grow old.'

They clinked glasses.

'Now it's my turn,' Dani said. 'To you, Monika. To your new life.'

'*Ja*, I'll drink to that,' Monika declared happily.

Nino chortled with glee at Monika's description of how Helmut had burst into the hotel room and found her with the Russian manicurist.

Naturally Nino would be amused, thought Dani cynically. Were all men so callous? Certainly her father would never have won any awards in the sensitivity department. Though in all fairness, Nino would never humiliate her the way Helmut had humiliated Monika. In fact, he probably would have jumped right into bed with her *and* the manicurist.

'At least you found a woman who knew how to satisfy you,' he said approvingly. He snapped his fingers for another bottle of champagne.

'I was desperate,' Monika said. 'Though I must admit, it was very . . . interesting. She had very nice breasts. I never thought much about women's breasts before. But I do like men better,' she added hastily.

'Well, good riddance to Helmut,' Nino declared. 'What an insufferable bore he was. And the worst part was he never wanted to party.'

'*Nein*,' Monika snickered, 'that was *not* his worst part. But now I'm rid of that liverwurst forever.'

'Your timing was perfect. Dani needs some cheering up after her little run-in with that fashion designer. Don't you, *cara*?' he soothed.

'I'd hardly describe the theft of my designs as a "little

run-in,"' Dani replied tightly. Nino knew how upset she'd been. How could he be so casual about it? She explained to Monika what had happened with Mr Reggie.

'Shameless, isn't it?' Nino clucked.

'Worse than shameless,' Monika said, squeezing Dani's hand sympathetically. 'It's criminal. The man's a fraud. A swine. Dani, you must be livid. What are you going to do?'

Dani flashed her a grateful smile. She'd been plotting her next move ever since she'd stormed out of Mr Reggie's office.

People would talk, of course, but she didn't give a damn. Most of all, they would ask why. According to the people who prided themselves on being in the know, Countess Dani diPortanova had everything she could possibly want or need.

But what did they know? No matter how wealthy her husband was, no matter how much he loved her, no matter how attractive or charming she might be, there were some things she didn't have.

Her designs back, for one.

Her name on the labels, for another.

And Mr Reggie's head on a silver platter, for a third.

But all that was going to change.

'I'm going to give that son of a bitch a run for his money,' she said defiantly.

Nino raised an eyebrow, appraising his wife.

'How?' asked Monika.

'I'm working on it.'

Through Maurice, Dani tracked down Irving Blatt, whom she remembered from the Passover Seders of her childhood. The brother-in-law of one of her mother's oldest friends, Irving was a second-generation *shmatta* salesman who had survived the hard way on Seventh Avenue.

70

Irving had taken his knocks along the way – and doled out a few, when necessary. Relying on his wits, his gut instincts, and sheer determination, he'd built I. Blatt and Sons into a solid business that sold medium-priced sportswear under a variety of labels.

By Seventh Avenue standards, I. Blatt was a small company. But it was profitable year in, year out, which, Irving reminded himself, was more than most of the schmucks in the rag trade could say. For almost thirty-five years, Irving had devoted himself to his company and dreamed of handing it over one day to his sons, Stuart and Howie.

But now that he had put the boys in charge of the two most critical areas, sales and production, Irving found himself with one thing he'd never had before: time on his hands. He was bored. And he didn't like it.

Nevertheless, when Dani phoned to invite him to lunch, saying she needed help with a problem she'd rather discuss in person, he almost told her no. As fond as he'd been of poor Sophie Lieberman, he couldn't imagine what he'd have to say to her daughter, whom he vaguely remembered as a fat, sad little kid.

His wife had mentioned some years back that Sophie's girl had married a rich *goy* from Italy. Probably broke her father's heart. Thank God her mother had been spared that tragedy. He could only imagine what kind of help she wanted – an introduction to some of his Seventh Avenue pals so she could buy her clothes wholesale? Or worse, maybe a job?

Irving sighed heavily and pretended to be leafing through his calendar.

'Please,' Dani pleaded. 'If you're too busy for lunch, I'll come to your office. At your convenience, of course. Just give me a few minutes.'

'Okay,' Irving said reluctantly. 'I can see you tomorrow

71

at three. But listen, honey, if you're looking for a job, we don't have any openings here.'

The minute she walked into his office, he was genuinely sorry he couldn't hire her. The fat little girl who had clung to her mother's arm had turned into a gorgeous, knockout broad – the kind he'd have given his right ball for when he was younger.

Dani had deliberately dressed to kill in her shortest mini and her highest heels. Maybe she had overdone the sex goddess bit. But her mother's friends used to kvetch about what a tough crowd the garmentos were, how they never gave anybody a break. From the look on Irving's face, it looked as if he wanted to give her one, and more . . .

'Thank you so much for seeing me, Mr Blatt,' she said sweetly, crossing her legs.

'Irving. Please call me Irving. How's your father? I haven't seen him since your mother's unveiling, may she rest in peace.'

'He's quite well. Still working. Perhaps you don't know he remarried.'

Of course Irving knew. His wife had almost had a cow when she read the wedding announcement in the *Times*.

'And to a girl young enough to be his daughter,' Gert had clucked, glaring at Eunice's photograph.

'Coffee? Tea?' Irving offered.

'No, thanks,' Dani said. 'The reason I asked to see you, Irving, is because I need some advice about your business.'

'*My* business?' Irving was immediately suspicious. A garmento didn't talk to his own father about business if he thought he'd become a competitor, much less the daughter of a long-dead friend. That was the law of survival on Seventh Avenue.

Dani smiled. 'Actually, I mean the trade in general.'

Irving brightened. 'Oh, you want to interview me . . . What? Are you doing a paper for school or something?'

Dani grinned. 'Irving, do I *look* like a student?'

So, she had a mouth on her. He liked that.

'It's a long story,' she said. 'I know you're busy, so I'll make it as brief as possible.'

She told him everything.

About her sketches. Mr Reggie's fashion show. Her plan.

For fifteen minutes Irving listened, not saying a word.

'Well,' she said finally, 'will you help me? I just need some direction – names, numbers, where to start . . . the basics.'

Irving absentmindedly ran his fingers through what was left of his wavy gray hair. 'Look, let me give you a piece of advice.'

Dani nodded eagerly, ready to absorb every word.

'Forget about Mr Reggie. Forget this crazy scheme of yours.'

'Wha – '

'Look, you've got a nice life. A husband, a home, plenty of money. What do you need the aggravation for? Like I said, forget about it. What's done is done.'

'But I *can't*!' Dani protested indignantly. 'On principle alone I can't drop it. Bad enough that he ripped me off in my own home. But even worse, he's making money off *my* designs, selling clothes that should have *my* name in them, not his.'

Irving shrugged. 'So what else is new? Happens all the time. Sure, the guy's a schmuck, but Reggie Bolt isn't the first and he sure as hell won't be the last son of a bitch thief in the business.'

Dani shook her head. 'I can't accept that. What if it happened to you? I bet you wouldn't let him get away

73

with it. And I would never be able to live with myself if I did.'

She was a nice girl, Irving thought, but *oy*, was she naïve.

'Look,' Irving said patiently, 'before you get any *meshuggeneh* ideas, let me tell you a thing or two about the *real* business.'

For the next two hours, Irving lectured Dani on the dubious pleasures of being a garmento. In response to her comments and questions, he played the role of grand inquisitor, devil's advocate, and doubting Thomas.

Finally, Dani leaned forward and said, 'I appreciate what you're trying to do, Irving, really I do. But trying to talk me out of it isn't going to help. Seventh Avenue is going to have to deal with me whether it wants to or not. I may look like a slick socialite, but forget appearances. That's window dressing. I'm smart and talented, and I've got the financial resources to succeed. So why not?'

Irving smiled. This was one determined broad. He liked that. Determination. Spunk. Money. She was right: along with talent, that was what it took to make it. He got up and stared out of the window behind him, looking down on Seventh Avenue. She was going to get into the business with or without him, he could see that. It took him less than a minute to make up his mind. His wife always complained that he was a soft touch. Maybe she was right, but so what?

Irving turned around. 'You really want to be a designer?'

'Absolutely,' she said without hesitation.

'Then be here tomorrow morning, nine o'clock sharp.'

Dani was stunned. This was far better than she had hoped for.

'Hey,' Irving said, 'you might as well learn it the right way, you know. With me as your teacher, you'll learn the business top to bottom, guaranteed. Besides, how could I say no to Sophie Lieberman's little girl?' *Especially when she looks like you* . . .

'Irving,' Dani said earnestly, 'I don't mean to sound ungrateful, but I have to be perfectly honest with you. I don't have the time for a long-term apprenticeship.'

Irving chuckled at her *chutzpah*.

'What's long term? If you're as smart as I think you are, and if you pay attention, you'll know enough of the fundamentals in a coupla months to do what you want.'

Dani extended her hand and smiled. 'Thank you, Irving. I promise you'll never regret this.'

'Three hundred and fifty thousand dollars,' said the Harry Winston jeweler, removing his loupe.

'I know those diamonds,' Monika told him firmly but politely. 'There are no carbon specks, no hairline fractures. They're worth more than that.'

The jeweler replaced his loupe and reexamined the necklace, more for formality's sake than anything else. They both knew she was right, but he always lowballed the initial quote. Most people didn't know the value of gems, even if they owned a fortune of them.

'Three hundred and seventy-five thousand, and that's final.'

'Four hundred.'

'Three eighty-five.'

'*Danke*,' Monika said, trying hard not to smile. Gloating would cost her money on the other pieces. Thank God she'd taken some time to learn about precious gems during her years with Helmut. It was finally paying off.

She was ensconced in a small private room on the second floor of Harry Winston's Fifth Avenue shop. Outside the room, down the hall, stood a security guard. Inside, neatly arranged on velvet-lined, cushioned trays in front of Monika and the Harry Winston appraiser, was a small fortune in jewelry.

The jeweler peered at a pair of earrings that matched the just-sold necklace. Monika sat back in the Louis XIV chair and waited.

'A hundred thousand,' the jeweler announced.

Monika was enjoying this. 'They're seven carats each, flawless D's. I'm sure you know that on the open market they'd be – '

'A hundred and twenty-five, and that's it.'

'They're yours.'

Inwardly, the jeweler marveled at his client's imperturbable manner. The woman was parting with hundreds of thousands of dollars' worth of one-of-a-kind pieces without so much as a tear or even a sigh of regret. He was accustomed to bitter divorcées and stricken widows whose highly charged emotional state usually permitted him to get the better part of the deal. But this blasé blond with the seemingly bottomless trove of treasures was giving him a run for his money.

Diamonds, rubies, emeralds, sapphires, pearls . . .

The negotiations continued.

Thank you, Helmut, she thought smugly, *for insisting I travel with all my jewels*. She congratulated herself, too, for remembering to claim the pieces, along with Helmut's stash of American dollars, from the Connaught safe before Helmut got to them.

She mentally calculated her profits so far and fought harder to control her smile of satisfaction. Most of the pieces she had purchased out of boredom – or, worse, sheer spite. A few, like the necklace she'd just sold for $385,000, had been birthday or anniversary presents from Helmut. Suitable gifts for the wife of one of Switzerland's leading industrialists. Gifts that had nothing to do with love or joy or respect.

Parting with each piece felt like throwing yet another shovelful of dirt into the hole where she was burying her life with Helmut. Dead and buried – good riddance to Frau Monika Bletz.

And it wasn't as if she was selling off her entire collection. She still had the jewels Karola had given her as part of her trousseau. From now on, whatever she wanted, she would just have to pay for with her own money.

And as soon as she found herself a place to live and got settled in, she would figure out a way to make that money.

She couldn't *wait* to begin earning a salary. She'd never worked in her life. It was going to be wonderful to try . . .

Walking briskly up Fifth Avenue two hours later, Monika finally permitted herself the smile she had been suppressing. She'd left instructions at Harry Winston to have her check for the proceeds of the sale, $1.4 million dollars, hand-delivered and deposited into her newly opened bank account at Morgan Guaranty Trust.

At last she was on her own! No more Karola. No more Helmut. And best of all, no more of Helmut's cold cock. For the very first time in her life she felt free and happy.

And the best was yet to come. She was sure of it.

She stepped off the curb at Fifty-seventh Street and hailed a cab.

'Where to, blond goddess?' the cabbie asked.

Monika winked slyly and gave him the address of the exclusive real-estate firm of Edward Lee Cave. Next on her agenda was to buy herself a home.

The headquarters of diPortanova USA occupied the entire thirty-fifth floor of the General Motors Building, prestigiously located at Fifth Avenue and Fifty-ninth Street. The offices had recently been renovated under

Nino's personal supervision. The latest issue of *Architectural Digest* had applauded the results.

The color scheme throughout was high-tech gray and black, the appointments all chrome and glass with expensive art hanging on the walls of the corridors and in the conference rooms. On clear, sunny days, the floor-to-ceiling windows offered sweeping views of Manhattan and beyond. It was all very European. Very Italian. Very Nino.

Nino's involvement in the design decisions had included hiring the new front-desk receptionist – a pert young redhead who had confided to him that her proudest achievement was being voted Miss Congeniality at the Miss Nebraska state pageant.

Nino had hired her on the spot.

Now her green eyes lit up as he walked through the double glass doors, and she lavished on him the dimpled smile that had won her the coveted title. 'Lovely morning, isn't it, Count?' she oozed.

Nino smiled and blew her a kiss. One day maybe she'd return the favor – around the shaft of his cock. He strolled down the long, plushly carpeted hallway to his corner suite, which overlooked Fifth Avenue and Central Park.

Never would he have imagined that he could actually come to *enjoy* the small pleasures of a daily office routine. The doting support staff, mostly female, so ready to do his bidding. The cachet of an impressive-sounding title. The air of subdued excitement and activity that meant the fortunes of the diPortanova family were rising, rising, rising.

Of course, it helped that he was free to come and go as he pleased. Take a month off to ski in Gstaad? Who was to tell him no? Sleep until noon and not show up until three? His prerogative. Cruise the Greek islands for a week or two? He could always keep in touch through ship-to-shore telephone.

Intermittently, Roberto grumbled, but they both knew he had no cause for complaint. Nino had always been very adept at playing with money, or rather, spending huge sums of it. But after he and Dani moved to New York, Roberto had made him responsible for handling one of the family's trusts. Nino had begun to play a different sort of money game.

The thrill of investment management was like the thrill of racing cars: the pleasure lay in the risk. Buying, selling, increasing one position, decreasing exposure in another – it was no different than accelerating and decelerating, whipping his car in and out of different positions at the track. The goals of both were the same: move ahead as swiftly and skillfully as possible.

He had good instincts, and within six months the trust's value had risen almost 18 percent. An exceptional performance, especially in a bear market. Pleased but still cautious, Roberto had gradually turned over to his son more and more of the family's portfolios. The big test had been the corporation's $70 million pension fund. In the two years since he had taken over its management, under Roberto's constant supervision Nino had shrewdly increased the fund's value to almost $100 million.

His personal secretary, Eileen, was his secret weapon. Eileen, who was single and fiftyish, commuted from Montclair, New Jersey, where she lived with her ancient parents. A devoutly religious woman, she prayed each night to the Virgin Mary for Nino's health and happiness.

Eileen had a face like a pit bull, a body like a toadstool, and a brain like a computer. She knew all of Nino's secrets – and would have submitted to torture rather than reveal any of them.

There was no way Nino could have functioned without her, and they both knew it.

'Coffee, Nino?' she said, getting up to fetch him his freshly brewed espresso as he strode by her.

'Please, sweetheart – and a Danish, *si*?'

As usual, the morning editions of the *Wall Street Journal*, the London *Times*, and Italy's *Corriere della Fera* were neatly stacked in the middle of Nino's otherwise clear desk. He turned on the Quotron machine, took a long sip of the steaming hot espresso, and quickly paged through the newspapers to check the latest movements in the precious metals market, stocks, and interest rates. Next he scanned the front-page news and the business sections, looking for clues to where the world markets might be heading.

Today he wasn't touching a thing. The recent portfolio shifts he had made were working beautifully. This past week the fund had earned another three million.

What was it the Americans said? If it's not broken, don't fix it.

'Eileen, would you get my father on the line, *prego*?'

Lately Nino had been making an effort to repair his relationship with his father. He had come to value Roberto's advice and phoned him often. Once they had finished talking business, they would turn to politics, sports, family matters.

'Your father's on line three,' announced Eileen.

Nino gave Roberto his weekly report on the pension fund's performance. The conversation, as usual, quickly turned to other matters.

'We have a houseguest,' Nino told Roberto. 'Our friend, Monika, Karola von Reich's daughter.' He didn't mention that Monika had left Helmut or under what circumstances. Roberto hated to hear about marriages breaking up. It went against his Catholic grain.

'How's *your* wife?' Roberto asked pointedly.

'*Dani* is fine.'

'Is she pregnant yet?'

'Papa, we have plenty of time for that. Dani says first she needs to do something with her life.'

There was silence on the other end of the line.

It was not a good sign.

The conversation went downhill from there.

Monika's waking hours were consumed by house hunting. Dani had begged her to live with them for a while. But Monika knew, even though there was an abundance of space, that three was a crowd, especially when two were a couple. Besides, she had always lived with somebody; it was about time she had a place of her own.

She'd immediately ruled out rental apartments, no matter how prestigious the address. Nor was she interested in buying any of the co-ops that the real-estate agent, Mrs Langer, a skinny, horse-faced woman, was so eager to sell her.

She'd had enough of people asking her questions, approving and disapproving, telling her what she could and could not do. Besides, she saw how the Dakota doormen kept track of Dani's and Nino's comings and goings. She craved privacy and anonymity.

'Very well,' said Mrs Langer, pursing her lips disapprovingly. 'I'll show you town houses. What a pity. I sold such a lovely one down in Murray Hill just last week.'

'Do you have anything on the West Side?'

The woman rolled her eyes. 'Trust me, dear,' she declared in a voice that could have cut glass, 'except for a few choice buildings on Central Park West, the West Side is an absolute *jungle*.'

They toured the Upper East Side in Mrs Langer's company car. Monika turned out to be a tough sell. 'Too far east of Fifth,' she said, turning thumbs down on a landmark limestone building.

'But you'd be next door to *Sutton Place*,' brayed the woman.

Monika toured town house after town house and turned thumbs down on them all. Too cold. Too shady. Too small. Too large. Too drafty. Too imposing. Too pretentious. Money was never an issue. What mattered to Monika was finding a house that was also a *home*.

The agent was in despair. If it weren't for the fact that Miss von Reich was a close personal friend of the diPortanovas . . .

'I'll know it when I see it,' Monika said firmly, still not discouraged after three long weeks of traipsing in and out of houses, up and down steep flights of stairs. 'What's next?'

The agent impatiently flipped through her notebook. 'I only have one more listing in this area, a four-story house on East Sixty-first. You cannot find a better location, dear. But quite honestly, I don't feel it's your sort of place,' she said firmly.

Monika was fed up with the woman's assumptions about how and where she should live. 'Show it to me anyway,' she snapped.

The brownstone was almost a hundred years old and looked its age.

'Charming, isn't it?' sniffed the agent. 'Of course, you would have rather an expensive plumbing job, and the floors are in terrible condition. But – '

'Are there fireplaces in all the rooms upstairs as well?' Monika interrupted.

Mrs Langer checked her listing and nodded. 'Shall we take a look at the upper floors?'

'I'd rather go upstairs by myself, thanks.'

She paced the empty rooms and gazed out the back

windows, which overlooked a tiny, unkempt garden with one lone apple tree. And saw what the real-estate agent could never see.

The house cried out for an owner who would love it, nurture it, care for it as she, Monika, had never been cared for or loved. Certainly it needed a great deal of work, but with some money and imagination, these rooms could be transformed into a beautiful, warm, welcoming home.

The back room, the one that overlooked the garden, had a south-eastern exposure. Good – she wanted a warm, sunny bedroom. She would paint it in warm, muted colors – maybe a sandy pink – and decorate it with lots of chintz. She visualized antiques, old English rugs, oils, ancient ginger jars, and books everywhere. A home that enveloped, soothed, protected, and caressed. The place was perfect.

Monika hurried downstairs to join Mrs Langer. '*Ja*, how soon can I close?'

The agent's eyes widened. 'Don't you even want to know the price?'

'No, you work out the details,' Monika said carelessly. 'I don't care how much it costs. I'll take it.'

Not even at the Clinique Etiole, when she had pushed herself like a machine to take off sixty pounds of fat, had Dani worked so hard.

Irving wanted her by his side every day without fail. 'Think of yourself as a sponge,' he'd say. 'Absorb everything.' He was a born teacher. 'At least you didn't waste your time at the Fashion Institute or one of those schools,' he told her. 'The only way to learn fashion is by getting your hands dirty and breaking a few nails.'

Dani broke more than a few. As the days and weeks went by, she was beginning to feel that she was fighting a losing battle. There was so much to learn, so much to do, never enough time. Late at night, after a day of following Irving around, then dashing off to a party with Nino, she would fall into bed and wonder whether she'd gone crazy. Exhausted though she was, she would lie awake for hours, recalling everything she had heard that day, fretting about finding time to design, to organize her first collection.

More and more she worried that she'd bitten off more than she could chew. It was all very well to threaten to take revenge on Reggie Bolt, but plunging feet first into the icy waters of Seventh Avenue was an altogether different matter.

Not even to Monika could she admit her worst secret fear – that perhaps Reggie was right. Perhaps she was nothing but a dilettante. Perhaps she was nothing more than a pampered rich man's wife who couldn't take the heat.

But Dani had underestimated her best friend's ability to see through her and guess her concerns.

'Your problem is you think you have to be a super-woman,' Monika correctly analyzed her. 'I grew up with a mother who ran a multimillion-dollar company. But she had lots of help. And she wasn't out dancing and drinking four or five nights a week.'

After all the stories she had heard about Monika's witch of a mother, Dani didn't know whether to be amused or insulted. 'Are you saying I should use Karola as my role model?'

'Heaven forbid!' Monika shuddered. 'All I mean is that you can let up on yourself once in a while. Take it easy. Let Nino stay out late if he wants to, but you're a working girl.'

The truth hurt, and Dani wasn't sure she wanted to

hear it from her former partner-in-mischief. 'Since when did you get to be so sensible?' she asked resentfully.

'Since I've had nothing better to do than think about my life and what I want to do with it.'

The fact was, Monika was right. If Dani was really serious about starting a company, even a small one, she couldn't manage it single-handedly. As she rushed off to yet another meeting with Irving, she realized that sooner or later she'd have to get help.

'Monika,' she said the next time they had a few minutes alone, 'what did Karola look for in her top executives?'

Monika didn't have to think twice. She and Dieter had sat through innumerable dull dinners listening to Karola rail on the subject of her staff. She ticked the qualities off on her fingers. 'Smart. Hardworking. Loyal. People she could trust totally. She used to rant about how hard it was to find such people.'

'In other words,' Dani nodded excitedly, 'people like you. Monika, you're the best person I know to help me organize and run the company. I can't pay until we start earning money, but please, please tell me you'll do it. You know what you always say about how we bring each other luck.'

We are very lucky, ja? Their private code that forever would summon up the memory of the sleepy drive from Lausanne through the night fog along the dark, winding road that led back to the Clinique Etiole. Those terrifying few moments when they'd been only a hairsbreadth away from crashing over the mountainside and plummeting many miles to their death.

Their friendship had been cemented that night. And now, surely as she knew she could design dresses that women would want to buy, Dani knew that together she and Monika could take on Seventh Avenue.

'Will you?' Dani persisted. 'Will you join me?'

Monika laughed. 'Oh, God. Do you honestly think I'd say no?'

They would make a great team.

It hadn't gone unnoticed by Mr Reggie that for several weeks now Dani diPortanova had been showing up, early in the morning, at 550 Seventh Avenue. At first, immersed in putting together his fall collection, Reggie didn't have time to consider the meaning of her presence in the district. But eventually the countess's daily appearances on Seventh Avenue began to disturb his sense of well-being. Anything that disturbed Mr Reggie affected his creativity. And creativity was his stock in trade.

Though Reggie had been shaken by Dani's invasion of his office and her hideous tantrum, he hadn't bothered to dignify her threats and accusations by repeating them to anyone, not even to Magee. But word had leaked out, no doubt via Étienne, his hairdresser, that Reggie and the usually amiable young countess had had a row.

Now that she was being sighted regularly on Seventh Avenue, tongues were wagging. 'What do you think she's up to?' his friends wanted to know. 'Surely the girl's not mad enough to try to get back at you?'

'Darlings, it's not for me to worry,' sniffed Reggie, wishing with all his heart that he could fire that gossip-monger Étienne for his flagrant betrayal. But Étienne was the best hair colorist in the city. And if Reggie's next collection turned out to be half as sensational as he suspected it would, the press would be banging down the doors of Mr Reggie's showroom for exclusive interviews and photo shoots. And he would need Étienne more than ever, for impeccable grooming was one of Mr Reggie's trademarks.

He commanded his loyal network of informants to dig

86

up some dirt on why the countess had become a Seventh Avenue regular.

A runway model who aspired to be Mr Reggie's design assistant came back with the information that Dani was spending her days with Irving Blatt.

'That old garmento?' Reggie snorted. 'What's she doing, giving him enemas?'

'Maybe he's grooming her to be his successor,' the runway model suggested, buffing her long, long nails.

'For chrissake,' Reggie snarled, 'every idiot on the street knows that man has two sons who've already taken over most of the business. Now get out there and bring me some information I can use!'

The model returned, breathless with excitement. This time she'd hit pay dirt. 'Countess diPortanova is putting together a collection,' she reported proudly, hoping this would finally land her the job she wanted by Reggie's side. 'Her own line of ready-to-wear high fashion. And she's doing it on her own, no backers.'

'Right,' snapped Reggie. 'And I suppose *you* still believe in the tooth fairy, huh? Her husband is more than very rich, dear heart. She is not – repeat, *not* – doing this on her own. *If* she's doing it at all . . .'

'I'm sure it's nothing to worry about,' the model assured Reggie, patting him on the shoulder.

'Who's worrying?' Reggie said contemptuously, brushing her hand away and wishing the bitch hadn't told him anything at all. He went whimpering to Magee for reassurance.

'You're a genius,' she reminded him.

'Of course,' he immediately agreed.

Magee checked her watch. 'The photographer from *New York* magazine is due here in less than ten minutes. You'd better go pull yourself together.'

Reggie nervously patted his hair and sucked in his slight

paunch. He was one of several top designers who were to be featured in a *New York* cover story on the industry. Magee was so right. He was a genius. Soon to become a certified star. And then it would be *Time* and *Newsweek* who would want him, and him alone, on their covers.

Chapter Four

New York

Dani had shrewdly hired a public relations whiz to publicize the formation of Countess Dani, Inc. But the official announcements, which were mailed out on December 15, 1974, could have been printed on toilet paper, and Dani would have gotten great press. The New York social grapevine had been buzzing for weeks that the young Countess diPortanova was headed for Seventh Avenue.

The columnists who religiously followed the antics of their favorite aristocratic couple made a huge fuss over Dani's latest escapade. Tongues wagged from Dubrow's Cafeteria in the heart of the fashion district to the backroom offices of Saks, Bloomie's, and Bergdorf's. Dani's friends and acquaintances talked endlessly of how marvelously clever it was of her to stage her own fashion show, let alone start an entire company.

Normally, the New York designers reserved time slots for their next shows six months in advance of the semiannual Fashion Week, which took place every October and April. *Fashion Calendar*, an industry newsletter that went out to tens of thousands of subscribers across the country, served as the scheduling clearinghouse. Traditionally, the more prominent designers were booked for the second week of the fourteen-day period. Retailers, fashion writers, and other interested parties dashed breathlessly from one show to the next up and down Seventh Avenue, taking notes and swapping stories on what they'd seen and heard.

There seemed to be a rule of thumb among the designers: the higher the price tags on their creations, the more extravagant and expensive the show itself. Some of the top couturier designers were rumored to drop half a million dollars in their attempts to woo their audiences. The hope was that the buyers would be impressed, the fashion writers inspired, and the socialites and celebs entertained.

It took some string-pulling by Irving before a time slot could be scheduled for Countess Dani, Inc. Not only was it an altogether new and unproven line, but Dani's request came in months later than the rest. But she was determined to have her first collection shown during Spring Fashion Week.

'All right,' the word came back from *Fashion Calendar*, 'we can squeeze you in on Friday afternoon of the first week. But only on the condition that, if necessary, you'll charter buses to get everyone over to the next show.'

'I'll charter helicopters if I have to,' Dani told them ecstatically. Now, where to hold the show?

'Piece of cake,' Monika said confidently. She'd attended hundreds of shows. Between herself and Dani, they could certainly dream up something.

They brainstormed late into the night, discarding one concept after another. Monika's favorite idea was to hold the show aboard a boat that would circle the island of Manhattan.

'That would take hours,' Dani pointed out. 'Besides, what if people got seasick?' She winced at the thought of the models throwing up on her designs. Instead, she wanted to set up a tent in the middle of the Great Lawn in Central Park.

'But what if it rains?' Monika asked practically. 'Can you see all those unhappy women squishing through the mud in their high heels?'

'Okay,' Dani conceded. 'Then let's move the show indoors, say to the Metropolitan Museum. I've been to some fabulous parties there.'

'*Ja*, what better backdrop for your designs than all those beautiful works of art!'

The sun was coming up over the tops of the buildings across Central Park, but before Dani allowed herself to slip between the sheets, she scribbled a note on the pad she kept next to her side of the bed: 'Call Met p.r. office re permission.'

Just as she was drifting off to sleep, Monika's words flashed through her mind like a neon sign: 'All those beautiful works of art.'

That would inevitably become the focal point of the show, diverting the audience's attention from her own creations. Because, face it, she might be good enough to compete with Mr Reggie, but she sure as hell didn't want to go up against the likes of Matisse and van Gogh, not to mention the Old Masters.

The answer, at six in the morning, was clear. For once in her life, Dani decided to opt for simplicity. Her designs had to be the most important part of the show. Nothing could be allowed to distract the audience from her collection.

Simple, of course, didn't have to mean cheap. As his contribution to the venture, Nino wanted to pay for the show. 'My gift to you, *cara*,' he said proudly. 'Spend whatever you need to make it memorable.'

Knowing Nino meant it, Dani gratefully took him at his word. She had taken a lease on half a floor in Irving's building at 550 Seventh Avenue, and she promptly hired a contractor and space designer. She set up a meeting with her contractor and told him, firmly but sweetly, that her showroom offices had to be ready by April 8. No delays and no excuses, she warned him, even if he had to pay the electricians, carpenters, and plumbers double overtime. She would make it worth his while.

Next she called her friend, Kim Wantanabe, her favorite instructor at the dance studio where she took classes five times a week. Kim was a bright, funny fireball of energy who really wanted to direct musicals. But Kim was realistic enough to know what her chances were of ever breaking into that exclusive, all-male charmed circle. 'Not to mention,' she told Dani over coffee, 'that I'm twenty-six years old and I look all of seventeen. People think I'm a kid. They never want to take me seriously.'

Dani took her seriously. Kim's technique as a teacher was equal parts drill instructor, cheerleader, and stand-up comic. For the hour and a half they spent in her class, her students worked hard. But they all adored her.

She was just the person to direct and coordinate Dani's first show.

'Me?' Kim gasped. 'Are you kidding? Because if you are, I'll never speak to you again.'

'I'm dead serious,' Dani promised her. 'Monika and I have enough to do without worrying about the lighting and music and making sure everyone's in the right place. Obviously, we'll have to work together and give you our suggestions, but – '

Kim was already digging into her bag for her notebook. 'Okay,' she said briskly, 'the designs are the most important thing, of course.'

'Of course,' said Dani. Now all she had to do was create the line.

It rained for three days straight, but on the morning of Dani's first show the sun was finally shining again.

'A good omen,' Monika decided.

But Dani couldn't seem to shake the sense of foreboding that had plagued her ever since Monika, a perfect size eight, had modeled the finished original samples. With a critical eye, she had examined the twenty-five pieces. Were her designs worth the tissue paper she had drawn them on?

Strutting back and forth in Dani's living room, Monika had rhapsodized about how beautiful she felt in the dresses, suits, and pants. But in this one area, Dani didn't trust Monika. She was too much of a fan, too convinced of Dani's talent, to be objective.

And now came the moment of truth. As she and Kim fretted and fussed and made last-minute adjustments on the models, she tried to calm herself with the thought that, after all, she *had* already proved to herself that she was a designer. Now all she had to do was prove it to everyone else.

The contractor had bullied his crew into finishing ahead of schedule, and Dani was pleased with the results. She and Kim had agreed that delivery of the office furniture should be postponed until after the show. The space was empty except for the models' runway, which was covered in royal blue carpeting, and the three hundred rented chairs.

Behind the runway was the backdrop, painted a pale blue. The only other items in the large, empty space that would soon be transformed into the showrooms of Countess Dani, Inc., were enormous white vases and baskets filled with freesia, lilies, and baby's breath that graced the white-carpeted banquettes that had been built in against three of the walls.

Whether out of sheer curiosity or genuine interest, a large group had trooped up to the fourteenth floor to see the first showing of the Countess Dani line. Monika peeked through the curtain and quickly counted heads. 'A full house,' she reported to Dani . . . and then it was time to begin.

Kim had spent days carefully scripting the show, devising one script for the lighting, music, and stage cues, another for the choreography each model would follow on the runway. She had held a quick dress rehearsal early that morning. Now she signaled the first model to get ready, nodded 'good luck' to Dani, and pushed the 'play' button on the large cassette recorder.

The talking stopped and the members of the audience leaned forward, all with eager anticipation. Dani's show marked the end of a long week, the last stop before the beginning of an even longer week. Few of those present were actually rooting for Dani diPortanova; most assumed the show would make for good gossip, a 'novelty item,' amusing filler for a future article on where would-be designers go wrong.

'At least she's starting on time,' the head buyer from Bergdorf's whispered to her Neiman-Marcus counterpart. 'How about a drink as soon as we can get out of here?'

'I heard the countess is serving champagne after the show,' the Neiman-Marcus buyer whispered back.

'Isn't she celebrating a little prematurely?' murmured the woman from Bergdorf's with one eyebrow raised meaningfully as the first of Dani's models retreated to halfhearted applause.

The fashion editor for *Harper's Bazaar* had nudged a *Vogue* editor whose opinions were influential enough to make or break the collection. 'What do you think?'

'Let's hope the next one's better,' came *Vogue*'s clipped response.

From the row behind them, the *New York Times* style editor overheard their exchange. She leaned forward and said sotto voce, 'It's not. Look at that mess.'

Heads turned as the second model, dressed in a green linen miniskirt and matching linen jacket, sauntered toward them.

'I cannot believe I'm wasting my time here,' the buyer from Bendel's hissed to the director of fashion at Saks.

'The poor woman,' said Saks.

'Poor she is not,' a representative from *Paris Match* said with a chuckle.

'Is it just me?' asked a new and still insecure buyer from Bloomingdale's, 'or is this as ordinary as I think it is?'

'She should have stuck to what she's good at – designing parties, not dresses,' pronounced a giggling young social-ite who hungrily coveted Dani's position as the queen of their set.

Another design was paraded out. The model turned, showing it off for all to see. Then, just as quickly, she was gone.

The applause was politely restrained.

Another design on another model.

The applause was faint.

It grew fainter with each successive outfit. Before the show was even officially over, people were standing, gathering their handbags and their notebooks. A few were yawning and looking at their watches, totally ignoring what was being shown on the runway. Kim quickly propelled Dani out on the stage to take her bows. It was the most humiliating moment of Dani's life. Half the showroom was already empty. Three models were still waiting in the wings with other outfits to show. Smiling woodenly, she held back the tears until she could sneak away and cry in private. Backstage, she didn't miss the look in Maurice's eyes, the look she remembered too well from her childhood. It spoke volumes about disappoint-ment, disapproval, embarrassment. Once again she had lived up to his worst expectations.

In her typically awkward way, Eunice tried to be kind.

'Bravo, darling,' she said soothingly. 'They loved it. You could just see it in their faces!'

It certainly wasn't love that Dani had seen in the audience's faces. 'Be right back,' she called behind her and ran blindly to the ladies' room.

Locking herself in a stall, she sat down and pulled her knees up to her chin, taking great big gulps of air, trying not to hyperventilate. Rocking back and forth in pain, she didn't even feel the tears streaming down her cheeks.

Echoing again and again in her head was Maurice's laughingly scornful comment, uttered years earlier when she had modeled her very first design for him: *'She'll never be a Coco Chanel . . .'*

'She'll never be . . .'

No, she thought miserably, *but I never wanted to be Coco. All I want is to be Dani Lieberman diPortanova, designer. My own original self.*

The door to the bathroom opened, and Dani could hear several pairs of high heels clicking across the tiles toward the mirror.

'She'll be through in three months,' predicted a vaguely familiar voice.

'Probably less,' another declared.

'What could she have been thinking? How utterly embarrassing.'

'Then it'll be another new hobby. You know how she and Nino are, flitting from one thing to the next. Why doesn't she just stick to dinner parties and nightclubbing?'

'Did you see that logo of hers?'

'A bit *de trop*, don't you think?'

There was laughter all around.

The next day, Mitchell Barton, who wrote *WWD*'s most widely read column, 'One Ear to the Ground,' summed up Dani's show: 'I didn't realize we had been invited to Countess diPortanova's new showroom for a wake. She

promised us a collection – she never let on she'd designed
it for the Salvation Army.'

Mr Reggie also unveiled his new fall collection during
Fashion Week. The collection was hailed as his greatest
triumph to date. The 'fashion mafia' – members of the
press and the buyers for the major stores – finally con-
ferred upon him the unofficial status of Star Designer, a
much-coveted designation reserved for a select group of
designers.

'A combination of Halston and Galanos,' raved the
New York Times.

'Quintessentially himself, but with a dash of Dior and a
hint of Saint Laurent,' swooned *Women's Wear Daily*.

He was all of them and none of them, the foreign press
wrote in a dozen different languages. A true original. An
American who was clever enough to use the best Parisian
accents.

He was *the* designer of 1975, the buyers enthusiastically
concluded, besieging his office with so many orders that
his operations computer jammed.

Mr Reggie loved every minute of it.

What a fool he'd been to have wasted even a moment
worrying about Dani diPortanova. Her show had been
worse than a flop; it had nailed her coffin shut and, with
it, had buried any aspirations that bitch might have had
of being a designer. Honestly, how he loathed people who
thought it was so easy just to whip up designs that the
American public would want, as if they were following a
McCall's pattern. The fools!

'I guess a famous name doesn't guarantee success,'
mused Magee.

'Of course not,' Reggie agreed emphatically, mentally
counting his blessings: A smash collection. Rising fame.

More money than he had ever hoped for. And Rah Rah waiting for him at home.

Rah Rah.

All Reggie had to do was think about Rah Rah, and his cock began to harden. Rah Rah was easily the most beautiful man Reggie had ever slept with. He was a surprise package of sex. Unfortunately, the package came COD.

Rah Rah was a hustler.

'I'm supposed to pay for getting *your* rocks off?' Reggie had asked in disbelief after Rah Rah had blown him in the men's room at the Four Seasons last fall when he'd unveiled his spring collection.

'I gave you a freebie this time,' the boy had said, flashing his devastating grin. 'Special introductory offer. But after that, it's two hundred and fifty dollars a pop.' He had handed Reggie his business card.

'Skip it,' Reggie had said indignantly and stormed out of the rest room.

But a week had gone by, and Reggie couldn't get the image of Rah Rah out of his mind. He loathed the thought of paying for sex, especially when there were so many boys who would die for the chance to screw a name designer. But Reggie did not want just any boy. He wanted Rah Rah. Finally, he succumbed. He picked up the phone and dialed Rah Rah's number.

At first they spent one night a week together, all Reggie felt he could afford. But before long, once a week simply wouldn't do. Rah Rah was an impressively hung beauty who knew how to please in and out of bed. He was habit-forming, and Reggie quickly became an addict. When he began to indulge twice a week, sometimes three, his accountant started asking questions.

'Just shut up and write the checks,' snapped Reggie. But he pleaded with Rah Rah for a discount. After all, wasn't he more than just another trick? Didn't they have something that went beyond mere sex? Did money have to be at the heart of each of their dalliances?

Rah Rah would not budge. Reggie didn't discount his clothes for his customers, so why should Rah Rah discount his cock?

Reggie raged and cursed and cried. But not even his tears moved Rah Rah, whose motto was 'Pay before you play.'

Reggie's expenses continued to mount.

When he wasn't hustling, Rah Rah was shopping. In New York the best place to shop on a Saturday afternoon was Bloomingdale's. Not because of Bloomie's fabulous, trend-setting assortment of home furnishings, food, and clothing, for which it was justifiably famous, but because of the *action*.

On this afternoon in May Rah Rah had checked out the scene and been winked at more than a few times, but no one had caught his eye. Some days were like that. As a consolation prize, he stopped in at the Ralph Lauren boutique to pick up a pair of Lauren's khaki shorts, which were cut just right to show off his well-muscled thighs.

A full head of blond, straw-textured hair hiding behind a pair of mirrored Ray-Bans and a baggy sweatshirt stopped him dead in his tracks.

Rah Rah edged closer to get a better look.

It was Spike Stone, the English rock star. Rah Rah couldn't believe it. Spike Stone was the hottest rocker since Mick. Rah Rah owned every one of Spike Stone's albums.

Spike was all alone – no bodyguards, no sexy chicks, no groupies.

'Give me every one of those whaddyacall'em . . . those

yachtin' sweaters in size medium,' Spike told the salesman in his unmistakable cockney accent.

Swallowing hard and speaking with more confidence than he felt, Rah Rah said coolly, 'I was thinking of buying one of those sweaters, but you just took all of them in my size.'

Spike Stone lowered his sunglasses and openly appraised Rah Rah – the expensive cowboy boots, the tight faded jeans that barely hid the strategically located bulge, and the T-shirt that strained to contain Rah Rah's well-developed pectorals.

'That right, eh? I s'pose I could give you one, but my motto is – if you want something, you've got to bloody well work for it. I got a show tonight at the Garden, but you can always come by my suite at the Plaza afterward and show me how badly you want it.'

Rah Rah gulped. 'The sweater – or you?'

'Both.' Spike chuckled.

Tonight . . . He was booked to spend the night with Reggie, who had made a big deal about the dinner party he was throwing to celebrate the success of his new collection and to introduce Rah Rah to his closest friends. Reggie would have a screaming shitfit if he skipped out on him.

But Spike Stone was an opportunity Rah Rah didn't want to miss. Fucking Spike Stone at the Plaza Hotel was the big time, the reason he'd come to New York.

'Okay,' Rah Rah said casually, as if it hardly mattered to him, 'tonight after the show, the Plaza.'

Spike tossed a thick wad of bills down on the counter. 'Right, then, keep the change,' he told the dazed salesman who had just toted up a bill for $2,655. 'Send the lot to me at the Plaza. I'll be there till Monday.'

He winked at Rah Rah before he left. 'And I'll see *you* later, luv.'

'Right,' Rah Rah muttered, 'later.'

Spike Stone's breezy invitation was like a dream come true. For an instant he regretted having to cancel on Reggie, who had fast become his best customer. But regrets would only get in his way, and Rah Rah was a young man in a hurry with one eye always on the future . . .

Until he was seventeen Rah Rah – then known as Ellis Hughes – had never traveled more than fifty miles from his hometown of Lake City, Florida, where his parents had struggled to raise him and his five younger siblings on the money his father earned as a state highway patrolman.

His parents' dream was to see their children graduate from college, so after high school Ellis enrolled at the University of Florida at Gainesville. To pay for his housing, books, and fees, he worked as many hours as he could spare as a waiter. But he was always short on cash, especially for extras like movies and dates.

Walking across campus one day during his sophomore year, Ellis was approached by a man who told him he owned a club downtown. He was looking for young, good-looking guys who could dance and who wanted to pick up some extra money on weekends. Ellis thought, Sure, why not? But when he showed up for his first gig he quickly discovered that 'dancing' really meant 'stripping' – and the club was for men only.

At first he balked at the thought of peeling down to the buff, but the club owner urged him to give it a try for a couple of weeks. Ellis was a smash. The patrons all but drooled every time he moved his perfectly sculpted body in time to the music. Their enthusiastic cheers earned him his nickname, Rah Rah.

Not only did he fast become the most popular dancer in the club, but also he was besieged by requests from well-to-do businessmen for 'private dances.' By now Rah Rah was savvy enough to know that most of the private dancing took place in hotel room beds, but the businessmen paid well for his services – often as much as two hundred dollars a night, almost half of what his daddy made in one week.

Instead of going home to Lake City during semester breaks and vacations, Rah Rah headed south to Miami where his boss owned another club and where the money was even better. A lot of the customers, tourists from New York, assured Rah Rah that he had some highly attractive assets that could mean big bucks in the Big Apple.

He was only one semester shy of graduation, and he knew it would break his parents' hearts if he dropped out of school. But the lure of earning a clear three hundred and fifty dollars a night was too tempting to resist. So he made up a story for them about an offer from a modeling agency ('Great way to earn money for graduate school'), promised to enroll at New York University to finish his degree, and took off for New York.

Rah Rah didn't regret his decision for a minute. He had a terrific one-bedroom apartment with a view of the East River, a summer share in a house on Fire Island, and a good, steady income that promised to get even better, thanks to customers like Reggie Bolt. Poor Reggie. Rah Rah hated to disappoint him, but Spike Stone was . . . well, Spike Stone.

He made his way through the crowded first floor to the pay phone near the front doors of the store and dialed Reggie's private number.

'I can't make it tonight, Reggie,' he said with genuine regret. 'Something's come up.'

There was a long silence at the other end of the line.

Reggie was aghast. Planning this dinner party had been his chief obsession for the last month. He had invited twenty of his close friends, all of whom had been clamoring to meet the new man in his life.

He had hired *the* hottest caterer in the city. The most *expensive* caterer, too. 'The hell with what it costs,' he'd said grandly. The party was a double celebration – of his ascent to stardom *and* of his acquisition of a sweet and exquisite boyfriend.

That same boyfriend who was now telling him that something had come up.

Reggie felt sick. If Rah Rah didn't show, he'd never hear the end of it from his friends. He could hear them cackling among themselves. 'Poor old Reggie, he's such a star he can't even keep one boy in his stable . . . I always knew that Rah Rah sounded too good to be true . . . a figment of his fevered imagination . . .'

It pained Reggie deeply to have to plead, but caught between the greater and lesser of humiliations, he all but fell to his knees and begged.

'Please, Rah Rah . . . you know how important this dinner is to me, how much I've been counting on you to be there . . . You promised.'

Rah Rah felt a touch of remorse, but Spike Stone was a much bigger fish than Reggie Bolt could ever hope to be. 'Let's make it tomorrow night instead, okay?'

'*No!* I need to see you *tonight*. And I *expect* to see you tonight. No discussion.'

Rah Rah didn't like to be pushed. 'Hey, wait a minute, man,' he pointed out, 'you don't *own* me.'

Reggie cursed silently. They had had this conversation before. But he could own Rah Rah, in a manner of speaking, could have exclusive rights to his time if he bought out Rah Rah's option. Buying out his option meant making it worth Rah Rah's while to stop hustling for life. To do that, Reggie would have to fork over $250,000 in cash, the sports car of Rah Rah's choice, free room and board, and the promise in his will of another $250,000 from Reggie's estate.

The idea was absurd, Reggie had declared unequivocally when Rah Rah gave him the terms. Absolutely unacceptable. He didn't have that kind of money to spend on boys, no matter how pretty they were. A gift of cash, such as he made to Rah Rah whenever they saw each other, was one thing. But this was prostitution. Besides, Reggie didn't have to buy love. He could have anybody he wanted.

The trouble was, as they both knew, he wanted only Rah Rah.

Buying out Rah Rah's option would be a very expensive proposition. His accountant would raise hell. But dammit, the man worked for him, not the other way around. And if that's what it took in these mercenary times to ensure that Rah Rah didn't break any more dinner dates, perhaps he should pay the price. For then he would own Rah Rah, lock, stock, and barrel.

Reggie liked the sound of that *a lot*.

In the days and weeks that followed her show, Dani felt like the laughingstock of New York. Each day she dutifully tried to make the rounds of the major store executives and the buyers to whom Irving had introduced her. But all she got from them was the usual excuse about how busy they were. In the evenings, wherever she went with Nino, she was sure people were talking about her, snickering about her collection, dishing her the way her so-called friends had dished her in the rest room of the showroom.

Lingering looks, muffled giggles, sympathetic pats on her hand . . . Dani saw and felt them all, and was convinced that she had become the biggest joke in town. When she complained to Nino, he tried to reassure her.

'*Cara*, nobody's talking about you. Nobody even *cares* about the line.'

His words were well intentioned, but instead of making her feel better, they twisted the knife deeper into her wounded pride.

At galas and fund-raisers and black-tie affairs, she would corner key fashion people, some of whom she'd known socially for years, and try in vain to persuade them to take a risk with her line. Eventually they began to flee in the other direction as soon as they saw her coming. And when they stopped taking or returning her phone calls, Dani had all the evidence she needed to declare her first venture onto Seventh Avenue a complete and utter failure.

The only thing worse than creating a stir, she thought miserably, was creating no stir at all. Unfortunately, she had succeeded at that.

The slights triggered off the long-buried hurts of her childhood. Suddenly she was once again Maurice's fat, ungainly, unloved daughter. Only this time she had made a fool of herself, not within the narrow frame of Maurice's affections, but on the much larger canvas of the New York social and fashion establishment.

But there was another difference, too, she sternly reminded herself. At the Clinique Etiole she had emerged from her fat-encased cocoon transformed into a beautiful svelte butterfly. The new Dani didn't have to slink away to her room and sink into a cake-induced coma of depression. The new Dani could soar on a pair of gossamer wings that were reinforced with self-confidence and lined with steely determination.

But before she could soar, she would have to figure out where she'd gone wrong.

Thinking back on the months that had preceded her show, she didn't have to dig far to find the answer. Even with Monika's help, there had been too much to do, too much to worry about and remember. Her calendar was proof of how distracted she'd been. All those meetings and lunches and drink dates, the long days spent with Irving, the late evenings out with Nino.

No wonder she had flopped, she thought bleakly. She hadn't allowed herself enough of what she needed most – time to create, to be inspired, to think about colors and shapes and movement, to consider what would make her clothes special . . . unique.

She had neglected to concentrate on the most basic element of the fashion business: creating *good* designs.

The critics had been right. Her designs were dull. Absolutely ordinary. Uninspired. But the applause that had greeted the originality of her designs at Mr Reggie's October show still rang in her ears.

And that, too, was where she had gone wrong. She had been so determined to beat Mr Reggie at his own game that she had missed the boat.

'So you're not an overnight sensation,' Irving told her one afternoon when he stopped by his protégée's offices. 'Welcome to the club. A little taste of failure isn't the worst thing in the world. Makes you a little hungrier for success, doesn't it? But next time around, remember – you're a designer first and a businesswoman second. And speaking of business, if you want the retailers to pay attention to your *next* collection, you better get your ass in gear and hustle up some orders for this collection.'

'It's not as if I haven't been trying,' she complained, staring down at Seventh Avenue, the avenue of so many dreams. 'Nobody returns my calls unless it's to set up a social engagement. They couldn't care less about Countess Dani, Inc.'

Irving was unsympathetic. 'You think I haven't had doors slammed in my face? And I'm not even a celebrity.

Come on, *bubelah*, get off your piss pot. Here,' he said gruffly. 'Maybe this will help.'

Dani unwrapped the package he handed her. Inside was a new copy of *Sheldon's Retail Book*.

'In there,' Irving said, 'you'll find the orders for your first collection. Now get on the phone and start calling those buyers – everyone from here to Pasadena. And don't you dare give up. *Farshteyst?*'

Dani nodded. She understood.

She and Monika divided up the states and pitched the Countess Dani line until they were hoarse. Countless times a day they told the voice at the other end of the line, 'We'd love to have you drop by the showroom when you're in town.'

With the women, they shamelessly played up Dani's title and all but promised entrée into New York society. With the men, they relied on the breathy, sexy come-hither voice and whatever else it took to lure them into the showroom where sandwiches, fruit, beer, champagne, sodas, and coffee were always available to the tired, hungry buyers who ventured in to see the line.

The major chains, most of which were owned by conglomerates, all but ignored her. The smaller independent retailers were the only ones who came through.

The trickle of orders was not enough.

Mougins, France

Roberto diPortanova liked to pontificate to Nino and his sisters about the importance of a good solid marriage – a marriage like the one he enjoyed with his wife of thirty-four years. But what he liked even better was a good fuck with one of his several mistresses.

As a devout Catholic, Roberto regularly went to mass

107

and knelt before the altar to ask forgiveness for his sins. As a true Italian, he knelt just as regularly before the altar of a mistress's mass of pubic hair.

Frequently the rest of the body belonged to Karola von Reich.

In the early sixties, Karola had decided that von Reich Industries needed to diversify and that the manufacture of electric heaters was a suitable market into which the company could expand. After several years in the market-place, von Reich Heaters had consistently lost money because, Karola was chagrined to realize, the name to beat was diPortanova Ltd. Simply put, the diPortanovas produced better, cheaper heaters.

The next logical step, of course, was to acquire the competition. Karola sent an envoy, one of her vice presidents, to make the proposal.

Roberto diPortanova was incensed. Serious suitors didn't send messenger boys to do a man's work. Or a woman's. Roberto sent the envoy packing.

Karola was irritated but undeterred. She knew all about Roberto diPortanova and how to deal with men of his ilk. Though her closets were brimming with unworn made-to-order outfits, all numbered and cataloged according to season, color, and designer, she had Marc Bohan of Christian Dior fly into Salzburg to custom-design her a new wardrobe of suits and dresses. Then she headed for Rome.

In her luggage was a peace offering – a double-barreled rifle, custom-made by her best craftsmen at von Reich Munitions. Roberto's name was engraved in gold on the butt. Karola saw it as a practical gift: If he refused her deal, she boasted, she'd shoot him.

Roberto had no intention of selling, but he was eager to meet the infamous Karola von Reich. 'Ballbuster,' his own executives called her. 'A hard-hearted bitch with brains and the kind of looks you don't easily forget.'

When she arrived at his office, her blond hair clipped as short as a man's, her long legs conspicuously displayed beneath the gray pinstriped miniskirt of her suit, he was amused to see that she lived up to her reputation.

As soon as she shook his hand, he knew he was going to fuck her. It was only a matter of time.

He laughed with pleasure when she presented him with the rifle. 'An excellent gift,' he said, pretending to take aim. 'I like to hunt.'

'As do I,' Karola purred, crossing one leg over the other and exposing the black lace garters that held up her stockings. She had already made up her mind. If she couldn't fuck him in business, she would fuck him in bed.

Roberto didn't like Karola, but he admired her. She was the first woman he'd ever met whom he couldn't dominate. She knew how to fight dirty. She challenged him. And Roberto always rose to a challenge. And he satisfied her in a way that no other man, least of all her husband languishing in the sanitarium, had satisfied her.

They were a perfect match.

They met whenever and wherever their schedules permitted. Sometimes they rendezvoused at Karola's villa in Mougins, just up from Cannes where the von Reich yacht was moored. The villa was small by Karola's standards, with only twenty-four bedrooms. But it served its purpose – a place to hold intimate meetings, whether for business or pleasure, that were better off unpublicized. This time, the occasion was purely pleasure.

As usual, when they hadn't been together in a while, Karola and Roberto had sex immediately and quickly. Later they would go at it again more slowly, teasing and tormenting each other with all the tricks in their sexual repertoire.

Karola lay spent atop the tangled satin sheets. Through the open French doors that led to the terrace, a light May breeze fanned her nude, sweaty body.

'You've put on some weight,' Roberto told her. 'That's good. I prefer my women to look well fed.'

Then he bent over and began to lick her nipples until she was moaning weakly. Satisfied that he had left her hungry and ready for more, Roberto abruptly stood up and went into the adjoining bathroom to take care of other, more pressing matters.

At any other time, Karola would have been stewing over his cruel jab about her weight, especially because it was true – she had gained several unwanted kilos. But this time the joke was on him. It was all she could do not to snicker aloud.

In a basket next to the toilet, she had planted the latest international edition of *Newsweek*, artfully folded open to a story about Roberto's daughter-in-law and the clothing company she had just launched. Karola knew Roberto only tolerated the girl – he rarely even mentioned her – and he loathed the publicity she and his son generated.

Karola wondered whether Roberto knew about his daughter-in-law's latest stunt. If not, he would in a moment. She smiled happily. Roberto tended to get too smug, even with her. She liked to remind him that she, too, could play his game.

Lighting a cigarillo, she glanced at the Cartier clock next to her bed, counting the seconds.

Roberto didn't even bother to flush the toilet before he came charging out of the bathroom, brandishing the article. 'I suppose this amuses you!' he shouted, hurling the magazine at her.

'What on earth are you talking about?' she said, yawning.

'Don't play innocent. *Somebody* must have been reading it.'

'Oh,' Karola said sweetly, 'you mean the article about your daughter-in-law's new venture?'

'You know exactly what I mean,' he snapped, sitting down on the side of the bed, his cock bobbing limply.

'Roberto, why you permitted your son to marry that dreadful girl I cannot imagine,' Karola said, lazily examining her nails. 'I'll never forget how she filled Monika's head with the most idiotic ideas when they spent time together at the Clinique Etiole. I almost had to handcuff her to Helmut, she was so headstrong. And now this.'

Roberto saw an opening and seized it. 'Karola, you never did tell me why Helmut divorced Monika.'

'We were talking about *your* daughter-in-law,' Karola firmly reminded him, 'and why you sanctioned such an unsuitable marriage.'

Roberto stalked out of the room without answering Karola's question. He was not about to tell her or anyone else why he had finally allowed Nino to marry Dani . . .

Roberto had been incensed when Nino and Dani arrived at the diPortanova estate in Asolo and announced their engagement. How dare his only son even consider marrying an American – not to mention an American Jew! It was unthinkable! Roberto had unequivocally refused to give his consent.

Dani had flown back to New York, heartbroken and in tears. Nino had stormed out of the villa without so much as a good-bye to his father and sped south to Rome in his Lamborghini. There he checked into the Hotel Hassler on the Piazza Trinita dei Monti.

Trying to forget his sorrows, he stayed awake night after night, making the rounds of the discos – Jackie O', Il Dito al Naso, and other favorite haunts. But a week went by and still he couldn't forget Dani. Spending hundreds of lire shopping on the Via Condotti didn't help. The only way to blot out his misery was to drink himself unconscious.

One night while he was guzzling champagne at the Hassler bar, a handsome redheaded American seated a few stools away sent him a bottle of Taittinger's. Nino raised an eyebrow but didn't object. After they had shared yet another bottle of champagne, the American drunkenly placed his hand on Nino's shoulder and invited him up to his suite.

Nino shrugged and thought, Why not? Heaven knew he was never going to bring this one home to meet the family.

Roberto also happened to be in Rome that night on business. After a late dinner at exclusive El Toula, he was standing outside his room searching his pockets for the key when two guests blindly stumbled past him. Roberto glanced up and recognized Nino, obviously drunk.

Roberto was about to call out to his son, but Nino and his companion walked right by, totally engrossed in each other. Roberto watched as they stopped in front of a door farther down the hall.

The redheaded man squeezed Nino's ass, then kissed Roberto diPortanova's son on the lips.

Roberto couldn't believe what he was seeing.

Worse yet, Nino didn't object!

He wrapped his arms around the man and passionately returned the kiss.

Trembling with disgust and anger, Roberto told himself that he must have been mistaken. It couldn't have been Nino. He hurried into his room and telephoned the hotel operator, who confirmed that Gianni diPortanova was indeed registered. Roberto sank down on the bed, his breathing labored.

His only son . . . a froscia!

An hour went by and then another.

112

Finally Roberto knew what he must do. Even worse than Nino marrying Dani Lieberman would be for Nino never to marry, never to bear a son. Roberto could not permit that to happen.

He picked up the phone and placed a person-to-person call to New York.

'Miss Lieberman, this is Roberto diPortanova.'

He heard her gasp. After her chilly leave-taking in Asolo, certainly he must have been the last person she ever expected to hear from.

'Is Nino all right?' she asked.

He cleared his throat. 'Of course. Miss Lieberman, tell me the truth. Do you honestly love my son?'

'Oh, yes! I'm crazy about Nino.'

He had changed his mind, he told her. She could marry his son, but on two conditions: their children were to be raised Catholics, and she was to make sure to keep Nino happy and completely satisfied.

'Do you understand me, Miss Lieberman?' he had asked her. 'Do you think you can fulfill those conditions?'

'Yes, yes,' she had ecstatically agreed. Children were something that belonged to a distant future. As for keeping Nino happy – of course she would. They were madly in love – and she was the happiest girl in the world.

But now, three and a half years later, there *were* no children, Roberto reminded himself, no tangible signal that all was well and . . . normal between Nino and his wife. Instead of a new baby, there was a new company – Countess Dani, Inc.

Standing on the sun-drenched terrace off the west wing of Karola's villa, Roberto grimaced as he puffed on his cigarette. Naturally the girl had chosen to capitalize on a noble title that was hers only through the privilege of

113

marriage. And even worse, to have coupled it with that ridiculous, boyish nickname she insisted on using.

Americans were all alike. So brash. So vulgar. Roberto stubbed out his cigarette.

From inside the villa, Karola beckoned . . .

By June, Dani knew that unless she could pull a rabbit out of her hat, she was facing total ruin. The orders for her fall collection were in, and the figures were 70 percent below her original projections. Another season like this, she thought gloomily, and she would be finished as a designer. Even worse, the corporation bearing her name would be bankrupt.

As it was, her company was losing $50,000 a month, and that was on top of the original $400,000 capitalization loan she owed the bank. Of course, Nino had offered to bankroll the entire operation, negating the need for a bank loan, but Dani had refused. He had helped her stage the first show, and that had been a disaster. Any future disasters, God forbid, would come out of her pocket, not his. That was only fair. Still, no amount of fiddling with the figures would reduce her fixed expenses – office rent, salaries for Monika, her samplemaker, her finishers, the receptionist who doubled as the showroom model, entertainment, lights, phone – the basic costs of operating a business.

And manufacturing. Dani had contracted out her first collection to a manufacturer in Queens, one of the few who could find time for her order. Later she understood why the contractor had been available. Irving had warned her about quality control and had urged her to look around for another contractor. But she was desperate to get the line finished and shipped before June 30, the cutoff date after which stores could cancel their original orders.

When the garments came back, at least a third of the collection was mis-sized, badly pieced, sloppily made. Dani and Monika stared in horror. Over and over, they had pitched quality to the buyers.

And now . . .

'*Liebchen*, we have to fill those orders,' Monika told Dani. 'Let's hope this is the worst of it.' She held up one especially mismatched dress as if it were a bloody rag.

'And have my name on that? Forget it,' Dani said angrily, furious with herself for not having listened to Irving. 'I'd rather not fulfill the order and hope the buyer comes back when we have a better collection than risk losing the customer forever with a shoddy piece of crap like that.'

She and Monika had their first business disagreement over the issue of quality versus unfulfilled orders. But Dani was, after all, the boss. And so, what few orders she had were reduced by another third.

Dani and Monika finished shipping the first collection on June 29, 1975, from the back of the building on Seventh Avenue. Along with the rest of the staff, they stayed up until four in the morning packing and labeling the last of the shipments. Nino's conspicuous absence was in protest against Dani's decision to drive up to Connecticut later that day.

'But, *cara*,' he complained, 'we've been invited to Saint Tropez for the month, and you need a vacation. Besides, we have obligations, and I don't want to go without you.'

'I have work to do, Nino,' Dani defended herself. 'It's time I designed some real clothes.'

'Can't you design there? On the beach?' he cajoled.

'In Saint Tropez, in the summer? Are you kidding?'

Nino knew she was right. The nonstop parties, the

drinking, the drugs . . . Most nights people danced until sunrise, then slept until noon and spent the afternoon drying out by their villas' pools. Besides, Dani was adamant. She had work to do. She couldn't afford to present another collection like her first one. That was the fastest route to becoming yesterday's news.

July and August were dead months as far as the fashion industry was concerned. Fall had been shipped, and spring wouldn't be presented until October. She had two months to recoup, to figure out where she'd gone wrong and how to prevent that from happening again. By the end of August, she needed a set of sketches for a spring collection that would prove to the critics that she wasn't a figment of her own imagination.

She and Nino had bought a house in Roxbury, Connecticut, on an impulse one beautiful fall weekend two years earlier. A two-hundred-year-old restored farmhouse, it stood at the top of a hill that provided a view for miles of the Connecticut countryside and the neighboring Berkshire Mountains. Fifteen acres of meadows, streams, and stands of birches and evergreens separated the diPortanovas from their next-door neighbors. It was a perfect place for solitude and privacy. With Nino happy and probably in trouble in Saint Tropez, Dani would be all alone, except for the caretaker and his wife, who did the cooking and light cleaning.

July was hot, even in Connecticut, but Dani was up with the sun every day. Some mornings she rode one of the horses for an hour or so; other mornings she jogged several miles along the dirt path that led to the pond.

And then she went to work. After a light breakfast, she would arrange herself by the pool, armed with a bottle of Bain de Soleil suntan lotion, a wide-brimmed straw hat, her sketch pad, and her colored pencils. At lunchtime, her housekeeper tiptoed out to leave her a plate of fresh fruit and cheese and a pitcher of iced coffee. In the early evenings, she rode again, swam, returned phone calls, and ate dinner on a tray in front of the television.

One weekend Monika came to stay, and they partied for two nights all over Litchfield County. But when Monika departed promptly on Monday at noon, Dani was left again to her solitude.

She hadn't spent so many hours alone since that terrible time after Sophie's death, but now she found that she was enjoying the experience. Life with Nino was like a non-stop roller-coaster ride – the highs and lows came so quickly that she never had a moment to catch her breath. Now that she had stepped off the ride, if only temporarily, she was rediscovering the calm that came from sitting still.

After a couple of weeks, she had a stack of sketches, but nothing that added up to a collection. Something was wrong. Good ideas just weren't coming.

On long walks through the fields and along the country roads, she pondered the problem. Fishing for a clue, she called Monika, who was, as always, supportive but otherwise unhelpful. Monika had a natural instinct for business and administration, but the creative burden was Dani's alone.

The answer, when it came to her, was so easy and obvious that she couldn't understand why she hadn't seen it before: her first collection lacked a voice . . . a direction. It was a scattershot mishmash of designs, none of which really worked. A collection without a theme was like a car without a drive shaft. It went nowhere. And hers hadn't.

But not so the designs that Mr Reggie had stolen. She had conceived those designs, which *had* received praise and applause, for a very specific market – Dani diPortanova. She had created them because designers weren't offering her clothes that had any snap or glamour.

117

Worse, she couldn't wear the same outfit all day – to go shopping or to lunch – and also later, for cocktails and dinner. She almost always had to change three times a day to keep up with her schedule. That was fine for a lady of leisure, but what about a twenty-one-year-old woman on the go?

Dani mulled it over. More and more of her friends, if they weren't just graduating from college, were working in offices. Their lives were complicated and fast-paced. And not all of them had the perfect size six or eight figure.

Certainly there had to be a way to design comfortable, flattering, feminine outfits that could carry these busy women through a long day and still be appropriate for all but the most formal evening occasions.

She sketched well into August, using up pad after pad of paper. It was as if nothing else in the world existed except the circle of space that included herself, her pencils, her sketches.

Finally she was as satisfied as she would ever be. She put down her pencil and stared critically at the dress that would be the center-piece of her fifteen-piece collection. She was so exhausted emotionally from thinking about and perfecting the design that when she got into her red Jaguar and headed back to New York, she still didn't know whether her creation measured up to the standard she'd set for herself. And she wouldn't know until the dress was unveiled at her spring collection showing in October.

If the dress didn't measure up, she was through.

Chapter Five

The second collection was not a hit.

It was a smash. Bigger than anything Seventh Avenue had seen since the miniskirt.

The pièce de résistance, the 'Drop Dress,' so christened because of the way it slipped over the head and shoulders, brought the audience to its feet in a rousing, standing ovation.

Even by Seventh Avenue's standards, the cotton knit dress was a stroke of genius. Not a single button or zipper distracted from its well-sculpted lines. The boat-neck collar was oh-so-slightly revealing and sexy. The dress flowed so easily that it seemed to breathe. Best of all, it was flattering to almost any woman, whether she was the perfect fashion industry standard size eight or Dani's former size, fourteen.

Whether worn belted, sashed, or loose, the drop dress was more versatile than anything the fashion-buying public had seen in years. And with a price tag in the neighborhood of $125, the Drop Dress, available in a variety of colors, was affordable as well as imaginative.

Women's Wear Daily raved, 'Countess diPortanova's designs make many of this season's other American offerings seem irrelevant. The collection as a whole – and in particular what will no doubt come to be seen as her signature dress – succeeds brilliantly because it appeals to a hitherto unrecognized market: designer sportswear for women whose idea of "dress for success" goes beyond gray flannel suits.

'Here are clothes for women on the go, for discriminating women on their way to the top, designed by a discriminating woman who is clearly a designer to be watched. Countess diPortanova has managed to give us outfits that can make the transition from daytime to evening wear, from business or social luncheons to dinner and the theater. We predict that the "Drop Dress" will find its way into the closets of fashion-conscious women all over America.'

How right they were.

'Drop Everything – The Drop Dress Is Here!' screamed the headlines on the style pages of every major newspaper in the country.

The New York Times enthused, 'The centerpiece of Countess diPortanova's collection is a startlingly practical but sexy dress that can be worn for day or evening.'

Diana Vreeland, the doyenne of American fashion editors and trendsetters, said, 'On the right woman, the "Drop Dress" has the "drop dead" look.'

Dani immediately adopted her comment as the tag line for her ad campaign: 'Drop them dead with the Drop Dress.'

Fascinated by the twenty-one-year-old immigrants' daughter who had married into aristocracy, whose life was a fairy tale of endless glamour and limitless money, shoppers responded to her pitch.

Who could resist? Everyone wanted to own a Countess Dani – and in quantities that were astounding.

Even Irving Blatt, who thought he had seen everything, shook his head in disbelief. Buyers for the major department and specialty stores – the people whom Irving had warned would be tough sells after her disastrous first

120

season – flooded the Countess Dani showroom with orders.

To think that Dani, who just six months before had been on the verge of ruin, should suddenly be the darling of the industry! And all before even one order had been manufactured or shipped. He was proud and delighted for her, though he couldn't help but pat himself on the back for having recognized her talent.

The rest of the Seventh Avenue designers, by nature an insanely jealous lot, were less thrilled. At best, snipped the sour-grapes crowd, Dani was just another celebrity of the moment. If she was lucky, her name might carry her one more season before she sank without a trace, as so many others had. She was a socialite who wanted to play designer, they clucked.

Through the grapevine, Dani heard it all.

'Just ride it out,' advised Irving. 'Deliver what you've promised, and the joke's on them.'

She swore to Irving that she would.

Clive Churchill-Manley, New York society's premier interior designer, had worked his ass off to achieve the elegant, homey English country look Monika von Reich had requested. The result was nothing short of dazzling.

He didn't come cheap, but Monika didn't care. What was money for, if not to enjoy? She had given Clive free rein, and he had gladly run with it.

He had hired an architect and an army of contractors. The plumbing and wiring had been ripped out and replaced, the walls torn down, rebuilt, painted, and papered. The floors had been stripped and refinished, the roof replaced.

Cabinetmakers had built brand-new pine cupboards and beams for the kitchen, then carefully stained them so that they looked like antiques. A crew of landscape architects had transformed the weed-choked backyard into a miniature English garden.

From among his best antique sources, galleries, and private collectors, Clive had amassed some of the finest pieces of his career. A week's junket to London and the surrounding English countryside had yielded two Louis XV stone mantels, Chinese porcelains, gilded consoles, heirloom rugs, and a crate full of Old English paintings.

The work had taken months, but Clive had transformed the dilapidated town house into a warm and colorful home, the kind of home Monika had always craved. Now he wanted to get paid.

Waiting for Monika to join him in her living room, Clive grunted with anticipated pleasure. A bottle of Dom Pérignon champagne was chilling in the sterling silver ice bucket he'd bought her as a house-warming gift. Two crystal goblets stood on the mahogany rent table he'd found for her just outside of Bath.

Soon she would arrive for his 'presentation,' as he liked to call it.

Clive had learned from bitter experience that, no matter how rich his clients were, they didn't like to pay their bills. But he had to pay his. Thus, he made a ritual out of personally presenting his statement, tastefully itemized on Clive's gray linen engraved stationery with the distinctive coat of arms emblazoned at the top.

The coat of arms was as phony as the rest of his family history. But his real surname, Jones, lacked cachet. And he'd known when he started out in London, more years ago than he admitted to, that success as an interior designer to the very rich depended on snob appeal as much as on talent.

With the help of a very discreet plastic surgeon, Clive looked the part of distinguished English designer. He dieted and exercised with a discipline that even Monika's mother would have admired, and dressed so stylishly that he regularly made the 'Best Dressed' list. When he was between wives, as he was now, he was every hostess's favorite candidate for extra man at the dinner table.

But if Clive had his way, his availability would soon be coming to an end. He had made up his mind that he wanted more from Monika von Reich than payment for services rendered.

She had everything he fancied in a young woman: a succulent pair of tits a man could wrap his hands around, a face that showed up well in photographs (essential for garnering publicity at all those benefits and galas), and most important, what he privately called Money with a capital M.

He'd made his usual inquiries and liked what he heard: heiress to one of Europe's great industrial fortunes, recently separated from her wealthy Swiss husband (nobody seemed to know why), best friend of Dani diPortanova.

If his instincts were right, as they invariably were, she was ripe for his plucking.

Glancing at the carpenter who was filling in a flaw in the molding with some plastic wood, he said, 'Hurry up, there. Miss von Reich should be here any moment, and I want everything finished before she arrives.'

The carpenter, who had worked for Clive before, had his boss figured for an A-1 jerk. He noticed the champagne and the way Clive kept inspecting himself in the gilt-framed mirror over the mantelpiece and figured out that Clive had the hots for Miss von Reich.

'Sure thing, Mr Churchill-Manley,' he said and nodded obligingly.

He had no intention of rushing. Rick Flood knew how to read women, whether they were society dames or mick Irish from south Jersey, like him. One thing he was sure of, Monika von Reich wanted him. Wanted him badly. And he'd be damned if that ass-licking limey was going to have her . . .

After being burned by the shoddy production of her first collection, Dani had lined up a first-rate manufacturer for the fall collection. But when the orders for the Drop Dress started to pour in, the manufacturer said no.

'What do you mean, *no*?' Dani screamed into the phone. 'We made a deal! You can't renege on me. I'll take you to court!'

'Hey, lady,' the manufacturer calmly pointed out, 'you were talking about producing ten thousand pieces, max. Now you're telling me you got almost that much for your *first week* of selling. I wish I could help you out, but I can't handle that volume. You got to find someone else. Go talk to the big boys.'

'You son of a bitch,' Dani swore. 'You can't get away with this. You'll ruin me!'

'You're wasting your breath, honey. Save it to find someone who can fill your orders.'

At the end of the third week, when orders were topping twenty thousand and still climbing, Irving gave Dani a list of manufacturers and said, 'Feel free to use my name.'

Unfortunately, his name didn't help. Dani and Monika placed phone calls to factories from Worcester, Massachusetts, to Greenville, South Carolina. It was the same story everywhere. Nobody was willing to take on the line. Their plant time was already committed to other designers with equally heavy production jobs.

'It's a great position to be in, honey,' a rep from one of the country's biggest manufacturers told her. 'I hope you find someone. It'd be a shame if you didn't.'

'Thanks a lot,' Dani said bitterly.

'Yeah, yeah, sure you got the orders, doll,' another

manufacturer told Monika. 'But so do Calvin and Leslie Fay. I can't bump them for you. They've been with me for years. Come back next season. We'll line up something then, all right?'

'Like hell we will,' Monika shouted, slamming down the phone.

Dani offered the manufacturers exclusive deals on future collections – collections she promised would be even more lucrative than this one – if they could only accommodate her. She got nowhere. The bottom line was that every free minute of plant time had been booked months earlier by the major designers.

'But I didn't know three months ago I would be a *major designer*!' she said in frustration.

'Hey,' one manufacturer said, 'others should be so lucky. You're gonna be rich and famous. Somebody'll take you on.'

Her dream was turning into a nightmare. If she didn't find a manufacturer, her collection, her company – worst of all, her name – would go down the tubes.

She brought her problem home to Nino, expecting sympathy and support.

Nino had something else on his mind. Roberto was coming to New York. He had requested that a dinner party be organized in his honor.

'*Cara*, I'd like you to arrange the dinner. I'll help you, of course.'

Dani stared at Nino as if he had just suggested she take a swim in the Hudson River. 'Are you crazy? I'm already in over my head. Or haven't you noticed?'

He had. Their sex life was almost nonexistent. 'I'm your husband, and I need your help. You can find the time – as you always do.'

'For your information, I'm running a business,' she said icily. 'You ought to know. You cosigned the loan.'

125

A big mistake, Nino realized. His father had given him hell for permitting Dani to set up her own company. If Roberto were ever to discover the whole story . . .

'Look,' Dani said, trying to make peace, 'you're always talking about how efficient your secretary is. *She* can help you make the arrangements.'

'She's *not* my wife. You are. It's your place to do it.'

'What the hell are you talking about?' she exploded. 'My *place*? That shit sounds as if it came straight out of Roberto's mouth!'

It had, but Nino wasn't about to tell her that.

'I know it would please my father if you arranged the dinner party,' he said stiffly.

'Since when are you so concerned about what would please your father?'

'Since he gave us permission to marry.'

Months of anger and resentment suddenly boiled out of control. Dani hit low. 'Maybe he should have saved his breath. Maybe you'd be better off with a woman who'll be happy to stay home while you're out catting around,' she raged.

'Maybe,' Nino said, his eyes glinting with fury.

They stared at each other wrathfully. In almost four years of marriage, they had never quarreled with such venom. Their insults slashed back and forth across the room.

'You're a pigheaded snob, just like your father.'

'My father was right. All you care about is money!'

'Go tell it to one of your girlfriends!'

'At least *they* give me what a man needs!'

'Bastard!' she hissed.

'Bitch!'

She picked up the first thing she saw, a sixteenth-century Chinese bowl full of potpourri, and threw it against the bedroom wall. The delicate hand-painted bowl shattered into hundreds of tiny glittering fragments that fell to the floor like a misty spring rain. Dani stared in horror at the shards strewn across the rug. How could she have been driven to destroy this beautiful one-of-a-kind object? Was her love for Nino also on the verge of being destroyed?

Despair clutched at her heart, and she burst into racking sobs. 'Nino – '

He grabbed her in his arms. '*Cara, cara,*' he whispered tenderly, 'let's not fight.'

'Oh, Nino, I'm sorry, I'm so sorry.'

'Never mind, it doesn't matter,' he said, holding her tightly and stroking her back.

'Nino,' she whimpered guiltily, 'I feel terrible. Wasn't that bowl appraised for twenty thousand dollars?'

'Don't worry, I had it insured for thirty. We just made money on it.' He laughed carelessly and kissed her cheeks, still wet with tears. She looked so sad and stricken . . . his American beauty. At that moment, more than anything in the world, he wanted her naked beneath him. His desire immediately translated into a pulsing erection. No matter how many partners there were – and there were many – Dani was his wife. The woman he loved. She still got him hotter faster than anyone else he'd ever slept with. '*Cara, cara, mia cara,*' he cooed.

One hand found its way beneath her silk panties. The other deftly unbuttoned her silk shirt and searched inside her bra until his fingers closed around a breast. He teased her nipple, pulling it this way and that until she was breathlessly pleading with him to fuck her.

'Yes, yes,' she urged him. She had almost forgotten how she felt when he touched her. It had been much too long since the last time.

He gently pushed her down on the bed, so that her long

legs dangled over the side. Then he took off her shirt and bra and tugged her skirt and panties down over her hips.

Naked, Dani stared at Nino through gray eyes dazed with lust, silently telling him she was his.

Nino knew what she wanted, even if she herself had forgotten. He quickly stripped and fell to his knees in front of her, burying his head between her thighs.

'Aaah,' Dani groaned blissfully. All her worries about finding a manufacturer, about delivering merchandise on time, flew out of her head as Nino's mouth closed over her moist, aching triangle. His tongue, which had been this way so many times before, knew all her secret, hidden, most sensitive places.

He didn't stop probing, kissing, sucking, until she came, convulsively, crying out his name.

Then it was his turn. His cock, hard as a steel rod, was immediately sucked up into her, enveloped by her hot wetness. She pushed upward to meet his thrusts.

This time they came together . . .

Grateful for the French he'd learned all those years ago in Paris, Mr Reggie greeted the maître d' at Le Cirque with a magnanimous smile and a hearty '*Bonjour!*'

It was the lunch hour. The dining room, with its distinctive beige and peach monkey murals in the manner of the Singerie Room of the Palace of Versailles, was packed. But while the Old Guard and the nouveaux riches cooled their heels at the bar waiting to be seated, Mr Reggie was immediately ushered to his table.

From the moment the doors had first opened a year ago last March, in 1974, Mr Reggie had sensed, with the same nose that made him a fashion trendsetter, that Le Cirque would score as the 'in' place to dine. To buy himself some reservation insurance, he'd done something so simple, so appallingly déclassé, that the social set would have blanched, had they ever known.

He had slipped the maître d' a tip of one thousand dollars. Enough, he had rightly calculated, to cover himself for a year or two. Now, strolling through the dining room, nodding his head in acknowledgment of the many familiar faces, he thought smugly that without the maître d's goodwill, he, too, would have been kept waiting for a table. And that would *never* do.

Money still talked. One had to know the language. Like connections. A man had to know which ones to make and keep and which ones to cut off.

His favorite connection was already at the table – Mitchell Barton, the feared and fawned-over columnist of Seventh Avenue. Mitchell was a few years younger than Mr Reggie, in his early thirties, and everyone read and feared his column, 'One Ear to the Ground.' In the past he had printed the lowdown on everyone from Halston and Diane Von Furstenberg to Oscar de la Renta. He was universally treated like royalty because finding oneself the subject of an unfavorable item in a Mitchell Barton column was like getting hit with a ground-to-air missile. Ever fearful of where his next missile could be aimed, no one dared cross him.

But among the gay garmentos, the joke was that while Mitchell might have one ear to the ground, he always had his ass in the air, looking for a fuck.

Reggie had obliged him in that area with a double-headed dildo, Reggie at one end, Mitchell at the other. He was sure that Mitchell was longing for another session, but Reggie and Rah Rah had already gone at it that morning.

Then again, maybe Reggie would invite Mitchell home with him and pull out the dildo, just as a gesture of generosity and friendship. It *had* been quite a while. Rah

129

Rah liked real flesh, not toys, so for months all of Reggie's paraphernalia had been gathering dust under the bed.

'Mitchell, that tan! How divine,' Reggie said, smiling as he sat down.

'Key West,' Mitchell explained.

'Of course,' Reggie said, signaling the waiter for drinks and menus. He hadn't had time lately to get to the Keys, but that wasn't any of Mitchell's business. Besides, Reggie stayed perpetually tanned with his suntanning booth, which he kept in a small room off his office. Reggie had discovered that one of the joys of earning money was spending it. Especially on oneself.

Lunch was more of a ritual than a meal. Drinks arrived. Vodka martinis straight up. Their orders were taken. Then the dish began.

'His name is Rah Rah?' Mitchell asked, raising a tastefully plucked eyebrow.

'A nickname,' Reggie explained.

'One would hope. Is he a cheerleader or something?'

'No, just a companion.' Reggie wasn't about to mention he had to *pay* for the companionship.

'How's his cock?'

'Enormous and cut,' Reggie replied proudly.

Mitchell finished off his martini. Another round was ordered. 'I don't know where you find them. All of my tricks end up being two inches, hard. Have you ever tried to jerk someone off with a pair of tweezers?'

'Well, that's certainly not Rah Rah.'

'How do you take him?' Mitchell teased.

'Like these drinks, darling – straight up!'

They both cackled wickedly.

Appetizers arrived. Pasta primavera for Reggie, carpaccio Toscano for Mitchell. All the while a steady stream of acquaintances made their way to the table, bearing verbal invitations to parties, dinners, cocktails. Scraping.

130

Bowing. Ass-kissing. The two men handled them diplomatically, promising nothing, but making all of them feel as if they had committed to everything.

'Being in demand is so hard,' Reggie said, twirling his pasta.

'Agreed.' Mitchell sighed.

Neither would have had it any other way. They were young, brash, talented, and powerful. Sought after and envied. One for his talent, the other for his ability to make or break talent.

In many ways, Reggie and Mitchell were a lot alike . . .

Mitchell Barton had hitchhiked to New York from Houston in 1968, determined to make a name for himself as a designer. His family, Southern Baptists who had never strayed from their hometown, had begged him to stay, telling him that New York was a wild, bad town. Sodom and Gomorrah.

Their warning was music to Mitchell's ears. He had repressed his sexuality for the first twenty-five years of his life. He was determined not to repress it for the next twenty-five. New York was the only place to go.

For three years he camped out in a sixth-floor walk-up with little heat and even less hot water and a roommate who lived in a hashish haze. After serving several stints as a lowly design assistant, he watched his dream of becoming a designer begin to fade.

Others were making it, but not Mitchell. For whatever reasons, other people got the breaks. Or had the money. Never suspecting that perhaps his lack of success was due to a lack of talent, Mitchell grew bitter. Seventh Avenue had looked him over and found him wanting as a designer. But they hadn't seen the last of him.

He got himself hired as a copyeditor at WWD and looked around for greater opportunities. His abilities, he

131

soon discovered, lay in making friends and gaining their confidence. Thanks to his carefully cultivated contacts, he soon had his own column and a reputation as one of the most influential voices on Seventh Avenue.

Mitchell knew that would last only as long as he was hot. And he was determined to stay hot, even if it meant burning a designer or two.

'Well,' Mitchell asked over chef Jean Vergnes's chocolate soufflé, 'any news?'

Reggie smiled. Familiar as he was with Mitchell's background and his particular sensitivity to overnight-sensation designers, he knew which buttons to push to set in motion a blistering column. He was about to push a few, but he had to be subtle. The fact that they were occasional fuck-buddies worked in his favor, but business *was* business. If the game was too obvious, Mitchell might bow out.

'No, nothing, really,' Reggie said, sounding bored. Calculating every word. 'And you? You're the only one in town who hasn't gone gaga for the Drop Dress or whatever the hell it's called.'

'It's a fluke, nothing more. Dani diPortanova is a one-dress designer, mark my words. You think a title, connections, and money make her a designer?'

'Of course not.' Reggie sniffed. 'But the way the press is falling all over themselves, you'd think she was another Chanel. It's certainly an about-face from last spring when they skewered her for that joke of a collection. The question is, how can she meet the demand? Nobody's mentioned the fact that she didn't bother to line up a manufacturer who could handle the volume. Now she's running around at the last minute trying to find someone. It's amateur night.'

Reggie helped himself to the last bit of soufflé. 'Take it

132

from me, Mitchell, that company isn't going to last. The business end is being handled by a rich-bitch Austrian friend of hers. They tell me the girl can't even speak English. Her last job was wife to a Swiss industrialist. What does a divorced blond bimbo know about fashion? Other than how to shop? It's absurd. Especially when you and I have to *work* for a living.'

Mitchell thoughtfully sipped his cognac. 'Tell me more,' he said.

The afternoon wasn't going at all as Clive Churchill-Manley had planned.

The carpenter was still hard at work when Monika arrived.

Worse, she declined Clive's offer of a tour of the house.

'But surely you'll have a drink with me,' he said, pointing to the champagne. 'Now that everything is ready for you, my dear, we must drink to the end of one of my most enjoyable projects – and to beginnings . . .' He lowered his voice meaningfully.

'Certainly, *ja*,' she said graciously, wishing Clive would give her the bill and get out. She had more important things to think about.

Like the carpenter.

'What's your name?' she had asked him the other day when she caught him staring at her.

He flashed her a crooked grin. 'Rick Flood, at your service.' He had a mop of shoulder-length black curls, held in place with a makeshift headband, and a nose that looked as if it had survived a fight or two. His tight T-shirt revealed his bulging biceps, and his even tighter blue jeans hugged his ass and left no doubt as to the heft of his cock.

Monika couldn't stop thinking of him. She had even told Dani about him.

'You have a crush on the guy,' Dani teased her. 'You have the hots for Rick Flood.'

Monika dreamed up a list of woodworking alterations as an excuse to keep him around.

She had a hard time breathing when he was nearby.

Now he caught her eye and winked boldly.

Since getting free of Helmut, she'd gone out with dozens of men and slept with more than a few of them. But not a one had made her cream in her jeans the way Rick Flood did when he stared at her with those smoldering brown eyes. He looked almost . . . dangerous.

She wondered what he was like in bed. Aggressive? Tender? Passionate? Kinky? The possibilities were deliciously endless.

Clive droned on. Monika didn't hear a word. She was too consumed with images of Rick Flood whispering in her ear about what he was going to do to her, undressing her, his lips brushing against her naked body, his hands caressing her breasts, his mouth kissing her between the legs, his tongue –

'Monika?'

'*Ja?* Sorry?'

Clive looked at her sharply. Didn't the silly bitch know that any one of his female clients would jump at the chance to be Clive Churchill-Manley's next wife? He'd paid a small fortune for the ice bucket. He didn't make such gestures for just anyone.

Annoyed and wanting her to sense his displeasure, he said curtly, 'Could you just initial here, and then I'll be off.'

Monika glanced at the total – $600,000. It did seem rather a lot of money . . .

Ah, well, there must still be plenty left in her trust fund. When she was married, Helmut, of course, had taken care of all the bills. Before that, Karola had managed her financial affairs. This was all new to her. She'd never realized how expensive it was to be rich.

She scrawled her initials across the bottom of the page and smiled faintly. 'Clive,' she said, rubbing her hand against her forehead, 'I am having the most dreadful headache. I think I must go lie down on my new bed with a wet washcloth. We will talk soon, *ja*? And *danke, danke*, for all your help.'

Clive didn't give a shit about her headache, but he felt a sure thing slipping out of his grasp as she steered him to the front door.

'I'm concerned about you, my dear,' he said gravely. 'Please take care of yourself. Let me get rid of that damn carpenter for you. I'll tell him to come back when he won't bother you.'

'No, no,' Monika assured him, 'he's no bother at all. Not to worry.'

'I *do* worry about you, Monika,' Clive simpered, kissing the back of her hand. 'Promise me we'll have dinner soon. Somewhere . . . *intime*?'

Monika nodded vaguely and quickly closed the door behind him. The pompous old fool, hoping to seduce her. It was all she could do not to laugh in his obviously lifted face. She'd had it with these self-important people who thought she was a commodity to be taken care of and properly 'handled.'

From here on in, she was strictly on her own and downwardly mobile. Years ago she had read in one of Karola's dirty books that the most erotic perfume a woman could wear was her own vaginal scent. 'Eau de pussy,' the writer had called it. Now seemed an appropriate time to test his theory.

Stripping off her panties, she stuck two fingers deep inside herself, withdrew them dripping wet, and generously dabbed the sticky juice behind her ears, at the base of her neck, and between her breasts.

Ready for action, she smoothed her black leather skirt down over her hips and slowly returned to the living room.

She picked up the bucket that held the champagne (it was, after all, Dom Pérignon) and smiled politely at the carpenter. 'Mr Flood, could you come upstairs with me?' she asked. 'I need your help. There's something in the bedroom that needs screwing . . .'

'We have to talk,' barked Jerry Allen, the motor-mouthed public relations ace Dani had hired to promote Countess Dani, Inc.

'Sure . . . what's up?' Dani cradled the telephone under one ear and prepared for his assault. She knew she was lucky to have Jerry working for her. He was one of the best around. But that didn't mean she had to like talking to the man.

'Don't you read your own trades?' he asked. Twenty years in the business, and he was still surprised by how dumb his clients could be.

'I have enough to worry about,' Dani said wearily. 'What are they saying about me now?'

'I hate to do this to ya, kid,' he began. In Jerry's lingo, that meant he was about to hit her with a shot of bad news.

He read Dani the pertinent item in Mitchell Barton's latest column. It was snide, condescending, rife with innuendo and gossip. Most of it wasn't true, but that was beside the point.

'That son of a bitch!' she swore, sitting up.

'How much of this is fact?'

'Jerry, you know better than anyone. We're looking for a manufacturer, and . . . we'll find one.'

'So where'd he dig up the rest of this crap?' Jerry

136

growled. 'I'd like to put a permanent muzzle on his so-called source.'

'I can think of at least one person who has it in for me.'

'Gotcha,' Jerry said. 'Look, if this were just a cock-and-bullshit story about you and Nino, I'd say fuck it. But Countess Dani, Inc., is a business. Bad press can make or break a company a lot easier than a marriage. We're going to have to nip this in the bud. Pronto. I've got some ideas. When can we meet?'

When Roberto diPortanova was in New York, business was anything but usual at diPortanova USA. Comman-deering his son's spacious office as well as his secretary, Roberto took control: issuing orders, demanding figures, calling meetings, scrutinizing details, creating general havoc. If there was a method to his madness, Roberto alone appreciated it.

Everyone dreaded Roberto's visits – most of all Nino, who ran himself ragged, doing everything he could to ensure that his father was kept satisfied and happy. Tonight Nino would be hosting a dinner at the 21 Club in Roberto's honor. With Dani otherwise engaged, he had had to take care of the arrangements almost single-handedly, assisted only by his secretary, Eileen.

The guest list was limited to twenty of Roberto's closest New York friends and their wives. CEOs. Company presidents. Investment bankers. A couple of attorneys. Dull people by Nino and Dani's standards. Important people by Roberto's. People to whom appearances were everything.

Seated in the office that was his for the duration of Roberto's stay, Nino prayed that the evening would be a success. If it wasn't, he knew his father would never forgive him.

But the minute Roberto left town, Nino promised himself, he would hop the first jet south to the Caribbean.

Roberto's motto was 'Work hard and get ahead.' Nino's motto was 'Work hard, play hard, and stay hard.' He was way overdue for some playtime.

The intercom buzzed. He pressed the button, and Roberto's booming voice filled the room.

'Everything is set for tonight's dinner, Nino?'

'*Sì*, Papa. The private dining room at Twenty-One.'

'*Bene*,' Roberto said approvingly. The 21 Club wine list offered several of the diPortanova family's finest wines. 'Nino?'

'*Sì*, Papa?'

'Get there early to make sure everything is in order.'

'*Sì*, Papa, of course.'

The dinner party had been called for eight o'clock. As Dani was dashing out the door that morning, Nino told her he wanted them both at the 21 Club no later than seven-thirty. Earlier if possible.

'This is important, Dani,' he reminded her. 'Just this once, we must be on time.'

She blew him a kiss. 'No problem, hon. I swear it.'

By six-fifteen, Nino had finished bathing and was getting dressed for the evening. He put on a white silk dinner shirt, the ruffles perfectly starched and pressed; a burgundy silk ascot, newly arrived from Turnbull & Asser; trousers from his favorite tailor in Rome, to match his custom-made dinner jacket; and velvet slippers with the diPortanova coat of arms stitched across the toes.

He deliberated a moment in front of his jewelry case before choosing a pair of burnished gold studs to fasten the cuffs of his shirt. From his collection of watches, he chose the very thin gold Polo Piaget.

The watch needed setting. He checked the time.

Six-thirty. Where, he wondered, taking a hefty gulp of finely aged scotch, was his wife? Certainly not here, where she should have been by now.

A red-hot wire of worry stabbed at his gut. He knew he should have called to remind her again. But he'd been chasing his tail all day at the office. With Papa calling the shots, he'd barely had a second to take a piss.

Six-fifty. Late was one thing, but this was ridiculous!

He fetched the bottle of Glenfiddich from the wet bar in his dressing room and poured himself another glass. She couldn't have forgotten . . . Even Dani wasn't that irresponsible.

He grabbed the telephone and punched the numbers for the night line at the showroom. Busy . . . and again, busy. Two minutes later, still busy.

'*Basta!*' He slammed his fist down on the night table. The hot wire twisted deeper in his belly. How dare she treat him like this. Outrageous!

For Dani's sake, he hoped it was Monika who was tying up the line.

She could forget about taking a shower. As for wasting time trying to decide what to wear, she could forget that, too. He would choose her outfit, and if that didn't suit her, fuck her!

Nino diPortanova, reduced to playing lady's maid to his wife. Why wasn't she home taking care of him and making babies, as Papa insisted she should be?

He stormed into her room-sized closet and yanked off the evening-gown racks a strapless bronze lamé Saint Laurent original. Her gold high-heeled sandals. The matching compact purse. The hell with underwear. She could go naked underneath the dress for all he cared, just as long as she looked presentable.

Seven-fifteen. Their car would be waiting downstairs in front of the courtyard gates. His jaw tightened angrily. It would serve her right if he left without her. But then, God forbid, she might not show up at all. He would never hear the end of it from his father, who would consider her absence an affront to the entire family, not to mention an insult to Nino's manhood.

He tried the showroom again. This time the line was clear. No busy signal, but no answer, either. It rang and rang and rang. Finally, he heard 'Countess Da – '

'Monika, it's Nino. Dani's left, I hope?'

'*Ja*, sure. About half an hour ago.'

'*Cazzo!* Where the hell is she? She should be here by now!'

'Where's here? Are you at the Four Seasons?'

'The Four Seasons?'

'*Ja, ja*, she's having dinner with Jerry Allen, our public relations man.'

'She's what?' Nino exploded with more Italian curses and slammed down the receiver.

The Four Seasons, long accustomed to having patrons' dinners interrupted by phone calls, hooked up a telephone to Dani's table.

Nino didn't bother with hello.

'What the fuck do you think you're doing at the Four Seasons?' he shouted. 'You and I are supposed to be at Twenty-One right now.'

'Oh, shit!' She held up a finger as a signal to Jerry that she'd be just a minute. 'Nino – '

'Get the hell out of there and over to Twenty-One. *Immediatamente!*'

Dani took a deep breath. 'Nino, listen to me. I can't come. I'm sorry, but – '

'No! *You* listen! You know what this evening means to me. You are my wife – Countess diPortanova, *sì*? And you owe it to me – *owe* it to me, you understand? – to be by my side. Don't you dare humiliate me like this.'

140

'Humiliate you? For God's sake, they won't even miss me. Nino, for once in your life, act like an adult and think about someone besides yourself. I have a business crisis that can't wait.'

'There's *always* a fucking crisis,' Nino snarled. 'If I'd wanted to live in an emergency room, I would have been a goddam doctor!'

'Nino, please don't shout. I got killed in "Ear to the Ground" today. Somehow they got wind that I haven't been able to find a manufacturer, and now all of Seventh Avenue knows. My whole company could go down the drain. I have to act fast, control the damage . . .'

He had heard enough. He would have to invent a story to cover for her. Roberto had blistered his ears for not having told him about Countess Dani, Inc. Now he was sure to see through the bullshit and demand an explanation. Then would follow yet another tirade about what a fool he'd been to marry an American girl whom he couldn't properly control.

She had failed him once too often. He wasn't about to forgive and forget.

'Very well,' he said icily, throwing back the last of his drink, 'I'll go without you. But I must tell you, Dani, this little hobby of yours has gotten out of hand . . .'

He was right, Dani thought miserably, putting down the phone. But from the very beginning he had encouraged her. He'd seen firsthand how much work it took. The long hours. The anguish. She had slaved to get her company off the ground, to create designs that the public would buy. And she loved every minute of it, no matter how time-consuming and difficult the work might be.

No way was she going to give up.

The awful truth was that 'this little hobby' of hers was beginning to be a lot more fulfilling than her marriage.

It was all she could do not to burst into tears. Dani diPortanova, spotted crying at the Four Seasons . . . That certainly would give people something to talk about.

Angry and upset, she didn't eat a bite of dinner. But she did get business done.

'You don't want to lose the momentum of your positive publicity,' Jerry told her, cutting into his chicken paillard. 'You gotta nip this thing in the bud and fast. The best way to neutralize the damage is by announcing who your manufacturer is, but you can't do that until you find one.'

'We're working on it,' snapped Dani.

'But when will you have someone?'

'Jerry, *please*. If you can spring a manufacturer out of your hat, I'd be happy to do business with him.'

'I can't, but you've got to, kid.'

Nino didn't eat much dinner either. But everyone else enjoyed the food. All the guests, with the exception of Dani, showed up. Roberto basked in the company of his fellow power brokers.

By midnight everyone was stuffed, drunk, and happy. The women were chattering away about fashion and shopping. The men were swapping corporate war stories and ribald jokes, which their wives pretended not to hear.

'What happened to your wife?' Roberto demanded as soon as they were alone in the backseat of his stretch limousine.

Nino cringed. This was the moment he had been dreading. 'She had a business crisis.'

'Really?' Roberto's voice dripped contempt. 'Her business takes precedence over you and your family?'

There had been extensive press coverage throughout Europe about Dani's company and the new collection. And whatever articles Roberto might have missed, Karola was sure to send him.

He was still furious about how Karola had trumped him by breaking the news to him about the company's formation.

'Certainly not, Papa. My needs always come first for Dani,' Nino lied, 'but this once she had an emergency.'

'Once is too often. You've got to make her toe the line. Once a woman gets out of hand and sees she can get away with it, it gives her the upper hand.'

Nino had heard it all before.

'The man loses. And then,' Roberto spat with disgust, 'you become nothing more than a *cornuto*!'

Nino flinched at his father's choice of words. *Cornuto*. A pussy-whipped man. The lowest level to which an Italian male could sink. He straightened his shoulders and declared indignantly, 'Papa! I am still the man of my house.'

Roberto seriously wondered. 'What was the emergency?' he inquired.

Nino told him about the column. 'Worst of all,' he said, 'it's true. She can't find a manufacturer, and she's sitting on millions of dollars' worth of orders. If the Drop Dress really takes off, possibly tens of millions.'

Roberto's world was one of 'can do,' not 'cannot.'

'Why can't she find one?' he asked practically.

'She had a very reputable fellow in Brooklyn all lined up, but his is a small factory. He couldn't possibly handle the volume. Last season she could barely give the collection away. Now the customers are pounding down the door. Nobody expected this kind of response.'

Roberto listened in silence. Usually the diPortanova name commanded instant respect, not to mention action. Obviously the girl was doing something wrong. Probably pushing too hard to cut a deal.

On the one hand, he didn't approve of his daughter-in-law's company. A young girl like Dani should be producing grandchildren – heirs to carry on his lineage. She was

143

living up to all his worst expectations of her, and he was reluctant to give her any encouragement.

On the other hand, he was in a position to help her. His brother Aldo was married to a baroness whose family owned the largest clothing manufacturing company in Milan. Fiorucci, Krizia, and Armani were among her customers. If he helped the girl, she would be even further in his debt, which would give him some control over her business.

As the limousine glided to a stop in front of the imposing dark Dakota, Roberto smiled at his son. 'Have your wife give me a call. Maybe Aldo's wife can make time for her at their factory in Milan.'

Nino was overwhelmed by Roberto's generosity. Ever since he could remember, his father had rescued him from difficult predicaments. Now he was doing the same for Dani. Irritated as he was with her, Nino couldn't wait to break the news that he and Roberto were about to save her hide.

'Papa! *Grazie, grazie!*' he said fervently.

His gratitude grated on Roberto's nerves. Curtly he told his son, 'Don't mention it.'

Salzburg, Austria

'Roberto?' Karola's voice sounded as smooth and silky as the warm oil her masseur was liberally applying to her body. 'How was your trip to New York? I trust it was fruitful.'

Flat on her stomach and bare-assed naked on the massage table in her *schloss*'s private gym, Karola had Roberto on speakerphone. As she spoke, Massoud worked his magic, soothing and releasing the knots of tension.

144

Roberto knew Karola didn't give a damn about his trip. He wondered what was really on her mind. But he bided his time, savoring the zinger he had in store for her.

'I was thinking,' she said lazily, as Massoud began working his way up her legs, 'that when next we meet I will tie you up. You would like that, *ja*, Roberto?'

'Karola – '

Imagining him ensconced behind his desk in his office, Karola laughed silently. 'I will tie you up, and what shall I do with you? Suck your cock? Would you like that? Or perhaps, Roberto, I will whip you.'

'Stop it!' Roberto hissed into the phone.

Karola seemed to have a sixth sense for catching him in the middle of important meetings when he could ill afford to be distracted by her stream of filthy talk, to be caught squirming with a hard-on like a horny schoolboy in front of his associates . . . And what if someone should over-hear? But her descriptions of what she would do to him – or what she wanted done to her – drove him wild.

At Massoud's signal, Karola shifted onto her back. Relaxing as his strong, capable hands kneaded her aching muscles, she said, 'Or perhaps I will finger your asshole as you come between my breasts. By the way,' she said and casually changed the subject, 'I heard the most amusing rumor the other day and I thought, I *must* share this with Roberto.'

'And what was that?' Roberto asked coolly.

'They say you've asked Aldo's wife to find room at her factory for your daughter-in-law.'

Though he never would have admitted it, Roberto admired Karola's ability to ferret out information. She seemed to have well-placed sources throughout Europe. But he didn't appreciate being second-guessed by anyone, particularly a mistress. Most particularly Karola von Reich.

145

'I'm glad I've amused you, Karola,' he retorted. 'The rumor is true. For now, yes, I have decided to help the girl. *I* don't abandon family. And speaking of family, I, too, heard an amusing story – about your daughter.'

'I'm not interested,' she spat.

'I'll tell you anyway. It's a pity about her marriage, but I understand she's doing very well. She bought herself a town house in New York, and she's working alongside Nino's wife. She must have got her business sense from you.'

'She got nothing from me.'

'That's not what I hear.' Roberto chuckled.

'What's that supposed to mean?' demanded Karola.

It meant nothing – purely a stab in the dark. But he had struck a nerve. He instantly decided to find out from Nino, who was sure to know, why Monika was now the ex-Frau Bletz. It could prove . . . amusing.

Grudgingly, Karola asked, 'How long has she been in New York?'

So her tentacles didn't reach that far. He had the answer, but better to leave her hanging.

'Forgive me, Karola,' Roberto said politely, 'but there's another call I must take. So good talking to you. I'll see you next week in Mougins, *si*? *Ciao!*'

The line went dead.

Karola sat up abruptly and pushed Massoud's hands away. 'Enough,' she commanded.

Massoud helped her off the table and handed her a towel. After five years of serving as Karola von Reich's personal masseur and physical trainer, he knew better than to argue with his employer. He also knew enough about her personal life that he could have blackmailed her for lots of money. But Karola was already paying him handsomely to do his job and keep his mouth shut.

146

'He thinks he can outsmart me,' she fumed. 'I promise you, Massoud, I'll have his balls.'

And Massoud knew that, one way or another, she would.

Lake Garda

It took considerable string-pulling for Roberto to persuade his sister-in-law to take on the production of Dani's line. But when Dani telephoned him in Lake Garda, he had good news for her.

She couldn't thank him enough.

'Just as long as you honor the agreement we made when I consented to your marriage,' Roberto told her, 'your business will be welcome at the Milan factory.'

New York

As another season and another collection came around, Dani took her clothes on the road for the charity show circuit. She hit San Francisco, Beverly Hills, Dallas, and Palm Beach.

She and Monika had become fixtures at the Kennedy Airport warehouse. Dressed in their cashmere sweaters, jeans, and sable coats, they spent endless hours sorting out and routing the orders.

They quickly learned the lingo of Seventh Avenue.

'What's your best body?' a rep asked Dani.

'I beg your pardon?'

'Body, baby, *style*. I want to see your best-sellers and the fabrications they come in.'

'Today I've got a long pencil for you,' another buyer told Monika.

147

Monika cocked an eyebrow and said smartly, '*Ja*, you want to pull it out and show me?'

The buyer roared with laughter. 'Big pencil means a big order.'

Monika blushed and reached for an order pad.

'We have this body at one hundred and five dollars, this at one twenty-five . . . this dress has the two-shoulder treatment, which is going to be all the rage.'

'Love it, cookie. Give me an exclusive and I'll take fifty.'

'Mauve, that's our strongest booking.'

And so it went.

When running a five-million-dollar company became too much for just Dani, Monika, and a receptionist, they hired a couple of assistants. Dani concentrated on designing and marketing, while Monika took charge of accounting and production, fulfilling her old fantasy of being a businesswoman.

By their fourth season, with the Drop Dress selling better than ever, Dani introduced a lurex version for more formal evening wear. It, too, was a hit. The dress was well on its way to becoming a perennial best-seller, quite possibly a classic design . . .

One Saturday afternoon Dani dropped into Saks with Eunice to look for a birthday present for Maurice. He already had enough ties, he didn't wear cologne, and he'd bought a Burberry raincoat on his last trip to London. But Eunice knew he'd love a new sweater, a cranberry red handwoven cardigan like the one he'd admired but couldn't find in his size at Harrods.

They went upstairs to the men's department. Dani had just pointed to one she thought he might like when she heard a familiar voice loudly whine, 'Why we're paying retail is beyond me!'

Parading down the narrow aisle toward her was Reggie

148

Bolt, his arms piled high with sweaters. Behind him she saw a very cute blond actor type.

She and Reggie hadn't spoken since that awful confrontation when she'd accused him of ripping her off. She'd never forgotten his parting shot as she'd slammed out of his office. 'Cunt!' he'd shrieked after her. Though they'd attended many of the same parties and shows, they'd always made a point of avoiding each other.

But there was no escaping him. In a moment she would be face to face with the man who had unwittingly launched her career.

'What do you think I am,' he was berating his blond friend, 'a bank? Here, you carry some of these.' He thrust a few of the sweaters at the boy, who seemed to take Reggie's carping with good humor.

He didn't notice her until they were only a few feet apart. 'Reggie,' she said, 'it's been a long time.'

Reggie looked as if he'd just stepped in dog shit. 'Yes, it has. Thinking about starting a menswear line, Countess? I hope Nino's not your model. If he is, you should be over in Better Dresses. Let's get out of here,' he snapped at his friend. 'There's a bad smell in the air.'

Dani took a deep breath. 'Oh, don't rush out. I don't bite. Besides, I never did properly thank you.'

'What are you talking about?' he demanded, trying to push past her.

'It's all because of you that I'm in the business.'

Reggie smiled tightly. 'Really? I'm delighted to have been an inspiration. Now, if you please – '

'Inspiration?' Dani laughed. 'Reggie, you really have forgotten that *I* was the one who *inspired* so much of your spring 'seventy-five collection.'

'Indeed? You must be getting old. Your memory fails you.'

'Just as your imagination failed you that season?' Dani

shot back. 'Ah, well, that's all water under the bridge now, isn't it? We're both doing so well.'

'Yes, but some of us are here for the long haul. We're not mere flash-in-the-pan fashionplates. Now get the fuck out of my way.' He stormed past her. His friend, looking very embarrassed, followed close behind.

'Heavens,' Eunice gasped. 'Such language. How unpleasant for you.'

'Oh, Eunice,' Dani said with a laugh, 'I've been waiting for that moment for a long, long time. C'mon. Let's find Maurice a sweater.'

Part Two

Chapter Six

Dani drummed her fingernails against the glass top of her Parsons-style desk. The surface was clear except for a multi-line telephone, her calendar, a neat stack of sketch pads, a basketful of pens and pastel pencils, and a picture of Nino in a sterling silver frame. The frame had been a gift from the president of Cartier – no doubt his first step in a courting dance to win a licensing agreement.

Usually the phone was ringing off the hook with calls from the retailing executives who regularly checked in with her, from the fashion writers who had quickly discovered that they could depend on Dani diPortanova for a good quote and an even better story, or from one of her forty employees. But the calls were being held this morning so that Dani could give her full attention to the account executives from the advertising agency of Hellman, Ltd. For almost thirty minutes they had been talking nonstop, flashing one board after another under her nose. Whether or not they knew it, they were about to wind up their presentation.

For despite their high-powered reputation, Dani was unimpressed by any of their ideas for a new Countess Dani advertising and promotional campaign. She was further unimpressed by the total absence of women from their creative team.

Fellows, this is, after all, November 1977. And Countess Dani's line is designed specifically for the growing numbers of working women.

The Hellman guys were the fifth agency she'd seen in as many days. After a while they all began to look the same. Only the name of the agency changed. Her patience was wearing thin. Since setting up shop four years ago on Seventh Avenue, Dani had learned to speak her mind. Now she leaned forward and said, 'No. It's all wrong. You don't understand me.'

Taken aback by her bluntness, the gray flannel-suited men fell silent in midsentence.

'How can you come in here looking for my business when you don't know what we're all about? Didn't you do your research?'

As the ad men pleaded for a second crack at her account, Dani stood up to signify that the meeting was over. 'No,' she told them in a voice that meant business. 'We need an agency that can get it right the *first* time. In this business, it's rare that we get a second chance. Believe me, I know.'

Very occasionally Dani wondered what she would have done if her Drop Dress hadn't worked. Then she'd immediately wipe the thought from her mind. She wasn't interested in second-guessing the past. Her sights were set on creating trends for the future.

She had traveled light-years since introducing the Drop Dress, which five seasons later was still billing ten million dollars in wholesale business a year. The Countess Dani line – fresher, more stylish, more practical than anything else on the market – had revolutionized the way American women dressed. Her fiercely loyal customers returned season after season, many of them to buy the entire collection. Clearance sales were almost unheard of, and when they were needed, the retailers dreaded them. Normally staid women would turn the events into wrestling matches – punching, pulling, kicking their way to the limited number of reduced items.

Dani shook her head in amazement when she read the reports about the fights that erupted in such hallowed retail institutions as Neiman-Marcus, I. Magnin, Sakowitz's, and Saks. That anyone would literally fight over a dress – *her dress* – was hard to imagine.

These were exciting times for her. She relished her newly achieved power. Manufacturers and licensors, all vying for a piece of her name and her business, lunched her as often as she would consent. Conglomerates wooed her, trying to persuade her to sell out. But power was worth something only to those who held it. The Drop Dress had created her destiny as a designer, but the trick was to control that destiny.

One lesson she had learned quickly was the value of publicity. Each time a story appeared, orders jumped. When *New York* magazine proclaimed her 'The Countess of Seventh Avenue' in a cover story about her and Nino, sales in the New York area quadrupled, as did advance orders for the next season.

Thus the importance of hooking up with the right ad agency.

The first time she had gone shopping for an agency, on the heels of presenting her premier collection, doors had slammed in her face all over town. 'Too small,' they told her. 'Not enough billing.'

Eventually she had found herself a two-person shop, just starting out, that had expertly handled not only the Drop Dress campaign but the subsequent collections as well. The agency, a husband-and-wife operation, had developed into a tiny powerhouse, in large part thanks to Countess Dani's business. But recently the couple had decided to seek the true meaning of existence. Wishing Dani much peace and happiness in this life, not to mention in all her future lives, they had left for a commune in Colorado. Even before they shaved their

155

heads and took new names, word of their departure had spread quickly up and down Madison Avenue. This time around, the big agencies were lining up to snag the Countess Dani account. Thus far none of them had managed to capture the image Dani was seeking.

Ushering the ad men out the door, she turned back to Monika and Kim Wantanabe and asked, 'Well?'

The expressions on their faces said it all. No need for further discussion. What she would have done without the two of them, Dani couldn't imagine. Monika, vice president and director of production and marketing. Kim, director of promotion and special events. They were her two closest business associates and her closest friends as well.

Kim's inexhaustible energy and irrepressible sense of humor had proved a lifesaver time and again. She'd been working full-time for Countess Dani for two years, and Dani frequently blessed the day she'd had the good sense to hire Kim to direct her first show. But Dani also knew that Kim still nursed her dream of becoming a producer. It was no secret that she was always on the lookout for a suitable opportunity.

And Monika was, quite simply, indispensable. The calm at the center of Dani's storm. Even when all hell was breaking loose and yet another crisis had Dani tearing at her hair, Monika somehow managed to remain unflappable.

She joked about her Teutonic heritage, claiming to be genetically imperturbable. Whatever the reason, Dani was grateful for her shoulder, which was always there to be leaned on.

'What a bunch of old farts!' Kim said, rolling her eyes. She consulted her calendar. 'We have another one scheduled for tomorrow afternoon. Let's hope and pray they have more on the ball than the rest of the jokers.'

'And don't forget Ian McAdam,' Dani said. 'I have him down for dinner tonight. The guy wouldn't take no for an answer. Speaking of food, who's for ordering some lunch?' Dani suggested.

'Sounds good.' Kim nodded. A tiny size four no matter how much junk food she scarfed down, Kim was hungry the minute she finished eating.

'Count me out,' Monika told them. 'I have a date.'

Dani and Kim exchanged sly, knowing smiles.

'A one o'clock quickie?' Dani joked.

'I thought I heard someone say something about a carpenter,' Kim chimed in.

'*Ach*, you're both jealous,' Monika scoffed amiably. 'I'm meeting him at a restaurant. All we're going to do is eat and talk.'

'Eat what or whom is the question,' Dani teased. 'Make sure you sit in a dark corner. The way you two go at it, you could get arrested for creating a public spectacle.'

To Monika's surprise, Rick Flood had turned out to be a long-playing one-night stand. Almost three years now. What began as a lark had developed into an enduring relationship, though what he meant to her she couldn't or wouldn't say. In bed, he was alternately tender and demanding. The sex was explosive. Out of bed, he confused her utterly. His breezy informality verging on insolence masked a warm, sympathetic nature that looked for the best in people and accepted them for who they were. Monika's barbed quips usually sailed right past him.

'Save that stuff for your uptown boyfriends,' he'd tell her.

She never made a secret of the fact that she dated – and slept with – other men. Just as Rick no doubt slept with other women, though when he had time she couldn't imagine. For Rick had a dream that consumed him like a bright, hot flame. He wanted to be a rock star. He was positive he was going to make it. Someday he was going to stand on a stage and play his guitar, and crowds were going to cheer. Someday his records were going to sell millions of copies. Each one a platinum. Someday he was going to be very, very big.

In the meantime, he made good, steady money as a carpenter, slept with Monika whenever their schedules allowed, and spent every spare moment playing his guitar and writing songs. Every so often, his band – the members all high school buddies – got a gig at a college frat party or in one of the bars down by the shore.

The last time she'd seen him, he'd casually mentioned that he was thinking of heading west to LA where the music scene was easier to break into. How would she like to come along?

And leave New York? Her job? Her friends? Her home that she loved so much? Absurd even to think about it. Besides, she'd confided to Dani, their romance read like the back cover of a paperback romance. Could a rich European girl from the right side of the tracks find happiness in the arms of a south Jersey boy?

Nein, she declared. Impossible. Rick was the guy she fucked. He was her pal, someone to depend on. But certainly she wasn't in love with him.

'Are you sure about that?' Dani probed, distressed at the thought of losing Monika to the West Coast, but even more, wanting her to be happy. 'Not that I have much expert advice to offer on the subject of men and true love.'

No one but Monika knew that the glittery fabric of Dani's marriage was slowly but surely unraveling. Dani kept up a good front and still managed to fool the gossip-hungry tabloids and bitchy columnists scratching about in the dirt for scandal. But it was only a matter of time before one of Nino's 'little' indiscretions became big press.

Ironically, she still considered Nino her best friend. She loved him and was sure she always would. Whether they could live together was an altogether different question. Nino didn't mind a bit if she spent her days at the office – so long as she was available to party with him at night. He correctly pointed out that her customers were the very people they partied with and that the more often her picture appeared in the newspapers, the more free publicity she garnered.

Still, she couldn't socialize six or seven nights a week *and* run a company. It didn't matter how good her staff was or how much help she hired at home. She was beginning to feel as if she was always putting out brushfires – a crisis at the office would almost inevitably set off sparks between her and Nino.

As often as possible, she stole long weekends with Nino in Europe or the Caribbean, or at the house in Roxbury. But frequently she felt as if she was running in two directions at once. It was hard to be romantic, even so far from home, when she had fabrics, colors, delivery dates, and the next collection forever on her mind. And heaven forbid if she tried to talk to Nino about what was worrying her! He didn't bring his business problems home with him, and he expected his wife to play by the same rules.

Dani had come to accept that Nino considered it his God-given right – his macho duty, even – to have affairs with other women. Monika had explained to her that among upper-class Italians, such liaisons were de rigueur.

What she didn't know couldn't hurt her, she firmly told herself. And if that was the price she had to pay for Countess Dani, Inc., she was willing to do so. Especially since she had no choice. Occasionally she wondered how Nino would react if she had some extramarital fun. Not that she had either the time or the inclination. Making love with Nino had lost none of its magic.

But one morning when Nino had jetted south for a birthday party on Eleuthera and Dani was late leaving for the office, the phone rang. She grabbed the receiver and was greeted with 'Hi, is Nino up yet?'

The caller had a breathy, girlish voice Dani couldn't place.

'Sorry, he's not here. Who's calling?'

'A friend . . .' A coy giggle, then, 'You're not his wife, are you?'

'Damn right, I am,' Dani snapped.

'Oooh, then I guess there's no message.' Another giggle and a sharp click.

Dani slammed down the phone, ready to kill. How dare he give their home number to one of his girlfriends!

When the phone rang again a few seconds later, she picked it up and snapped, 'Don't you *ever* call here again. Is that perfectly clear?'

'You were expecting somebody else, *ja, liebchen*?'

'Monika? I'm sorry! I thought you were one of Nino's girls. Now he has them phoning him at home.'

'*Ach*,' Monika said, 'bad boy. Very bad manners. I'd give him a good spanking.'

Dani laughed bitterly. 'I swear to God, if I thought it would do any good, I *would* spank him. It's either that or divorce the bastard.'

But both of them knew that that was an idle threat. For the diPortanovas, divorce was the ultimate scandal.

Reluctantly, Nino had grown accustomed to Dani's success as a designer and to all the responsibilities that entailed. While he resented how much of her time the business took from him, he rarely complained. After the Drop Dress collection, there'd been some rough times and a lot of fights. But in the end, he had decided there

160

were worse things than losing a wife and gaining a businesswoman in bed.

Besides, he was discovering his own pleasures.

Among the jet set there existed a select corps of rich, powerful, and beautiful men. Most had made it to the top in television, motion pictures, fashion, banking, law, medicine. They were more than merely famous. Their names appeared regularly in newspaper headlines, on movie screens, and on expensive clothing labels. They were the 'mauve mafia' – men who preferred the company of other men. The sexual revolution of the seventies had made them social power brokers even among the straight ruling elite.

They flew from continent to continent in search of fun. They threw the most lavish parties. They frequented the best underground discos and after-hours clubs, and they were always the first to know about the newest drugs. Naturally, Nino was enthralled by them.

Increasingly, they had become a part of his life. Increasingly, there were rumors in the press.

Rio de Janeiro, Brazil

Carnival, 1978. Four in the morning. The packed dance floor of Help! – Rio's hottest disco, facing the ocean in Copacabana.

As strobe lights turned their every movement into an eerie slow-motion film, thousands of revelers boogied to the sounds of Zulema's disco hit, 'Giving Up.' Nino, wearing only cowboy boots and skin-tight jeans, shook his sweat-drenched head of hair and laughed when two garishly dressed drag queens grabbed him by the waist and whirled him around with them. High as a kite from

161

nonstop drinking, popping, snorting, he was having the time of his life.

'Giving Up' faded and 'One Night Affair' quickly fired up. The crowd, which security guards were estimating to number at least three thousand, went wild. A beautiful mulatto woman, dancing topless, shook her enormous breasts in Nino's face and offered him a hit off her poppers.

He greedily accepted. The rush was fast and overwhelming.

'Good, *sim*?' the woman screamed above the noise, taking a hit herself. Reeling from the effect, she staggered into several young boys standing behind her, spilling their drinks.

The boys cried out in mock horror and pushed her back to Nino.

'*Sim!*' Nino grinned. 'But I have something better.'

From his jeans pocket, he pulled out a small vial of coke and sprinkled a small mound on her left nipple. He took a hit, then licked the nipple clean. The dancers around him urged him to take another hit. Nino obliged, this time off the right nipple.

The woman giggled and yelled, 'Like my titties?'

She buried his head between her boobs and the crowd closed in, blanketing him with the musty-sock smell of poppers and sex and spilled booze. Anonymous tongues licked the sweat off his neck, his chest, his back. Unseen hands groped at his groin, his ass, his nipples.

Hard cocks, encased in jeans, rubbed against Nino's ass, sending their signals, while women's tits were served up before him. It was a sexual smorgasbord, and Nino was the biggest glutton of all.

Damn shame, he thought blurrily, *that Dani isn't here . . . have fun, just like in the old days before . . . before Countess Dani, Inc. . . . Life is so wonderful . . .*

162

And then he passed out.

When Nino awoke the next morning in his suite at the Copacabana Palace, he had a hangover the size of the Amazon, and he remembered nothing that had happened the previous night. But a series of phone calls brought him up to date. Somehow he had connected up with a coke dealer who had not only laid him off a kilo but had also sold him a Lear jet.

Yes, indeed, the concierge matter-of-factly informed him, as if such things happened every day. Early that morning Nino had authorized a wire transfer for four million US dollars.

A jet? Nino grinned. How convenient! What a fun toy. He'd never owned a jet before. He hired a pilot, snorted half a gram of coke, loaded the jet up with some of his newfound friends, and took off for Carnival in Trinidad.

New York

News of Nino's antics preceded him to New York with dispatches from the press about the festivities and personalities of Carnival. Dani was heartsick.

'How could you just *buy* a Lear jet?' she greeted him furiously. 'Did you think it was like buying caviar at Balducci's? And smuggling in that kilo could have landed you fifteen years in Attica. You're insane!'

Nino shrugged his shoulders. '*Cara*, it's good to see you again,' he replied calmly.

There was nothing left for her to say. Besides, her driver was waiting downstairs. She was already late for an appointment.

It was none of his wife's business how he spent his money, but Nino couldn't hold a grudge. So in the late afternoon, after sleeping off the effects of Trinidad, he headed downtown for Dani's office in a Ferrari he'd recently purchased. Driving past a flower shop on Columbus Avenue, he double-parked and hurried inside to buy an enormous bouquet of their prettiest spring assortment. The delicate aroma of roses, tulips, and lilacs filled the car and buoyed Nino's spirits. And then he noticed a sign from heaven that this was his lucky day – a parking space was waiting for him right in front of her building.

Dani was talking animatedly into the phone when he was ushered into her office, but she waved and held up a finger, mouthing 'I'll be done in a minute.'

The minute dragged on into five, then ten.

'Yes, Mr Chen,' she kept saying. 'That won't be a problem, Mr Chen . . . No, Mr Chen . . . Yes, I'm sure we can work all that out face to face.'

She rolled her eyes and shrugged her shoulders, signaling her exasperation with Mr Chen, whoever he might be.

Nino listened with half an ear to what sounded like the opening round of negotiations, perhaps for a licensing agreement. A cute young assistant in a clingy mini-Drop Dress scurried in and thrust a piece of paper under Dani's nose. The girl waited as Dani, never skipping a beat in her conversation, read the memo and quickly scribbled an answer.

On her way out of the office, her back to Dani, the girl winked at Nino. She had large, sassy eyes, and something about her smile and the way she moved reminded Nino of Dani at age eighteen.

Finally Dani said good-bye to Mr Chen and hung up.

Nino grabbed the bouquet from behind his back and presented it to her with a flourish.

'Oh, they're beautiful,' Dani said, taking a deep whiff. 'Nino, I'm sorry. I was out of line this morning. It's just that I worry about you. But I guess if you really want a jet – '

'*Cara*, forget about it.' Nino gave her a long kiss and let his hands play over her ass. 'Listen, I have a marvelous idea. Let's have dinner tonight at Chez Antoinette, just the two of us. Very romantic, *si*?'

Dani stayed in the circle of his arms but shook her head regretfully. 'Nino, that sounds great. I wish I could, but I have a business dinner that I can't cancel – '

'Then I'll join you,' Nino said, enthusiastic as a puppy. 'We'll have a great time . . . drink lots of champagne, get your guest a girl, a boy, whatever he wants, show him a time he'll never forget.'

'That's sweet of you, Nino,' Dani said, playfully ruffling his hair, 'but this is strictly business, and he sounds very formal. You'd be horribly bored.' *And in the way*, she thought guiltily. 'How about tomorrow night?' She glanced at her calendar. 'Whoops, that's no good either. But we could do it night after next.'

Nino bristled. 'What? I need an appointment to have dinner with my own wife? This is bullshit!'

'Nino, please. You know I don't have a choice.'

Still feeling the effects of too much booze, drugs, and sun, Nino snatched the flowers out of her hand. 'You *do* have a choice. But your choice isn't me. I'll give these flowers to someone who knows how to treat a man properly!'

'Nino, listen to me . . .'

But he was already gone.

Rah Rah loved tooling around the city in the silver Mercedes 450 SL convertible Reggie had bought him. Where better to check out the action on this unseasonably warm day in March than from behind the wheel of his $45,000 baby? Cruising the streets of New York, he could get himself into a lot less trouble than cruising the floors of Bloomie's or Saks. It was also much less exhausting than pumping iron at the New York Health and Racquet Club, where Reggie had bought him a membership so he could stay in shape.

Rah Rah cranked up the volume on the tape deck. 'Love to Love You, Baby' – his theme song – boomed out of the convertible's open top. As Donna Summer oohed and cooed in stereo, pedestrians craned their necks to catch a glimpse of the driver. Hidden behind his mirrored Ray-Ban sunglasses, Rah Rah smiled contentedly. He saw the envious stares, the curious eyes checking him out. Was he a celebrity? Or merely rich? What had he done to earn such a major-league set of wheels?

If only they knew.

A year ago Reggie had finally bought out Rah Rah's option. Lawyers for both sides had negotiated a twenty-page contract that spelled out the terms of their relationship. The package included the Mercedes, free room and board in Reggie's Sutton Place triplex penthouse apartment, and a check for $250,000 deposited in Rah Rah's name at the Morgan Bank. The check was Reggie's insurance that Rah Rah would quit hustling and belong only to him.

It was a good deal, as such deals went, and Rah Rah knew it. He'd never planned to make a career out of hustling. He was all too aware that he'd be done for with the first hint of wrinkles, thinning hair, and a paunch. That money was his future, and he intended to make it grow. But first he sent his parents a check for $125,000 with a note that read, 'I made a smart move on the stock market. Hope this helps.'

'We appreciate the money,' his dad wrote back, 'but be careful, son. Don't let those New York sharpies pull a

166

fast one on you.' Nobody was pulling anything on Rah Rah.

'Love to Love You, Baby' segued into Gloria Gaynor's 'Never Can Say Good-bye.' Which was what he wouldn't do, as long as Reggie paid him his annual cost-of-living increase, which was coming due next month. Reggie would scream like a banshee when reminded. The greater success Reggie achieved, the stingier he became. Not to mention demanding.

Rah Rah considered the increase battle pay.

Still fuming, Nino flung the flowers onto the passenger seat, turned over all 268 horses under the Ferrari's hood, and furiously shifted out into the middle of Seventh Avenue, ignoring the blaring horns and screeching tires behind him. Let the other cars crash, he thought angrily. He didn't give a fuck. All he wanted was to get as far the hell away from Seventh Avenue as possible.

He should have stayed in Trinidad, bought a house on the beach, and worked on his tan. Dani probably wouldn't even have noticed his absence. She was never home. All she did was work eighteen hours a day. And for what? Not because they needed the money, that was for goddam sure. He cursed the day he had encouraged her to get into the goddam business. Cursed her for staying in it.

Life was too short for this shit.

He shifted the Ferrari again, floored the accelerator, and bolted across Thirty-fourth Street. Turning onto crowded Sixth Avenue, he peeled uptown, heading he wasn't sure where. On all sides of him other cars wheeled in and out of the lanes, but Nino hardly paid them any attention. He didn't have to. A Ferrari sent out a signal: Back off. Keep away. In New York, people listened to money.

He considered the evening ahead of him. Absorbed in

deciding what would provide the best salve for his injured pride, he noticed too late that the light had changed. *Slam!* went his foot on the brake . . . but not fast enough to avoid smashing into the rear of the car ahead of him. Metal screeched against metal as Nino fought with the wheel.

'Putana Eva! Merda!'

Loudly vowing vengeance on New York City drivers, his wife, her company, and for good measure the entire fashion industry, he jumped out to inspect the damage.

What a perfect way to end the day – wrecking a $75,000 car with fewer than two thousand miles on it.

He stalked over to the car whose fender was crumpled against his. Music blared.

'Can you turn that down?' he shouted angrily. He opened his mouth to deliver a furious earful.

The dazed driver removed his Ray-Bans and peered up at him.

One glimpse of the young man's face, and Nino's rage faded like a nimbus cloud in the wake of a summer storm . . .

Leaving the office to go to dinner, Dani was still brooding about Nino and his parting shot. It seemed as if all they did lately was rip at each other. Her parents had managed to stay happily married for many years. Why couldn't she? Of course, her mother hadn't been in charge of a multimillion-dollar business. Sophie's main preoccupation had been Maurice's happiness and well-being. No doubt Nino would be much happier if she stayed home and catered to his needs the way Sophie had to Maurice's. So she could end up like Sophie, miserable and depressed?

No, she'd walked away from that role too long ago to reapply for the job.

The elevator stopped on the twelfth floor, home of I.

Blatt and Sons. A pretty young woman got on the elevator, opened her green eyes wide as if startled, then smiled ingratiatingly.

Though she didn't recognize the girl, Dani smiled back. She had rosy cheeks and a pleasant face framed by light strawberry blond hair.

'Of all the days for me to bump into you in the elevator – when I'm not wearing my Drop Dress. I cannot tell you how much I admire you,' gushed the young woman. 'You're a genius.'

'I don't know that I'd go that far,' Dani replied, glad that *someone* at least appreciated her. 'But thank you for the kind words.'

'Oh, no,' the woman said earnestly. 'You're being too modest. One day women all over the world will reach into their closets and pull out a Countess Dani.'

'That's lovely of you to say.'

'But how rude of me not to introduce myself. I'm Barbara Hester. I work for Irving Blatt.'

'What a coincidence! Irving got me started in the business. You can learn a lot from him.'

'Oh, I intend to,' Barbara Hester said enthusiastically.

Barbara Hester's heart was pounding with excitement. Ever since she had first set eyes on Dani diPortanova almost a year ago, she had all but memorized every story she could find about the one designer she most admired and her rich, handsome husband.

'How is Irving?' Dani asked. It had been a couple of months since she had seen or spoken to Irving, who had lost some of his punch after his wife's death a year and a half ago.

'Oh, fine,' said Barbara Hester. 'He's such a wonderful person. An inspiration to all of us who are just starting out.'

The elevator door opened on the ground floor.

'Well, best of luck to you,' Dani said, rushing off to dinner. 'See you around.'

'See you around,' Barbara Hester echoed. She lingered a moment in front of the building. *A lot more than you think . . .*

All but ignoring his steak tartare, Ian McAdam pulled out a yellow legal pad and drew rough sketches of the ad campaign he had in mind for Countess Dani, Inc. His ideas about her company's image and direction spilled out so quickly that Dani was left with no choice but to listen.

She sipped her wine and studied the man seated across the table from her. Though not conventionally handsome – he was shorter than average, and his features were uneven – something about how his face lit up and the way he used words was downright . . . sexy.

Was he married? she wondered idly, checking his ring finger. Not that the absence of a ring meant anything. Nino never wore his wedding band. Anyway, she had never cheated on Nino, and she wasn't about to start now. Still, Ian interested her. If she were single and he were available, she could imagine . . .

'. . . don't you think?'

'Pardon?' she blushed guiltily. 'I'm sorry, I got distracted for a moment.'

'Bored?' He laughed, as if to say, *Not with me, you couldn't be.*

'No, no,' she protested, 'not at all. Please, what were you saying?'

'What I perceive as the message behind your designs: Dare to be powerful, feminine, sexy!'

'Absolutely! That's it!' she agreed excitedly. 'I couldn't have said it better myself.'

'But you can deliver it better than anyone else.'

'What?' She stared at him, puzzled.

'You're your own best advertisement, Dani. You're everything you're telling other women to be. You have on one of your designs now, right? It looks terrific on you. You ought to fire those models who don't hold a candle to you for style. *You* should be the spokeswoman for Countess Dani.'

Stunned by his suggestion, she considered the idea. And bumped up against the image of fat little Dani Leiberman smiling into the camera's unforgiving lens. She began to shake her head no. Then she stopped and took another look through the camera and thought, *But I'm the only one who still thinks I'm that little girl. Maybe he's right.*

'Okay,' she said, 'it's an interesting concept. A definite possibility. Ian, I like the way you think.'

He pushed his plate away impatiently. 'Dani, I have a funny reputation on Madison Avenue. I'm the first to admit it. I've turned down accounts, potentially *lucrative* accounts, because' – he rubbed his forefinger and thumb together, searching for the right words – 'the mix wasn't right. But when I feel something happening between me and the client – bingo! I know we can go all the way together. That's why I wanted to meet you. Trust me, Dani. There's terrific chemistry between us. I can feel it. Can you?'

Dani gulped and nodded. Chemistry . . . But what she was feeling had nothing to do with advertising. Suddenly she wanted to reach over and hold his hand, kiss his fingers, be kissed . . .

By Ian McAdam? Whom she'd met just two hours ago? What the hell was happening to her?

She looked up and found herself staring into a pair of warm, friendly green eyes. No, she told herself sternly, there was no secret message hidden there. Ian McAdam wanted her business, not her body. The buzz she was feeling was strictly a one-way current.

Or was it?

'Care for a nightcap?' he asked as they were leaving Chez Louis.

'I better not,' Dani said. *Or we might do something I'd regret.*

'Another time, then.' He had a crooked, engaging grin that was hard to resist.

She gestured to her limo and said, 'Can I drop you somewhere?'

Ian gave a long, appreciative whistle. 'Nice. But no, thanks. I could use a walk. It's been a stimulating evening. But let's talk tomorrow.'

A walk sounded great. She wondered where he lived. Somewhere on Central Park South? Or maybe near her on Central Park West? Maybe Fifth Avenue? A fantasy flitted through her head of the two of them strolling hand in hand up Central Park West. Toward the apartment she shared with her husband. The fantasy abruptly faded.

'Right,' she said, all business, and shook his hand briskly. 'It's been a pleasure, Ian.'

'And the best is yet to come,' he assured her.

She had recently seen a psychologist interviewed on 'Today.' The author of a book, *How to Flirt with Your Husband*, the psychologist felt there was no harm in women flirting with other men, even getting turned on by them, so long as they brought the buzz home to their husbands.

'I'm buzzed,' Dani told herself. 'And I'm bringing it home to Nino.'

Every marriage had its problems. Hers only seemed worse because the press liked to play them out in living color. The challenge was to find solutions. Compromises.

She and Nino hadn't had sex in several weeks. No

172

wonder they were going at each other. She would apologize to him for her crazy schedule. They would stay up all night making love, do it in every position they could think of – in the Jacuzzi, in the shower, hours and hours of lovemaking.

She would take the morning off and go to brunch with him . . . then maybe make love some more.

But when she got home, the huge duplex apartment was dark. Their bed was empty. She checked her desk, the message machine, and blinked back tears of disappointment.

No note.

No messages.

No Nino.

At four in the morning, stuck on the New Jersey Turnpike in the front seat of Rick Flood's broken-down van, Monika gave up any hope of sleep that night. Ah, well, there were more important things in life . . . like going along for the ride to the south Jersey club where his band, the Justice League, had played a gig.

She took another swig of Budweiser and made a face as the metallic taste hit her tongue. Drinking beer out of cans was one American custom she would never get used to. Not to mention that the beer tasted nothing like the beer she'd grown up drinking in Salzburg.

'The tow should be here any minute,' Rick said. His voice was hoarse from the beating it had taken during the four hours he had given his all to the audience. Just a small, out-of-the-way bar, but it was precisely the kind of place that had launched another local boy, Bruce Springsteen.

He gently flicked one finger across her cheek. 'Tired?'

'*Ja*, a little,' she admitted. March was always a rough

month, with the deadline for Fashion Week, 1978, looming just ahead. The relentless pressure made the days seem endless. No wonder so many people on Seventh Avenue lived on uppers and diet pills. She closed her eyes, pretending to nap, and thought about their conversation at lunch hours earlier.

'I've made up my mind,' Rick had said. 'If I hang around New York too much longer, I'll be stuck for life. By this time next year I want to be in LA. You ought to come with me, Monika.'

His eyes burned into hers, challenging her to disagree.

He was so proud, so independent. So determined not to let her make things easier for him. Again and again she had told him, 'It's only money.'

'Your money,' he'd say. 'Keep it. I don't care how rich you are. I pay my own way.'

But for once she intended to overrule him and have *her* way.

She opened her eyes and chugged down the rest of the Bud. 'I want to go away next weekend – a vacation, *ja*? With you.'

He eyed her curiously. 'Did you have anything special in mind? Besides the obvious, of course.'

'*Ja*, I would very much like to go to the Bahamas. My treat.' She forestalled his objections. 'A birthday present.'

'But my birthday's not till October,' he reminded her.

'Details,' she scoffed, sure she had won.

'What's so special about the Bahamas?' he wanted to know.

'Paradise Island,' she said. 'Gambling. Like in Cannes.'

One long, hard look at Nino – the custom-made clothes, the expensive watch, the pricey haircut, the car – and Rah Rah knew he'd hooked himself a rich fish. As soon as

174

they'd agreed that the accident had been the fault of both of them, he said, 'I could use a drink. How about you?'

Drinks led to an invitation to Rah Rah's impeccably furnished penthouse coop on the Upper East Side, and to more drinks. By tacit mutual consent, their tongues found their way into each other's mouths. Nino's hands quickly moved south.

But Rah Rah pulled back. 'I have to tell you something,' he said. 'This house – it's not really mine. It belongs to the man who . . . who keeps me. But he's away tonight, so if you'd like to make a financial arrangement for the rest of the evening . . .'

What an amusing idea, thought Nino. He'd never paid for sex.

They easily settled on a price and moved the party upstairs to the bedroom where Rah Rah proceeded to give Nino his money's worth. Hours later they broke for supper – French toast and fresh strawberries, prepared by Rah Rah and served at bedside on an eighteenth-century silver tray.

'Your patron knows how to live,' said Nino appreciatively. He helped himself to more champagne from the wine bucket on the Federal-style drum table next to the bed.

A display of silver-framed pictures caught his eye. There were many familiar faces – socialites, entertainers, a couple of political wives, the mayor of New York. Some were autographed.

In every photograph, one man was prominently featured.

Mr Reggie. His wife's sworn enemy.

'Your boyfriend?' he asked, pointing to Reggie. Had he tried, he couldn't have dreamed up a sweeter form of revenge on his wife and the man who had inadvertently created the monster she'd become.

175

Rah Rah nodded. 'Do you know him?' A note of worry crept into his voice. If Reggie ever found out that he had taken a little extra on the side, he'd be out of a home faster than he could blink. Thank God he was out of town for the night.

'By reputation only. I'm married to Dani diPortanova,' Nino said, howling with laughter. The joke was made no less delicious by the fact that he couldn't share it with anyone but Rah Rah.

Irony added spice to their fucking. By the time they were finished, the peach-colored silk sheets lay stained and crumpled on the floor.

In the light of day and sober, Rah Rah realized how close he'd come to kissing the gift horse good-bye. 'I'd better trash these sheets,' he said. 'Reggie's very suspicious. It's been fun, but we probably shouldn't see each other again. You understand, don't you?'

'Of course,' Nino said. Besides, buying sex more than this once didn't suit him. When he started having to pay for it regularly, he would get out of the game.

'And if our paths should happen to cross . . .' Rah Rah began uncomfortably.

Nino winked. 'Don't worry. You can trust me.'

Lake Garda, Italy

The damning evidence, forwarded to his attention courtesy of Karola, lay neatly stacked in front of Roberto diPortanova. The bitch was more efficient than a clipping service, he thought, as he riffled through the pile of newspaper articles and grainy black-and-white photographs. Photographs of Nino, cavorting about half-naked in Rio, hamming it up with a bunch of *finocchi*. Men who weren't really men. Homosexuals.

176

Alone in his office, Roberto's cheeks burned with anger and shame. He glared at a particularly loathsome picture of Nino, drunkenly leering at the camera from the arms of another man. That a son of his should parade his perversion for all the world to see and laugh at the diPortanova family . . . this was sheer madness!

At Christmas, Roberto had quizzed Nino about his relations with his wife, who mercifully had stayed in New York, claiming business pressures. But whatever his failings, Nino was loyal. If he was unhappy with Dani, he wouldn't admit to it. Though that was hardly the point. With the trail of clues Nino left scattered in his wake, Roberto didn't need a road map to be pointed in the direction of the obvious.

His son's unfortunate impulses could be controlled only if he was accorded the proper respect and devotion. No wonder the boy didn't feel like a man. His wife had stolen his pants and was intent on wearing them herself.

Roberto had no choice. He simply could not permit such behavior to continue. His daughter-in-law had reneged on her part of their bargain. But how to handle the situation, that was the question.

177

Chapter Seven

New York, 1978

When the morning mail landed on the front desk at I. Blatt & Sons, Barbara Hester didn't even bother to look up.

'I. Blatt,' she said with a sigh, 'I'll connect you.'

As usual, the phones were ringing off the wall.

After singsonging 'I'll connect you' for what seemed like the thousandth time, she disconnected the call. Screw 'em. She'd blame it on the phone company. She was fed up with playing Ma Bell. Two years on Seventh Avenue and she was no closer to realizing her dream of becoming a designer than when she'd first started. Her patience was running thin.

On top of handling all the phones, she was supposed to sort out and distribute the mail. 'By lunchtime, please, Barbara,' her boss kept reminding her. As if she were sitting around doing her nails.

Glancing at today's stack, she drew a quick excited breath when she saw the cover of *People* magazine, dated July 2, 1978. Emblazoned across the top was the headline: 'Dani And Nino – Famous, Scandalous, And Getting Richer By The Minute.'

The photo featured Countess Dani and her husband dashing to or from some event. Dani in an emerald green, sequined version of the Drop Dress. Nino in a tuxedo, one hand on Dani's arm, hustling her along, carrying an open bottle of champagne in the other hand.

Three lines jangled, all at once, but Barbara Hester

ignored them. They could ring until hell froze over for all she cared. She pressed Hold, temporarily silencing the phone, and hurried off to the ladies' room, magazine in hand. A nice juicy story full of gossip and information about Dani diPortanova, her role model . . . *that* couldn't wait until her lunch hour. With the urgency of an alcoholic stepping up to the bar, she quickly paged to the cover article.

She hadn't had a chance to speak to Dani except for that one time in the spring when they'd all too briefly shared an elevator. But they would speak again, of that Barbara Hester was certain. And in the meantime, she was determined to find out everything she could about Dani diPortanova. She wanted to get to know her better than the countess knew herself.

Just because she was currently the reigning Countess of Seventh Avenue didn't mean she couldn't one day be dethroned.

Dani preferred to read the *People* story in the privacy of her apartment, so early that morning she'd had her housekeeper, Elvira, pick up the current issue at the corner newsstand. The cover photo had been taken at the cocktail party held just last month to publicize the first series of commercials that Ian McAdam had shot for Countess Dani, Inc.

Ian had had his way. All three of the sixty-second spots, set to air nationally at the beginning of August, featured Dani as spokesperson and model. Dani pushing Drop Dresses, pushing sportswear, pushing herself. Initially uncomfortable in the starring role, she had been put at ease by the director, who had shown her how to make love to the camera, not shy away from it.

Even she had been pleased with the end result. On screen, she exuded confidence in herself as a woman, and

179

she reeked of sexuality. Ian was predicting that once the spots began airing, sales would jump by 25 percent the first month.

With a critical, knowing eye, she studied the magazine-cover photo of herself and Nino. They both looked harried, and Nino looked drunk. Or maybe it was simply that she saw what others could not.

The article itself was equally deceptive. Some of what the writer had dug up on them was the usual gossip and exaggeration, but some of the stories were true. With her permission, her father and Monika had allowed themselves to be interviewed. Dani had figured that way at least some of the information would come directly from sympathetic sources.

There was a nice quote from Irving, recalling their first meeting and praising her energy and imagination. That dear man, she'd have to call and thank him. Via the public relations director for diPortanova, Ltd., Italy, a chilly 'no comment' came from Roberto. Thank goodness for Roberto's hatred of publicity. She had no illusions regarding how he felt about her and her company. But the writer had done her homework and dug up the fact that Roberto had refused to toast his son and new daughter-in-law at their wedding reception. His silence gave her plenty to conjecture about.

There were comments from members of Dani's staff, from fashion writers and retailers. A nice plug from Halston and a pat on the back from her friend, Diane Von Furstenberg. Best of all was an 'I knew her when' from a man who'd gone to high school with her.

'We always knew she was very bright and talented,' said the man, who was now a City Council member. 'We've all been rooting for her ever since she went into business.'

What a crock of shit, Dani thought. The man had been

one of the leaders of the pack of boys who had called her names and tormented her about being fat. '*Rooting for her,*' *my eye! Probably wants to get clothes at wholesale for his wife.*

Missing, of course, was an important piece of information that the writer had chosen not to share with her readers – the fact that the story had been written with the full cooperation of Countess diPortanova and her public relations firm. Publicity – good, bad, even indifferent – meant increased profits.

Dani skimmed the pages, pausing to look at the accompanying photos.

A shot taken immediately after the wedding ceremony. The expression on her face was one of unalloyed rapture as she gazed blissfully at her new husband.

The two of them, recently arrived in New York, splashing in the fountain in front of the Plaza Hotel.

Shots of their famous third wedding anniversary party, with the limos lined up for several blocks outside the Dakota.

Dani, almost in tears after her first show.

Dani and Monika, both of them wearing the first version of the Drop Dress and clowning for the camera in front of the Saks Fifth Avenue window that featured her first line.

Nino at Carnival in Rio with the boys . . . not looking his best.

Dani, dressed in an evening gown of her design, accepting the Coty in 1977.

Nino, last fall at his Fifth Avenue office. Dani sometimes wondered how, despite his frequent absences, he continued to handle his family's money successfully.

Nino, in Rome in May of this year. During a routine customs inspection at Leonardo da Vinci Airport, he'd been arrested for possession of cocaine. There was a shot of Roberto diPortanova arriving at the police station after driving from Lake Garda with a phalanx of attorneys. Thanks to Roberto, Nino had gotten off with a hefty fine and no jail sentence. According to *People*, as father and son left the courthouse, Roberto had commented, 'She's not a normal woman, and you're not a normal man!'

A terrible picture of Dani raging at Nino in the middle of the Studio 54 dance floor a moment after Nino had walked out of the ladies' room with an eighteen-year-old debutante who, the article said, was drunk, giggling, and missing her dress.

Dani remembered the night. Wasn't it only her bra that the girl had been missing? The paparazzi had captured the shouting match that had ensued between Dani and Nino. The next day the headline on the front page of the New York *Post* had screamed, 'Designer's Royal Feud.'

Naturally, sales had rocketed.

The *People* reporter wrote, 'The more outrageous or controversial the diPortanovas' behavior, the faster the merchandise flies off the racks. Over the past three years, Countess Dani, Inc., has increased its retail sales on the average of 40 percent a year. Dani diPortanova's company is a machine generated by publicity and oiled by strikingly simple but alluring designs that keep her well-heeled customers coming back for more, season after season. Three years after Dani first introduced the revolutionary Drop Dress, 20,000 women a week are still buying the design.'

Twenty-five thousand, she thought proudly, *but who's counting?*

The piece was moderately accurate, with one exception – the closing paragraph: 'The golden couple of the decade seems to have reached an understanding. Nino has his life, Dani has hers. Neither will do anything to jeopardize either his relationship with his family or her soaring success as a designer. One source close to both of them said, "Theirs is the best marriage of the seventies I've seen. It's what every marriage should be – one of convenience."'

Some convenience, Dani thought, tossing the magazine. Her marriage was rapidly coming apart at the seams.

Cannes, France

From childhood, when she and Dieter had summered with their nanny in Cannes, far from Karola's short leash, Monika had been intrigued by the glittering white fortlike building that housed the Palm Beach Casino. As a teenager, she had regularly sneaked in to play the roulette wheel until just as regularly she would be spotted and kicked out. But smitten with the sense of taut excitement born of fortunes being won or lost on a throw of the dice, Monika invariably took her chances and came back for more.

Helmut had characterized gambling casinos and the people who frequented them as 'depraved.' He'd forbidden her so much as to step foot inside. Since her divorce, she'd been making up for lost time in the Bahamas, Monte Carlo, wherever gambling was legal. In July, the slow season on Seventh Avenue, Cannes had been the natural choice for a much-needed vacation.

On this, her final night in Cannes, she'd swept her blond hair up into a knot and put on a ruby red strapless gown designed by Bill Blass. Her ears glittered with brilliant pear-shaped diamond earrings, and a matching choker circled her tanned neck. Now, crossing the threshold of the main game room, she surveyed the scene and licked her lips in anticipation.

The late hour meant that the casual players had left for

183

dinner or dancing. The tables were dominated by serious gamblers, who were piling up chips and stuffing wads of money into the pockets of their dress pants. Many of them greeted Monika with a nod or a smile. They had known her all her life from the European vacation circuit. The world of the wealthy and privileged being small and gossipy, almost everyone had heard she'd split up with Helmut. Only a few were tactless enough to ask after him.

Monika smiled politely and left it at that. No sense spoiling a good evening, the perfection of which was marred only by Rick's absence. Back in the spring, they'd spent a long weekend in the Bahamas, possibly the best three days of her life. They had motorbiked all over the island, gone swimming, and made love in the early afternoon when the sun was too strong for tanning. At night they'd gambled in the casino on Paradise Island.

Though he obviously enjoyed himself, Rick wasn't as enamored of the scene as Monika. When she had suggested another weekend jaunt, he'd said no, thanks, claiming obligations with his band. Besides, he reminded her, he couldn't afford to vacation in the style to which she was accustomed. And he wasn't about to let her pay for him on a regular basis. Monika loved him for his pride and his stubborn refusal to take money from her. But sometimes he infuriated her.

She hadn't even bothered to invite him along to Cannes – where the *real* gambling happened – because he was working on a demo tape. Maybe that would finally give his career the push it needed. And when he became a rich and famous rock star, she'd let him pay for everything, if that would make him feel better.

In the meantime, she wanted to have fun.

Over the course of the last couple of nights she had lost more than $60,000 dollars playing baccarat, blackjack, and roulette. But tonight she felt lucky. Her gambling blood was flowing. The baccarat table beckoned. She sat down, taking seat number four at the long oval table. The shoe was chopping from Bank to Player to Bank to Player. Monika made some bets, tried to switch at the right times to catch the rhythm of the chopping shoe, but didn't quite get the hang of it. She quickly lost a couple of thousand, then a couple thousand more.

So much for baccarat.

'Better luck next hand,' said an Austrian prince, an old chum of her brother's. He relieved a passing waiter of two glasses of champagne and raised his glass to hers. 'You're looking radiant, Monika. New York must suit you. How's Dieter?'

'He's very well,' Monika said, her mind still on the last hand she'd squeezed out.

'Is he still taking photographs?'

'*Ja*, he is,' she lied. She had no idea what Dieter was doing these days. When last heard from, he was stoned on dope and sleeping on the beach in Goa.

'Excuse me,' she said to the Austrian prince. 'I think I'll try my luck at blackjack.'

Blackjack treated her more civilly. She quickly beat the house by almost $15,000, but after another few minutes, she decided she was bored.

It was time for some real action. Time to play craps. Monika circled the room until she sniffed out a hot table where the house chips were low. She grabbed an open railing in the dice pit, lined up so she could get the dice first coming around the stickman, and put down a stack of $500 gold chips.

A man whose pinky finger was weighted down by an enormous ruby ring threw a six. Several people around the table backed up their bets and bought all the numbers. The stickman looked at Monika expectantly. She picked up the dice and threw them against the far end of the table.

Rotten luck. Seven out. The worst of catastrophes for a craps player. The man with the pinky ring had lost $7,000. She herself had flushed $14,000 down the drain.

'*Encore une fois, mademoiselle?*' asked the croupier.

Monika nodded. Yes, she'd give it another shot. She heaped a stack of gold and black chips on her table rack, bet $2,000 on the line, backed up her number, and bought all the numbers for $2,000 apiece. The dice were hers for the next fifteen minutes. Then the numbers came up bad again.

Seven out.

She'd lost over $30,000.

Wounded but still not defeated, she played another round, determined not to make this her third losing night in a row.

And another. And still another.

It took her only half an hour to lose another $55,000 and run out of chips.

'*Je le regrette*. I'm sorry,' said the croupier, 'but your credit is up.'

Credit up? Monika ignored him. Certainly he couldn't be speaking to her. She was a von Reich, had been a loyal patron at this casino since she was a teenager. Screw them. They could just extend her credit. Monika turned back to the table. She lined up, and the dice came around. The croupier picked up a house phone and called the ladder man above the tables, who phoned upstairs.

A firm no came back from the house manager.

'I'm sorry, Mademoiselle von Reich,' the croupier said politely.

Unfazed, Monika unhooked the diamond choker from around her neck and dropped it in the table rack. There were gasps and murmurs all around.

'Mademoiselle, we don't accept jewelry. Perhaps – '

A man reached over and picked up the choker. Casually he dropped $25,000 in gold chips in the rack and gestured to Monika to go ahead and place her bet.

'It's been appraised at fifty-five,' Monika said coolly, noticing that he was young and darkly attractive.

The man smiled and dropped another $30,000 worth of chips in the rack. 'My mistake,' he said. 'Have fun.'

'*Danke schön.*'

Monika placed her bet, bought her numbers, and rolled. But the dice continued to come up against her. Her pile of chips dwindled down to zero.

'I'm so sorry. This isn't my night,' she said to her benefactor.

He placed his hand over hers. 'Don't worry. I'll cover you for the rest of the night.'

Their eyes met.

'*Ja*, all right.' She could feel the heat from his hand sparking off the heat within her.

Intoxicated by the thrill of rolling the dice, Monika lost track of time and of how much money she was winning or losing. Nothing mattered or existed except the roll of the dice, the croupier's calls, the table in front of her, the man beside her handing her more champagne, feeding her more chips.

She awoke the next morning with a powerful hangover in a bed that was not her own. She had very little memory of how she had come to spend the night in these unfamiliar surroundings. Her friend from the casino lay next to her, still sleeping. Then it all came back to her – his suggestion that she join him for a nightcap in his suite at the Carlton, another bottle of champagne . . . the girl who had appeared suddenly and joined them in bed.

Monika groaned quietly and rescued her evening gown, which she found lying on the floor by the bed. Not stopping to wash her face or comb her hair, she threw on the dress and quickly tiptoed out of the room.

It was Sunday. She had a flight to catch back to New York. Back to work. Back to Rick. Back to the real world.

New York

Barbara Hester consoled herself with the thought that though she was only a receptionist, she'd learned a lot in the time she'd been working at I. Blatt. That was no coincidence. She'd asked plenty of questions, read *WWD* religiously, and shamelessly eavesdropped on the showroom conversations. And people said southerners were hard to understand, she thought to herself in amusement, listening to the garmentos greet one another in their peculiar mixture of English and Yiddish.

'Schlepping *shmattas* again, Abe?'

'You got it, *bubelah*.'

'It's dreck, sonny. All dreck.'

'What are you, a *meshuggener*? Always kibitzing. You know this line is going to go through the roof.'

'*Fun dein moil in Gott's oyren.*'

Barbara especially liked that one: 'From your lips to God's ear.'

When she heard Stuart Blatt call her 'the cute *shiksa* at the front desk,' she went to Carole, the house model, for an explanation.

'He means you're not Jewish, honey,' Carole told her. 'That's a rarity around here. Be careful, though. He'll take you out, sleep with you. But don't get your hopes up. When it comes to closing the deal, he'll never marry a shiksa.'

188

'Thanks, Carole,' Barbara Hester said sweetly. 'I don't know what I'd do without you.'

Returning to the switchboard, she thought, *What a stupid bitch*. She didn't give a shit about Stuart. She had much bigger fish to fry.

In the meantime, she kept busy paving the way for her future. A couple of evenings a week were taken up with courses at the Fashion Institute. She quickly discovered that, though she had an innate sense of fashion, designing was not one of her great talents. But the knowledge didn't hamper her ambitions. If anything, it fueled them.

There was more than one route to the top. Her design instructor came on to her, and she let him have his way. By the end of the semester, she was at the top of her class. Not that she deserved the high marks, but Barbara figured that for what she'd had to put out in bed, she could have earned an honorary degree.

Occasionally she dated I. Blatt salesmen or customers, but she never slept with any of them. After all, they couldn't do anything to advance her career. She allowed them to take her to Broadway plays and out to dinner afterward, but she soon tired of the food at Mamma Leone's and Joe's Pier 52, the guaranteed paw on her breast as they tried to cop a feel when they kissed her good night.

Still, she had to remind herself, she'd come a long way from Henderson, North Carolina, and the farther away, the better . . .

Barbara Mae Hester had grown up in the Henderson slum of Moccasin Bottom, hardly a stone's throw from the cotton factories. Until the day she'd arrived in New York a year and a half ago with $2,000 in cash, she'd answered to 'Bunny,' an appropriate nickname for a little girl with big buck teeth.

Incest was a way of life in Moccasin Bottom, and Bunny's daddy was also her granddaddy. Ernest was a mean, bitter man who made his living by throwing cucumbers into the salt-curing tanks at the Heinz Pickle Plant. Bunny's mother, Irma Rae, also worked at the pickle plant, grading cucumbers.

The Hesters didn't make much money, and home was a drafty shack whose wooden floors had cracks so wide that Bunny could see the chickens scratching the ground beneath her feet. For as long as she could remember, Bunny knew she was different from the rest of the folks in Moccasin Bottom.

If only her life could resemble the lives she saw on 'Leave It to Beaver' and 'The Patty Duke Show.' Since she couldn't vent her anger on her parents, her baby sister Verna became the target of all her rage. She beat her with a belt, forced her to swallow dirty pennies or eat mud pies, and when Verna went crying to their mama, Bunny beat her harder next time to keep her quiet. She hated her life there, hated her parents and her younger sister.

To escape from the poverty and ugliness that surrounded her, she spent all her free time at the Leslie Perry Library across the street from the courthouse. She loved books that told her how rich people lived. But her favorite stories of all were about poor girls who grew up to be rich women.

She pored over the fashion magazines, memorizing the descriptions of the elegant clothes, absorbing the details about what rich people ate, how they entertained themselves, where they spent their vacations. When she discovered Town and Country and Architectural Digest, she almost died of joy and envy.

She swore to herself that one day she, too, would live that life. But certainly not in Henderson or anywhere else in North Carolina. While her friends in Moccasin Bottom dreamed of making the fifty-five-mile trip to Raleigh,

Bunny fantasized about moving to New York, where everyone was rich and all the women were thin and beautiful. Well, she was thin, and she knew she could be beautiful if she could afford to get her teeth fixed. People were always complimenting her on her big green eyes and her strawberry blond hair, which she washed every other night without fail.

As soon as she turned sixteen, Bunny got a job working afternoons at Blair's, Henderson's best women's clothing store. She made full use of her employee's discount, and no matter how short of money her family might be, Bunny's closet was filled with smart and sophisticated outfits.

Blair's founder and owner, Jeremiah Blair, was one of Henderson's most distinguished senior citizens. Poor Jeremiah had been alone ever since his wife left him for another man ten years earlier. The widow ladies of Henderson had all tried to catch him in their fluttery silk-lined nets. Bunny was pretty near certain she could succeed where the older ladies had failed. Any time her employer happened by Better Dresses, the department where she worked, Bunny would push her ample breasts forward until the buttons on her blouse were about to pop. She would purr, giggle, and wiggle her ass as she paraded back and forth in front of him.

Jeremiah couldn't resist her approach.

Soon Jeremiah was showering his 'little bunny rabbit' with gifts of clothing and jewelry and taking her out to dinner in Raleigh. When she smiled, her teeth glittered with metal braces, paid for by Jeremiah Blair. In return, Bunny gave Jeremiah her virginity.

Sex, Bunny had read in the magazines, was exciting . . . mysterious . . . at its best, a moment of great intimacy shared by two people who loved each other. What the magazines hadn't talked about was the way Jeremiah's

191

penis, even at its most erect, looked like a long pink balloon that had been losing air for two days. When he came, the semen dribbled out like the last few drops of water from an old hose.

Bunny shut her eyes and endured the encounters in disgusted silence, but when Jeremiah asked her to lick the drop of sticky white gunk hanging from the tip of his dick, she flat-out refused.

According to Cosmo, *she was supposed to soar on the wings of an orgasm. She didn't even know what an orgasm felt like, but she didn't give a damn, just as long as Jeremiah kept giving her gifts and her bank account continued to grow.*

Three weeks before Bunny's high school graduation, Jeremiah handed her a diamond ring and asked her to do him the honor of becoming his wife. Bunny was horrified. She had far bigger dreams than staying on in Henderson, North Carolina, as Mrs Jeremiah 'Geritol' Blair. But she smiled sweetly and put up with another session of his half-flaccid lovemaking.

As soon as Jeremiah was fast asleep and snoring, Bunny grabbed her clothes from his closet, packed them in his Hartmann suitcase, and helped herself to $200 from his wallet to add to the $1,800 she had already managed to squirrel away. Softly closing the door behind her, she turned her back on Bunny Hester and the life she despised. From the moment she climbed aboard the Greyhound bus bound for New York, she never looked back.

She took a room at the Barbizon Hotel for Women and started pounding the pavement, hoping to find a job in one of the big department stores she'd always dreamed of visiting. The pay was low, however, and she was warned that only a few got very far. Better to start off with a $200-a-week job as the receptionist at I. Blatt & Sons. Seventh Avenue was an entirely different story, the other girls told

her, depending on how tough and ambitious she was.
  After all, look at Dani diPortanova.

Barbara had never spoken to Irving Blatt except to say good morning and hand him phone messages. But for months she'd watched him carefully while he did business with his cronies in the showroom. Though his sons, Stuart and Howie, were running most areas of the company, Barbara's radar was aimed at Irving. Not because she hoped to move up at I. Blatt & Sons, but because Irving was the one person who could give her what she wanted most . . . the inside track to Dani diPortanova.

Once again, Nino was making headlines. Bad enough that Dani was constantly gossip-column dish, but Nino's lack of discretion was getting to be front-page chow. This time one of his tricks had taken off with Nino's new toy, a $150,000 Aston Martin Lagonda.

After Dani bailed Nino out of jail on charges of public intoxication, he indignantly described how he'd generously shared a half a gram of coke with the boy, whom he'd met at an after-hours club. After that they had decided to take the car for a spin, at a hundred ten miles per hour, around the island of Manhattan.

Nino had to take a leak, so they pulled over by a meat-packing plant on the West Side. No sooner had he unzipped his leather pants and taken aim at a wall than he heard the four-cam 5.3-liter V-8 engine roar to life.

'So long, sucker,' the boy yelled as he raced the car toward the West Side Highway.

Three days later the boy turned up in Key West, Florida, joyriding with his lover.

By now the story had been kicked to page five of the *Post*, and the car was on its way home. But Dani was still pissed.

'You're lucky the bastard only stole your car,' she snapped at Nino. 'One of these days one of your sponge-cake boyfriends or girlfriends is going to kill you.'

'And what do you care, *cara*?'

'I care a lot! Blond is a hair color, Nino, not a life-style.'

'What do you know about life-styles? You, the – what do they call you? – the Countess of Seventh Avenue! You'll never have to worry about money or fame. You've used my title not only to make a fortune but to surpass me in celebrity. A pretty hard feat, *si*?'

'How can you say that?' Dani cried, hurt but knowing he was partly right. 'I'm doing this for us, and at least I'm in control of my life. Look at you. You've lost weight and you look like shit. Every time I turn around, you're doing another line of coke or popping tranquilizers to bring you down. You don't know whether you're coming or going.'

'Bullshit. I'm in complete control, just like you,' Nino said, straightening his shoulders. '*Ciao, cara*. Go bust some balls on Seventh Avenue today.'

Walking briskly through the lobby of her office building, Dani considered the subject of balls. Forget busting 'em – she'd be happy to fondle a pair. The way things stood these days between Nino and herself . . . she had just about had it with men. None of them, except maybe Ian McAdam, had the guts to stand their ground with her. They were always deferring to her, afraid to say what they really thought or wanted.

Ian, on the other hand, spoke his mind, but he was so charming and bright that she didn't mind his blunt talk. Plus he was a brilliant ad man. Too bad he was engaged to be married, which explained why he'd been such a gentleman during that first dinner. Or maybe she just didn't turn him on.

The other men she met in business weren't so immune

194

to her charms. Just the week before, she'd gone to a meeting with a vice president from Burlington House who wanted to better the L'Eggs offer for a licensing agreement for Countess Dani hose. Burlington's terms included an advance of $2.5 million for the use of her name, against a 7.5 percent royalty for every unit sold. Dani would also retain design approval and the right to quality control.

She said she'd think about it overnight.

Afterward, the vice president had asked, 'Want to have a drink?'

She'd agreed to the drink but declined his suggestion that they adjourn to his place on Park Avenue.

He'd said, 'Well, what about your place?'

These were the seventies. Being up front and doing one's thing seemed to matter. Subtlety was out. But was subtlety what she yearned for? Would she have said yes if the guy had come on to her with smooth talk and finesse?

Hell, she didn't know what she wanted. Yes, she did. She wanted her husband back – the man she'd fallen in love with, not the one she lived with now whose major interests seemed to be bimbos and cars.

And drugs.

A pain seared her heart. Nino's use of drugs had crossed the line from recreational to almost habitual. More than once she'd commented on that, then pleaded with him to stop. He'd shrugged her off with a laugh. She'd mentioned the Silver Hill Clinic in Connecticut, where a couple of fashion people she knew had detoxed. He'd told her to stop being so uptight and then had gone on a binge that was worse than the last one.

Short of baby-sitting him every hour of the day, which she obviously couldn't do, Dani was fresh out of solutions. But dammit, he was an adult. Besides, she couldn't control him. She didn't even dare try.

Face it, she told herself, *he's nothing but a spoiled child, and you're having to grow up very quickly*.

She sighed and walked into her office. A dozen telephone messages were already waiting for her, and it wasn't even nine o'clock.

Lake Garda, Italy

Roberto diPortanova's secretary placed an envelope in his in-box, and Roberto knew immediately it was from Karola. No doubt another clipping. He could imagine Karola cackling as she sealed the packet. Inside was a copy of *People* magazine as well as a page from the New York *Post*, a dreadful headline about Nino's Aston Martin Lagonda being stolen. Nino hadn't mentioned that little episode when they'd spoken earlier in the week. Not even bothering to read the stories, Roberto grunted and shoved the magazine and the clipping into his shredder.

So, Karola thought she'd trumped him again. He would have to fuck that bitch but good the next time he saw her, teach her a thing or two about when to stop baiting him. Perhaps that was why he found her so irresistible. She needed to be tamed. And, he thought smugly, if anyone could do it, it was Roberto diPortanova.

Remembering how she had cried and begged for his cock up her ass, Roberto began to get hard. Yes, indeed, the next time he saw his cunty *Frau*, he was going to stick it to her. And he was going to stick it to his daughter-in-law as well. Metaphorically, of course.

He'd already set the wheels in motion. Yesterday he'd put in a call to his sister-in-law in Milan and persuaded her that it would be in the best interests of the family if she were to cease production of the Countess Dani line.

196

Dani was to be notified right after the long holiday weekend that Americans referred to as Labor Day.

Roberto roared with laughter at the irony. No labor after Labor Day!

Fire Island, New York

'Ouch!' wailed Mr Reggie, 'be careful with my moles! Jeez, you think my skin's made of rubber?'

No, Rah Rah thought, squeezing more lotion onto Reggie's back, *but it's already beginning to look like it's made of leather*. He rolled his eyes at Mitchell Barton, Reggie's houseguest, who was also intent on catching some rays.

Reggie lay flat on his stomach on a lounge chair by the pool of his recently purchased beachfront home. Located in the exclusive Pines section of Fire Island, the place was a spectacular monument to conspicuous consumption. Reggie had bought the house and an acre property in the spring for just under $600,000 – a gift to himself in anticipation of the deal that would definitively establish him not only as America's hottest fashion designer but also as Seventh Avenue's sharpest businessman.

The renovations had taken all summer. Determined that the decor exemplify the latest in 'beach chic,' Reggie had had the interior completely gutted and redesigned. Now, on the last official weekend of summer, he was finally able to enjoy the fruits of his investment. Self-confessed perfectionist though he was, even he couldn't find fault with the results. The restful color scheme was a harmonious symphony of pale pinks, sands, and beiges, and the mood was one of utter simplicity almost to the point of starkness. Huge seashells, starfish, and tapered candles in varying lengths predominated.

'I call it "relief from clutter,"' Mr Reggie had explained to the editor from *The New York Times Magazine* who was interested in photographing the house for an upcoming article on beach homes. 'I desperately needed a place where I could unwind and get away from all the colors and patterns of which my life is composed. I come to the beach to relax. I made myself a promise – *never, ever* to do business on Fire Island.'

Ah, but promises were made to be broken. Reggie had chartered a seaplane for the weekend so that his lawyer, accountant, and business manager could join him at the house. While he suntanned and swam, they were spending most of the weekend indoors, poring over the book-length contract that promised Mr Reggie fame and fortune beyond even *his* wildest imaginings.

This deal far surpassed the standard licensing agreements whereby various companies paid royalties for the privilege of manufacturing and selling leather goods or ties bearing the Mr Reggie name. If all went as it should – as it was *destined* to – Reggie Bolt would be selling his entire business, the whole pie, the Mr Reggie trademark included.

True, he would have to get corporate approval before he was allowed to put his name to any new designs, but what Reggie would receive in return would be the financial backing he needed to keep his company marching confidently into design history.

Far above his head, at the top of a huge flagpole visible from all points on the beach, a flag bearing the Mr Reggie logo flapped wildly in the wind.

'Isn't that flag fabulous?' Reggie asked Mitchell. 'It lets everyone out here know that this is *the* flagship house in the Pines.'

Rah Rah thought it let everyone know what an egomaniac Reggie was, and he said so.

Mitchell sipped his margarita and laughed in agreement with Rah Rah.

'Listen,' Reggie hissed, 'I don't give a fuck what you two think. If I wanted to, I could take the flag down and they'd *still* know this was my house. You know why? The design. The place has class. Reeks of it. You don't need to wave a flag or read about it or whatever to see that. *Some* people have to stick their fucking twats on the covers of magazines like *People* to advertise who they are,' he said, taking a slow sip of his heavily doctored Long Island iced tea. 'I don't have to do that. The world already recognizes me for who I am. And if they don't, I wouldn't want them to know me anyway. Besides, the next time you see me on a magazine cover, it's not going to be that gossip rag. It'll be *Time* or *Newsweek*. Those are the only two that count.'

Rah Rah and Mitchell exchanged sympathetic glances as Rah Rah continued coating Reggie with sunscreen. Reggie had been mouthing off hysterically ever since Dani diPortanova had been covered by *People*. When the issue first hit the newsstands, he'd fired his public relations firm, only to rehire them the next day and demand that they get him a cover. Since then, he'd railed almost daily about the magazine.

Personally, Rah Rah had been delighted with the story. He'd thoroughly enjoyed the night he'd spent with Nino and thought it was a kick that Nino hadn't lost any of his spark since then. Maybe they'd hook up again sometime.

Reggie shooed him away, sat up, and began punching figures into the calculator he'd taken to carrying around with him.

'Mike,' he bellowed at his lawyer, who was inside paging through the agreement, 'what did you say was their last offer on the annual payout schedule?'

Mike yelled out an answer.

Totally absorbed in his figures, Reggie whipped his hand across the calculator. 'God, I am going to be so rich! Rich, do you hear me?' he crowed triumphantly. He got hard just thinking about the money.

Rah Rah needed some relief. He dived into the pool. Mitchell followed close on his heels.

'Unbelievable!' Reggie shouted to no one in particular. 'It's like printing money! How am I going to spend it all? God, how I love this business!'

Mitchell, who earned a relatively modest $34,000 a year, swam over to Rah Rah and muttered, 'If I have to hear one more time about how rich he's going to be, I'm going to hold him, his calculator, and that fucking contract underwater until he drowns.'

Rah Rah shook his head. 'No, don't do that. He's wondering how he'll spend it all? I think I can come up with a few ways – '

'Rah Rah!' Reggie bellowed. 'More lotion!'

'Then again,' said Rah Rah, 'drowning's not such a bad idea. I mean, I *am* provided for in his will.'

Cosmo had counseled Bunny Hester to take a share in a summer house, while *Glamour* had touted Bermuda and the Hamptons as the chic spots to spend holiday weekends. But even frugal Bunny couldn't afford to travel far from New York on her meager salary. And she was damned if she was going to share a house with a bunch of people she didn't know, and have to worry about whose turn it was to buy the groceries.

But what no magazine had told her was how to get through those sultry weekends when she was going crazy with boredom and heat, when she was sure she was the last white person left in New York. And the holiday weekends were the absolute worst – there were just so many movies and museums she could bear to see, and the sun at the beach seared her skin like a hot dog that had been left too long on the barbecue grill.

So Bunny had spent most of the Labor Day weekend sulking in her room at the Barbizon, plotting her escape from I. Blatt. When the alarm clock rang on Tuesday morning, she was glad to get up and go to work.

A faint breeze followed her into the building, and Bunny thought, *Thank God for September*. August in New York had almost made her forget why she'd ever come north. She recalled all the long summer nights when she sat alone in her room with the window open to catch a breeze. The noise from the street, of people laughing and talking and having fun, made her feel lonelier than a fawn lost in the woods without its mama in the middle of hunting season.

She inserted a new blotter into her desk pad, flipped to a new page on her calendar, and stuck a cheery smile on her face. New month, new season, renewed resolve to get moving. Enough sitting around and feeling bad for herself. That wasn't how she'd pulled herself out of the muck of Moccasin Bottom, she sternly reminded herself.

Then the phone rang, and it was back to business as usual. The first call of the day was from Carole, Howie Blatt's secretary, who also doubled as the size eight fitting model. She'd gotten food poisoning from eating clams, she said. She was too sick to come to work. Bunny was sure she could hear a guy's voice in the background. Carole probably just wanted an extra day off.

'Sure, sure, I'll tell them,' Bunny said impatiently, cutting off the girl's string of apologies and explanations. Bunny hated her. Carole's father had grown up with Irving, and Carole got away with murder because of that childhood friendship. Bunny could give herself a new name, even a new history that omitted all mention of

Moccasin Bottom and fathers who raped their own daughters. But one thing she couldn't give herself was a credible link in the chain of family connections that led to the top of Seventh Avenue.

When the showroom manager walked in, Bunny handed her Carole's message.

'She said *what*?' screeched Lillian. 'That bitch! She knew damn well I needed her here first thing this morning. I've got a bunch of buyers from Texas scheduled to see nighties in exactly one hour. Now, what the hell am I supposed to do? Model them myself?'

The question was obviously rhetorical, because if her life depended on it, Lillian couldn't have fit into the size eight samples – or even the size fourteens. But before Bunny could open her mouth, Lillian was snapping her fingers and saying 'C'mon with me, Barbara! Hurry up! Belle.' She shouted at one of the saleswomen, 'Grab the switchboard, wouldja? I got another job for Barbara to do.'

'Go to the mountains for the weekend,' Irving Blatt's sister and brother-in-law had urged him. 'It's already two years that you're alone without Gert. There are plenty of women dying to meet a handsome man like yourself.' Sick of their nagging, Irving had finally caved in and booked himself for Labor Day weekend at Grossinger's, the Catskill Mountains' most famous and enduring resort.

Driving up the New York State Thruway on Friday afternoon, he'd admitted to himself that he *was* lonely and wouldn't mind meeting a nice lady, someone he could invite out to dinner, maybe once in a while take to the movies, have some fun, and get warm next to in bed. A classy lady, with a little more spunk than the blind dates he'd recently endured.

But despite Grossinger's reputation as a paradise on

earth for singles looking to become doubles, the three-day weekend had been a bust. Irving came home without any phone numbers, only a killer case of indigestion to show for his efforts.

His sister called him at the office first thing Tuesday morning and said brightly, 'So . . .?'

'So no more of your smart ideas,' Irving growled. 'Three days of nothing but rich food and blue-rinse pussy. I may be sixty-four years old, but I can still do better than that.'

He hung up on her shocked silence and smiled with bitter satisfaction that lasted only as long as the next attack of heartburn. Irving shook his head and went searching for Maalox.

Walking through the showroom, he stopped as he always did to survey his domain. Business was good. At least he had that fact to comfort him. He waved at an old friend, one of the buyers from Sanger-Harris, who waved back. She mouthed, 'Hot,' as the model sashayed across the floor in a revealing seashell-pink nightgown and matching peignoir.

Nice, thought Irving, *very nice*. Stuart and Howie had argued with him about doing the collection in pale colors – pearl grays, blush roses, dusky blues. 'Won't fly,' they'd declared in unison, defying him to contradict their business school wisdom.

Ha! Irving snorted. M.B.A. degrees, laminated and hanging on the wall, might make a good impression, but when it came right down to fashion business sense, he still had a thing or two to teach his kids. They were smart boys, but it wouldn't hurt them occasionally to listen before they opened their big mouths. How often, for example, did he have to remind them to check their projections with Lillian, who'd been with him for over

203

thirty years and was worth her considerable weight in gold?

Lillian had these buyers wrapped around her little finger. *She* was telling *them* what their orders should be. They were obediently writing down her numbers like secretaries taking the boss's dictation.

The model reappeared, wearing Irving's favorite outfit – a two-piece, shorty pajama set harking back to what they'd called 'baby-dolls' in the late fifties. But these pajamas had left 'cute' behind and were downright seductive. Especially on this girl, with her smooth, slender legs and sweetly rounded tush.

He turned to one of the salesladies and whispered, 'New model?'

'She's just filling in for Carole. You know her – the receptionist, Barbara Hester.'

Funny, he'd never really noticed her before. Such a pretty girl, especially now when she caught his stare, smiled, and flashed her big green eyes at him.

Irving felt a hardening that wasn't in his arteries.

For the first time since starting her company, Dani had taken some time off, a two-week vacation with Nino – ten days in Portugal, followed by several days stretching through the long Labor Day weekend at the house in Connecticut. She badly needed the holiday, and even more urgently, her marriage needed mending. She couldn't stop Nino's drinking, but she could remind him that *she* was the woman he'd pledged his love to. And vice versa, of course.

'Like a second honeymoon' was how she described it to Monika. 'We made love every day, sometimes twice. Honestly, Monika, it's incredible what a great couple we are when we put our minds to it.'

'Your minds?' snorted Monika. 'Is that what you

thought you were doing? Now I know why you haven't had that baby Roberto's always asking about.'

'Very funny. Speaking of Roberto, I didn't invite you into my office just to catch up. I also wanted you here for moral support. I have a call in to Asolo.'

'He doesn't know yet?'

'No. Today's the day. Oops.' She grimaced in response to her secretary's buzzer. 'That's probably him now.'

'Hello? Yes, this is the Countess diPortanova. Yes, I'll hold . . . Roberto, how are you? . . . Fine, yes, we had a lovely trip. I'm sure Nino's already told you all about it . . . Yes, I *know* he and I need more time together. Why do you think we took this vacation? Roberto, never mind about that. I have a business matter to discuss . . . Oh, really? What were you planning to call me about? . . . You *what*?'

She listened quietly, shaking her head and mouthing to Monika, *Wait till you hear this!*

When he was finished telling her his news, Dani said, 'Perhaps you'd like to think you were motivated by a desire to save my marriage, but I'm sure that's only half the story. The fact is, Roberto, that not all women are as stupid as you'd like to believe. If that were the case, I'd never have lasted in this business. As much as I've appreciated your help, I've always known it was only a matter of time before you'd pull exactly this kind of stunt. And I'm pleased to say you can't hurt me, Roberto, because I don't need your sister-in-law's factory. I'm one step ahead of you. I've already lined up a new manufacturer. In fact, a letter went out to Milan this morning notifying them to that effect. My best to the family, Roberto.'

She hung up the phone, shaking, and looked up at Monika. 'He'd already convinced Giulietta to stop production of our line. That bastard! We could have been left high and dry.'

'But we weren't,' Monika said practically. 'And all because you were smart enough to get your ass over to Hong Kong to line up a manufacturer.'

'It still hurts, Monika. He's my father-in-law, and he treats me as if I'm the enemy. I'll never understand it. It's not *my* fault his son is such a . . . a flake!' She smiled ruefully. 'Well, I guess the last laugh's on him, especially since Hong Kong's prices are so much lower than Milan's. You're definitely satisfied with their quality? No lingering doubts?'

'None at all, *liebchen*, I promise you.'

Dani let out a breath of relief. 'Okay, good. You know, I never thought it was such a hot idea to have a business involvement with the family, but at the time I had no choice.'

'*Ja*,' Monika agreed. 'Look at how my mother managed to swallow up all our cousins' companies.'

Dani absentmindedly tapped a pencil against her desk. 'Karola and Roberto are actually a lot alike. Can you imagine if they ever got together?'

Monika roared with laughter. 'I shudder to think of it.'

Chapter Eight

New York, 1979

'Who died?'

Howie Blatt jerked his thumb toward the dozens of red carnations spread like a blanket across Barbara Hester's desk.

'We should be so lucky,' his brother Stuart said sourly. 'You think the old man ever gave Mom so much as a box of chocolates on Valentine's Day?'

Howie grimaced. Their father's five-month-old relationship with Barbara was a sore subject for both boys, despite the fact that Irving was looking better than he had in years.

'And I feel better, too,' he'd told them in no uncertain terms when they'd objected to his bringing Barbara to Stuart's son's bar mitzvah.

'But, Dad,' Stuart had pleaded, 'she *works* for you. Is that smart, mixing business with pleasure? People will talk.'

'So let 'em talk. You're inheriting the company. What else do you want from me? So I'm getting a little action with a girl who's sexier than both your wives put together. Stop clucking like a couple of old ladies and leave me alone.'

'I only hope he doesn't drop dead in the saddle,' muttered Howie, viciously punching the elevator button.

'Or, God forbid, marry her.' Stuart rolled his eyes heavenward.

The elevator door opened in time for them to be spared

the sight of Irving, dapperly dressed in a new checked sports jacket, sneaking up on Bunny and planting a sloppy wet kiss on her cheek.

'It's time for lunch, *bubelah*.'

Bunny flashed Irving a winsome smile. 'Lunch already? How time flies. Oh, Irving, honey, thank you again for these gorgeous flowers,' she gushed. 'I'm the luckiest girl in the whole wide world.'

She buzzed for her lunch-hour replacement and waited for Irving to help her with her coat.

'Let me guess,' she said archly. 'Siegel's, right? We ate at Dubrow's yesterday.'

'Wrong, my little *bubelah*. Today we go crosstown to Murray Hill. For Valentine's Day, something special for my Valentine.'

'Murray Hill?' Bunny asked, curious but pleased that Irving was finally using a little imagination. She was sick of the three or four fashion-district restaurants the garmentos frequented, where Irving inevitably bumped into one of his old cronies who would chew his ear off in Yiddish, leaving Bunny to stew over what they were saying.

Not that she gave a damn whether people were gossiping about how much time she and Irving spent together. Irving had quickly gotten over his initial embarrassment at being seen in public with a woman young enough to be his granddaughter. Now he regularly took her out not only at lunch but for dinner as well, usually to Joe Allen or Broadway Joe's, often followed by an evening at the theater or a movie.

Because men weren't allowed upstairs at the Barbizon, they had sex only on the weekends, when Bunny slept at Irving's home in Forest Hills. Screwing Irving was no thrill, but it was better than being stuck in her room at the hotel with no money.

Irving was a much more energetic lover than Jeremiah Blair, and Bunny endured Irving's ardent coupling with as much feigned enthusiasm as she could muster. It was an investment in her future, she consoled herself, trying not to shudder as his tongue probed between her reluctantly parted legs. She was still only a receptionist, earning $300 a week, but she was getting ready to hit Irving for a promotion. Maybe today, she mused, as she snuggled closer to him in the back-seat of the cab that was negotiating its way through the congested noon-hour traffic. Yes, she decided, she'd ask him today at lunch. Unless, of course, Irving gave her a really expensive piece of jewelry as a Valentine's Day present, and then she might be better off waiting another week or so.

'Here we are.' Irving motioned to a building on the corner of Lexington Avenue and Thirty-sixth Street. He handed the driver the fare plus a generous tip.

'Thanks, pal,' grunted the cabbie.

'Thank *you*,' Irving replied, rubbing his hands together with excitement.

They had stopped in front of a nondescript red-brick apartment building that resembled hundreds of others on the East Side. There was no sign of a restaurant, fancy or otherwise. Bunny didn't get it. She'd been looking forward to a pleasant lunch in a cozy, quiet restaurant with waiters gliding over to do her bidding.

'Irving,' she sulked, 'couldn't whatever you have to do here wait until after we eat?'

Irving smiled, waved at the doorman, and steered her to the elevator.

'What I have for you is *better* than food,' Irving chuckled gleefully.

Bunny fumed silently. *This damn well better be good, Irving baby, because I'm starving.*

'Fourth floor,' Irving announced. He bounded off the

elevator, led her down the hallway to Apartment 4B, and dangled a set of keys in front of her. 'Happy Valentine's Day, doll face.'

The apartment was a typical furnished New York studio – a combination living room-bedroom, which couldn't have been more than seventeen feet square. It wasn't anything *Architectural Digest* would have featured, but it could have passed muster in *Apartment Living*. The pink and orange couch, mirrored wall, and chrome accessories weren't exactly Bunny's idea of chic, but she could tell that some thought and money had gone into the place. A teak wall unit held a TV set, a stereo, and a bar, which was stocked with Dewar's, Irving's favorite drink.

'Booboo, I don't understand,' Bunny murmured, the picture of sweet confusion. She thought, *If he doesn't say this is mine I'm going to kill the old goat*.

Irving took her in his arms and kissed her passionately. What a wonderful, innocent little girl. In all the years he'd been married to Gert, she'd never turned him on like this little girl did. And she was so ambitious! Always asking questions, observing, taking notes . . . Her hunger to learn the business reminded him of Dani diPortanova. He'd told her so, and she'd seemed pleased with the compliment.

The taste of Irving's mouth told Bunny that he hadn't let his dentures soak long enough the night before, but she tried to ignore the sour odor. Compared to Jeremiah and all his problems, Irving was a piece of cake. Pulling away from his eager embrace, she took another look around.

'Do you like the apartment?' he asked, worried by her silence.

'Yes, but I don't understand . . .'

'Barbara, this is all yours! No more Barbizon Hotel. No more living out of a suitcase. It's a sin for you to be living like that when I can afford better for you. You deserve a real home. Come see the rest of it.'

He guided Bunny around the room, pointing out the bathroom, the tiny closet, and the louvered doors, which were latched shut.

'The kitchen?'

'Yes.' Irving beamed. 'But there's more than just the kitchen in there, doll face. My special Valentine's Day present.'

Two piles of fur were balled up on a piece of newspaper in the middle of the tiny kitchen. It took a few moments for Bunny to realize that what she was staring at was not a fur coat, as she'd hoped, but two fluffy dogs. She'd never owned a dog. Didn't they cost a lot to feed? And what about vet bills? And who the hell was supposed to walk them?

She stifled an impatient sigh. Sometimes Irving could be such an old fool.

'Oh, booboo,' she simpered. 'They're so cute! But two?'

'Sure, to keep each other company when you're not home. The people at the pound told me they were from the same litter, and I hated to separate them. It would be like breaking up a family.'

Bunny bent down to pet the dogs, and they woke up, wagging their tails. Happy for the attention, they licked her hands and pawed at her suede skirt. 'They're awfully fat and furry. What kind are they?'

Irving shrugged. 'They told me, but I forgot already. What difference does it make? A dog's a dog. But I took care of their shots and tags, and there's a big bag of Puppy Chow in the closet. So, what do you think? Do you like the place? Is it okay?'

'Okay? Oh, Irving, I love it! You're too good to me!'

Irving planted another sour kiss on her lips. 'And you're

too good to me,' he whispered, taking Bunny by the hand and leading her over to the sofa bed.

The two little puppies waddled close behind them.

Watkins Glen, New York

Playing the money game with the diPortanova trust had lost its thrill. Nino needed a new kick, and it didn't take long before he was flirting again with his first love, professional sports cars.

Long before he'd met Dani, Nino had wanted to race professionally. Thanks to Nino's skill behind the wheel combined with the diPortanova money, entrée into the racing world would have been relatively easy. But his marriage to Dani had intervened. Since then, while he hadn't been behind the wheel, he'd certainly made it a point to attend all the big annual races: the French Grand Prix in Le Castellet, the Indy 500, Le Mans, Brands Hatch, and Watkins Glen. Through the years he'd made friends with his heroes, world-class greats like Bobby Unser, Mario Andretti, Brian Redman, Carlos Maco, and Jacky Ickx, men for whom speed and competition were a way of life. Every time they raced, they defied death, a dangerous game that Nino was eager to play, too.

After convincing his father that sponsoring him and providing a car and a race team would be great advertising for diPortanova, Ltd., Nino started training. That was in January. Since then he'd cut down on his consumption of booze and coke, given up the all-night partying, and hired a personal trainer to come to the apartment five mornings a week to work with him in his private gym. The results were beginning to show. He'd lost weight and firmed up his pecs and abdomen. He was feeling great – hard and tough and raring to go.

Now came the big question: Was he good enough to get past the qualifying rounds, the results of which would determine whether he'd be in the real competition two days later here at Watkins Glen in upstate New York? Today's rounds were crucial. One slip could mean an end to his chances. Anxiety about today's qualifying rounds had turned his usually unflappable nerves into putty, and he'd been pissing all morning. Alone in the bathroom, he cursed himself for the drinking he'd done last night. A couple of drinks had somehow turned into what must have been a bottle of scotch. Champagne, too, if his memory served him correctly – and he wasn't altogether sure it did this morning.

He was due in the pit in five minutes, but his stomach was churning. Tiny fingers of fear pulled at his gut, and when he closed the zipper of his shiny red fireproof Nomex suit, his fingers trembled. *Cazzo!* The first rule of race driving was to relax, to be the emotional equivalent of an empty glass. Anything else, and he risked losing control. Couldn't let that happen . . .

Hidden away on the top shelf of his locker was a sterling silver flask. After unscrewing the top, he gulped down a healthy dose of scotch.

Instantly he felt calmer.

But the booze dragged him down, so he dug deep into his canvas sports bag until his fingers closed around a tiny vial of coke, hidden there for just such an emergency. Four quick snorts and he was feeling no pain. Scotch and coke – an unbeatable combination. Like a good martini. *Hold the olive, bartender. Just another line, please.*

Climbing into his Alfa Romeo Tipo 33, Nino felt ready to take on the world. He adjusted his helmet, flashed a thumbs-up to his crew, and pulled out of the pit. The coke and scotch kicked in as he roared onto the track.

He jigged left, clipped a right-hand apex, and went

213

down hard on the throttle. By the time he'd brought the car up to 200 miles an hour and had put the first couple of laps behind him, he was taking the contoured track with ease.

The flagman signaled the laps – five . . . seven . . ten . . .

After twelve laps Nino was moving up fast on a March Formula One on the inside track. He backed off the throttle and downshifted to fourth, keeping his foot well away from the brake. He eased the car left, rocketed around the next turn, and opened up on the throttle as soon as he hit the high-speed back straight.

He was closing in on a Lotus Formula Three and a Matra, with a Ferrari edging close behind, pushing hard to overtake him. Nino took his foot off the accelerator for a millisecond, dropped back slightly, and made a quick, dangerous cut in front of the Ferrari. He roared past the Lotus and Matra and closed in on the lead, a Surtees.

A quick glance in his mirror told him that the Formula One was moving up fast on the inside, within striking distance of overtaking him. Nino was doing over 210 miles an hour and accelerating, but he was losing ground fast.

The Formula One moved up . . . then the Ferrari.

Nino tightened his grip on the wheel and glanced right, weighing his options, deciding to work his way left into the inside track to block the Formula One. Did he have enough room to shoot through the space between the Formula One and the Surtees? He blinked his eyes, trying to focus on the distance, trying to calculate the crucial number of feet that separated victory from disaster. At these speeds, even a minor collision meant an almost certain accident – the kind of fiery crash that few men had ever walked away from. That was a chance he would have to take.

He floored the accelerator.

The Alfa shot forward.

The instant his rear grazed the Formula One's front end, he knew he'd made the wrong move.

But it was already too late . . .

Monika and Rick stood at the end of a long line of people waiting to pass through the metal detector at the United Airlines Terminal at Kennedy Airport. Over one shoulder, Rick was carrying a battered blue canvas bag. His favorite guitar, in an ancient case, was slung over the other shoulder. The line was moving slowly, and for once Monika was glad for the delay.

She'd been dreading this moment ever since Rick had told her he was moving to Los Angeles. Thanks to the demo tape he'd cut last summer, he'd finally gotten the big break he deserved – a recording contract with MCA Records. Monika was thrilled that all his hard work was paying off, but she still didn't understand why he had to leave New York.

'They have studios in New York,' she'd pouted. 'Why can't you cut the album here?'

'Because LA is where the action is, baby,' he'd told her again and again. 'Besides, you can always fly out on weekends to visit me.'

But they both knew she wouldn't. Dani and Kim were convinced that Rick, a diehard New Jersey booster if ever there was one, wouldn't last more than a month or two in laid-back LA. But Monika's instincts told her otherwise. He'd already rented a house in West Hollywood, found himself a roommate, and shipped ahead the rest of his equipment and clothes.

To mark his first recording contract, Monika had bought him a tiny silver pin in the shape of a guitar, encrusted across the top with four tiny diamonds.

215

'I thought guys were supposed to buy the jewelry,' he'd said when she'd presented it to him.

'*Ach*, forget that macho shit. I can afford it,' she'd told him.

How she was touched to see the pin on the lapel of his denim jacket. Why did she care so much that Rick was leaving? she wondered. She'd hardly slept with anyone else since they'd met, but it wasn't as if they were in love. She wasn't even sure there was such a thing. Certainly not based on the couples she knew best.

Her parents? If that was togetherness, she'd take a life of solitude, thank you very much.

Dani and Nino? Perhaps they still loved each other, but it was no secret that Dani went her way and Nino went his.

Kim had a boyfriend, a screenwriter, but they seemed to fight as often as they made love.

She had always assumed that Rick was just a temporary thing, a stimulating diversion until she met a man who was more her style . . . whatever that style might be. The image of her perfect man grew fuzzier the longer she lived in New York.

Perhaps she should be paying more attention to the men who escorted her to the dinners and parties she was required to attend. They were all wealthy, well-educated, and attractive – and crashingly dull. After an evening with one of them, Rick felt like a cool, fresh sea breeze blowing into her bed.

Damn! She was going to miss him.

It was almost Rick's turn to put his bags on the conveyor belt and walk through the detector that would separate the passengers from their well-wishers. 'I guess this is it,' he said, his voice gruff with suppressed emotion. He smiled his big lazy grin that never failed to get her wet. 'I meant what I said, you know, about your coming out to live with me.'

Impossible. She could no more leave New York and Countess Dani than Rick could give up his dream of being America's number one rock star. She was second-in-command of a company that showed every promise of one day being able to move into the celestial ranks occupied by Calvin Klein, Ralph Lauren, and Perry Ellis. Dani depended on her, and Monika lived and breathed the business, crazy and hectic though it was.

But it was nice to know she was wanted. All her life she'd felt unloved – until Rick had come along in his scruffy jeans and T-shirts. He'd wooed her with his haunting rock ballads and love songs. And now, just as she was getting used to him, he was leaving her.

He grabbed her in his arms and she buried her face in his neck, soaking in his odor, which smelled better to her than the most expensive cologne. He kissed her, and she savored the lingering taste of him in her mouth. He was going to make it, she could feel it. And they would stay in touch for a while – phone calls, Christmas cards, an occasional visit – until eventually the connection between them would be broken.

'I'll call you in a couple of days, baby,' he whispered. 'Take care. Stay out of trouble.'

'*Ja*, you, too.'

Tears welling up in her eyes, Monika popped Rick's demo tape into the cassette player of her Jaguar and headed out of the Kennedy parking lot. Rick's voice – driving, powerful, sexual – filled the car. She turned up the volume, then abruptly ejected the tape. Rick was history. Time to move ahead. When she stopped at a red light, she fumbled among the cassettes until she found one of her favorite Marvin Gaye tapes.

Just ahead, a plane flew across the roadway and soared west into the setting sun. Rick's plane? Was he thinking about her? She remembered the way he'd looked in bed last night . . . how he'd touched her face, played with her breasts, kissed her between –

Quickly she erased the thought.

She couldn't do this to herself or she'd lose her mind.

Lonely and looking for company, she'd almost called Dani from the airport, but she'd hung up before anyone answered. Probably she and Nino were out celebrating his results at Watkins Glen. Wherever they were, she wished she were with them. She sure as hell didn't feel like spending this evening all by herself.

Fingers of pink and lavender streaked the April sky, and the air was springtime mild. It was the perfect evening to take a romantic stroll down Fifth Avenue, or to have dinner *à deux* at a sidewalk café. She couldn't remember the name of the English poet who'd called April the cruelest month, but he obviously knew what he was talking about.

The lights of the Triborough Bridge winked at her in the fading dusk, summoning her back to Manhattan, back to where the action was. And she knew exactly where to go to find it.

Lucky's, the oldest and most exclusive private gambling club in the city.

On one of her regular jaunts to the Paradise Island Casino, an acquaintance had told her about the club and later given her an introduction. After her background was checked and her credit investigated, Monika was invited to become a member, along with the Wall Street high rollers, city and state government officials, Hollywood and Broadway luminaries, and the 750-odd men and women who were wealthy enough to come up with the $50,000 membership fee.

Rick thought gambling was a loser's game where the house always came out on top. He was wrong, but she didn't bother arguing with him. Lucky's was her little secret where she played to win and often did. When she lost, she kept on playing. The higher the risk, the greater the thrill.

Yes, she decided, turning south onto the East River Drive. Lucky's it would be tonight. The perfect place to recover from Rick's departure.

Nino slowly returned to consciousness. Foggy with pain and medication, he tried to speak, but his mouth felt as if it were stuffed with cotton. He yawned, and the pain almost forced him under again, but his thirst demanded to be slaked.

'Aargh,' he groaned. 'Water . . .'

'The nurse said you could suck on this.'

An ice cube found its way to his lips. Nino sucked greedily at the moisture and opened his eyes to find Dani hovering above him. His right arm was strapped across his chest, an IV tube was attached to the left, and his head throbbed worse than ten hangovers.

'What the hell – ' Suddenly it all came back to him. 'The guy in the Ferrari . . . is he okay?'

Dani nodded and lost control of the storm of tears that had been threatening ever since she'd gotten word of Nino's accident. She'd taken the diPortanova USA chopper, a Sikorsky S-76, straight from the city less than twenty minutes after the call came.

'I've never been so worried in all my life,' she said, sobbing, perched gingerly on the side of his hospital bed. 'Never! I begged you not to go back to racing! You could have been killed!'

'Oooh, my head . . .' he moaned. '*Cara*, I'm too wicked to die young. Where am I, anyway?'

'Ithaca Medical Center. You were incredibly lucky, you know. You suffered a concussion, broke an arm, three ribs, smashed your head up pretty badly . . .' She ticked off his injuries.

'At least I'm alive.' He smiled weakly.

'Barely. Do you remember what happened?'

'Bad luck. I miscalculated and made a stupid move.' He grimaced and reassuringly patted her hand. 'It could have happened to anyone.'

She bit her tongue and said nothing for a few minutes, trying to let him get his bearings a little more. Finally, softly, she said, 'Nino, you can lie to everyone else, but please, not to me. Your doctor told me he found traces of coke and alcohol in your blood.'

'Dani, I only did a couple of lines. It was no big deal, believe me,' he pleaded, trying to bluff his way past her anger.

'Nino, please . . . I'm your *wife*. You were out so long that I had time to speak to our lawyers. The race officials are bound to find out about the blood test. Ditto the insurance people. The other driver will probably sue, though perhaps you can settle out of court for several hundred thousand. All because of a few lines? You're addicted to it.'

'Addicted?' He'd had a swig or two of scotch. That didn't exactly make him an alcoholic. A few lines – that made him an addict?

'Oh, never mind!' She gestured impatiently. 'Why do I bother? Talking to you is like talking to a child!'

She snapped open her handbag and pulled out a pocket mirror. 'Look at yourself! Do you like what you see?'

The face that stared back at him was swollen and grotesquely bruised. His left eye sported a shiner that was all the colors of the rainbow. His forehead was swathed

220

in an enormous bloodstained bandage. No wonder she was looking so upset and worried.

'I swear, Nino, if I had any brains or guts, I'd leave you!'

Through eight often stormy years of marriage, Dani had never threatened to leave him. Her quiet, resolute tone impressed him as much as the words themselves. And he had to admit she had reason to be angry with him. No driver worth his salt used liquor or drugs to pump himself up before a race. Artificial stimulants dulled the reaction time. Even the rankest amateur knew that.

'Perhaps I made a mistake.'

'A *mistake*?'

'Excuse me, Countess.' Nino's private nurse poked her head in the door. 'Your husband's due for his next injection. If you'll just wait outside a moment . . .'

'That's all right, I was just leaving.' Sadness etched across her face, Dani leaned over and kissed Nino's cheek. 'It's late, Nino, and we both need sleep. I didn't mean to tear into you like that. I know you're in a lot of pain. But so am I, watching what you're doing to yourself. I'll be back first thing in the morning.'

She shrugged on her fur coat. 'Here's my number in Ithaca,' she told the nurse. 'Call me if there's any problem whatsoever.'

'Dani, wait – ' Grunting from the pain, Nino pushed himself up on one elbow. 'I love you, *cara*. That's the truth.'

'I believe you, Nino. But I don't know how much longer I can stomach the rest of the lies.'

Nino was awakened by a nightmare about the crash that he preferred not to remember. His nurse, who sat reading in the corner by the light of a tiny lamp, gave him a few sips of water and asked whether he needed more butalbital for his head. Though every muscle in his body was screaming in pain, he said no. He wanted his mind clear to think about what Dani had said.

There had never been a divorce in the diPortanova family. The idea was unthinkable. He was sure she still loved him, in spite of everything. And he loved her. Perhaps she wasn't quite the woman he would have imagined himself married to – a woman like his mother or his sisters – but she was his wife, and, more than that, his friend. He needed her by his side more than he needed the coke or the booze.

He'd tell her so in the morning.

Lucky's was located on East Seventy-fifth Street, in a venerable four-story brownstone that resembled all the other well-tended houses on the block. Its staid exterior belied the atmosphere that lay beyond the front door, whose armor plate was nicely concealed by a rosewood veneer. The owners had spent millions of dollars on the decor to create an opulent ambience that was reminiscent of a Venetian palace. The walls were covered with bleached Louis XVI Revival *boiserie*, and the floors beneath the gambling tables were made of imported Italian marble.

The gambling activities were arranged by floor in order of ascending importance and amounts of money laid out. The gaudy slot machines and roulette wheels were relegated to the first floor. Lively poker games were played in a back room on antique English card tables. Marble *atlantes* stood against the walls behind them.

Craps and blackjack were played on the second floor, at tables surrounded by highly polished brass railings. Giltwood Chippendale chandeliers sparkled above the baccarat table on three, as well as on the hallowed fourth floor, where personal fortunes were nightly lost and won at the highest bet-limit games.

Monika loved Lucky's. She loved being greeted by name by the elegantly uniformed doorman and ushered into the green felt foyer where the butler would hurry over to say 'May I take your coat, Miss von Reich? Care for a drink, Miss von Reich? How are you this evening, Miss von Reich?'

No matter how down she was feeling, the sight of the other women swirling past in their colorful evening gowns and the men in their evening jackets never failed to raise her spirits. As she approached the gambling tables, the tensions of her day would fall away and she could almost taste the sweet fruits of the victory that could be hers.

Once she had asked Nino what drew him to racing.

'I crave the rush,' he had said. 'It's like nothing else I know.'

Monika had understood exactly what he meant. She got her rush from gambling.

Roberto glared at the Aaron Shikler portrait of his daughter-in-law, which hung over the fireplace in his son's library. The painting dominated the book-lined room. Dani's gray eyes dominated the painting, and her audacious smile seemed to mock Roberto and everything for which the diPortanovas stood.

The ancient open-well grandfather clock had just struck five, and Roberto was tired of waiting. He threw down the early edition of the *Daily News* and pressed the buzzer to summon Elvira.

'Yes, sir?'

Roberto had been barking orders at the staff from the minute he'd arrived two hours earlier to visit his convalescing son, and the servants were all eager to see the last of the older diPortanova.

Roberto pointed an accusing finger at the clock. 'My daughter-in-law was supposed to be home by four-thirty.'

Elvira thought that obviously he didn't know his daughter-in-law very well. The countess couldn't be on time if her life depended on it. 'Yes, sir. She probably got caught in traffic. Would you care for some tea or coffee, sir? Or a drink, perhaps?'

'Nothing. Just tell my daughter-in-law I want to see her the minute she comes in.'

Elvira fought the impulse to curtsy and hastily retreated.

This was Roberto's first visit to the apartment. Despite his many business trips to New York, he'd never seen fit to accept any of his son's invitations to join them for dinner at home. What would be the point? He spent time with Nino at the office, and Dani – if he saw her at all – would join them for the obligatory formal dinner at his suite in the Sherry Netherland.

Now that he'd seen Nino, he was eager to be on his way. He'd fulfilled the purpose of his visit – he could, in good conscience, assure his anxious wife Benedetta that their son was alive and in one piece. No thanks to his daughter-in-law, he brooded, who was even now gallivanting about the city when she should have been home taking care of Nino.

He didn't care how many stories he read about her runaway success or what excuses Nino made on her behalf. The girl was an incorrigible fortune-hunting social climber, and Roberto had every intention of telling her so. For far too long, hoping for news that a child was imminent, he'd held his tongue. But no more. Today he would give Dani a short course on her responsibilities toward her husband.

He switched on the television set and impatiently flicked the buttons on the remote control in search of a news report on the Wall Street closing prices. Instead, he got a smiling blond correspondent gushing about a fashion show at Saks Fifth Avenue that had drawn celebrities from the Social Register and the entertainment industries.

'. . . backed up by a huge advertising budget and an ad that features the same woman whose name appears on the back pocket of every pair of jeans,' burbled the reporter. 'An ad that is bound to create controversy among consumers who believe that what Countess Dani diPortanova is selling is sex, not product.'

A moment later Roberto had the dubious pleasure of seeing the ad: Dani paraded across the screen dressed in a plain white T-shirt, tight, tight jeans, and high-heeled boots. Her hips undulating to the rhythm of a wailing saxophone, she took three steps forward, then slowly turned her back to the camera. The camera zoomed into focus on her behind. Then Dani turned around again, licked her lips suggestively, and purred, 'I make the tightest jeans in the business. Sure it takes a while to get them on . . .'

A man's well-muscled back, naked from the waist up, moved into view of the camera.

Dani threw back her head and delivered the punch line: '. . . but that doesn't mean you can't get them off in a hurry.'

A close-up of the man's hand reaching over to pull down the zipper filled the screen.

Roberto trembled with rage as he zapped the Off button on the remote control. '*Cazzo!*' This time his daughter-in-law had utterly surpassed herself in bad taste and lack of judgment. There was no question in his mind about what the girl was selling – and it had nothing to do with clothing. She was behaving like a whore . . . a most desirable whore, he had to admit. He momentarily imagined that it was *his* hand unzipping her jeans, squeezing her luscious ass, fucking her until she begged for mercy.

225

Roberto laughed aloud at the image. No doubt *he* could teach her a thing or two about how a *real* man made love.

Dani heard Roberto's laugh as she rushed down the hall to the library and hoped that meant he was in a good mood. She caught a glimpse of her face in the mirror and put on a falsely bright smile. Roberto would be only too pleased to catch her looking upset. She would die before she'd give him the satisfaction of knowing that she'd spent the last hour fending off questions from the press about Nino's accident. The reporters had hounded her at Saks, where she'd spent the afternoon presenting her new jeans line. Unfortunately, they cared more about her husband than the jeans. She caught herself – oh, God, she should be *glad* they cared so much about Nino, even if the interest was only prurient.

'Roberto!' She greeted him with outstretched arms and the briefest peck on the cheek. 'Sorry I'm late. Midtown traffic is awful! Can I offer you a drink?'

'You kept me waiting long enough that I had a chance to see your new ad on TV,' Roberto said in a voice that was frosty with anger. 'And no, thank you, to the drink. I only stayed to talk to you. Then I have to be on my way.'

'Oh,' Dani said, trying to look disappointed. 'I thought you'd join us for dinner. Did you have a nice visit with Nino?'

'He seems to be recovering,' Roberto said flatly.

'Yes, his doctor's very pleased,' she assured him.

'More pleased than I am,' Roberto retorted.

Dani sighed and settled herself on the sofa, anticipating another one of Roberto's diatribes on the sanctity of marriage and on herself as failed wife. She'd hoped that just this once he'd forgo the opportunity to pontificate.

But no such luck.

Just as she'd expected, Roberto blamed her for Nino's accident. 'It would never have happened if – '

'If I'd been a proper wife and stayed home.' Dani could recite the lecture by heart, since she'd already heard it so often. For Nino's sake, she usually kept her mouth shut, pretended to listen, and did mental calculations of projected sales and expenses.

Roberto flashed back to the picture of Dani's denim-clad ass, offered up on national television as a treat to be lusted after by hundreds of thousands of American men.

'My son is lying upstairs, broken and in pain, and you behave like a slut!' thundered Roberto. 'No wonder he crashed! A man can take only so much humiliation! You've shamed him every chance you've had!'

Stung by his venomous criticism, Dani burst out, 'Roberto, that's not fair! If anyone's behaved shamefully, it's Nino.'

'How dare you! You money-grubbing – '

A flash of anger loosened her tongue. 'Don't! Don't start something you don't want to finish, Roberto. For years I've put up with all your bullshit prejudice, and I've about had it. Now you be quiet and listen to me – only what I'm going to tell you isn't one of your ugly lies. It's the truth!'

'What could you possibly tell me about my son that I don't already know?' sneered Roberto.

'That he's a drunk. An alcoholic. Not to mention a coke addict. And *that's* why he almost killed himself at Watkins Glen. As soon as he's well enough, he's going to check himself into a rehabilitation clinic to dry out and overcome his addictions.'

'I don't believe you,' Roberto said, genuinely shocked that Nino would agree to such a thing. He remembered the rumors about how Karola had forced her husband into a mental hospital so she could take over the business . . . Certainly his daughter-in-law was capable of a similar

227

scheme. He turned on her, his eyes blazing. 'This is your doing, isn't it?'

'Go ask Nino,' Dani calmly replied. 'It was his decision.'

'Nino?' Roberto declared with contempt. 'All his life that boy has been coddled and bamboozled by women. He may *think* it was his decision, but you and I know better, don't we, young lady? You think you're pretty damn sharp because you've had a couple of lucky breaks in business – backed by *my* money, I might add. But it takes a great deal more than luck to outsmart me. I don't yet know what your dirty little game is, Dani *Lieberman* diPortanova, but you can rest assured I'll find out. And when I do, I'm going to ruin you – once and for all!'

He was out of the library and gone from the apartment before Dani had a chance to say another word. Which was just as well because she was trembling with such fury and hurt that she was likely to have burst into tears had she tried to speak. Instead she wearily rubbed the back of her neck and tried to compose herself before she went to check on Nino.

What a day! The jeans launch had been a smash, far more successful than she and Monika had ever anticipated. Scores of women had attended the show at Saks, then stayed around long enough to buy two, three, four pairs of the jeans that fit as no pair of Lee's or Levi's ever had.

'Darling, you've done it again!' they'd gushed. 'Genius, sheer genius!'

Dani was quick to admit that Monika was the real genius behind the concept. After ruining yet another pair of silk pants at one of Rick's gigs, she'd wondered aloud to Dani why she couldn't find a pair of pants that were both sexy and well fitting. Rick lived in his blue jeans, but she'd yet to find a brand that didn't make her feel as if she were auditioning for a cowboy movie.

'Maybe we could get one of the seamstresses to whip up a pair for you,' suggested Dani.

'For me and the rest of your customers,' Monika had said with a gleam in her eye. 'Designer jeans . . .'

'. . . by Countess Dani!'

Jeans that hugged a woman's hips and ass and flattened her stomach. Jeans she could wear for so many different occasions that she wouldn't mind paying twice the price of the competition. With any luck, the best-dressed tushes in America would soon be screaming 'Countess Dani.'

It was a revolutionary concept, and it would take a leap of faith on the part of the consumer. But these were the seventies. If a designer could get away with sticking his or her name on jeans and not have the product deemed 'downscale,' there were fortunes to be made. If Dani's instincts were right, as they almost always were, she was on the cutting edge of another national sensation.

'Excuse me, Countess,' said Nino's nurse, who stood in the doorway. 'Your husband is awake and asking for you.'

Dani pulled herself out of her reverie and nodded. 'Thank you, Ellen. I'll be right there.'

Everything would work out all right, she reassured herself as she walked down the long hallway to their bedroom. Nino would soon be well, and her business would continue to thrive. And Roberto would keep out of her way. She'd outsmarted him once before. She could do it again if she had to.

Just let him try to stop her.

Bunny popped open a can of Tab, set it down carefully on a coaster on her coffee table, and prepared to enjoy herself. She'd been waiting for this moment ever since the mail-room boy had thrust the box of business cards into

229

her hands just as she was leaving for dinner with Irving. She'd fidgeted through dinner, then pleaded a splitting headache to keep him from staying over, as he often liked to do.

Now she carefully lifted the cover off the box, held up one of the cards to the lamp at the side of her sofa bed, and gazed with reverence at the inscription: 'Barbara Hester, Design Coordinator, I. Blatt & Sons.'

Her face lit up with a satisfied smile. As much as she hated it, putting out for Irving was definitely helping her career. This was her second promotion in six months, and it was a plum job. She'd had to beg Irving to consider her for the spot, especially since it was already filled by a young woman whose performance was excellent – but Bunny knew there was more than one way to perform excellently.

'Can't you find something else for her?' she'd coaxed Irving.

'But, shnookums, Howie and Stuart would wonder . . .'

Screw Howie and Stuart, she'd thought.

Bunny had locked the door to Irving's office and knelt at the side of his desk. 'Booboo,' she'd purred, unzipping his pants and suppressing a shudder as she moved his penis toward her mouth, 'shnookums has a present for you . . .'

Bunny was still worshiping her business cards when she felt a pair of tongues drooling saliva all over her bare legs.

The dogs.

Those hateful creatures. They shed. They teethed. They cried. They ate. They ate more than Bunny could ever have imagined puppies eating. And when it rained . . . the mud alone was a nightmare. The paltry-sized bag of dog food that Irving had left in her pantry had lasted exactly three days. The dog food bills had increased in direct proportion to the puppies' growth. Fearing tapeworms, Bunny had taken the dogs over to the East Side Animal Hospital.

'No tapeworms,' the vet had cheerfully assured her. 'Just happy, healthy Saint Bernards.'

'Saint Bernards!' In her tiny studio? Bunny was appalled. How could Irving have done this to her?

Irving named them Bernie and Bennie, but Bunny always thought of them as 'the beasts' . . . two enormous, slobbering beasts who ate everything in sight and refused to be housebroken. They simply wouldn't respond to Bunny's shrieking cues. Day by day, they were slowly destroying her home. They chewed open her pillows and left a trail of feathers strewn about the apartment. They teethed on her television cable cord and telephone wires and knocked over floor lamps. Urine stains streaked both sides of her couch.

But worst of all, they left Bunny presents everywhere – enormous piles of dog shit. Bunny screamed and cursed Irving, and swatted the beasts with newspapers. The dogs stared lovingly at her and wagged their tails. Finally she was paying attention to them.

Tonight, in her excitement over the business cards, she'd forgotten to buy more dog food. They were probably hungry again, which was why they were pawing at her skirt and licking her legs.

Just like Irving. She smirked.

Sure enough, their bowls were empty.

'Don't you ever quit eating?' she snapped at them.

They stared up at her, pleading for sustenance.

Through her window Bunny could see that it was raining, and she'd left her umbrella at the office. No way was she going out in this foul weather for dog food. Tonight the beasts could diet. It wouldn't hurt them to lose a pound or two.

They planted themselves at her feet, panting with anticipation, their ugly bloodshot eyes occasionally darting to their empty bowls.

They're like living garbage disposals, she thought, searching her nearly empty cupboards for any kind of Puppy Chow substitute. Coffee . . . tea . . . a can of soup . . . not even a tin of tuna fish.

Too bad. For all she cared, they could starve to death, and then she'd be rid of them. But how would she explain that to Irving? She took another look and came up with a bag of Doritos. Oh, what the hell? Tearing open the bag, she distributed the chips equally into the two bowls.

'There, you hideous beasts! I hope that satisfies you!' she hissed. 'Now leave me in peace.'

As she picked up the new issue of *Cosmo*, she could hear the dogs wolfing down the Doritos and greedily lapping up water. But soon she was too absorbed in an article about Dani diPortanova even to notice them padding about the apartment. Then suddenly they were pawing at her again. They'd brought her a little gift. One of them had something dangling from the side of his mouth.

Bunny peered closer.

'Oh, my God!' She gagged.

The beast had his teeth clamped down on a soiled sanitary napkin.

'Drop it! I said, drop that, God damn you!' she screamed. 'I hate you both, you disgusting animals!' Now they were going through her garbage. Was there no end to the trouble they caused her? What if Irving had been here? It wasn't as if they didn't have chew-toys to gnaw on. She'd bought them shopping bags full of rubber bones, which they never even looked at.

Screw 'em! Using the rolled-up *Cosmo* to prod them along, she shoved the dogs into her tiny bathroom and slammed the door shut. Now, at least, she could have some peace. The dogs pawed noisily at the door, begging to be let out. Bunny ignored them. Let them suffocate, she thought, turning back to her article.

She bet Dani diPortanova had never had to put up with old men, wretched dogs, and a cramped apartment.

Life was so unfair. Her road to success was going to be a hard and tortuous one, unless she found herself a shortcut.

And fast.

'Your check, sir,' said the waiter, presenting Reggie with a brown leather folder.

The restaurant – northern Italian cuisine and expensive – was located in the heart of the theater district and had opened just two months ago. Reggie had expected the management to pick up the dinner tab, as many places did for the VIPs whose movements were followed by the paparazzi and gossip columnists. Press for the star was sure to mean press for the restaurant or club or whatever establishment the star deigned to visit.

Obviously this place wasn't eager to attract Reggie's sort of crowd. If they couldn't be gracious enough to pay for his dinner, they could forget about his continued patronage. The food was rather good, but for his money, they could shut down tomorrow.

He sneaked a peek at the bill and gritted his teeth. How did restaurants get away with charging such ridiculous prices? Meanwhile, everyone else at the table – Rah Rah, Mitchell, a stand-up comedienne who was wearing his clothes in her hit Broadway show, and a rich-bitch debutante with great coke – pretended to be engrossed in conversation. Naturally *they* weren't about to offer to pay. He knew what they were thinking: *Let Reggie pay. He's good for the check.*

Bunch of gold-digging cheapskates.

Matching the waiter's flourish, Reggie whipped out his gold American Express card. The dinner wasn't a total loss. At least he could use it as a tax write-off.

Outside, in front of the restaurant, a stretch Lincoln limousine with dark-tinted windows awaited him. The limo was his twenty-four hours a day, three hundred sixty-five days a year. It was one of the perks he'd insisted upon before he'd sold his company to Megacorp, the multinational conglomerate that owned everything from baseball teams to Mexican resorts. Limos, as he so often reminded Rah Rah, were the *only* civilized way to travel.

'Kiss, kiss. *Ciao, ciao!* Good-bye, precious.' Reggie bumped cheeks with his guests, hugged the women, and waved his farewells. Leaving them to get home by whatever means they could, he gratefully sank into the cushioned comfort of the car.

'Would you hurry up, Rah Rah!' he snapped, pulling at Rah Rah's expensively tailored sleeve.

Rah Rah shook off his hand and turned on the limo's television, as he always did when he and Reggie were alone together.

'Must you?' Reggie said with a sigh. 'Pour me a stiff vodka, would you?' He nodded toward the well-stocked bar.

What he really wanted was a line or two of coke. The gram the debutante had slipped him under the table was burning a hole in his pocket, but Rah Rah didn't approve. Both Rah Rah and his housekeeper, Lydia, were constantly nagging him about the evil of drugs. Idiots.

Cocaine was nothing more than a delightful recreational sport. But because of them, he had to watch where and when he tooted. If he was smart, he'd fire the both of them.

Reggie switched on a movie, *Rebel without a Cause*.

234

'Now there's a man I could get into,' Reggie tried to needle Rah Rah.

James Dean's leather jacket set Reggie to musing about his first lover, the leather queen. Those were the days. He wondered whether the guy still had the dog collar he'd asked Reggie to wear . . . Perhaps he'd do leather jackets for his next collection. Yes, he thought with a flicker of excitement. Leather jackets for women, but maybe he'd have one made for Rah Rah and include him in the show. He rather liked the idea of his boyfriend being paraded down the runway in full view of all the society gals who were his great fans.

As the limo turned onto Times Square to head east on Forty-fourth Street, Reggie glanced out the window.

'Stop!' he bellowed into the intercom connected to the driver's compartment.

The driver slammed on his brakes.

'What the hell – ' sputtered Rah Rah, spilling a Pepsi all over himself.

'That goddam bitch!' Reggie raged. He pointed with a trembling finger at the most erotic ad he'd ever seen, splashed across an enormous billboard that dominated the sky. Affixed to a skyscraper high above Times Square, the billboard featured a blowup of a man's hand pulling down the zipper on a pair of women's jeans. It was clear that the woman wasn't wearing any underwear; her nipples were highly visible beneath her clingy white silk blouse. The copy was simple: 'Countess Dani Jeans.'

Clustered on the streets below the billboard, scores of pedestrians stared up at the stunningly sexy photo that dominated the corner of Seventh Avenue and Broadway.

Reggie grabbed the car phone next to him and furiously punched the home phone number of his advertising agency account executive.

As soon as he heard her voice, he screeched, 'Have you

235

seen Dani diPortanova's ad in Times Square? What do you mean, *no*? Did it ever occur to you to move your ass out of your high-rent office on Madison Avenue and take a good look at the real world? I want you to get yourself over here *tonight* to see what the bitch has done. Then buy me the biggest fucking billboard space you can find in this area, because I want to see one of my ads up there by the end of the week. And it better be hot or you're *fired*!' He slammed down the phone and ordered the driver to move on.

'If you don't calm down, you're going to give yourself an ulcer,' Rah Rah remarked.

'I don't get ulcers. I *give* them,' Reggie snapped, now craving the coke more than ever. 'That diPortanova bitch has some balls. Thinking she can trump me on my turf. How dare she, the flash-in-the-pan cunt!'

'What do you care what she does? She doesn't even do couture. And you're every bit as successful a designer as she – '

'Listen, bimbo, she is *not* a designer. She's a fraud. A fake. A whore who'll sell her name to anyone. She's been in the business two minutes and thinks she can take over the whole fucking world. And I am *far* more successful than that bitch will ever be, got it? Honestly, that you could ever speak of us in the same breath really makes me wonder about you.' Steaming, Reggie stared at James Dean on the television.

Rah Rah turned a cold shoulder on Reggie for the rest of the ride home. He hated it when Reggie called him a bimbo and treated him as if he were a piece of dumb blond meat. Who the fuck did he think he was? He was tempted to give Reggie a swift poke in the jaw, but Reggie would probably get off on the rough treatment.

Instead, Rah Rah sulked in silence, likewise staring at the movie, knowing that Reggie couldn't bear to be ignored. There was no arguing with Reggie when he wound himself up into one of these moods. Rah Rah had two choices – live with it, or move out. One day soon he would move out, and Reggie would be left to wonder why.

In the meantime Rah Rah sucked Reggie's cock, saved his money, bided his time, and looked forward to the day when Reggie Bolt would sleep alone.

Chapter Nine

Silver Hill, Connecticut

'My name is Nino, and I am an alcoholic.'

The hardest sentence Nino had ever uttered.

For two weeks he'd wanted to stand up in front of the group and say those words. For two weeks he'd been too stubborn and scared to admit the truth. But he'd listened to the others speak up, heard their stories, so different from and yet so similar to his own.

The denial. The lies. The anger and guilt. The waking up in strange beds, without any memory of what had happened the night before. The accidents . . .

The day a young woman with tears running down her face described how she'd crashed her car into a tree after an afternoon of alternating shots of vodka with lines of coke, and killed her infant daughter, Nino decided he, too, could find the courage to stand up and talk.

Puffing nervously on a cigarette, he reminded himself that these people understood. They'd been through it themselves, which was why they were patients at Silver Hill, the expensive private substance-abuse hospital set in the middle of the upper-crust community of New Canaan, Connecticut. Silver Hill was a revelation to Nino. In Wilton House, the cozy white clapboard residence reserved especially for alcoholics, he was surrounded by people like himself. People of wealth. People of privilege. People whose famous names and titles he recognized instantly. People who were, as he was, alcoholics and substance abusers.

Admitting it was the most difficult part of the program. More difficult even than the hellish three days spent in detoxification. Neither the memories of the pain from his accident nor his doctor's warnings had prepared him for the tortures he'd had to endure in order to cleanse the toxins from his body. He shivered and shook and vomited and begged for 'just one drink . . . it'll be my last, I swear it!' Finally, the crisis point was passed, and then the real healing began.

There'd been denial and anger: *I'm not a drunk. I just like to have a good time. Everybody gets tanked every now and then . . . I just happen to have opportunities to do it more often. Alcoholics are bums who roll around in the gutter. I'm a diPortanova, one of a long line of vintners. Alcohol is in my blood.*

Then came the guilt and embarrassment: *There were so many nights and so many parties where I couldn't even find the door to leave. I spilled drinks, pawed at the women, pawed at the men . . . How did I ever get invited back? How did people ever put up with me?*

Then, once the barriers were down, he was faced with the truth: He was a rich, spoiled playboy. A party boy who stayed too long at one too many parties and became a drunk and a doper.

The truth was sobering enough. But at Silver Hill, where there was strength in numbers, Nino was gradually finding the courage to stay sober and face himself.

And to think about what he really wanted to do with his life. It was an excruciatingly painful process, but exhilarating as well. He was more in control, more alert, more in touch with himself than he'd been in years.

More in touch with Dani, too. Family members of Silver Hill patients were strongly encouraged to get involved in the treatment program, so twice a week Dani drove to New Canaan for the group meetings. Listening

239

to Nino and his fellow participants, Dani couldn't help but admire their courage and honesty. Nino was beginning to talk to her about his fears and doubts . . . about himself, about her, about their marriage.

They *wanted* to stay married – on that they both agreed. And he assured her that, Roberto's vicious remarks to the contrary, he didn't believe she was responsible for his accident or his drinking.

'I'm sick. I have an illness. But it's not your fault, and I'm going to recover,' he said, staring into the murky depths of the Silvermine River, which ran through the grounds of Silver Hill. On this beautiful day in June, the longest day of the year, though it was already past eight, the sun still glinted on the water.

'I can't help but wonder what my part has been in all of this,' Dani admitted, taking his hand and twisting his fingers around hers.

Nino shrugged. 'What's more important is that we not continue to play the same crazy games with each other. I'm not your bad little boy.'

'And I don't have to be the worried parent, always nervous about what mess you've gotten yourself into.'

'That's right, which is all the more reason why you should take a few days off next month and fly out to Los Angeles with Monika.'

For weeks Monika had been begging Dani to go with her to the West Coast when she went to visit Rick.

'Okay, okay.' Dani laughed and held up her hands in surrender. 'You and Monika are relentless – and very convincing. If you're sure – '

'I'm sure. And I want you to use the jet.'

The Lear jet Nino had bought in Rio on an impulse was a sore point between them. Dani refused to use it except when they traveled together, and then only because Nino wouldn't fly any other way. To Dani, the jet represented

240

the worst of Nino's excesses, and she hated the fact that its previous owner had been a drug dealer.

Nino thought she was crazy to subject herself to a commercial flight when she could have all the comforts of home and fly at *her* convenience instead of the airline's.

Time and again, they'd fought over this issue.

Now she asked herself if she was trying to teach Nino a lesson by refusing to use the Lear. At the previous group meeting, the leader had gently pointed out to her that she had to give up trying to get Nino to change. Only Nino could change Nino.

'I suppose it does make more sense,' she conceded.

'Of course it does. Besides, that's what it's there for. I'm not paying the pilot seventy-five thousand dollars a year to stay grounded.'

He put his arm around her waist, and they strolled in companionable silence toward the shade trees that bordered the property.

'Pretty here, isn't it?' said Nino.

'Beautiful.' Dani breathed in the fresh June air and threw back her head to gaze at the azure sky.

'I bet you're wishing you could duplicate that color for your next collection,' Nino teased.

'No, not at all.' Her gray eyes were serious, her expression almost solemn. 'I was thinking . . . how much I've missed making love with you.' Her voice caught, and she stared away from him toward the trees, as if embarrassed by her admission.

'Ah, *cara* . . .'

He put his hand under her chin and gently forced her to meet his gaze. 'It's been such a while, hasn't it? Dani . . . no, my darling . . . oh, no, don't cry . . .'

With his palm he wiped away the tears that flowed recklessly down her cheeks. Then he gently kissed her lips and whispered, 'My love. I've missed you, too.'

She'd almost forgotten how right it felt to fold herself into his arms, to bury her face against his neck. Memories of the first time he'd held her and made love to her aboard the von Reichs' yacht at Cannes came flooding back. They'd been so happy and innocent then. Now they were no longer innocent, but they could still be happy again.

'Nino, Nino, I love you,' she murmured. 'I've never stopped loving you.'

'I love you, too, my darling . . . I have a marvelous idea,' Nino said with a mischievous lilt to his voice that Dani hadn't heard since their early days in New York. 'Come with me.'

He grabbed her hand and laughingly pulled her along a path between the trees until they stumbled onto a narrow clearing. Breathless and giggling, Dani watched Nino tamp down the tall grass to make space enough for them to sit.

He plucked a pale blue forget-me-not and stuck it through the clip that held her hair back from her face. 'Your corsage, Countess. I know these accommodations are a little rougher than what you're used to, but I thought perhaps we could . . . you know . . .'

She'd never seen him so shy, and that made her want him all the more.

'Oh, yes, Nino,' she whispered. 'Yes, yes, yes.'

They lay down together on the grass, their lips just barely touching, searching each other's eyes for reassurance.

With a feather-soft touch, he brushed his fingers across her forehead, her delicately arched eyebrows, her cheekbones, and the pucker above her lip. 'You're shivering.'

'So are you.'

'Are you cold?'

'Not cold . . . nervous. I . . . I feel like a kid again.'

As the sky turned from azure to violet to velvety blue,

they kissed for what seemed like forever. Carefully at first, tenderly, then with a deepening passion that sent shock waves of desire rippling through Dani's body. Nino's probing tongue made her impatient to feel him naked against her, and she reached up to unzip his pants.

'Slowly, *cara*, all in good time.' He smiled, carefully unbuttoning her blouse and helping her out of her skirt and panties. He stripped off his own clothes, spread his shirt on the ground beneath her, and said, 'Here, lie on this.'

He kissed the beauty mark just above the nipple of her right breast, then very deliberately teased first one nipple, then the other until she was gasping with pleasure. Aching to feel his hardness between her fingers, she groped for his cock. But he brushed her hand aside and bent his head between her spread legs, breathed in her musky scent, and greedily sucked her wetness.

Dani moaned, and then suddenly she came, the spasms so quick and sharp that Nino could actually feel them against his tongue. Afterward, he pulled her up to sit facing him. She kissed him and tasted herself on his lips. 'Your mouth smells like cunt.'

'Do you like it?'

Her answer was to push him gently to the ground and take his penis in her mouth. She ran her lips up and down the length of the shaft and lightly tickled his balls with the tip of her tongue.

Nino stared up at the sky, conscious of nothing but her tongue pleasuring his cock. Finally, half asking, half commanding, he growled, 'Now,' and hurriedly rearranged himself above her.

'Fuck me, Nino . . . Please, fuck me hard,' she groaned.

Night was falling all around them as they rediscovered the familiar sweetness of their lovemaking. Nino came

243

first, his cries piercing the stillness. And then Dani cried out a moment later, her climax triggered by his.

There was no need for more talk. They'd communicated on a level far deeper than words could ever touch. They held each other for a few more minutes, and then, because Nino had a curfew, they brushed the grass off their bodies and quickly got dressed. They walked back to Nino's cottage in silence.

'Look, a full moon rising.' Nino pointed to the eastern sky. He kissed Dani and whispered, 'Safe journey.'

'Safe journey,' she echoed.

Nino had had the interior of the Lear completely overhauled and redesigned in leather and polished woods in shades of tan and soft brown. There were two bathrooms (one of which had a Jacuzzi), a bedroom, a fully stocked bar, a galley suitable for preparing gourmet meals, and a warm, large, comfortable living area. The two flight attendants, one female, one male, were both young, good-looking, and very tan. Almost a matched set, Dani pointed out to Monika.

Monika caught Dani's eye and nodded toward the young man. 'Straight?'

Dani laughed. 'Interested?'

Monika shrugged. 'Flight insurance.'

After a remarkably smooth takeoff, the young man brought out a platter of cheeses and fresh vegetables.

'And to drink, Countess? Your usual?'

Dani nodded.

'What can I get you, ma'am?' he asked Monika.

'Mmmmmm,' she purred, 'something nice and stiff . . .'

The attendant's eyes widened, but a smile spread across his face. Dani decided he was definitely straight.

'. . . like scotch on the rocks.'

'Coming right up,' he said and disappeared into the galley.

'Already revving up your engines for Rick?' Dani teased.

'Maybe . . .' Monika stretched out lazily on the tan suede couch across from Dani. 'Let's just hope Rick doesn't need a tune-up.'

'Are you getting cold feet about surprising him?'

Monika shrugged. 'Every time we talk, he tells me come any weekend, I'm always welcome. But you never know . . .'

Dani couldn't believe Monika was taking the risk of dropping in on Rick without any notice. But Monika was definitely a risk-taker, except when it came to the business, which she approached with absolutely sound judgment.

The attendant returned with their drinks, Perrier with lime for Dani and scotch for Monika, served on a silver tray in cut-crystal glasses, the initial D engraved on each.

'He *is* cute,' Monika said when they were alone again.

Dani giggled. 'I think you want to have your cake and eat it, too.'

'I don't want to eat any cake, *liebchen*, I just want a bigger piece of the pie.'

'The pie may be a flavor you don't want to eat,' warned Dani in a feigned stern voice.

'Just as long as there's *lots* of whipped cream.'

Dani kicked off her high heels and sliced into the Brie. 'I have to admit it – this is the only way to fly.'

'Amen!' Monika raised her glass. 'To our success, present and continued.'

'And to happiness.' Which didn't necessarily come hand in hand with success, though she wasn't complaining about the star treatment she was getting these days. This was a far cry from the old days of unreturned phone calls and having to convince buyers that the Countess Dani line would sell in Oklahoma. Now she had retailers, the press, and would-be licensors waiting on her every move.

Los Angeles

Success also meant Dani was instantly recognized at the desk of the Beverly Hills Hotel five hours later, where she and Monika had booked adjoining pink bungalows. Dani took a quick shower and couldn't wait to get outside and take a drive to the beach in the rented Mercedes 450 SL which she'd had waiting at the Burbank Airport. In New York, the forecasters were gloomily predicting another week of 'the three H's' – hazy, hot, and humid. Here the weather was glorious – clear blue sky, sunshine, and temperatures in the high seventies.

She knocked on Monika's door. 'Did you track down Rick?'

Monika's radiant smile was all the answer she needed. 'I caught him on his way out to a rehearsal. But he says he can't wait to see me.'

'Are you sure you don't want to be alone with him, instead of having me tag along?'

'*Ach*, don't be silly. We'll have plenty of time together. He has to play tonight, but not until later. He wants to take us all out to dinner.'

'All?'

'His roommate, too. Jack something. Rick said he's trying to break into modeling, so at the very least he'll probably be great to look at across the table.'

Dani made a face. New York had an abundance of aspiring models. Whenever they found out who she was, they invariably slipped her one of their cards with the line, 'If you ever need me for an ad . . .' Some of the more brazen of them even said, 'If you ever get tired of your husband, look me up.'

Sure. Why model for money when you can marry into it?

'Please, say yes,' Monika urged. 'We'll have a great time. He's making a reservation at Morton's.'

'The man must be trying to impress you. Morton's is one of the trendiest places in LA. They're so hot they don't even list their number in the phone book.'

'He says he's been doing very well out here. I think he wants to make up for the few times he let me take him out in New York.'

Rick arrived at the hotel promptly at eight in his black Jeep. Monika was so excited to see him she could hardly breathe. She rushed down the carpeted and covered open-air entrance of the hotel, brushed past several uniformed valets handling the traffic coming in off Sunset, and fell into his arms. She instantly felt at home.

LA had certainly been good to him. His pasty white New Jersey skin was tanned a golden brown, his dark hair was sun-streaked to a light brown, and his well-sculpted pecs looked as if they'd been getting regular workouts. But he was still dressed in the same jeans and plain T-shirt with the sleeves rolled up to his shoulders.

He finally released Monika and planted a big kiss on Dani's cheek.

'You look gorgeous!' Dani told him. 'Like a movie star!'

Rick grinned and helped them into his Jeep. 'Everyone's into their health and bodies out here. They have me going to the gym five times a week and eating things I never even heard of before. Tofu! Jicama! Bean sprouts! You ever hear of a Jersey boy eating bean sprouts? But I feel terrific. It's the best thing that ever happened to me. Besides meeting Monika, of course.'

'I'll agree with that,' Monika said. She'd missed him so much in her bed. There were lots of other men in her life, but none of them could do for her what Rick did.

Morton's was bustling with activity. Dani looked around the large, pastel-colored restaurant filled with ficus and palm trees and recognized many of the faces. She herself was recognized by more than a few people, some of whom waved or lifted a glass to greet her. She was especially pleased to see that her designs were well represented.

Rick's roommate, Jack Andrews, was already seated at their table near the front of the restaurant, beneath a huge palm tree. Rick hadn't said much about Jack except that he was 'kind of young, a nice kid.' He was also very handsome, with smoldering good looks and hair the color of coal hanging to his shoulders.

The waiter greeted Rick by name. 'Care to see a wine list? Or should I bring you the California Chardonnay?'

'Yeah, the Chardonnay, definitely.'

'You come here often, Rick?' Monika asked.

'Often enough.' He shrugged. 'One of my pals knows the manager, and we kind of got to be friends.'

Dani smiled at Jack. 'Have you done any runway shows?' she asked, tearing off a piece of hot bread and buttering it.

'No, mostly local print ads for the department stores, that sort of thing. But I just got my first big break – four pages in next month's *Vogue* with Cheryl Tiegs.'

'Nothing like starting at the top,' said Dani, impressed. 'I'll have to look out for you.' Sweet, she thought. He knew who she was, of course, but he was being cool about it. Not star-struck. Or if he was, at least he hid it well, which was a refreshing change from the men who were always bowing and scraping and trying to curry favor with her.

The appetizers arrived: fresh mozzarella and tomatoes in basil and two orders of oysters. Then pasta primavera, lamb chops, grilled chicken, and medallions of veal in a wine sauce.

'Everyone says the food here is as good as anything you can get in New York,' said Jack. 'One of these days I intend to find out for myself.'

'You've never been to New York?' asked Monika, barely able to take her eyes off Rick.

'No, I was born and bred in California. Lived here all my life, except for a couple of years at prep school up in Seattle.'

'Does your family live around here?' Dani asked.

Jack's face seemed to darken momentarily. 'Uh . . . yeah, sort of. Actually, I don't have much to do with them. Parents can be hard to deal with sometimes, know what I mean?'

'*Ja, ja*, I certainly do!' Monika nodded sympathetically. 'I could write a book on the subject.'

Jack turned back to Dani. 'Are you here on business or pleasure?'

'Pleasure mostly. Business only because I can't ever seem to turn off that part of my brain. But I guess you could say that basically I'm here as Monika's chaperon,' Dani said with a wink.

'Does that woman look like she needs a chaperon?' Jack smirked.

Monika and Rick were lost in each other's eyes, all alone on their own planet. Dani was thrilled to see Monika glowing. She was always pooh-poohing any suggestions of serious romance between herself and Rick, but Dani didn't quite believe her. She never looked quite as relaxed or happy as she did when Rick was by her side.

'It looks as if your friend's going to be tied up for the next few days,' Jack said. 'Let me know if you get bored or lonely. We could . . . uh, hang out, go to the beach, grab a burger, whatever . . .'

'Sure,' Dani said, surprised by his boldness. Was he flirting with her? He was just a kid, probably not even twenty. But he was sweet to offer his company. She couldn't even remember the last time she'd just 'hung out' with a man other than Nino. The thought of it, as busy as she knew she could otherwise be, was very appealing.

After dinner, they drove over to the Black Teddy, where Rick and his band had a regular gig four nights a week.

'Good money, good exposure,' Rick explained. He introduced the group to the club's manager. 'Hey, c'mon backstage and say hello to the guys,' Rick said, jostling through the crowd, many of whom greeted him by name. Three of the band members had been playing with Rick for years, and they greeted Monika like a long-lost friend.

'This guy's been pinin' away out here. It just ain't been the same without you,' Frankie Cordova, the bass player, assured Monika. 'We missed you, honey.'

'And this is our latest addition, Katie Quinn, the one other mick in the crowd. She plays a mean tambourine and puts up with a hell of a lot from the boys.' Rick grinned.

Katie Quinn was a slim-hipped redhead with freckles and an easy smile. She wore faded jeans, a denim work shirt, a black leather vest, and white high-top sneakers, and she somehow managed to make the clothes look positively elegant.

Dani saw the sneakers and thought, *What a great idea!* They looked just like the ones she'd worn when she was a kid. She hadn't bought a pair in years, but she remembered how comfortable they were. Sharp-looking, too, with jeans, or the right pants. Maybe she could design her own line and show them with her next sportswear collection.

Monika saw the way Rick smiled at Katie and immediately wondered if they were sleeping together.

The question nagged at her all through Rick's first set, even after he introduced her to the audience and then said, 'Monika, I wrote this song for you and I'm playing it tonight for the first time.'

'Golden Girl' was a haunting, ironic ballad about a beautiful, rich golden-haired girl who seemingly had everything – except a family and a man who loved her. When he finished singing, there was a moment of hushed silence before the crowd burst into exuberant cheers and whistles. Her eyes wet with tears, Monika clapped with them and threw Rick a kiss of thanks.

Rick winked and twanged his guitar. Immediately the band launched into a spirited medley of several songs she recognized from the soon to be launched debut album, *Hot and Sticky*. He and Katie cavorted about the stage, mugging suggestively as they shimmied their hips and bumped their behinds in rhythm to the music.

Monika knew Rick had his pick of the groupies who hung around the clubs, and she'd never given much thought to whether he was sleeping with other women. But she couldn't ignore the sparks that flew between him and his harmony singer. The band sounded better, more together, than they ever had, and clearly Katie deserved a lot of the credit for that.

'They're terrific!' Dani screamed above the din of the crowd. 'Rick and Katie are quite a team!'

Monika forced a smile and nodded. *Ja, quite a team* . . .

At 2:00 A.M., after three encores, the Justice League

251

hit one last exuberant chord, waved at the audience, and left the stage.

'Hey,' Jack shouted into Dani's ear, 'time to leave the lovebirds alone. Can I give you a ride back to your hotel?' He hardly gave her a moment to tell Monika she was leaving or say good-bye, just grabbed her hand and steered her to the front door. 'How about a bite to eat? Better yet, let me take you for a ride through the Hollywood Hills.'

Just like that.

No discussion.

Before she knew it, Dani was in Jack's Corvette convertible, riding up Mulholland Drive. It was a perfect night for a drive. A round yellow moon hung low in the sky, so clear and star-studded it could have passed for the painted backdrop of a movie set.

Jack pulled off the road and gestured to the city lights glittering below. 'Pretty special, huh?'

'I've been to LA so many times, and I've never taken this drive,' Dani admitted. 'It's beautiful, Jack. Thanks for bringing me up here.'

'My pleasure. Thanks for coming.'

Dani closed her eyes. She felt slightly light-headed. Was it jet lag? Or something more powerful than a simple disruption of her body's inner clock . . .?

Jack's boyish naïveté, his lack of sophistication, appealed to her. If she were the cheating kind . . . but she wasn't, she reminded herself and abruptly opened her eyes. The full moon gleaming overhead took her back to that night in June, a month ago, when she and Nino had made wonderful love in the grass. Midsummer night's madness? No – sanity. To succumb now with Jack would be madness.

'Jack?'

'Yes?' He leaned forward.

'I don't mean to be rude, but I'm exhausted. I think I should be getting back.'

'Are you sure?' Jack's voice was low and hopeful.

Dani rubbed her thumb against her burnished gold wedding band. 'Absolutely positive.'

Lunch in the Polo Lounge. While Dani waited for Monika to show up, she had a phone brought to her dark green upholstered banquette – banquette number one – to return some of the calls that had come in that morning.

Twenty minutes late, Monika slid in next to her.

'You're late,' Dani teased. 'That's a first. Must have been some night.'

'*Ja*, some night,' Monika said sourly.

'No? What went wrong?'

Monika made a face and signaled the waiter for menus. She hardly understood it herself. She and Rick had made a quick getaway, picked up a six-pack of beer and a pizza to go – Rick was always starving after he performed – and hurried back to the hotel. At first everything had been wonderful. They sat in the bathtub, drank beer, fed each other slices of sausage pizza, all to prolong their anticipation of the inevitable moment when they finally fell panting into each other's arms.

Sex with Rick was the best. By the time the sun rose over a smog-covered city, they'd made love twice and fallen into an exhausted sleep.

'Sounds great.' Dani sighed enviously. 'What's the problem?'

'I asked him to tell me about Katie.'

'Katie?'

'The girl from his band. The redhead.'

'You think they're sleeping together?'

'All Rick would say is that it's ridiculous of me to be jealous of her. And that . . .'

253

'Yes?' Dani prompted her.

'That he loves me.' Monika spoke so quietly Dani almost didn't hear the words. 'We had a huge fight . . . That's why I was late.'

'I don't get it. He tells you not to worry about Katie, says he loves you, and you have a fight?'

'It's too complicated to explain,' Monika said miserably, wiping her nose with a linen handkerchief. 'We're not right for each other, that's all. I'm going to break it off with him. Dammit, where's our food?'

Two identical orders of the Beverly Hills Hotel's warm chicken salad with tarragon dressing and diet soda appeared just at that instant. Monika took one bite, then pushed the plate away. 'I can't eat a thing,' she moaned. 'Distract me, *liebchen*. Tell me what happened with you and Jack.'

'Absolutely nothing. Honest. I admit I was tempted. He's very sweet . . . and sexy. But I *am* married.'

Monika wanted to ask whether his marriage vows had ever stopped Nino, but they both knew the answer to that. Besides, Nino was Nino. Dani was Dani.

A beautiful young woman, currently starring on a prime-time soap, walked by their booth and did a double take. 'Dani diPortanova! I adore your clothes. I told our producer he has to let me wear some of your collection next season. I think you're terrific!'

'That's awfully nice of you. Thanks so much,' Dani said with a warm smile.

When the woman was barely out of earshot, Monika snapped, 'If she loves your clothes so much, why's she wearing Calvin Klein?'

'Hollywood.' Dani laughed.

'So if you weren't cuddling in bed all morning with Jack, what have you been up to?' Monika asked.

'Checking out the competition. Lina Lee. Giorgio.

Saint Laurent. Gucci. Bijan.' The famed Rodeo Drive stores where the salespeople all behaved as if they were doing the customers a favor by even acknowledging them.

'Did you buy anything?'

'No, but I came up with a brilliant idea.' Dani's eyes widened with excitement. 'Monika, do you know what they're missing on Rodeo?'

'What?' Monika sipped her soda, only half listening.

'Us!'

'Us?'

'Monika, pay attention – this is important!'

'I'm listening.'

'What Rodeo Drive needs is a specialty shop for women like you and me. A store that's chic but fun to shop in, where you don't feel as if they're checking out your Dun and Bradstreet as you walk through the door. A store that sells Countess Dani exclusively!'

'Like a boutique?'

'Exactly! A signature shop. We'll call it Countess Dani, plain and simple, and we'll carry all of our lines, including the licensed products. And we'll open one in New York – in one of the hotels, like the Pierre or maybe the Plaza. Retail anchors on both coasts.'

What Dani was suggesting was a daring and risky proposition. Too risky. 'I don't see it,' Monika said slowly. 'What do we really know about the retail side of the business?'

'We'll figure it out! I'm a quick learner – so are you,' Dani insisted. 'Besides, we'll hire the right people to run the stores. Think about it! Nobody's better at selling our product than we are!'

'It would mean a huge outlay of capital.'

'So?' Dani challenged her. 'We can afford it. We can easily get a loan if we have to.'

The give-and-take was typical of their partnership. Dani

was the more impulsive of the two, always ready to take the big leap, rarely bothering to check below for a safety net. Monika moved more slowly and cautiously. When it came to business, she was a firm believer in maximizing profits, minimizing risks.

'Impetuous American,' she'd shout at Dani in moments of high tension.

'Hard-core Austrian,' Dani would scream in response.

Their enormous success was born of their ability to find a middle ground where they could agree.

'Well?' Dani prodded.

Monika shrugged. 'I suppose it's worth considering.'

'Monika, what I love about you is your unbridled enthusiasm.' Dani's smile tempered her sarcasm. 'Come on, honey, let's go rent ourselves a piece of Rodeo Drive.'

New York

Irving's face was lit up like a Halloween jack-o'-lantern. 'Bunny, shnookums, I've got a big surprise for you.'

He patted his pants pocket.

Bunny was sick and tired of blowing him in his office. She thought, *Dear Lord, please don't let him whip out that ugly old thing of his*.

Irving reached into his pocket and pulled out two airline tickets, which he waved in her face. 'I need a vacation and I want you to come with me. What do you say to a week at a luxury hotel?'

'Oh, Irving,' Bunny said coyly, wondering what he had in mind, 'I couldn't possibly afford – '

'Don't talk nonsense. I'm paying for the whole thing. Don't worry, I can afford it. It's off-season, the travel agent got me a deal.' He shoved some brochures at her.

'Here's the place. The Grapefruit Tree Resort in Saint Croix.'

Saint Croix? As in the Virgin Islands?

Images of sandy white beaches and clear blue water filled her head. Sailing. Swimming. Snorkeling. Watching the sunset as she sipped a cool tropical drink. What would the folks back home in Henderson say if they knew that she, Bunny Hester, was going to spend a week at a posh resort in the Caribbean? She'd never even been out of the United States before!

'Booboo, I'm the luckiest girl in the whole world,' Bunny said breathily. She planted a delicate kiss on his forehead, then gazed at him wide-eyed. 'But what about the doggies?'

'What a sweetie you are to worry about the dogs. I know you'll miss them terribly, but we can board them at the vet. My treat.'

Damn right, his treat. Maybe she'd get really lucky, and they'd drop dead.

Bunny bought herself a black Countess Dani bikini, another pair of the Countess Dani jeans that were the rage of the country, and an evening gown that she couldn't afford but had to have. She gathered a trashy novel, new sunglasses, Bain de Soleil in every strength, and she was ready for fun in the sun.

But first they had to get there. On board their American Airlines flight, her hands shook as she buckled herself tightly into her seat belt, and she kept a firm grip on the armrests until the plane was off the ground.

'You're not scared of flying, are you?' Irving asked solicitously.

'Of course not,' Bunny scoffed, embarrassed to admit she'd never been on an airplane before.

Midway through the flight, the attendant brought over a bottle of champagne. 'Compliments of the crew. You're newlyweds, aren't you? We can always tell,' she said with a perky smile. 'Congratulations. Have a wonderful honeymoon!'

Irving winked at Bunny. 'I guess we make a good-looking couple.'

Bunny's already queasy stomach took a turn for the worse. Did they honestly believe she'd marry an old fart like Irving?

A minivan taxi transported them and two other couples from the Saint Croix airport to the Grapefruit Tree Hotel. On one side of the winding road lay the blue Caribbean. On the other, shaded by towering palm trees, were clusters of pink and yellow shacks surrounded by tiny dirt patches.

'What kind of people live like that?' clucked Irving, shaking his head.

Bunny shuddered. People like her and her family. The poverty on the island was depressing.

But not as depressing as the hotel. The Grapefruit Tree was a far cry from the posh resort of her dreams. In reality, it was a dump, with peeling walls and a sagging mattress. One thing the brochures hadn't lied about – the beach was pretty, what Bunny could see of it from the rain-splattered windows of their room. The day after they arrived, Saint Croix was sideswiped by a freak storm that was wreaking havoc across the Caribbean.

'We're very lucky,' the desk clerk assured them. 'We're getting only the tail of the hurricane.'

For four days the rain fell in torrents. Marooned in the room, all alone with Irving, Bunny felt as if she would surely go mad. Room service rarely answered her calls. When they did, instead of the champagne she requested, they brought her complimentary drinks of watered-down, sugary sweet rum punch.

Bahama Mamas, they called the drinks.

'But this is the Virgin Islands!' she screamed.

Irving was perfectly content to cuddle in bed, play cards, and have sex. Four days of sex . . .

He was an old man. Where did he get the stamina? she wondered bitterly. By the fifth day, she began to get paranoid. She was sure that room service was deliberately mixing up her orders. And the food was wretched, almost inedible.

On the sixth day, the rain finally stopped, and the sun came out. Bunny slathered herself with number fifteen sunscreen, grabbed a beach chair, and went to work on her tan. Irving stationed himself at her side. His few strands of gray hair flapped in the gentle breeze.

When she strolled up the beach to the bar for a diet soda, the cocky blond wind-surfing instructor leered at her and called out, 'How about a trip to Buck Island for some snorkeling? I'll show you something real pretty.'

His tongue flickered across his lips.

She wasn't a strong swimmer, but anything was better than another long day of Irving.

But Irving had other ideas.

'Shnookums,' he said, looking up from his James Bond thriller, 'what do you want to run around for? We came here to relax, swim, get a tan, and a little bit of you-know-what.'

He winked.

Bunny smiled gamely and thought, *A little bit?*

Dani hadn't been back from Los Angeles two days when Eunice phoned to arrange their monthly ritual of dinner at Le Perigord.

'Your father's eager to see you,' Eunice told her. 'I think he's concerned about Nino.'

Then why couldn't Maurice himself have phoned to ask

259

about Nino? But Dani said only, 'Fine, I'll get us a table for Thursday at eight.'

Making the reservations meant she'd pick up the check, which Dani preferred. It was her way of reminding her father that she had, in fact, succeeded at something other than marriage.

Le Perigord was bedecked with elegant white tablecloths and a smiling, bowing maître d' who greeted Maurice by name and kissed Dani's and Eunice's hands. Waiters respectfully mentioned the specialties of the day as if they were introducing celebrities who deserved to be applauded.

For Dani, Le Perigord was redolent with memories of her childhood. The food was superb, but the taste in her mouth was bitter whenever she thought of the many dinners she'd endured as an overweight adolescent with Maurice presiding at the head of the table.

'Too fattening. Order the broiled Dover sole,' Maurice would scold her when she'd ask for the escargot, dripping with garlicky butter.

'You're already too zaftig,' he would say with a grimace when Dani wanted the duck with orange and brandy glaze. 'Crème caramel?' he'd hoot when the waiter offered the dessert menu. 'Don't you have any self-respect?'

Maurice never changed. He still treated her like a child and tried to order for her whenever they were out together.

'My daughter will start with the house salad, dressing on the side. Then the fresh swordfish, broiled, please. And broccoli will be fine as a side dish. My wife will have . . .'

But Dani had grown up. Now she dared to contradict him.

'Papa, I would appreciate it if you'd ask me what I'd like to eat before you order.'

Maurice raised an eyebrow. 'You still have to stay away from fattening foods. You're thin now, but who knows? One day you'll be – '

'Fat again? I don't think so, Papa.' Dani smiled. 'But if I am, it will be my problem to deal with, won't it?'

Eunice lit a cigarette. She hated disagreements and couldn't understand why Dani didn't humor Maurice the way she did.

Maurice ordered steak with béarnaise sauce.

'Maurice, that's too rich,' Eunice said quietly.

'Eunice, please.'

'What's going on?' Dani was surprised to hear Eunice contradict Maurice.

'He doesn't watch his cholesterol the way he should. I beg him to, his doctor begs him to, but he ignores us.'

'I'm perfectly fine,' Maurice said irritably.

The sommelier brought over a bottle of Châteauneuf-du-Pape, uncorked it, and poured a small amount for Maurice to taste. 'Monsieur Lieberman?'

'Good, very good. Nice choice, Marc.'

'Speaking of wine, how's Nino?' Eunice asked, puffing nervously.

Dani thought, *Thanks for opening Pandora's box, Eunice.* 'He's coming along nicely, thank you. Silver Hill is a wonderful place, and their program is excellent for him. Of course, he's getting a lot of support, especially from me and his doctor.'

Maurice took a bite of his duck liver pâté. 'Why waste all that money on a clinic? That's what I don't understand. If you spent more time with him at home, wouldn't he get the kind of help he needs?'

Now she was getting it from both sides. If she hadn't known better, she would have sworn that Maurice and

Roberto were checking in with each other. Chalk it up to both men's old world ways.

'Papa, the staff at Silver Hill is made up of professionals who are used to dealing with these problems. I'm not.'

'I don't know,' Maurice said, shaking his head. 'The way you young people treat each other today . . . out of sight, out of mind. Now, if I had packed your poor mother off to some clinic when she was dying, I could never have lived with myself.'

That was a low blow, even coming from Maurice.

'Papa,' Dani said weakly, 'there's quite a difference between Nino and Mama. He's *not* dying.'

She stiffly excused herself to go to the ladies' room, barely holding back her tears until she was safely hidden behind the door of the nearest stall. After all these years, with all that she'd accomplished, one well-intentioned comment from her father and she was a little girl again, blubbering in the bathroom.

How much more would it take for him to see her for the woman she was, instead of his fat, awkward daughter who could never do anything right? *Dammit, Papa*, she thought, flushing the toilet, *can't you just once in my life give me a break?*

She washed her face, reapplied her makeup, and came to a decision. She'd come too far to let his remark slide by. Along with everything else she'd acquired along the way, she'd gained too much self-respect to swallow Maurice's criticisms. She'd had it with Roberto and she'd had it with her father, too.

Throwing back her shoulders, she pasted a forced smile across her face and returned to their table. 'Papa,' she said, her voice tight with tension, 'Nino is not going through this alone. He's getting the best possible medical care money can buy. While I don't expect you to

262

understand, I'll thank you to keep your opinions to yourself.'

Maurice blinked in shock. His daughter had never talked back to him like this. Her eyes, so similar to his own in color, defied him to argue with her. So, perhaps he'd been a little harsh.

'How was LA?' Eunice asked, quickly changing the subject.

'Terrific.' Suddenly ravenous, Dani took a large bite of swordfish. 'I'm thinking of opening a store there, on Rodeo Drive. Also one in New York, maybe in the Plaza if I can get the space.'

'Ohhhh,' Eunice said, arching her neck as if she were a Modigliani model. 'What a cute idea.'

Cute? That was hardly the adjective Dani would have chosen to describe opening two very expensive stores. But the reaction was typical of Eunice, who liked to skim across the surface of life, never dipping her toes into any unpleasantness or complications.

'Why anybody would want to go to Los Angeles is beyond me,' Maurice grumbled. 'But you seem to know what you're doing with that business, making money hand over fist.' He reached over and shyly patted her hand. 'People are always asking me about my rich daughter. Do you know what I tell them, Dani? I say, "My daughter didn't have to marry wealth. She was born rich." It's true. You inherited your fashion eye from your mother and your business head from me. I'm very proud of you, Dani.'

Dani was so touched by her father's almost unprecedented expression of love that she could hardly speak. 'Thank you, Papa,' she finally choked out. 'That means a lot to me.'

One waiter glided over to clear their plates away while another materialized with dessert menus.

Dani waited for Maurice to order the usual three coffees. But this time he surprised her.

'Some dessert, Dani?' he asked, his eyes twinkling. 'How about the crème caramel?'

Chapter Ten

Piraeus, Greece

Roberto was having a bad summer. First there was the matter of Nino, who'd been virtually incommunicado ever since he checked into that drying-out clinic. Roberto had mounted a relentless campaign of angry phone calls and telegrams threatening lawsuits against his daughter-in-law and the people who ran the place. But to no avail. Nino couldn't be reached.

This was all his daughter-in-law's doing, Roberto was sure of it. How typical of that Jewish vixen, always wanting to be in control. Nino was no alcoholic. Roberto's imagination was running riot with hideous images of what might be happening to his son at Silver Hell or Hole or whatever it was called. What if his son was being held against his will, being given drugs to disorient him, to make him believe he was sick or crazy?

And now there was this business of having committed himself to a cruise aboard the yacht of Kuwaiti arms merchant Salim Abu-Faud. One of the world's wealthiest men, Abu-Faud had often purchased large consignments of wine from the diPortanovas through a discreet middleman. Still, the invitation to sail the Aegean for a week with him had come as a surprise. Roberto's wife, Benedetta, was thrilled. She'd heard all about Abu-Faud's yacht, named for his wife. To spend a week aboard the *Fatima*, with its almost mythic splendors – the Olympic-size swimming pool, the ten-foot-wide bed in the master bedroom, the disco that comfortably accommodated five hundred guests, the specially designed onyx and gold fixtures in each of the one hundred bathrooms, the private beauty salon, the satellite communications system, the helicopter landing pad . . . This was luxury of a kind that impressed even the discriminating Benedetta.

She had flown to Milan to have herself properly outfitted in the latest cruisewear and had almost driven her husband crazy with speculation as to who the other guests might be. Royalty? Heads of state? Entertainers? Secretly, Benedetta prayed that Frank Sinatra would be aboard.

It gratified Roberto to see Benedetta so excited. She was an excellent woman, a model wife, and he took pleasure in making her happy. Personally, he would have preferred to spend the week at their summer villa in Asolo. But no sane human being said no to an invitation from a man as rich and powerful as Abu-Faud without having a very good reason to do so.

They had flown to Athens and been ferried from the airport to the port of Piraeus in one of Abu-Faud's limousines.

'Who else do you suppose will be aboard?' Benedetta asked Roberto for the umpteenth time.

Roberto shrugged and smiled indulgently at his elegantly coiffed wife. Benedetta brought honor to the name of diPortanova. But then, of course, she came from a family of aristocrats whose lineage was as exalted as his own. One's heritage and background were what mattered; romance quickly passed, and sex could always be obtained elsewhere. Roberto and Benedetta hadn't slept together in years. So what? They were as close as brother and sister. He respected her as he'd respected his mother. If only their son had found himself such a wife . . .

'Welcome, welcome!' Abu-Faud himself waved them aboard the *Fatima* after they had passed through the metal detector and had their names checked by the security men at the bottom of the canopied gangplank.

'Count diPortanova. And this beautiful woman must be the lovely contessa. You do me honor.'

Abu-Faud was slightly stooped, completely bald, and ugly in a way that women seemed to find very sexy. He had tiny, thin fingers that played constantly with a strand of worry beads, and he wore a black patch over his left eye. Rumor had it that the eye had been plucked out by a hawk, set on him by a business rival.

'Please, my humble home is yours. Whatever you wish . . .' Abu-Faud gestured at a crew member dressed in white, standing at a discreet distance. 'Your valet will provide it for you.'

Famous for his legendary generosity, Abu-Faud meant what he said. Sex, drugs, food, wine – a guest had but to ask and any whim could be satisfied.

'How soon do we sail?' asked Benedetta, charmed by her host's warm, gracious manner.

'As soon as my last guest has arrived. And, as the Americans say, speak of the devil. Here she is now.'

Roberto and Benedetta smiled and followed his gaze.

'*Guten Tag*,' Karola called cheerfully.

Roberto's mouth went dry. Karola . . . What in hell was she doing here? He'd mentioned the cruise to her, and she'd never said a word . . . *That bitch!* he thought furiously. Was this precisely Karola's idea of a joke? How she must have relished the idea of surprising him. He gritted his teeth, horrified at the thought of spending a week on a yacht, no matter how large, with his wife *and* his mistress.

'Karola,' Abu-Faud enthused, 'welcome, welcome. I'm so delighted you could accept my humble invitation. Permit me to introduce you to the Contessa diPortanova. Of course, you already know her husband, Roberto.'

'Of course,' said Karola, looking radiant, dressed in a white linen Givenchy suit. She extended her hand to Benedetta. 'So glad to meet you, Contessa. Your husband and I are old, old friends, so to speak.'

'Oh, really?' Benedetta smiled and looked to her husband for an explanation.

Roberto thought he would piss in his pants. What crazy stunt was Karola up to now?

'But of course,' Karola purred, her expression turning sad. 'When my husband became . . . ill, and I was forced to take over the business, I needed the advice of someone I could trust. Mutual friends suggested I put myself in your husband's very capable hands.'

Benedetta beamed. 'I hope he was helpful.'

'Oh, he was,' Karola said earnestly. 'He gave me exactly what I needed. Roberto – you don't mind if I call you Roberto? – it's a pleasure to see you again after all this time.'

Roberto managed a tight, thin smile. 'The pleasure is all mine . . . Frau von Reich.'

'Come, come!' Abu-Faud boomed. 'None of this formality. And truly, the pleasure is *mine* for arranging this little surprise reunion. Though I must give Karola some credit for planting the seed of the idea. So delightful to have you all together here. Shall we join the other guests above deck for a drink?'

'Sounds marvelous,' gushed Karola, linking arms with Benedetta. 'We must have a chat and get to know each other better. Something tells me we have a great deal in common. Coming, Roberto?'

Roberto's face was pale with suppressed fury. 'Right behind you, Karola.'

Benedetta, oblivious to the tension, smiled contentedly. Roberto worked too hard, and on top of it all lately

268

there'd been all that trouble about Nino. Aboard the yacht, he would finally be able to relax.

Abu-Faud's guest list read like a cross section of the international Social Register. No Frank Sinatra, but Benedetta hardly minded. There were so many other amusing people to meet – an English duke and duchess (he was ninth in line to the British throne); a German Olympic weightlifting gold medalist turned movie star and his wife, the daughter of a former American vice president; the head of a Swedish auto firm; and a world-famous photographer of nudes.

'But where's Abu-Faud's wife?' Benedetta whispered to Roberto after the introductions had been made. 'Where's Fatima?'

'Back home in Kuwait with their three daughters. Their religion doesn't permit her to be seen unveiled in public.'

Karola overheard and added, 'That's not the only reason Fatima's not here.' She pointed discreetly at a young brunette sunning herself on the deck. 'That's Abu-Faud's mistress.'

'No!' Benedetta was shocked. 'What kind of a man flaunts his infidelity for all the world to see!'

Karola shuddered. 'I cannot imagine. Bad enough that he should even take a mistress, don't you agree, Roberto?'

'Indeed,' Roberto said stiffly, itching to smack Karola's smiling face.

Dinner was a sumptuous feast concocted by Abu-Faud's chef, who'd been trained by famed French chef Paul Bocuse. The parade of dishes was as lavish as the formal dining room, which boasted a pair of Picassos and an astonishing Renoir nude. Afterward, the guests were invited to choose between two movies in the twin screening rooms. Determined to avoid Karola, Roberto waited to see which she picked before heading in the opposite direction.

But he knew better than to underestimate Karola's formidable talents for making trouble. Sure enough, as the *Fatima* gently rode the waves of the Aegean, Karola played an elaborate cat-and-mouse game with Roberto and the unsuspecting Benedetta. She stalked them in the swimming pool, in the billiard room, on the sun decks, in the gym, and on the picturesque islands at which they stopped to explore and shop.

On their fourth day out, Abu-Faud scheduled an expedition to Andros, the northernmost island of the Cyclades. The launches ferried his guests back and forth to the island. Roberto, determined to spend one day without Karola, took his time getting ready. But just as their launch was ready to take off, Karola came hurrying down the stairs toward the boat deck.

'Hallo!' she hailed them. 'I missed my ride. Would you mind terribly if I joined the two of you?'

'Not at all,' Benedetta called back, waving her over.

'Can't we have a moment's privacy on this trip?' Roberto muttered.

Benedetta frowned. She rarely criticized her husband, but it wasn't like him to be so ungenerous. 'Have some compassion, Roberto,' she gently chided him. 'The poor woman has had such a difficult life, and now she's all alone.'

Roberto scowled but kept his mouth shut as Karola, wearing only a skimpy gauze shirt over her tiny bikini, stepped into the launch and settled herself next to him.

'Such a lovely day. I do hope I'm not intruding?' Her voice wavered uncertainly.

'No, no,' Benedetta assured her. 'We couldn't be more delighted. Isn't that right, Roberto?'

'Uh . . . quite right.'

Karola was seated so close to him that he could smell her scent, and when she leaned forward to adjust the strap of her sandal, he could hardly restrain himself from reaching over and cupping her breasts in his hands. Ah, to touch those breasts . . . to play his tongue over those large, pink nipples . . . His cock began to harden, and a low moan escaped his lips.

'Roberto?' Benedetta looked concerned.

'A twinge of heartburn,' Roberto said quickly. He shifted his legs to cover the bulge in his shorts.

'Stop by my cabin when we get back,' said Karola, her voice buttery-smooth with sympathy. 'I have just the thing to take care of that.'

The capital town proved every bit as picturesque as Abu-Faud had promised. But the charms of its Venetian fort and modern art museum were lost on Roberto. Trailing behind his wife and his mistress, burning with lust, he longed to grab Karola, throw her down on the marble-paved square, and fuck her beneath the blazing afternoon sun. It was all he could do not to excuse himself, find a men's room, and quickly masturbate to relieve his aching balls.

But no, he decided. Karola was begging for it. Revenge would be sweeter if he waited.

They got back to the yacht in plenty of time for a nap and a shower before cocktails. Roberto sat down on the bed next to Benedetta and grimaced.

'What's wrong?'

'Nothing serious. Another attack of heartburn.'

'Oh, Roberto . . .' Benedetta couldn't bear the thought of her husband in pain. 'What about Karola's pills? Shall I go get you some?'

'No,' said Roberto. 'You rest. I'll get them.'

He rapped sharply on Karola's stateroom door. As if she'd been waiting for him to appear, the door swung

271

open immediately. Karola stood in the doorway stark naked.

'I wondered how long it would be before you showed up.' She laughed.

'Get inside before somebody sees you like that,' Roberto hissed, shoving her into the room and slamming the door. 'You're crazy!'

'*Ja*, and that's what you love about me.' She arched her back, taunting him with her naked body.

Either she was mad or he was.

'You shameless bitch, what in hell are you doing on this yacht? Are you here to torture me? You could at least respect – '

'Oh, Roberto, shut up,' Karola whispered, snaking her arms around his waist. 'I'm here because I want Abu-Faud to invest with me in a missile plant or two.' She unzipped his pants and fumbled for his cock. 'Ah, I've found your missile . . .'

Her tongue flicked in and out of his ear. Roberto groaned as her fingers worked their way up and down his throbbing penis.

'Karola, I want to fuck you! Now!'

'And so you shall.' She grabbed his hand and led him over to the bed. 'Champagne?' An open bottle of Louis Roederer Cristal was cooling in an ice bucket.

'No more games, Karola. Lie down and spread your legs.'

'*Ach*, I love it when you talk tough with me,' Karola growled.

He groaned as he came in contact with her moist outer lips, but he held himself back, sliding the tip of his cock up and down across her slit.

'You want me, Karola, don't you? Admit it, bitch! You want me!'

'*Ja, ja*, I do,' she breathed.

272

'*Puttana!* Whore! Here, have me!'

Quickly, he was inside her, oblivious to anything but satisfying his own burning need. He thrust – once, twice, a third time, and he came in a thunderous explosion that left him panting for air.

'Ahh, *ja*! Now me, *ja*!' Karola gasped, frantically gyrating her hips and trying to capture the last seconds of his erection.

Roberto pulled out abruptly. 'You're still hot?'

'*Ja, ja*, you know I am. Make me come, Roberto, cool me off, I beg you.'

Roberto smiled and scooped up a handful of ice chips from the ice bucket. 'Maybe this will cool you off, Karola.'

She howled with shock as he rubbed the crushed ice up into her vagina.

'See you at dinner, Karola.'

The glass she threw missed him by an inch.

'Too much sun,' clucked Benedetta, when Karola didn't make it to dinner. 'But at least you're feeling better, aren't you, Roberto?'

Roberto nodded gravely. 'Yes, my love. Much better.'

New York

Bunny smiled happily and cut deep into her New York strip steak, cooked so rare that blood filled the bottom of the plate. No matter what kind of restaurant Irving took her to – French, Italian, seafood – Bunny ordered steak, 'rare, please, don't overdo it.' But tonight, as a special birthday treat (she was turning twenty-one, though even Irving didn't know how old she was), Irving had decided to take her to the Palm, one of New York's most famous steak houses.

273

The Palm was short on atmosphere and long on jowly men in three-piece pin-striped suits talking business over their martinis and filets mignons. Aside from herself, Bunny counted only four other women, all of whom were dressed like high-class whores.

'Whaddya think they are?' snorted Irving when she pointed them out to him.

'Are you sure you don't want a taste of my steak?' Bunny asked, knowing full well that Irving had a hard time chewing the meat because of his dentures.

'No, no, you go ahead and enjoy,' said Irving, picking at his charred salmon steak. At these prices, they could at least give him a nice piece of fish. But as long as his little shnookums was happy . . .

'Some fried onion rings?'

He shook his head. 'I love 'em, but they repeat on me. So, birthday girl, you like this place?'

'Mmm, yes. Thank you so much, booboo.'

Irving grinned. He couldn't wait to see the expression on her face when she opened her birthday present.

'Irving, did you tell Howie and Stuart you were giving me a raise?'

'Shnookums, let's not get into this again. You know I'd give you the money if I could.'

'What I know is that I deserve that raise. I work harder and stay later than anyone else in the company. Right or wrong?'

'You're right, you're right. But we have certain procedures and budgets – '

'Screw the budgets!'

Irving looked around, distressed. 'Barbara, please . . .'

'Sorry.' Bunny forced a smile. This wasn't the time to lose her cool. 'I really am sorry, Irving. It's just that sometimes I feel so unappreciated . . .'

She let the thought dangle in front of him as the waiter came over to clear away their plates.

'A piece of chocolate cheesecake, please. A *big* piece,' Bunny told the waiter.

Irving reached across the table and took her hand. '*I* appreciate you. But they give the raises.'

'Oh, booboo, I thought *you* were the boss.'

Oy, this little girl of his was relentless. 'I am, shnookums, but they're part of the business. Tell you what. I promise I'll talk to them tomorrow.'

Bunny stifled a sigh. 'Of course, Irving.' She saw right through him. It was like her father used to say – there wasn't a lot of milk left in this cow.

'So. Did lots of people call to wish you happy birthday?'

'Oh, the usual.' Including a collect call from her mother, the cheapskate. Doing her best imitation of a Long Island accent, Bunny had told the operator, 'I'm sowwry. Bawbawa's not here. I don't know when she's gonna be back. Bye-bye.'

Probably old Irma Rae had in mind to use Bunny's birthday as an excuse to ask for money. Everyone in Moccasin Bottom assumed she was rich, just because she lived in New York. To hell with them.

'I got you a little present,' Irving announced, pulling out a tiny gift-wrapped package.

Bunny held her breath when she saw the box was from Fortunoff. *Please, not an engagement ring*, she prayed. That would spoil everything.

A pair of diamond hoop earrings winked up at her. 'Oh, Irving, what a wonderful surprise. They're absolutely beautiful. I've never owned anything this expensive.'

'Nothing's too good for my little shnookums.' Irving chuckled. 'You deserve the best.'

'Now I have a little surprise for you, booboo.' Bunny ducked her head shyly. When she looked up at him, her eyes glistened with tears. 'Irving, honey, how would you feel about being a daddy again?'

Irving stared at her in horror. What, was she kidding? A father? At his age? And with a girl hardly old enough to be his daughter? Hadn't she taken precautions?

'You're not – '

Bunny nodded demurely.

Oy vey . . . What a *shanda*! He picked up his napkin and dabbed at the sweat on his forehead. He was crazy about Barbara. She made him feel alive and happy. But to have a child by her? He'd have to marry her! How would he ever face Howie and Stuart, not to mention his sister and brother-in-law?

'Barbara, are you sure?'

'Of course I'm sure, Irving,' Bunny murmured. 'I guess with all our . . . you-know-what, we slipped up. So what is it you say? *Mazel tov!* Right?'

Irving's bowels quivered with fear. 'Barbara . . .'

Another minute and he'd lose his dinner right here at the table.

'You're not happy, booboo?' Bunny asked, her voice flat and emotionless. 'You don't want me to have your baby? It's because I'm a shiksa, isn't it?'

'No, no, that's not it.'

Bunny swallowed a forkful of cheesecake. 'Irving, I'm not some little plaything you can knock up, then throw away. You owe me, Irving. You really owe me.'

Irving's hand shook as he reached for his water glass. This was the sweet little girl he'd taken under his wing, promoted, set up in her own beautiful apartment?

'I could have an abortion. But it'll cost you some money to kill this baby,' Bunny warned him, taking another bite of cheesecake. 'For the abortion, not to mention my mental anguish.'

His bowels rumbled ominously. A cold sweat broke out

all over his body. Little fingers of pain zapped his chest. 'Fine. Whatever you want, Barbara. I . . .'

Irving looked so sick and miserable that Bunny almost relented. But then she thought about Moccasin Bottom and how hard she'd had to fight to claw her way out of that squalor. She clenched her fists in her lap and plunged forward. 'Love isn't cheap, Irving, and neither am I. I want a lump-sum payment of five thousand dollars and a one-year paid lease on the apartment. Plus a new job with Dani diPortanova.'

'Dani diPortanova? How do you know she's looking for someone?'

Bunny shrugged. 'I don't. But with the glowing recommendation you're going to give me, she'll find a place for me in her company.'

Somehow Irving found the strength to sign for the bill and stumble out of the restaurant. Bunny took his arm and steered him to a cab. 'Don't worry,' she chirped. 'This will all work out for the best. Night-night, booboo.'

Booboo was right, Irving thought miserably. The biggest booboo he had ever made. What a horse's ass he'd been. If this story *ever* got out, he'd never be able to show his face on Seventh Avenue again. Five grand to buy her off . . . shit! He didn't give a damn about the money, but to have been played for such a fool . . . And then to pawn her off on Dani, who'd become like a daughter to him. Even now that she was such a big-shot star, she still called him for advice. Barbara was right; if he said the word, Dani would hire her.

God forgive me, but . . . Barbara was a hard worker, he consoled himself. A quick learner. And smart.

Too smart. The hell with chasing young pussy. From now on he was going to stick to nice Jewish widows.

* * *

277

Making the move to Countess Dani, Inc. was Bunny's greatest coup so far. Even though I. Blatt and Sons and Countess Dani, Inc. were only floors apart, they were miles apart in every other way.

The place had class. Real class, from the crisp ivory linen stationery with Dani's signature scrawled across the top in what looked like bloodred lipstick to the marble bathrooms and the all-white showroom and offices. Even the kitchen was classy, with a built-in microwave oven and a refrigerator stocked with soda and mineral water.

No expense was spared to make life pleasant for the staff, most of whom were young and energetic. Not like I. Blatt, where the majority of the employees, with the exception of Howie and Stuart, had one foot in the grave. Irving all but had his casket picked out. Thank God she didn't have to put up with any more of his denture-breath kisses or his fossilized tongue probing between her legs. Sex was so disgusting. She didn't know why *Cosmo* and all the other magazines made such a big fuss about something so messy, so crude, so animalistic.

But all that was behind her, now that she'd arrived at Countess Dani, the Cadillac of the fashion business. And one day she was going to drive it all the way to the top.

How she would do that she hadn't quite figured out yet. She knew Irving had touted her to Dani as an all-around fashion whiz, but the truth was, she wasn't really much of a designer. Sure, she had the mechanics down and she'd taken a design course at FIT, but there were other people at Countess Dani who had a lot more talent than she did.

Shrewdly, she took herself off to the library and read volume after bound volume of *Vogue*, dating back to the thirties and forties, looking for ideas to help her create something 'original.' She stayed late at the office, after everyone else had left, and pored over the other assistants' designs. Sometimes she would even slip into Dani's office and poke around her desk, reading memos and glancing through her sketch pad – which was how she discovered, late one night, Dani's preliminary sketches for her upcoming spring line.

Rough though they were, Bunny felt a jolt of excitement. Shoulder pads gave a new twist to the classic Drop Dress. The narrow-lapeled jackets harked back to the fifties. Pants were cut very narrow toward the ankle. Dani had whimsically added skinny ties and teased beehive hairdos to the drawings. Annie Hall with a sense of humor.

At the bottom of one page she'd scribbled herself a note: 'New Wave. Blondie, Red red red red red. Talk to Monika re CBGB, also new name for cosmetic line.'

Bunny puzzled over the note, then quickly copied it onto a scrap of paper to figure out at her leisure. Slowly she was learning her way around Countess Dani, Inc., figuring out which people to trust, which ones to watch out for. Kim Wantanabe seemed okay, but that snotty Monika gave her the creeps. The other girls on staff interested her only as people to have lunch with and trade rumors with. But as friends? Forget it. Unless they could give her a boost to the top, she wasn't interested.

It was two in the morning at Lucky's, and the quietly frantic action was just beginning to wind down. As usual, for some the night had been a disaster. For others, Monika among them, it had been the kind of night that more than made up for all the money she'd lost that week.

Though by nature not a superstitious person, when she played baccarat – as she had this evening – she consistently bet bank, which more often than not gave her winning hands. Even better, tonight she'd found herself up against three other Lucky's regulars as well as a guest, a Brit whom she recognized from Cannes. The woman was a 'steamer' – a mediocre gambler who was always chasing losing bets. The steamer had brought Monika luck, along with a neat little pile of chips that added up to $30,000.

Not bad for an hour's work.

She could barely contain her glee as she gathered up her stash. 'Madam, gentlemen' – she nodded to the croupier and the other players – 'it's been a pleasure.'

'Oh, screw you, Monika,' replied Buzzy Standish good-naturedly. Buzzy was the heir to an American industrial fortune so vast that he frequently gambled away in a night the equivalent of one assembly-line worker's annual salary.

Monika patted Buzzy on the shoulder. 'I'll see you again tomorrow night, *ja*?'

'Tomorrow is Friday. I'm going to Monte Carlo for the weekend, remember? Sure you won't change your mind and come along?'

She was sure. Monte Carlo was always fun, and Buzzy was a superb host, but he had weird ideas about sex. Nipple clamps and champagne enemas weren't Monika's idea of a good time in bed.

'Thanks just the same. Perhaps we can have dinner next week?'

The steamer threw down her cards and glared at Monika. 'I've had it. I hope *I* don't see you tomorrow night.' She stalked away angrily.

'What's her problem?' Buzzy snickered.

'Win a few, lose a few.' Monika shrugged. 'I have to go to work in the morning. 'Night, boys.'

Unseen by her, the croupier had signaled the ladderman, who immediately picked up the phone next to his chair. 'She's leaving now,' he murmured into the receiver.

Monika's heart was racing with excitement. It always

felt like this when she won big – the thrill that came from having beaten the odds, the exhilaration of knowing that tonight she would be adding to the stash of mad money she kept in the wall safe in her bedroom.

She loved the intimacy of Lucky's. Seated around the baccarat table or playing roulette, she and the others never discussed their daytime lives. All that mattered was what was happening to them here, tonight, at this moment.

Once in a while she wondered whether she was spending too much time and money at Lucky's. But then she'd remind herself she had plenty to spare. Besides, sooner or later she was bound to hit it really big and recoup whatever she might have lost.

No, she told herself as she waited for the elevator to take her to the first floor, she didn't have to worry. Especially not after a night like this.

'Ms von Reich?' Scott Devane, the manager, suddenly materialized next to her. 'I see you've had a good evening.'

'About time, don't you think?' She smiled to show she was joking. Devane was reputed to be a former mathematics child prodigy who carried in his head a computer bank of gambling odds for any number of games and hand variations.

'Won't you join me for a celebratory drink?' he said. 'There's something I'd like to discuss with you as well.'

Monika glanced surreptitiously at her watch. It was getting late, and she had a staff meeting at eight-thirty the next morning. But Scott Devane rarely socialized with the members. Something told her she would be wise to take him up on his offer.

Devane's office on the fourth floor was decorated as elegantly as the rest of the club. Monika sat down on a suede-covered beige Louis XV chair. Devane, thin and fastidious in his custom-made tux and Cartier love brace-let, sat opposite her. They shared Dom Pérignon from a bucket between them.

'You enjoy our little place, do you, Ms von Reich?' Devane smiled expansively.

'*Ja*, it's quite . . . stimulating.'

'You tend to do well here, Ms von Reich. Really better than most who play on those floors.'

'I try. It's luck, I guess.'

Devane took another sip of champagne. 'Maybe, maybe not. Some people are born gamblers. You, Ms von Reich, are one of that elite group. You shouldn't be so modest about your abilities. But you really deserve more of a challenge than what's offered downstairs. You should be playing up here on the fourth floor. You know that, don't you?'

The hallowed fourth floor, where the stakes were higher, the potential rewards all the greater.

'Your membership can easily be arranged,' Devane continued, picking a tiny fleck of lint off his trousers.

'Membership?' She'd had to pay a healthy fee to join Lucky's, and the annual dues weren't cheap. 'I don't understand. I'm already a member.'

'Yes, of course, but we like to think of the fourth floor as a . . . a club within a club. There's a one-time fee, good for a lifetime. Certainly it wouldn't be a problem for you, Ms von Reich.'

Was it her imagination or had Devane purposely emphasized her name? Obviously, everyone knew she was Karola von Reich's daughter. She had no idea what else they knew. Probably they assumed she was worth millions. What a joke. At the rate she was going, it wouldn't be long before she had to dip into her capital.

'How much is this one-time fee, Mr Devane?'

282

'Nothing that will put a dent in your wallet, Ms von Reich. A mere one hundred thousand dollars.'

A hundred thousand dollars? Were they crazy?

'That's rather a lot of money.'

'For some, perhaps. Not for you, I'm sure.'

'Quite frankly, I'd rather spend the money gambling on the other floors.'

Devane's smile reminded Monika of a dog baring its fangs. 'I'm not sure that's quite possible, Ms von Reich. We've very much enjoyed having you as a member here. But you've had a good run these past few months, better than average and . . . well, people are beginning to talk.'

'Talk? Talk about what?'

'Oh, you know, just the usual gossip. It comes with the territory when you have so many strong egos with so much money at stake. But there are those who wonder if you're not backed by the house.'

'But that's absurd!'

'You and I know that,' Devane said unctuously. 'But I'm *sure* you understand how such a rumor, if allowed to spread, could damage our reputation. Our members would lose faith in our honesty. Our credibility would be shot to hell. After that . . . well, you get the picture.'

Monika got the picture, all right. Either she put up the hundred thousand or she could forget about ever again gambling at Lucky's. In any language, that added up to blackmail. 'I don't really have a choice, then, do I?' she said, trying hard to sound casual.

Devane looked shocked. 'But of course you do. After all, you're not dealing with a bunch of thugs or hoodlums.'

'Let me get this absolutely straight. If I want to continue playing here, I must play on the fourth floor, *ja*? Otherwise, I am no longer welcome as a member?'

'Correct, Ms von Reich. Absolutely correct.'

* * *

Dani knew she had her work cut out for her. It was just a matter of time before the jeans market would be glutted. Word on the street had it that everyone and his brother would soon be putting his name on jeans. Calvin Klein. Gloria Vanderbilt. People nobody had ever heard of before, like Sasson and Jordache. Even Studio 54 was supposed to be merchandising its own line. Dani gave the jeans market another couple of years at most before the party was over.

The novelty and convenience of her other big money-maker, the Drop Dress, had finally worn off, and sales had peaked a season ago. Dani was amazed that the dress had lasted as long as it had. If Countess Dani was to continue to hold on to – better yet, increase – its share of the marketplace, Dani needed to give her public something hot, something that was more than just another new collection. She needed an entirely fresh concept.

If her instincts were right, she had every reason to believe that what she would be presenting at her next show would do exactly that. So far, she reminded herself when she lay awake worrying in the middle of the night, she'd been uncannily accurate about such things. What she liked, the American public liked. What she dared, they dared. What she wore, they wore.

But with the show just six weeks away, she couldn't help but wonder whether she was going too far in the direction of inventiveness. The new styles were startling enough in themselves. Maybe she was going too far out on a limb by holding the show at CBGB, the grungy downtown club that was home to the burgeoning New Wave and punk music scene. What on earth would her wealthy, sophisticated invitees think when they emerged from the minivans she'd rented for the occasion and found themselves on the Bowery? And if they recovered from that shock, how would they feel about Blondie, the New Wave band Kim had arranged to have play at the show?

Dani had listened to Blondie's albums, caught their act at CBGB and Whisky-a-Go-Go in LA, and fallen in love with their funky, trashy nouveau 1960s sound. She was especially taken with their bleached-blond lead singer, Debbie Harry, who projected a sultry, sexy know-it-all image that captured for Dani the spirit of her next collection.

A new decade was coming. People were looking to make a change. Women were getting weary of conservative, play-it-safe dressing. Dani sensed they were looking forward to having more fun and feeling more glamorous. The discos were full every night, but Dani was more intrigued by the tongue-in-cheek glamour at CBGB and its more chic cousin, the Mudd Club. Still, the idea, which had sounded so brilliant late one night when she'd presented it to Monika and Kim, now struck her as possible fashion suicide.

What hadn't lost its brilliance was the electric shade of red that was to be the cornerstone of her new cosmetics line. Another daring idea – to launch the line in conjunction with her spring collection, to present them as a unit, one complementing the other. She had Ian McAdam working overtime to develop an ad campaign that would neatly and dramatically tie together the new styles and cosmetics.

'Maybe we could get Debbie Harry for our print and TV ads,' she suggested to Ian.

'I want you to do it,' Ian replied. 'You always have been, always will be, your own best advertisement.'

But all the advertising in the world wouldn't help if she didn't come up with a name for the cosmetics. She'd already brainstormed with Ian, Monika, and Kim for hours at a time, their suggestions becoming increasingly absurd until they were giddy with laughter and exhaustion. Finally she'd decided to open up the discussion to the rest of the staff.

'Quiet, please,' she said, calling the meeting to order.

Twenty-one pairs of eyes stared at her over mugs of coffee.

'Yes, I know these early-morning meetings are hell, but this one's worth losing sleep over. Check out this color, folks,' she announced, as her assistant handed out swatches. 'Red hot! As brilliant as a tropical sunset. The hottest, most electric red to come along in years. We're doing it in lipstick, nail polish, blush, shadow . . . the works. And it's meant to be worn with these designs.'

She pulled away the cloth that was draped over the easel next to her and slowly flipped through the designs.

Silence settled over the room as her design, marketing, and production people, most of whom were seeing the collection for the first time, studied them closely.

The styles were more detailed, more polished versions of what Bunny had found on Dani's desk during one of her late-night prowls. But since then Dani had added something else that beautifully tied together the collection. She'd created leotardlike bodysuits, similar to what dancers wore, but these would be fashioned out of the finest jersey and cotton knits, carefully coordinated with the rest of the pieces in the collection.

'Here it is,' Dani said with a broad wink. 'Our "fuck me" wear.'

The staff erupted in applause and whistles.

'I'm glad you like it. As many of you probably know already, we're doing mostly black and white, grays, and shades of red. All of it will work with our cosmetics.'

More cheers and whistles.

'But we're sunk if we don't come up with a name for the line. One that's sexy and provocative, that'll make our customers feel as if they're being just a little bit wicked when they buy our product. Monika, Kim, and I have driven ourselves crazy trying to figure out just the right angle on this. Now we're turning it over to you. Give it some thought. Oh, and by the way, you name the line, and there's a two-thousand-dollar bonus for you.'

Bunny waved her hand, asking to be recognized.

'Yes? Barbara, isn't it?' said Dani.

Bunny smiled shyly. 'Well, I don't know about ya'll,' she declared, 'but it shouldn't be too hard to find the right name for this line. That red, combined with those designs, is hot enough to give me hot flashes.' She blushed. 'Not the bad kind, of course.'

'Hot Flash . . .' Dani rolled the name around on her tongue. 'Hot Flash! What do the rest of you think?'

Murmurs of approval circulated around the table. Kim nodded her agreement. Even Monika, who usually took her time saying yes, looked impressed.

'All right, then. Nice going, Barbara!' Dani announced. 'Okay, everybody, let's get to work on Hot Flash.'

Just as she did every morning, Irving's secretary, Myrna Nussbaum, sorted through Irving's mail and deposited it neatly in his in-box.

Irving barely noticed. He barely noticed anything these days; he simply went through the motions of discussing things with Howie and Stuart, then left the office, his head hanging low.

To see her boss so depressed was killing Myrna, who'd carried a torch for him since the day she'd started working at I. Blatt thirty-four years ago, fresh out of high school. She knew it was all the fault of that little blond hussy, with her phony smile and fake southern accent. Barbara must have dumped Irving but good. He hadn't been the same since she'd left the company.

287

Myrna knew she could cheer him up if only Irving would give her half a chance. The poor man, schlepping out to Queens alone night after night, always eating in restaurants . . . No wonder he was constantly guzzling Maalox. If only just once he could taste her pot roast and noodle pudding . . .

'Good morning, Irving. Coffee? A piece of cherry Danish?'

'No, thanks,' Irving said wearily. 'Shut my door, will you, Myrna?'

When he was alone, he picked up the phone to call Barbara, then changed his mind as he did fifty times a day. Just to see how she was doing, he told himself. Call him an old fool, but he missed her. He couldn't sleep nights, thinking about making love to her.

'Good riddance to rubbish,' his sister had said, and she didn't know the half of it. But Irving still asked himself whether he should have done the decent, right thing and married her. Now he was sure it was too late. Often he wondered whether the baby had been a boy or a girl. He blamed himself that he hadn't even offered to go with her when she had the abortion. But she'd seemed so calm and unemotional, almost as if she didn't care. Poor thing, she was probably scared out of her wits and didn't want to show it.

He reached over and listlessly picked through the mail. One envelope, a bill from the East Side Animal Hospital, caught his eye. A mistake, of course. It should have gone to Barbara, but he'd always paid for Bernie and Bennie's visits to the vet. Probably his name was still on the account. *Oy*, he hoped nothing was wrong. He missed those little rascals, but better they should be with Barbara. She was so attached to them.

'Please forward,' he scrawled across the envelope.

Then, overcome with concern for the 'boys,' he impulsively tore it open and scanned the bill: 'Canine euthanasia – 2 dogs @ $25.00 each = $50.00.'

Canine euthanasia . . .

She'd had Bernie and Bennie put to sleep.

Those two beautiful creatures – dead! He ached with grief for them, and tears spilled down his cheeks. First the fetus, now the dogs. What kind of person could commit murder so easily?

Chapter Eleven

New York

'Forget anything even approaching conventional,' Dani told her troops. 'I want the Hot Flash line to be controversial from the moment we launch it.'

Controversy was the strategy that had always worked wonders for Countess Dani. Controversy created the kind of publicity that no amount of advertising money could buy. Controversy meant sales.

In the late winter of 1980, Dani launched the Hot Flash line with a $10 million ad blitzkrieg that showcased Hot Flash lipsticks, nail polish, and fragrance, in a red cut-glass bottle at $150 an ounce. The line took off so quickly that it stunned industry analysts, Dani's competitors, and even Dani herself.

The previous fall, the fashion press had praised her show at CBGB for its wittiness and imagination. The society ladies adored being 'kidnapped' to the East Village. The fact that Blondie's *Parallel Lines* album had gone platinum didn't hurt. Nor did the delicious après-show lunch of blintzes and pierogi catered by the Kiev, a Ukrainian restaurant just up the street on Second Avenue.

The infamous Countess Dani jeans ad that had dominated Times Square was replaced with a photograph, shot through a hazy red filter, of a nude woman who looked suspiciously like Dani herself. Long wavy hair tastefully covered the woman's breasts, and a thin white lightning bolt streaked across the photo, ready to strike right between the woman's legs. The copy: 'HOT FLASH, from Countess Dani.'

Then there were the television ads that aired nationally throughout the spring: Outside, the mist-shrouded grounds of a country estate. Somewhere nearby, the sea batters the shore. Move through a pair of open French doors into a beautifully decorated, very feminine bedroom. Dani is lying on a chaise longue in a diaphanous red negligee, holding a glass of champagne in one hand. Music that sounds like the cries and whispers of the night plays softly in the background. Dani takes a long, slow sip of champagne, a drop of which falls into her cleavage. Suddenly she drops the glass, which falls to the floor in slow motion, champagne flying everywhere. And then her hand moves down . . . out of view of the camera. And for an instant, her arm can be seen moving lightly, as if massaging whatever she has found there. Her eyes are half shut in ecstasy as she whispers through pouty lips, 'Hot Flash – makes lightning strike in all the right places.'

One national network refused to air the spot, and the other two asked Dani to edit it.

She refused.

The networks backed off and ran the ads as originally shot, though some of the local markets boycotted the spot. Some that didn't, particularly in the Bible Belt, were blasted from the local pulpits and found their stations being picketed by the faithful. Conservative columnists railed against her, questioning everything from her morals to her marriage. Ministers condemned her. Feminists picketed her offices on Seventh Avenue, claiming the ads were demeaning to women.

The wags on Seventh Avenue joked that the line should have been called 'Hot Flesh,' and the nickname got picked up by the media in their news reports on all the ruckus about the new line.

Dani posed for the cover of *Time* magazine in a Hot Flash dress. 'In Hot Water: The Selling of Hot Flesh,' read the headline.

A week later, *People* carried on about it in an article entitled 'Dani's Hot Flesh.'

Bill Blass called to congratulate her. So did Calvin Klein, Ralph Lauren, and Donna Karan. Halston took her to Le Cirque to celebrate. Oscar de la Renta sent dozens of very red roses with a note: 'Hot Flash Roses for the Hot Flesh Countess.'

Reggie Bolt was conspicuously silent.

Roberto diPortanova was not.

'My father called again,' Nino said.

Dani pulled on another layer of cold-weather running gear to defend herself against the low temperatures of this unusually chilly March morning. She hated the cold, but after two laps around the Central Park reservoir, she would feel energized for the rest of the day.

'More of the same?' she asked. When would Roberto ever learn that he had no say in how she ran her company? He was spitting mad about the TV ads. *This* time, he'd thundered to Nino, his wife had truly overstepped the boundaries of good taste.

'Umm.' Nino wrapped their down comforter more tightly around himself and watched Dani twist her hair back in a tight knot. 'You have a beautiful neck, *cara*. Come back to bed and let me kiss it.'

'Flattery will get you nowhere. I still have some self-discipline, even if you don't.' The words came out sounding harsher than she'd intended. *Nice going, Dani*, she chided herself. So much for her vow not to treat Nino like a child.

After his release from Silver Hill, they'd had an idyllic fall together, almost like a second honeymoon. As busy as she'd been gearing up for the Hot Flash launch, she'd managed to get away with him most weekends – to Connecticut, the Caribbean, California . . . anywhere they could relax together. They'd talked and laughed and made love as they hadn't in years. A couple of times she'd even sat in the stands at Watkins Glen, biting her nails, as Nino put one of his cars through its paces.

Watching him take the turns made her almost physically ill. But racing was what Nino wanted to do more than anything in the world. Sober, he was convinced he could earn a place in the record books.

And as far as she could tell, he hadn't had a drop to drink. Not so much as a glass of wine. No drugs. No extracurricular screwing, either.

But with the onslaught of holiday parties, Nino's hard-won sobriety had crumbled in the face of the gushing fountains of champagne, wine, and eggnog that greeted them at every event. Mindful of what she'd learned at Silver Hill, determined not to be a nagging wife, she had bitten her tongue when he asked for wine instead of Perrier.

'Just one, *cara*. Don't worry, I can control myself,' he'd assured her.

Like hell he could.

In all fairness, though, he was living up to his promise and keeping a lid on how much he drank. There'd been no crazy antics, no stumbling drunken scenes, no unexplained disappearances at the end of the evening. So far, so good. But she wore her worry like a second skin. Sometimes she'd slip as she had just now, and the anxiety would come spilling out.

'Bitch,' he said succinctly. 'That's what you really think about me, isn't it? That I have no discipline.'

'I'm sorry.' She knelt next to the bed. 'Do you hate me?'

293

Nino couldn't hold a grudge for long. 'No, I don't hate you,' he relented. 'Come back to bed.'

She sneaked a peek at her watch, saw she had a couple of minutes to spare, and lay down beside him. 'Nino?'

'Shh, I'm busy, *cara*,' he whispered, nuzzling her cheek and lips. 'You smell wonderful.'

'Nino,' she tried again, 'at the party tonight – '

'Party?' he mumbled, kissing her earlobe. 'What party?'

Dani sighed inaudibly. 'The one we're giving for the two hundred or so people who helped make Hot Flash such a huge success, remember?'

'Oh, *that* party . . .' He rolled away from her. 'I'm warning you, Dani. Don't – I repeat, *don't* – tell me not to drink. I'm a big boy and – '

She laid her index finger against his lips. 'Shh, it's nothing like that. I have a favor to ask. Please be nice to Barbara Hester.'

He groaned. 'Agh, that dreadful girl.'

Nino, who usually adored any woman with a nice figure and a pretty face, had taken an instant dislike to Barbara.

'That dreadful girl is the genius who thought up the name for the new line. What do you have against her, anyway?'

'She's a phony. I hate phonies. I can spot them a mile away.'

He wasn't altogether wrong. Just the other day Dani had taken Barbara to lunch at the Four Seasons. An autograph hound, wearing a Hot Flash jumpsuit and Hot Flash red nail polish, had stopped at their table and stuck a napkin under Dani's nose.

'You don't mind, do you?' she'd gushed.

'Not at all,' Dani had replied, scrawling her signature.

'It happens all the time, right, Dani?' Bunny had chimed in, giggling conspiratorially.

Afterward she had wondered about Barbara's comment. It was almost as if she'd wanted to make it seem as if they were close friends. Or maybe it was just her misguided enthusiasm and naïveté.

Monika, too, had her doubts about Barbara, whom she called 'pushy.'

But in a funny way, Barbara reminded Dani of herself – smart and ambitious but with a streak of insecurity that sometimes made her work overtime to prove she belonged, whereas Monika and Nino, who'd been brought up so absolutely sure of their place in the world, had little tolerance for Barbara's lack of polish.

'Nino, please promise me you'll be your usual charming self with her.'

'*Si, cara*, for you – anything.' He kissed her hard on the mouth, then threw back the quilt and pointed to his partially erect cock. 'Look.'

'Nice,' she said, her defenses weakening. It was so cold outside, so warm and pleasant here in bed. And what Nino had to offer was very tempting. 'I suppose I could run tomorrow morning.'

Nino reached underneath her turtleneck to undo her bra. 'I suppose you could,' he said, fondling her nipple. 'I promise, it'll be worth the wait.'

Magee collared Reggie at the elevators just as he was leaving to attend the quarterly Megacorp board of directors meeting at their corporate headquarters in Rockefeller Center.

'Reggie!' She was gasping for breath. 'Wait a sec!'

'What is it?' he asked, irritated by the delay. Although he was officially the president and chief executive officer of his corporation, at a salary of a million a year, he was shrewd enough to realize it wasn't smart to keep the big boys waiting. Especially when he was coming armed with

295

a very important shopping list of demands. He glanced at his gold Rolex.

'Listen, I just got off the phone . . . some really bad news on Malinda,' Magee huffed. 'She was hit by a car in the Village last night and is in a coma at Saint Vincent's.'

That was *bad* news. Malinda Mayer was a nineteen-year-old blond Nebraska girl turned Ford model whom Mr Reggie, Inc., was paying over $600,000 a year to represent them in their ads.

'Oh, Jesus – what a moron! How could she do this to me?' he snarled.

'Reggie! For God's sake, the girl is *dying*.'

'Oh, don't be so dramatic, Magee. Anyway, couldn't this have waited? Did you have to tell me now?'

Magee ignored her boss's truculence. 'I'm going downtown to visit her. What kind of flowers do you want to send?'

'Who cares?' he said as the elevator door opened in front of him. 'Just don't send lilies of the valley.'

He swept into Megacorp's fourteenth-floor boardroom five minutes late and shed his full-length sable coat on the empty chair next to him.

'Nice coat, Reggie,' commented the chairman, Frank Gladstone.

Reggie knew what that meant: *If it weren't for us, kid, you wouldn't be wearing sable, and don't forget it.* But he refused to be intimidated by these clowns in their boring three-piece Brooks Brothers suits. They needed him as much as he needed their money.

'I'm sorry I'm late,' he said, his voice thick with distress. 'But one of our models was in a dreadful car accident. She may be dying. I've been at the hospital all morning talking to her doctors, the family . . . Such a horrible tragedy.'

'That's too bad,' said Gladstone. 'How's it going to affect your ad campaign?'

'Small delay until we find a replacement,' Reggie said, pouring himself a glass of water. 'But don't worry. She's not the only face who can sell Mr Reggie. In fact, I'm not even sure she's right for the new sportswear line, so this may be a blessing in disguise.'

'Good.' Gladstone nodded, pleased by Reggie's pragmatic approach. 'There are plenty of pretty faces out there. This time do yourself a favor and hire someone who *is* right for the line. And before you leave, give my secretary all the information. We'll want to send our corporate condolences if she dies.'

'Of course. Now, gentlemen,' he said without stopping to take a breath, 'I'd like to propose something I've thought about for a very long time.'

'Reggie, we have an agenda,' Gladstone sternly reminded him. 'This is highly irregular of you.'

'Please, indulge me.' Reggie flashed the chairman his most charming smile. 'This project is *very* close to my heart. I hope you'll agree with me that the time has come . . .'

Before Gladstone had a chance to say another word, Reggie had pulled twelve folders out of his briefcase and was signaling to one of the assistants to pass them around the table.

'What you're getting,' he explained proudly, 'is my architect's preliminary rendering of the first Mr Reggie store . . . not just a boutique, but a full-fledged store that will sell nothing but Mr Reggie products. What better way to sell and promote this line than through stores we can control? Instead of fighting for retail space in Saks or Macy's, we'll have an alternative . . .'

As Reggie extolled the possibilities, the board members exchanged knowing glances. It was no secret to anyone who read the trades that Dani diPortanova was preparing to open two signature stores, one in New York and another in Beverly Hills. They'd been wondering how long it would be before Reggie approached them about stores of his own, and they were ready for him.

'Reggie,' Gladstone cut in, 'what you're saying is that Countess diPortanova is starting up retail operations, therefore you want to do the same, right?'

Reggie could barely mask his contempt for Gladstone's limited imagination. God, how he hated these corporate types. Always making comparisons, never able to forget the bottom line and soar with him to the limits of creativity.

'Not exactly,' he replied. 'From what I hear, her stores will be nothing more than tacky dumps. Mine – I mean, ours – would be housed in a landmark building, an old mansion, perhaps, with a look that speaks of very old money. Very chic. Very understated. Much like my own home.'

'Reggie, we did some checking of our own,' Gladstone lied. '*Our* sources tell us that Countess Dani's stores will be loss leaders. No way will she recoup her investment for quite some time.'

'Really?' Reggie asked, a smirk on his face. He couldn't wait to tell Mitchell Barton. Still, just because hers were projected to lose money didn't mean his would. After all, he was a far more renowned designer, an American institution . . .

'Of course you are better known,' Gladstone said, ready to throw Reggie a bone. 'I think we're all in agreement that it's time to expand, but not with risky signature stores. We'd rather develop a cash cow.'

Reggie nodded. He liked that phrase, cash cow.

'We want to create a new division: Mr Reggie Cosmetics, the cornerstone product being a very expensive fragrance that will knock the socks off anything else in the market. Face care, makeup, and hair care products will complement the fragrance and round out the line.'

'A fragrance?' Reggie yawned. 'You mean a cologne that you'd advertise as a stocking stuffer or give away as a free sample with bronzer? Oh, no. I could never put my name on something like that . . . it just wouldn't do. Besides, I don't know the first thing about fragrances.'

Frank Gladstone had anticipated Reggie's reaction. He snapped his fingers, and an aide read off the projected first-year revenues . . . revenues in the millions.

That changed everything.

'Really?' Reggie said with a sigh, studying his well-manicured fingernails.

So what if he didn't know a thing about fragrances? There were companies that did nothing but throw different ingredients into test tubes to create new smells. Certainly Dani diPortanova hadn't developed Hot Flash herself.

'Well, it *is* tempting, but I must have final approval of the fragrance, which must reflect *my* sensibility. It must have my special stamp on it. And, of course, a name that's as worthy as my own.'

'Actually,' Gladstone said as he delivered his clinching argument, 'we were thinking of calling it "Mr Reggie."'

Reggie flushed pink. Yes, of course. The perfect name. Classy, instantly recognizable. A completely marketable commodity. Just like himself.

'I think that might work,' he conceded.

Los Angeles

From day one, the Countess Dani New York store had seemed destined for success. Through a friend who handled commercial real estate, Dani had rented space, at an affordable price per square foot, in the southeast first-floor corner of the Plaza Hotel. Happily, the location put her right where she had envisioned herself – just a few quick steps from Bergdorf Goodman and Bendel's, at the northern end of the Fifth Avenue carriage-trade shopping district.

She had sailed smoothly through the complicated maze of hiring an architect and a contractor, then filling out and filing the building permits. Each step in the process had gone smoothly. Every problem was quickly resolved. She planned to open the store on February 14, 1981 – a Valentine's Day present to New York. She had no reason to suspect that wouldn't happen.

On the other hand, the LA store on Rodeo Drive was a complete disaster from day one.

'Is this God's way of punishing me for my arrogance in opening two stores at once?' she had asked Nino, after cataloging for him the latest set of seemingly unavoidable mishaps. 'The contractor tells me we're now three months behind schedule.'

'The contractor is probably robbing you blind' was Nino's analysis of the situation. 'I'll talk to him.'

'Thanks, but no. I should be the one to talk to him. It's *my* store, *my* responsibility.'

Once a month through the spring and summer, she had flown to LA to see how far the construction had progressed. Each time she went, she asked Monika to come along. Each time Monika declined the invitation.

'What about Rick? You two haven't seen each other in

300

ages. Absence makes the heart grow fonder, but this is ridiculous.'

'Rick who?' Monika's laugh had sounded more bitter than amused. 'I can't even remember the last time we spoke.'

Frequently Dani doubted her own sanity. Why hadn't somebody advised her against taking the plunge into retail, especially this double-barreled plunge? The answer to that was simple: She hadn't stopped to ask anyone. Hadn't it always been her policy to leap before she looked? And hadn't it always worked?

But at what cost? she asked herself, feeling increasingly anxious about being spread so thin. Worry number one, of course, was Nino. Every time his nose was stuffed and he blamed it on allergies, she suspected him of snorting coke. He was drinking again, too. And more than just a little.

As if she didn't have enough problems, the goddam contractor was giving her a hard time. The guy was a male chauvinist pig who talked down to her and calmly handed her excuses that insulted her intelligence. It was October already, and there wasn't a snowball's chance in hell the store would be ready for her target date of December first.

The electric saws whirred around her, and the whine of drills and pounding hammers *sounded* impressive, but as far as she could see, almost no progress had been made since her September inspection. The second floor was still a shambles, none of the plumbing was working properly, and they hadn't even begun to bleach the floors or the woodwork.

What exactly was this contractor doing all day? He was charging her a fortune for every hour his crew was supposedly on the job. Construction costs had already exceeded her original projections by 30 percent.

It was time to kick ass.

Victor, the contractor, assured her he was doing his best. She had to understand that it wasn't his fault they were three months behind schedule. 'The marble from Italy was late, and the plumber lost his wife in a fire,' he said when asked to explain the most recent delays.

If he wasn't lying through his teeth, she wasn't the woman who'd created the Drop Dress.

'I'm tellin' ya, honestly, Countess, a Christmas openin' is impossible.'

'It may be impossible for you, Victor, but it won't be impossible for another contractor,' she spat out. 'You've made excuses every step of the way. Your delays have cost me money – real money. You're fired.'

Victor stared at her. Was the broad fuckin' crazy? Firing him halfway through the goddam project? He'd built half the stores on fuckin' Rodeo Drive. Nobody fired Victor. He told her so.

'I just did,' she informed him. 'Get these men off my property and get the hell out of here. I'll see you in court.'

A phone jangled nearby. Victor grabbed for it. 'Hello? Yeah? Yeah, hold on.' He handed Dani the receiver. 'For you.'

'Yes? Hello, who is this? Wait . . . I can't hear you. Hold on a second.' She clamped her hand over the phone and shouted at the workers, 'Hey, you might as well quit now. I just fired your boss.'

The place got quiet quickly. She went back to her phone call.

It was her housekeeper, Elvira, in New York, stammering about Mr Nino not feeling well. A car had dropped him off.

'Is he sick, Elvira? What are you telling me?'

Finally Dani managed to pry it out of her: Nino, dead

drunk, had been dumped out of a speeding car in front of the Dakota.

'But not to worry, ma'am,' Elvira assured her. 'The doorman – Harry, it was – managed to get him inside the guardhouse and called me right away.'

Dani's lunch threatened to come up on her as she pictured Nino sprawled flat on his face like a burned-out bum. 'Whose car was it? What kind of crazy maniacs throw people out of cars?' she asked, frantic with worry.

'I . . . I don't know, ma'am. And Mr Nino's fast asleep. I just checked on him.'

'Did you call a doctor?'

'No, ma'am, I wanted to call you first.'

'Right, that was very good of you, Elvira,' Dani said mechanically. *Think!* she ordered herself. *Think what to do next. This isn't so difficult.*

Victor, waiting to continue their conversation, had planted himself a few feet away. The workmen stood around grinning at her as if she had a green face and purple hair. She ignored their stares and concentrated on the phone conversation.

'I'll call Dr Feld and tell him to be in touch with you if he thinks it's necessary. In the meantime, keep an eye on my husband. I'll be here or at the Beverly Hills Hotel. If there's a problem, find me. As soon as Nino wakes up, have him call me, all right?'

'Yes, ma'am.'

Dani could imagine Elvira in New York, nodding and twisting her apron, the way she did when she was nervous.

'And Elvira?'

'Yes, ma'am?'

'Thank you, Elvira . . . for everything.'

Dani hung up the phone. Thank God her housekeeper was so devoted to Nino. The stories that woman could tell

. . . She hoped Elvira never decided to write a book or talk to the tabloids.

A message from Nino was waiting for her when she got back to her bungalow at the Beverly Hills. She sat down cross-legged on the king-sized bed and with shaking hands dialed their number.

Nino answered on the second ring.

Dani burst into tears.

'Calm down,' he coaxed her. 'I haven't died yet.'

'That's not funny,' she snapped. 'You were thrown out of a car, Nino. You could have been killed. Who were those people?'

'No one special. Just people. Friends.'

'Friends? *Friends?*' she demanded, her voice rising to a shriek. 'You were buying cocaine, weren't you, Nino? And you were drunk! Falling-down dead drunk! How could you? After all your promises, how could you, Nino? Don't you care about yourself . . . about us? Or don't you give a good goddam about anything?'

'*Cara* – '

'Don't, Nino. Don't try to sweet-talk me. Not this time. Now, listen to me – '

'Dani! Shut up and listen to *me*. I understand you're scared and worried, and I wasn't about to sweet-talk you. What happened today was very bad. I *know* that.'

'You do?' She sniffled.

'I may be an alcoholic, but I'm not stupid. And I know what I have to do. I've already been in touch with Silver Hill. I'm readmitting myself tomorrow afternoon.'

Dani clutched at the telephone as if it were her lifeline to sanity. 'That's . . . that's wonderful. I'm so glad. Do you want me to come with you?' She was already reaching into the closet for her overnight case. 'I can be packed and ready to leave LA in half an hour.'

'What about the store? And all your business appointments?'

'The hell with all of that. You need me.'

'That simple?'

'That simple.'

'Okay. Then I'll see you in the morning . . . Dani?'

'Yes?'

'I'm going to beat this thing this time.'

'I know you will, Nino. And I love you. I always will.'

New York

Bunny was on a roll. First, the new job. Second, the kudos she got for coming up with Hot Flash. Third, she was collecting men as if they were so many business cards to stick in her Rolodex. She wasn't choosy. If the man was prominent and powerful, she dated him.

For Bunny, meeting men was like a game of dominoes. A stockbroker introduced her to an attorney who put her in touch with an investment banker who inadvertently set her up with the head of his investment banking firm. What interested her wasn't so much the companionship or sex but what her dates could offer her – gifts she would never have bought herself, dinner at the trendiest, most expensive restaurants, tickets to the best Broadway shows, occasional weekends in the Hamptons, Palm Beach, and the Caribbean. No more schlocky third-rate hotels like the Grapefruit Tree, thank you very much, Irving Blatt. From here on in, she was traveling strictly first class.

The ultimate goal, of course, was to meet and marry a man who was not merely wealthy but downright filthy disgustingly rich. A man who was drenched in money, who had so much money he had no idea how much he was worth.

And so she circulated.

Her current beau, as she always referred to her boy-friends, was a thirty-four-year-old mergers and acquisi-tions specialist, Hollis Worthington III. Bunny loved dating a man whose name ended in a numeral, who had graduated from the right schools – Choate and Yale – and whose parents, Main Line Philadelphians, were fre-quently mentioned in *Town & Country*.

Bunny took it for granted that Hollis was madly in love with her. Given the proper encouragement, he could probably stand up to his snooty family and marry her. But sweet as Hollis was, he wasn't Mr Right. True, he had gobs of money, but he still had to work for a living.

'Everything's tied up in trusts,' he had once explained to her.

Well, what the hell good were trusts if a guy couldn't get his hands on them whenever he felt the itch to spend? She wanted to marry a man like Nino, who worked only for the fun of it.

One point in Hollis's favor was that he seemed to dislike sex almost as much as she did. When they 'did it,' as Hollis would say, they invariably stuck to the mission-ary position – unless Hollis was drunk. Then he'd lurch his way south and munch on her pussy like a puppy gobbling up Alpo. Still, Bunny endured. She'd suffered far worse.

Besides, Hollis took her to such lovely places. The Helmsley Palace for afternoon tea. The Hotel Carlyle to hear Bobby Short. Regine's for dinner and dancing. Opening night at the Met. And one memorable night, to an anonymous-looking town house on the East Side that Bunny mistook for a private home.

'Honey, who lives here?' she whispered as a uniformed

servant ushered them into an opulently appointed foyer, the centerpiece of which was a chandelier dripping with crystal prisms.

Hollis chuckled indulgently. 'This is a club, Barbara, a very exclusive club that very few people in this city even know about.'

Through a doorway that led into a large room Bunny caught glimpses of men in tuxedos and women wearing designer gowns.

'What kind of club, Hollis?' she asked, unnerved by the possibility that this could be one of the notorious swingers' sex clubs she'd read about. She peered closer and found the answer to her question.

'Hollis, honey,' she drawled, 'this is a gambling club. You know that a little old working girl like me can't afford to gamble away money.'

Hollis patted her arm and steered her over to the gleaming brass elevator. 'Don't worry. I'll give you plenty to play with. Fourth floor, please,' he told the elevator operator. 'Big time tonight, Barbara,' he said with a wink.

Bunny simpered obligingly. First floor, fourth floor, it was all the same to her. God, she was tired. Her shoes were killing her. She couldn't wait to take off her bra and panty hose and snuggle up in bed with a good book.

While Hollis ordered drinks from the bar, Bunny took a long look around her. If only she had *half* the money it must have cost to decorate the place! 'Ready to roll?' asked Hollis, returning with her ginger ale.

'Hollis,' she said, 'will you excuse me? I have to go to the little girls' room.'

'All right, meet you over there at the baccarat table.'

The ladies' room was as elegant as the rest of the club. Dusty rose moiré fabric covered the walls. The vanities were lit with just the right kind of face-flattering light. From poring over the pages of *Architectural Digest*,

Bunny recognized the love seat as Chippendale and the washbasins as Sherle Wagner. A black woman in a maid's uniform was handing out fancy guest soaps and hot towels to the patrons.

Damn, Bunny thought. Why did they always put help in the rest rooms? Now she would have to give her a tip . . . and Hollis hadn't given her any spending money yet. Well, maybe she wouldn't tip the maid. After all, she didn't need any help wiping her hands.

Naturally, just because she had to pee like crazy, every one of the stalls was taken. She fluffed her blond locks in the mirror while she waited. She hoped this wouldn't be a late night. If Hollis wanted to have sex, she would tell him she had her period. She sure hoped he wasn't keeping track; she'd already used the excuse twice in the past six weeks.

She sighed. When the hell was somebody coming out? Impatiently she called out, 'Excuse me . . . are you going to be in there much longer?'

'I'll be right out,' replied a voice from behind one of the doors.

A familiar voice.

The toilet flushed, the door opened, and Bunny gasped. 'Why, Monika,' she said sweetly. 'What a surprise.'

Barbara Hester was about the last person in the world Monika ever expected to run into at Lucky's. 'What are you doing here?' she demanded, nervously clutching her diamond choker.

'Well, it *is* a free country,' Bunny snapped. 'Besides, my beau, Hollis Worthington the Third, is a member. Who are you with?'

Monika ignored the question. 'So lovely to see you, Barbara,' she said, pushing past her and hurrying out.

What was with that bitch? Barbara wondered.

Hollis had moved over to the craps table and was just

throwing a pair of dice when Bunny sidled up next to him. Across the way, Monika was seated at the oval baccarat table, her attention intently focused on the table's shoe, which was being passed in front of her.

'Hollis, honey,' Bunny purred. 'Do you see that woman over there, the blonde in the blue satin gown?'

Hollis glanced over. 'You mean Monika?'

Bunny covered up her surprise. 'Do you know her? She works with me. I ran into her in the ladies' room. It's just so funny to see her here.'

'Oh, she's here all the time. I hear she spends a fortune at the tables.'

'Yes, well, she's *very* wealthy. One of the von Reichs, you know.'

Hollis smiled knowingly. 'She'd better be very wealthy, the way she plays. She can't stay away from the tables. She was doing so well downstairs, they made her join the Fourth Floor Club. But apparently she isn't doing as well up here.'

Bunny decided to quiz him about the Fourth Floor Club another time. 'You don't think she's in trouble, do you?' she asked with grave concern.

'Who knows?' Hollis shrugged. 'I know *I* certainly couldn't drop that kind of money as regularly as she does. Here, want to roll the dice yourself?'

'Sure,' Bunny said enthusiastically. 'Hollis, this is such fun! I'm so glad you brought me here. This is such an education.'

'Stick with me, Barbara,' Hollis chortled.

'Oh, you know I will.'

But only for as long as she had to.

Silver Hill, Connecticut

On Christmas Day Dani drove out to Silver Hill to visit Nino. As a reward for the steady progress he'd been making in his battle against alcohol, he'd been given permission to leave the grounds. He and Dani decided to celebrate Christmas by having dinner at the Silvermine Tavern, a rustic New England-style restaurant overlooking a frozen brook and a snow-dusted field.

Dani had called ahead to reserve a table near the blazing fireplace, which added to the cozy atmosphere.

'Christmas in the country. You can almost hear Bing Crosby singing . . . Pretty tree, isn't it?' Dani pointed to the fir tree decorated with hundreds of tiny crystal balls and tinsel.

'Mmm. You're prettier,' said Nino, leaning over to kiss her. He turned to the waitress and asked, 'Isn't she?'

The waitress smiled. 'I recognized you as soon as you walked in, Countess. I know you from your ads. Your jeans are the *best*! Can I bring you two something to drink?'

'Yes,' Nino said right away.

Dani held her breath.

'Perrier with lime, please.' He smiled at Dani. 'And for you?'

'I'll have the same.'

'*Cara*, you really don't have to – '

'I need to keep my wits about me for the drive home.'

The dinner was delicious, the service excellent. But Dani was so absorbed in the unaccustomed pleasure of seeing Nino sober that afterward she could hardly remember what she'd eaten.

She entertained him with stories about the latest goings-on at Countess Dani. By now the battle lines had been clearly drawn between Monika and Barbara Hester.

310

'They're like oil and fire. If they end up in the same room, there are bound to be fireworks.'

'*Bene*. A little competition is good for your business. Now, what's the latest on the LA store?'

The albatross around her neck. She'd made good on her promise to take the contractor to court, but as for opening the shop by Christmas – she'd had to forget that. The new man she'd hired had sworn he could get the job done by mid-March.

'The Ides of March.' Nino chuckled.

'As in "beware of." But what about you?'

'I feel great,' he assured her. He was full of plans. 'I've decided to enter that race I told you about, the one in Buenos Aires in June. I can't wait to start training.'

'Has your doctor said anything about how much longer you'll be at Silver Hill?'

'He says it's up to me now . . . whenever I want to leave.'

'And . . .?'

Nino shrugged. 'Another couple of weeks. This time I want to do it right. I want to wait until I'm *sure* I'm ready. But don't worry, I'll be home before Valentine's Day.'

'I wasn't even thinking of that.' He knew her so well. The opening-night party for her flagship store at the Plaza was on schedule for February 14. She hadn't wanted to put pressure on him by mentioning it, but she was dying for Nino to be there with her.

He deserved to be. Without him, she never could have accomplished all that she had.

Pulling up in front of the Dakota later that evening, she found herself wishing she'd accepted one of the many invitations she'd received for the Christmas-night get-togethers. She'd given the staff a couple of days' vacation, and both floors of the apartment were eerily silent and empty. She hadn't even bothered to put up a tree.

Decorating the tree was something she and Nino had always done together, and besides, she'd been so busy.

If only Monika was in town, she thought disconsolately, poking around in the refrigerator for a bite to eat. But Monika had gone skiing in Utah.

'I must be getting sentimental,' she'd told Dani. 'I'm longing for an old-fashioned *gemütlich* Christmas. But not like the ones from my childhood,' she'd said with a grimace. 'At home we had the dreariest holidays. Karola always complained that the holidays only interrupted business, and our dog, Heinzie, would get confused by the Christmas tree and do his business indoors. Then Mother would go on a rampage.'

Dani laughed now, remembering Monika's stories. Maybe she should call Maurice and Eunice. No. She'd invited them to dinner on New Year's Eve. Two evenings in one week were more than she could take of Eunice.

She was being silly, she decided. She was Jewish. Christmas wasn't even her holiday.

In the end, she fixed herself a toasted bagel with smoked salmon, made a big bowl of popcorn, and opened a bottle of Chianti. Then she settled down in bed to watch *It's a Wonderful Life* on the VCR.

At the climax of the movie, when the whole town showed up at Jimmy Stewart's house to lend him their money and support, she began to sob as if she'd lost her best friend.

But why? she wondered, sniffling into a tissue. What did *she* have to cry about? Her life was wonderful. She lacked for nothing. And it was only going to get better and better . . .

Just when the social elite were sinking into the post-holiday doldrums, Dani kicked off 1980 with the splashiest party of the year. Three hundred people, from the mayor on down, received hand-delivered heart-shaped boxes of Godiva chocolates along with red velvet invitations to the opening of Countess Dani in the Plaza on the night of Valentine's Day.

'I love New York and my new shop at the Plaza!' proclaimed the invitations. 'Be a sweetheart and help me celebrate.' Dani had autographed each and every invitation with her now famous signature.

The ambience at the Plaza store was comfortable, warm, and friendly. The color scheme was subdued – ivory, tan, and sandy pink, with mauve accents. The furnishings were mostly French country pieces, bleached to their original natural finish. Overstuffed love seats and armchairs invited weary shoppers to sit down and revive their spirits with a cup of coffee or tea and petits fours served from sterling silver tea carts.

Countess Dani lingerie, sweaters, and tops in every size and color spilled out of the open drawers of antique pine chests. One corner of the shop was devoted to Hot Flash clothes and cosmetics. Models had been hired to wander about the shop, showing off the latest designs.

Tonight, in honor of Valentine's Day, red roses covered every surface, and red-foil helium balloons floated above the guests' heads. Each female guest would take home a specially designed heart-shaped crystal decanter of Hot Flash perfume to commemorate the occasion.

No expense had been spared to satisfy the party-jaded appetites of the invitees. There were magnums of vintage Dom Pérignon; mountains of beluga caviar served with sour cream and blini; wheels of the finest cheeses from all over the world; grapes, kiwi, strawberries, and raspberries flown in from New Zealand; and platters of heart-shaped Godiva chocolates, which had arrived only that morning from Belgium.

Dani swirled through the crowds in a clingy red silk

strapless evening gown of her own design. Her long hair was pinned back with a diamond and ruby clip, and she wore ruby earrings and a Barry Kieselstein-Cord sterling silver bracelet around one upper arm.

She was having the time of her life.

'I'm so delighted you could come,' she greeted the mayor. 'How am I doing?'

'Beautiful store,' the mayor declared, living up to his reputation as New York's number one gourmand as he helped himself to yet another heaping spoonful of the tiny pearl gray caviar and a generous scoop of sour cream. 'But I'm glad I don't have to pay the bills on it.'

Dani laughed. 'My accountant wishes I didn't have to, either! Try the raspberries with crème fraîche. It'll make you forget the budget crisis.'

Actually, she reflected as she turned to greet more of her guests, what she'd just told the mayor was only partly true. Her financial people had done an analysis of the market, and the results had convinced Dani and her accountant that within two years the New York shop could be turning a profit. The truth was, she didn't give a damn about the losses because her gut told her the store was in the right place at the right time.

She caught sight of her father chatting with the chairman of Lord & Taylor and wondered whether he was thinking, as she was, about Sophie. If only her mother could have lived to see this night. How she would have enjoyed knowing that her daughter had taken her place among the exalted ranks of Fifth Avenue retailers.

Nino, just back from Watkins Glen, where he'd spent a few days on the track with his Alfa Romeo Tipo 33, was making his first public appearance since his release from Silver Hill. The columnists were badgering him to admit that he was a drug addict, but Nino was taking their questions with good grace and a glass of ginger ale.

314

Finally he made his escape and materialized at Dani's side. 'Do you feel like Cinderella?' he whispered.

'Cinderella? Maybe . . . Barbara! How are you?' she greeted Barbara Walters with an airy kiss on both cheeks.

The paparazzi and Minicams captured the moment for the national news programs and tabloids.

'Dani, you look marvelous,' Barbara said. 'And the store! Too bad it wasn't ready in time for the show! The audience would have loved it.'

'Well, that's a good reason for a return engagement.'

Dani had appeared the week before on a Barbara Walters Special. The show had featured three tough women who'd become successful on their own terms, and she had shared the billing with Diana Ross and Jane Fonda.

Dani had talked candidly, sometimes painfully, about herself, her business, her marriage. Years ago, she'd told the television audience, Seventh Avenue had whispered that she was just another celebrity of the moment, one of the handful of promising young talents who blazed each season, then disappeared in a rash of bad debts and undelivered orders before the next season's Fashion Week rolled around.

Behind her back they'd predicted that she would drown in a sea of problems and bad press. And God knows, she had had her share of setbacks and depressed seasons. But each time she'd searched her soul and found the strength to bounce back and prove her detractors wrong.

'And I hope to continue to prove them wrong for as long as I'm in this business.'

The special had been the runaway ratings winner for the week, a fact that Barbara acknowledged with a raised glass of champagne. 'With those ratings,' she assured Dani, 'you're welcome any time!'

315

Other guests approached them to bestow their all-important seals of approval.

'I *love* the colors!' burbled a tall blond model from Texas. Her boyfriend, a sour-looking, infamous English rock star, eyed Dani appreciatively.

'What a simply marvelous location, darling,' gushed the perky co-hostess of a local morning talk show.

'It certainly beats Madison Avenue,' chimed the wife of a real-estate and hotel mogul.

Bunny hovered just behind Dani and Nino, almost hyperventilating from the shocking pleasure of being within spitting distance of Barbara Walters. She'd almost taken a step forward so that Dani could introduce her, but had chosen instead to stay in the background, perfectly positioned to be captured by the photographers and video journalists.

A TV reporter descended on Dani and Nino with an outstretched microphone, and Bunny was blinded by the blazing lights from the Minicam. She smiled ingratiatingly and wondered how many of the folks back in Henderson would catch her on television. She could just imagine the expressions on their faces when they recognized her, little ole Bunny Rae Hester, dressed to kill in a sexy black number by Calvin Klein and looking right at home in the midst of the most glamorous party of the year.

'Would you look at that little bitch, trying to worm her way into Dani's limelight?' Monika muttered to Kim.

Kim checked out the scene and said, 'She's too much. But somebody ought to tell her black's not her color.'

'*Ja*,' Monika agreed happily. 'Makes her look totally washed out.'

'She doesn't miss a trick, does she?' Kim noted as Bunny preened for the camera.

That was precisely what concerned Monika. Early in life, as a defense against Karola, she'd learned to watch

316

out for people, women especially, who thrived on intrigue and manipulation. Her alarm bells rang a loud warning whenever Barbara went into action, and she'd kept a nervous eye on the girl ever since they'd bumped into each other at Lucky's.

'Well, *you* look smashing. Red definitely works on you,' Kim assured Monika. 'Let me guess – Ungaro, right?'

'Right.' Monika nodded, wishing she felt half as good as she looked. In the midst of all this celebration and triumph, it was all she could do not to burst into tears.

'Tonight is for *both* of us,' Dani had said earlier in the day. 'As you've so often reminded me, we are very lucky, *ja*?'

'*Ja*, very.'

'I couldn't have done it without you, Monika. You know that, don't you?'

Maybe so, but she could hardly summon up the energy to match Dani's excitement. During the last month or two, she'd lost a bundle at the club, which was no big deal. Nobody's winning streak lasted forever. And it wasn't as if she was *deeply* in debt, though the rate of interest Lucky's charged her credit line was exorbitant. Unconscionable, really. But it was manageable, what with the steady income she accrued from her trust fund. Not as steady as it had been, but good enough to keep her going until the dice came up lucky again for her at the baccarat table.

It was only a matter of time.

No, her soon-to-be-repaid gambling debt wasn't the reason she felt as if she were dragging lead weights around after her, as if the smile she'd painted on her face was as phony as a circus clown's grin.

Maybe it was the recent spate of magazine articles

317

about her mother that had appeared in *Newsweek*, *Fortune*, and the *Wall Street Journal*. The bullshit Karola had shoveled out – and the magazines had bought – was enough to make Monika puke.

Karola von Reich . . . proclaimed international businesswoman of the year, a role model for women battling the prejudices of corporate America, '. . . forced to take over her husband's family corporation . . . rose to the challenge in the face of ongoing crisis . . . a woman far ahead of her times . . . a single mother who raised two children,' *Newsweek* had written.

Her public relations machine must have been working overtime to churn out that crap. Karola was probably on the verge of a monumental corporate acquisition and felt she needed the favorable press.

Only the *Wall Street Journal* had done its homework well enough to mention the connection between von Reich Munitions and the Nazi war machine, and to wonder about Karola's apparent estrangement from her two children, and the apparent lack of men in her life.

Well, Monika thought with sour humor, that was one thing she and Karola had in common. *Vogue* and *Glamour* referred to what she didn't have as 'a meaningful relationship.' Sex was easy enough to come by; an escort could be had in the time it took to make a phone call. But love . . . that was a far trickier proposition.

Ah, Rick, why aren't you here with me tonight?

Because he was otherwise engaged downtown at a sold-out show at Madison Square Garden, his first New York appearance since he'd moved to LA and cut two records, the second of which was sure to go platinum. Rick Flood was fast becoming the hottest, most audience-grabbing rock singer since Bruce Springsteen.

A pair of front-row center tickets to the concert had

arrived for her by messenger with a hastily scrawled note from Rick.

'Love to see you. Hope you enjoy the show. Love, Rick.'

Two seats to the hottest show in town, a favor from a former friend and lover. But it hurt that he hadn't called to say hi. She hadn't seen Rick in almost two years, couldn't even remember the last time they'd spoken. Ever since the night she'd picked that stupid fight with him about his backup singer, they'd drifted apart. Her fault, his fault . . . she didn't know anymore. But it didn't matter.

What did matter was that tonight, knowing he was in town, so close by, she missed him. For all of her talk about how different they were, she couldn't imagine anyone she'd rather have by her side.

'Oh, there you are, Monika,' said Buzzy Standish. 'I've been looking all over for you.'

'*Ja*, here I am,' Monika smiled gamely at her date. 'Having fun?'

'Great party. Love it.'

'*Gut*,' said Monika, linking arms with him. 'Let's go mingle. And afterwards we go to Lucky's, okay?'

About a thousand smiles, air kisses, and warm embraces later, when all but the hard-core party-goers and freeloaders were gone, Nino pulled Dani aside. 'Hungry?' he asked.

'Starving!'

'Me, too. Let's go home, raid the refrigerator, and go straight to bed.' He raised one eyebrow and leered at her suggestively.

'Sounds delightful. Let me just make sure everything's under control here. Kim?' she called across the almost empty room. 'If you don't need me anymore – '

'Everything's taken care of. Barbara's volunteered to

319

stay as long as I need her. Leave. Good-bye,' Kim said briskly.

'Okay, okay.' Dani laughed. 'Where's Monika?'

'Must have left.'

'Already?'

'Yes. And so should you.'

'She's tough,' Nino joked, holding the door for Dani.

'That's why I pay her lots of money to be my director of special events.'

Holding hands, they stepped outside into the cold, crisp night air and headed toward their limo, parked in the roadway in front of the hotel.

Though it was already past nine, many lights were still burning in the windows of the General Motors Building on the far side of Grand Army Plaza. On Fifth Avenue the traffic was light at this hour. To their left, looking north, they could see the entrance to Central Park, its perimeter lit up by old-fashioned gas lamps long since converted to electricity.

'Beautiful, isn't it?' Dani sighed. 'I really do love New York.'

'Come,' said Nino, taking her hand and leading her over to the fountain in the middle of the plaza. He fished in his pocket and pulled out a couple of pennies. 'Here, one for you, one for me. Make a wish.'

'What a romantic fool you are,' she teased, loving every one of his sweet sentimental gestures. Her heart felt as if it might burst with happiness and gratitude that they'd reached this moment together. Shutting her eyes, she tossed the coin into the middle of the fountain and stepped into his embrace.

'What did you wish for?' he asked, breathing in the delicious scent of her hair.

'That our joy would never end.'

Chapter Twelve

New York

Reggie deposited his keys on the Regency table in the foyer of his penthouse and sighed with the weary satisfaction of a valiant warrior who'd done his duty in the line of battle. He slipped his aching feet out of his handmade Italian shoes and left them for his housekeeper to pick up.

All afternoon, under the watchful eyes of a couple of bouncer-sized bodyguards, he'd been stuck behind the counter of the newly designed Mr Reggie Cosmetics section at Bloomingdale's, launching his new fragrance, Mr Reggie. Now all he wanted was to take a nice hot soak in his Jacuzzi, to ease his weary bones and wash away the millions of germs passed on to him by the press of people who'd crowded around to share in his glory.

Thanks to the glorious weather on this first official day of spring, the lunchtime event had surpassed even Bloomingdale's most optimistic expectations. At its longest, the line of customers had extended as far as the Lexington Avenue exit. Waiting patiently for the chance to chat with the legend himself were some of his staunchest fans (the ones who wore nothing but Mr Reggie, God bless their souls), as well as hordes of out-of-towners, stopping by to snatch a glimpse of real New York glamour. How he loathed them, with their sweaty hands and hideous hairdos and polyester blouses and eager smiles. They were so gross, so middle class, such an unwelcome reminder of the family he'd left behind in Queens.

They had drooled for his autograph, clutched him, kissed him, pumped his hand until he thought it would fall off. But spring for the hundred fifty bucks to buy his perfume? Forget it! He couldn't wait to be rid of them. Unfortunately, so much of their makeup and cheap perfume had rubbed off on him that he smelled as if he'd just blown in from a Village drag bar.

He dragged himself up the spiral staircase to the third floor of his apartment where the master bedroom and sitting room were located. The sitting room, like the rest of the house, was a luxurious mix of pearwood Biedermeier paneling, mahogany, brass, brushed steel and glass tables, and expensive Chinese carpeting. The room was lined with custom-designed bookcases filled with hardcover best-sellers, most of them unread. Hidden behind an antique Japanese screen was an enormous rear-projection television and VCR unit, on which Reggie could watch his hundreds of videotapes, more than a few of which were hard-core porn. There was also an exercise bicycle, which Reggie swore he'd use but never did, and a drafting table with sketch pads and pencils, also rarely used.

Not that he didn't *want* to sketch. He would have loved to. The problem was those bastards at Megacorp. Gradually, insidiously, Megacorp had been choosing to use fewer and fewer of Reggie's own creations, deferring instead to the design studios of the various divisions. Reggie was irked, and he didn't hesitate to let Frank Gladstone know it. Why the fuck had they bought his company, if not for his designs? After all, *he* was the genius behind the company's success, not the goddam studio heads.

'But of course you are,' Frank Gladstone would croon, all the while thinking, *We bought your name and image, you arrogant asshole.* 'You're the driving force behind every sketch that sees the light of day in this company.'

Then Megacorp would throw him a bone, yet another all-expense-paid excursion – to the Orient, Egypt, the Caribbean, Brazil, Tahiti – to soak up atmosphere and inspire him for new collections. Not that he would design those collections, of course. The execution of his inspirations would be left to the minions in the studio.

At the salary he was drawing, Reggie didn't dare complain too often, though he would have liked to see the Megacorp board members endure just one of these endless promotional personal appearances.

Shedding his tan bespoke suit, purple silk tie, and matching socks, Reggie shouted, 'Rah Rah? Reggie-poo is home!'

Just the thought of sex with Rah Rah in the Jacuzzi, the jet streams of hot water massaging their naked, writhing bodies, was enough to get Reggie's cock stiff. Reggie rubbed himself gently a time or two. 'Rah Rah . . .' he moaned.

The boy wasn't putting out as much as he used to – as much as he ought to – considering the sums of money Reggie paid for his services. At that price, they should have been fucking whenever Reggie wanted it – twice a day, if that was his pleasure.

Angry now, he screamed, 'Rah Rah! Where the fuck are you!'

Still no response. Bad enough that Rah Rah couldn't find the time to be by his side for something as important as the launching of his fragrance. The little hustler could at least have been home to greet him.

Reggie jabbed the button on his intercom, buzzing Lydia downstairs.

'*Si*, Señor Reggie?'

'Where's Rah Rah?'

'Dunno, *señor*. Acting class, mebbe?'

Acting class.

Fuck that. Rah Rah had of late gotten a bug up his ass about becoming an actor. Of all the stupid, cock-eyed notions! Acting was a dog's life – facing constant scrutiny, rejection, humiliation. It was a profession for masochists.

'Don't be stupid,' Reggie had advised when Rah Rah first mentioned that he'd signed up to take acting lessons. 'Why? You're not going to be an actor.'

'I'm bored. I need more stimulation in my life.'

Reggie winced. '*I'm* supposed to be stimulation enough. Besides, what about shopping and working out at the gym? Most boys would die to do just that.'

'What you're describing is a life-style. I want a career.'

'You *had* a career,' Reggie reminded him sternly, 'and I paid heavily to have you give it up. Now you want another one, and I suppose you expect me to pay for that, too.'

'No. I can afford to pay for my lessons.'

'I just bet you can,' Reggie retorted. 'You know what you are, Rah Rah? You're a dilettante, flitting about like a butterfly from one pretty thing to the next. Well, fine. Go ahead. Take your damn lessons. See if I care.'

He cared, but there wasn't much he could do about it. He loved Rah Rah, as much as he was capable of loving anyone. And if Rah Rah wanted to take lessons – though God knew he didn't have a snowball's chance in hell of becoming an actor – then Reggie supposed he'd let him. Better that than having him hang out at the gym where the pretty boys regularly stuffed their phone numbers in his workout pants.

After all the dough he'd paid out to keep Rah Rah in his bed, Reggie hoped that was *all* they stuffed in his boyfriend's pants. What a nightmare – Rah Rah in *love* with another man.

Fuck the Jacuzzi, he needed a drink. He jabbed his intercom. 'Lydia! Bring me a vodka on the rocks.'

So what if he was starting cocktail hour a little early? What the hell, he might even do a line or two of coke. For what he had to put up with from Rah Rah and those idiots at Megacorp, he deserved it.

Los Angeles

Countess Dani on Rodeo Drive finally opened on May 2, four and a half months behind schedule. From day one, the LA ladies flocked to the shop.

Dani had left nothing to chance. Before the shop opened its doors to the general public, she flew west and all but moved into the boutique for three weeks. On the phone most of the day, she called in every favor she could from her friends. For years she'd been giving them free samples of her designs. It was time they paid her back with their patronage.

The Hollywood wives held brunches, luncheons, and dinner parties in her honor, and chatted up the store to all their friends. The LA fashion elite, motivated by curiosity and their desire to be on the cutting edge of whatever was new and hot, dropped by to inspect the premises and 'do something nice for that adorable Dani diPortanova.'

Dani didn't give a damn what their motives were. As long as they spent money and made a habit of coming back, she was happy to have them. If she'd been less of a perfectionist, if she'd had less need to control the whole show, she might have been satisfied by the first month's sales. But she'd never been one to leave well enough alone. So she flew west again in June to do yet another round of publicity appearances and to announce Countess Dani's version of a loss leader.

From experience, she knew that even her wealthiest, most pretentious customers hated to turn down a bargain. Why not use Hot Flash perfume as a lure to increase traffic? She would give away a vial of the fragrance, which normally cost $150 an ounce, with every purchase over $2,000.

Word spread, and the volume for the first week of the giveaway increased by 25 percent.

'You're a genius, Dani,' Nino congratulated her all the way from Argentina, where he was in training to compete in a race later that month. He'd been gone for two weeks, wouldn't be back in New York for another two, and she was missing him desperately.

'Nope,' she said modestly. 'I just know my customers. So what's new in Buenos Aires? Are you having fun? Do you miss me? How'd it go today?'

'Yes, I miss you. Yes, I'm having fun. And it went splendidly today. But I am being such a good boy that my old friends don't recognize me. I've been here two weeks and I haven't been to one nightclub.'

That *was* a change. She said, 'I'm impressed. Nino, I wish I could be there with you, but – '

'I understand, *cara*. Don't worry. Maybe the next race,' Nino said. 'So, what's the gossip in Beverly Hills?'

'Oh, the usual. Who's fucking whom, who's fucking over whom. You know. Speaking of fucking, I bumped into an old friend of Monika's at La Scala – Rick Flood. *Love Handles* just went platinum. I'm having dinner with him tomorrow.'

'*Si? Bene*. Tell him Monika still loves him.'

'What? What on earth are you talking about? How would you know such a thing?'

'*Cara*, in matters of love, I have a sixth sense. Besides,

it's obvious from the look in her eye whenever Rick's name is mentioned.'

Dani wondered whether Nino had picked up on something she'd missed. Monika certainly did seem at loose ends these days, and when they got together outside the office, they inevitably talked shop. When was the last time they'd talked about anything personal? They'd both been so busy . . .

'You tell Rick to come back to New York, *si*?'

'No.' Dani laughed. 'I'll wait for you to tell him, okay?'

'Okay. I love you, *cara*. Talk to you tomorrow, yes?'

'Yes. I love you, too. And Nino?'

'I know. Drive carefully.'

She could hear him chuckling as he hung up the phone. Very funny. Often she wondered how the other racers' wives coped with the terrifying knowledge that their husbands were putting themselves in mortal danger every time they went out on the track. Why, out of all the professions in the world, did he have to choose racing? Because he was Nino, that was why. Nino, who'd almost run her over the very first time they'd met and who had courted her in his Lamborghini doing ninety-five miles an hour on the busiest boulevard in Cannes. She supposed it could have been worse. He could have been a test pilot.

Small consolation.

New York

Monika fanned her face with the sheet of ad copy Ian McAdam wanted her to proofread and return to him by the end of the day. The temperature in her office felt like ninety degrees, and the air conditioner repairman was saying it might be another day or two before he could get the parts he needed. She was dying to go home and take a cold shower. But she still had to proof the ad copy, and after that there were production schedules and the daily billing printouts to review. It never seemed to end.

She loved the business, but some days, like this one, the pressure was almost too much for her, and she would fall asleep in the car-service sedan that drove her home.

She was baking in this damn heat. Her foundation makeup had turned into a beige stream running down her throat, and her pink silk blouse was damp with sweat. When one of the bookkeepers called to say there was a problem with an employee's expense report, she was ready to snap.

'Can't you handle it?' she asked irritably.

'All we do is audit them, Ms von Reich. This looks like it's been padded, so it's something you'll have to take up with the employee.'

Monika sighed. As if she didn't have enough to do. 'Whose is it?'

'Barbara Hester's.'

Monika smiled. *Well, well. This might make the heat a little more bearable.* 'All right,' she said, 'if you'll send it up, I'll look at it right away.'

When the interoffice envelope arrived on her desk, she pushed aside the billing printouts, read through the expense report, and noted the accountant's flag. Barbara had bunched together two bills for the same restaurant, listing them as one item, though she'd eaten at the restaurant on different days. She'd also listed one person for both bills. The sum total was only $148, but the accountant had enclosed copies of the previous months' reports, which showed that Barbara's tabs routinely ran high.

The girl was either networking a lot or living off the company's coffers. Monika suspected it was a little of both. *Gut*, she would enjoy rattling Barbara's cage. She'd

328

always felt uneasy about the girl, especially since that night in the rest room at Lucky's. If she could nail her, all the better. She didn't need a southern-fried snake slithering through the company . . . especially one that she suspected could bite.

Barbara, looking rather withered from the heat, knocked on Monika's office door and entered. 'You wanted to see me?' She folded herself into the cream suede chair in front of Monika's desk.

Monika dabbed her handkerchief across her brow. '*Ja.* Accounting asked me to take a look at your expense report for last month. It seems there's a serious discrepancy here . . .'

Bunny, her insides trembling with fear, listened carefully as Monika went on about the various charges. She should have known better than to pad the goddam thing. How could she have been so stupid? But friends she'd made at other companies told her everyone did it, that it was considered a perk . . . untaxable income. And now they were going to fire her, and she'd have to find another job, without references and with a cloud of scandal hanging over her head.

She could see her dreams being flushed down the toilet, all because of a few lousy dinners she'd treated herself to. *Damn, damn, damn!*

'So,' Monika was saying, 'how do you explain the one listing, even though your American Express receipts show two different dates? And you've listed only one guest, somebody from the Color Institute, for both dinners.'

Bunny decided to go for broke and try to bluff her way out of the mess. 'Actually,' she gulped, 'it's very easy to explain, Monika. I took my contact from the Color Institute out twice, both times to Chez Pierre. I simply added the two tabs together and made one listing because it was easier . . . and since it *was* the same person, I honestly didn't think it mattered how the listing was done as long as it was . . . legitimate.'

The story sounded only vaguely credible to Monika, but short of making some phone calls to check up on Barbara, there was no way to prove she was lying. And if she did call around, she and the company could easily end up looking foolish and ridiculously cheap.

'*Ja*,' she said, not yet willing to concede defeat, 'I'm *sure* you were concerned with it being legitimate. Be warned, Barbara. We treat fraud very seriously around here. Any improprieties will result in your immediate dismissal.'

Bunny bristled. How dare this Austrian bitch threaten her when she was so valuable to the company! She'd show her a thing or two about threats! 'Believe me, Monika, the figures are legitimate. I'm not going to *gamble* away my chances in this company for a few dollars . . . which is more than I can say for some other people.'

'Exactly what do you mean by that?'

'Oh, nothing . . .' Bunny smiled and fanned herself lazily. 'It's just that I wonder how Dani and the banks who lend us money would feel if they knew that one of the people in charge of the company's cash flow gambles her own cash away almost every night. I mean, if you do it with your own . . . well, who knows . . .?'

Monika stared coldly at Barbara. The girl was a far bigger problem than she'd imagined. She had unbelievable balls. 'Listen to me. What I do on my own time is my business. It doesn't affect my performance or this company. Is that perfectly clear?'

Bunny stood up. 'Whatever you say, honey. But I'm willing to *bet* that one day it will. *Auf Wiedersehen*, Monika.'

Monika watched in disbelief as Barbara sauntered out.

* * *

330

The call came at eight in the morning, just as Dani was leaving for work. It was a reporter from Reuters. She couldn't believe what he was telling her.

'But surely you've heard already, Countess. Someone *must* have phoned you by now . . .'

Nino.

A race car crash.

Dead.

In Buenos Aires.

There wasn't enough air to breathe in her bedroom. The walls felt as if they were caving in on her. 'But . . . but I don't understand. There must be some mistake. I just spoke to him yesterday. He's going to call me today as soon as the race is over.'

'Terribly sorry to have to be the one,' said the reporter. 'I say, are you all right, Countess?'

Dani gently replaced the receiver and stumbled out of her room. Elvira, ashen-faced, was hurrying toward her down the hallway.

'Ma'am, I just put on the telly to catch the news and – '

'No,' Dani whispered. 'It's not true! It *can't* be true!'

Tears were streaming down her housekeeper's cheeks, and then Dani was crying, too. 'Maybe it's a mistake, Elvira. Maybe it was someone else. Did they say his name?'

The housekeeper, who'd loved Nino as if he were her own son, nodded wordlessly. Only her outstretched arms prevented Dani from crumpling to the floor.

Her worst nightmare had come true. Nino had been racing in a field of twenty at the Buenos Aires Autodrome before a crowd of fifty thousand fans. Three laps remained in the race. Nino was neck and neck with a Swedish driver. The two cars approached the dangerous high-banking turn at the north end of the oval. Just as the

Swedish driver was closing in, Nino had a blowout. Traveling at 170 miles per hour, his Alfa Romeo Tipo 33 fishtailed, then roared out of control, flipping over and over until it burst into flames.

He was dead before they pulled him out of the wreckage.

The next few hours were filled with frantic phone calls and activity, which Dani watched through a haze of grief. At some point her father appeared with Eunice, and then Monika was there, looking as if the wind had been knocked out of her. The three of them banded together to shield Dani as best they could from the flood of phone calls and telegrams that came pouring into the apartment.

'Roberto . . . does Roberto know?' Dani asked her father. 'Did anyone tell him?'

'Yes, yes,' Maurice soothed. 'Don't worry, it's all being taken care of.'

He didn't tell her that the diPortanovas had immediately claimed Nino's body. They'd sent a jet to Buenos Aires, and his charred remains were already being flown to Lake Garda, where the funeral was to be held. A very private funeral, a family spokesman in New York had coldly informed Monika. The family would prefer that Nino's widow not attend.

'The family can stuff it!' Monika had replied. 'Dani was Nino's wife, and she's going to the funeral, whether Roberto likes it or not.'

For once, Dani was willing to let the others take control. 'I can't talk to anyone,' she said over and over again. 'I'm sorry. Tell them I'm sorry.'

Trays of food appeared in front of her, but she couldn't eat. Maurice took care of the personal calls, Eunice handled the media, and Monika made all the travel arrangements and kept in touch with the office. Dani sat in the library, her head heavy and aching, thinking, *First Mama, now Nino*.

She struggled to make sense of his death. All his life he had courted danger. He had danced on the lip of a volcano, daring fate to push him over the edge. Finally fate had won, and he'd died doing what he loved best. But that knowledge gave her small comfort now as she ached to reach out and touch him. She would have been the first to admit that their marriage was far from the idyllic, glamorous fantasy the public believed it to be. But Nino had been her first love and the only man she'd slept with. Through even their rockiest times, she had never stopped loving him.

And now he was gone. She would never see him again, never again hear his voice, never turn over in bed and feel him next to her in the night. And, oh, God, the pain of knowing she still had so much to say to him, words that would have to remain unspoken.

Nino, Nino, you were my love. Always, in spite of everything. And we never even got to say good-bye.

The Lear jet stood like a lone, silent sentinel on the runway at Kennedy, waiting to begin the long journey to Italy. The crew had completed the final walk-around check, and the refueling truck, having filled the plane with enough fuel for the flight, had pulled away.

The midnight blue stretch limousine, its windows tinted dark, moved swiftly across the tarmac, well away from the dozens of media representatives who hung over the fence with their Minicams and zoom lenses. The limo pulled up alongside the jet, and the driver stepped out to open the rear door. Monika, wearing black, was the first to appear, reaching out a helping hand to Dani.

Dani, similarly dressed in black, her swollen eyes hidden behind oversized sunglasses, slowly emerged from the limo, looking like a sleepwalker. Climbing the steps to the plane, she stumbled and would have fallen, had Monika not been right behind her.

She'd been this way ever since the phone call that had brought her world crashing down around her with such swift surety. Her insides were trembling so violently that she almost couldn't trust herself to walk alone. But now, oddly, she found some small comfort in boarding the plane that had carried Nino to Buenos Aires. Here, next to his favorite reading chair, was the book he must have been reading, a biography of Churchill, the page still marked where he'd put it down. A spare racing helmet sat atop the walnut chest in the aft cabin. She went into their bedroom and picked up a framed photograph of Nino and herself relaxing by a pool, holding hands and smiling at each other. She couldn't remember now when the picture had been taken, but they both looked happy, and that was all that mattered.

'Dani?' Monika poked her head into the cabin. 'Maurice and Eunice just came aboard. We're ready for takeoff. Are you all right?'

How she wished people would stop asking her that. She didn't know what the proper answer was, because to tell them the truth would be to risk frightening them with the extent of her agony. When Sophie died, she'd cried and ached for her mother. But her mother's months of suffering had made her death seem almost merciful. By contrast, Nino's death felt like a cruel, crazy mistake.

From the moment they touched down in Italy, Dani was confronted by a media circus. A phalanx of bodyguards tried to shield her from the crush of cameras, microphones, and television lights, but it was impossible to escape their ghoulish scrutiny. Helicopters hovered overhead, and paparazzi on motorcycles followed their entourage all the way to the diPortanova chapel in Lake Garda, where the requiem mass was to be celebrated.

The chapel was crowded with people who had come from all over the region to pay their respects to Roberto diPortanova's son. Flanked by Monika and Eunice, with Maurice glowering behind them, Dani began to make her way down the center aisle toward the front of the chapel. An usher who had apparently been assigned to look out for her party stepped forward and blocked their way. With much bowing and shaking of his head, he explained that seats had been saved for them in the back.

Shaken out of her daze by such audacity, her temper flaring, Dani glared at the man, obviously one of Roberto's flunkies. 'I'm Nino's widow. I want to sit with the rest of the family,' she insisted.

The man rubbed his hands together nervously. 'I am very sorry. Not possible. You're not a member of the church. You must sit at the back. Please be so kind as to follow me.'

It wasn't worth arguing the point, she decided with weary resignation. She owed it to Nino not to cause a scene at his funeral.

Six pallbearers, none of whom Dani recognized, carried Nino's ornate walnut casket down the center aisle. Behind them, led by Roberto, were Benedetta and Nino's three sisters, all heavily veiled.

Roberto saw Dani as soon as he entered the chapel and silently cursed her for showing her face at his son's funeral. He was sure she was somehow responsible for the accident. Probably they'd argued just before the race, and Nino's judgment had been thrown off. Who could think clearly, being married to such a woman? She'd been nothing but trouble to him from the very start. Nino had deserved so much better, and now it was too late.

He glanced at the woman next to his son's widow, and

his heart skipped a beat. For an instant he'd thought it was . . . but no, she was far too young. And then he remembered through his grief that Karola's daughter worked with Nino's wife. What an irony. Did the Jewess know that a von Reich subsidiary had helped build the ovens in which so many of her kind had been burned?

He moved on, and the family slowly proceeded to their pew, before the altar.

The pallbearers rested Nino's casket on a platform at the foot of the altar, where the priest blessed it with holy water and incense. Then, solemnly, he intoned the ancient requiem high mass in Italian, consigning the bodily remains of Gianni diPortanova to the protection of the church and his soul to the Heavenly Father.

Dani felt oppressed by the heat and the cloying aroma of the incense. It was hard to connect the man she had loved with the ritual taking place in this tiny church. Through her tears she watched the family step forward to take Holy Communion. Roberto, then Nino's mother and his three older sisters. The women were hardly more than strangers to her. Most likely she'd never see or speak to them again. It was strange that at this moment she should feel closer to them than she ever had before. If only they could all sit down together to share their memories of the boy and man they'd loved so much. But she hadn't even been invited to join them at the house after the funeral.

The priest completed the mass, and the pallbearers retraced their steps, balancing the casket on their shoulders.

Dani, clutching Monika for support, found herself being swept along by the crowd outside onto the steps of the chapel, where the reporters were waiting, their mikes and cameras ready for action. Somebody jostled her. She stumbled and felt herself falling. Grabbing the nearest available arm, she looked up into her father-in-law's eyes.

Roberto glared at her with such a look of white-hot fury that for a moment she was afraid he might strike her.

'Don't touch me!' he commanded loudly. 'You! You sent him to his grave! If you'd been more of a wife instead of a greedy businesswoman, he might have stayed home. And he'd still be alive.'

Stunned by the depth of his hatred, Dani stood frozen, staring at him. The press captured the moment.

'Dani . . . Dani!' Monika grabbed her arm and pulled her through the crowd. 'Where are those damn body-guards? Excuse, please! Excuse!'

'Wait.' Dani reached out through the crowd to the casket being loaded into the hearse. 'I just want to say good-bye – '

'Not now, Dani,' Monika said gently. 'Now it's time to go home.'

New York

Bunny couldn't believe her luck. Bud Nelson, who directed Dani's television commercials for Ian McAdam, was a legend – the best in the business. He'd won more Clios than he could remember. He was also an ass-pinching lech who'd just split up with his third wife. He claimed he was fifty, but Bunny figured he was pushing sixty at the least. She didn't care. The older they were, the less demanding they were in bed.

Besides, right now Bunny couldn't afford to be too choosy, since that stuck-up bore Hollis Worthington III had just dumped her for a girl with the predictably cutesy name of Muffy.

'Our families have been friends for several generations,' Hollis had explained when he'd broken the news over dinner at the Four Seasons. 'Father feels I need to settle down and find a suitable wife.'

'Muffy's suitable, and I'm not?' Bunny had sneered.

Hollis had smiled weakly. 'Of course not. But Father's very picky about bloodlines, and – '

Bunny had picked up her bowl of split-pea soup and dumped it in his lap.

They hadn't spoken since.

So when Bud invited Bunny to be his date for dinner at the Central Park South penthouse apartment of a famous movie producer, Bunny had jumped at the chance. Screw Hollis Worthington III. She'd show him just how suitable she could be.

She'd read about the apartment in *Architectural Digest*, but still she wasn't prepared for the opulence – the museum-quality artwork, the period furniture that shrieked 'expensive,' the marble fireplaces, the gold-leaf ceilings, the sweeping views of Central Park. *Dear Lord*, she prayed, *let me not do something stupid like pick up the wrong fork at dinner*.

Dinner was served at four round tables set with sparkling Baccarat and gleaming Wedgwood. The conversation turned to Dani diPortanova as soon as the other guests discovered that Bunny worked at Countess Dani.

The international press had played to the hilt Roberto diPortanova's parting shot to Dani outside the chapel. Bunny hadn't seen the British and Italian papers that the elite were talking about, but everyone agreed that the American tabloids deserved the prize for the juiciest coverage.

'Shunned Countess Mourns,' the New York *Daily News* had screamed on the front page above a picture of Dani being led down the steps of the chapel by Monika.

'Dani's Deathblow,' roared the New York *Post*, alongside a photo of Roberto hissing at her through clenched teeth.

The *Women's Wear Daily* column, 'One Ear to the Ground,' reported that competitor Reggie Bolt had declared, 'Nino made a great career move. If only his widow would do likewise.'

Everyone at the table agreed that Mr Reggie's comment was by far the wittiest, albeit the bitchiest, bon mot any of them had heard in ages. Bunny joined in the laughter, all the while calculating what role to play. Loyal and devastated close friend? Well-informed but diplomatic insider? Clever, catty executive on the rise?

It was a tough call. She didn't know all the other guests or what their relationships were to Dani. *Be careful. When in doubt, don't play it out*, she reminded herself. She kept her mouth shut, smiled knowingly, and took in every word and gesture for future reference.

'So you work for that diPortanova broad, huh?' asked a deeply tanned man, dressed in California casual with lots of gold jewelry around his neck, who was seated to Bunny's left. He looked to be pushing middle age, and his bald head was covered by a few thin strands of hair that looked as if they'd been spray-starched across his scalp.

'Yes, I do,' she said, trying to remember his name.

'I'm Stan Moore,' said the man, pawing her leg under the table.

Bunny stifled a giggle. Men were all alike. All they wanted was a piece of ass.

'My friends call me Stan the Man. If you're lucky, little girl, I'll be Stan Your Main Man,' he said, squeezing her again.

Bunny turned on her southern belle charm and listened to Stan the Man brag about what a hotshot producer he was. Her computerlike memory filed away the information for future reference. One never knew . . .

After dinner, Stan slipped Bunny his card. 'Give me a call, sweetheart,' he said with a wink. 'We'll do lunch.'

'Oh, no, Mr Moore. I *never* call men,' Bunny protested sweetly. 'My mother told me that the gentleman *always* calls the lady.'

Stan chuckled. 'Listen, babes, even if you don't call, check out my show sometime. "Pot O' Gold" is the number one game show on television, and I'm workin' on a big mother that's gonna blow the other nighttime soaps off the map.'

'And what's that called?' asked Bunny, dodging the smoke from Stan's cigar.

'"The Seducers."' He leered. 'Get it?'

Dani was obsessed with the image of Nino's Tipo 33 tumbling over and over, then bursting into flames. When she closed her eyes, she could see the smoke, smell the burning gasoline, and hear his scream of anguish.

One night, flipping the TV channels, she happened upon a movie in the middle of a car-chase scene. She was mesmerized by the sight of the two cars, one in hot pursuit of the other, whipping around the deadly curves of a mountain. With tires screeching and gravel flying, the lead car suddenly took a narrow turn directly into the path of an eighteen-wheeler. A second later, the car plunged off the side of the mountain and exploded in a fiery ball.

She couldn't sleep for days afterward, wondering how long it took for a human being to die amid the flames. It was a question, she realized, that she really didn't want answered.

Among the piles of phone messages were several from Nino's lawyer, Ned Black, reminding Dani that he needed to meet with her to discuss the disposition of Nino's estate. The last thing in the world she felt able to cope with was talking to Ned about her husband's will. Somehow that made Nino's death feel so much more final and absolute. But she knew she had to face reality, and she supposed that some matters simply couldn't wait until the pain had lessened.

Sitting in the library across from Ned, with Monika by her side for moral support, she listened but could hardly take in the lawyer's dreary litany. So many words and numbers – stock transfers, trusts, offshore accounts, holding companies, dummy corporations. To her pain-numbed ears, it all sounded like so much gobbledygook.

'And so,' Ned concluded, sounding almost apologetic, 'the sum total of these various entities comes to only about sixty million dollars.'

Dani nodded automatically, wishing he would finish and leave so she could go lie down.

'I realize that amount must come as a shock to you, Dani. I'm sure you were expecting more from the estate, but your husband did . . . uh . . . spend rather a lot of it. Still, sixty million is enough to allow you to maintain your life-style, and you will, of course, have income from your own corporation.'

'Yes, yes,' she murmured, 'of course.'

Her head was pounding, and the sunlight streaming in through the windows hurt her eyes. She had always prided herself on how well she understood the financial intricacies of her own business, and she'd listened and asked lots of questions whenever Nino had talked about stocks and bonds. Now here she was behaving like the stereotypical befuddled wife who simply didn't have a head for these complicated money matters.

Ned cleared his throat and said, 'I realize this may not be the most appropriate time, but at some future date you will want to revise your own will . . . appoint a new executor.'

'I'm sorry,' said Dani, her voice quavering. 'I'm not feeling very well.'

Monika immediately came to her rescue. 'Please, I really don't think Dani should have to deal with this just now.'

'Quite right, quite right,' the lawyer agreed. He shuffled his papers and neatly stacked them in his briefcase. 'That's all, then. Dani, if you have any questions, just call me, any time, day or night. And again, my very deepest – '

When she stood up, Dani felt light-headed, as if she might faint. 'If you'll excuse me,' she pleaded, fleeing the room without a backward glance.

'What a tragedy,' said Ned. 'That poor woman. Nino's death was such a shock . . . a terrible loss for us all.' He handed Monika a manila file. 'Here are Dani's copies of everything we went over today. Could you be sure they're put away somewhere safe? I have the originals, of course, but I'd like her to have a set as well.'

Monika glanced at the label on the folder: 'diPortanova, Legal and Financial.'

'Tell Dani to be in touch about her will as soon as she's up to it, will you?' said Ned, shaking Monika's hand, his fingers lingering just an instant longer than was necessary.

'Of course,' agreed Monika. 'Thank you so much for coming by today, Mr Black.'

'Please, call me Ned. By the way, Ms von Reich, don't *you* hesitate to call if you ever need me.'

'I'll remember that,' Monika said. 'You're very kind.'

At the end of each day, Dani's assistant, Lance Turner, would fill up three color-coded folders with Dani's mail and telephone calls for Monika to take up to the Dakota. Occasionally, when a matter came up that required Dani's immediate attention, Lance would hand-deliver the folder to the guard in the gatehouse.

'Did they let you upstairs?' Bunny would grill him afterward. 'Did you get to see her?'

The answer was always no.

Bunny was sure that only a wimp like Lance couldn't get past that guard. She was dying to see for herself how Dani was doing, and she couldn't stand the fact that that hateful Monika was the only one with access to Dani. Given half a chance, she knew she could sweet-talk her way into Dani's apartment.

She didn't have long to wait before the perfect opportunity fell right into her lap. Her friend, the director of advertising at Saks, wanted to make a last-minute change in one of their cooperative advertisements. 'Just a teeny-weeny change, Barbara, no big deal,' said the advertising director. 'We're in a hurry. Couldn't you just sign off on it yourself?'

Not if she wanted to keep her job as fashion coordinator, she couldn't. But she didn't want the girl from Saks to know that. So she took a deep breath and promised, 'No problem, honey. I'll have it back to you right after lunch.'

To save time and money, she carried the ad boards uptown by express train to Seventy-second Street and almost ran the two blocks to the Dakota.

'Help you?' asked the guard in front of the building.

'You surely can,' she drawled, all soft green eyes and sweet smile. 'I have somethin' here that requires the Countess diPortanova's most urgent attention. She said to be sure to ask for you' – Bunny squinted at the man's nametag – 'Joe, 'cause you'd send me up right away.'

'Let me just call up and make sure – '

'Oh, please,' Bunny implored the guard, 'she's havin' a real important meetin' with my boss, Ms von Reich, and you don't want to be gettin' me in trouble now, do you, by interruptin' them?'

Faced with a smile like that, how could he say no? The guard broke every rule in the book and waved her through the iron gate without first calling upstairs for permission.

So far, so good, Bunny congratulated herself as she rode the mahogany-paneled elevator up to the fifth floor. She crossed her fingers for good luck and rang the doorbell.

'Yes? Who is it?' came a British-accented voice from inside.

'Barbara Hester, from Countess Dani. I have an urgent delivery for the Countess.'

The door swung open.

'You're supposed to leave whatever it is downstairs,' Elvira said crossly. 'Why did they let you up?'

Bunny thought, *Shut up and get out of my way, you old bag*. 'I told them it was an emergency. I need a signature right away – from Dani or Monika.'

'Wait here,' said Elvira, leaving Bunny alone in the foyer. 'Let me go check. What did you say your name was?'

'Barbara Hester,' Bunny replied, pronouncing each syllable very carefully, as if she thought the woman was deaf.

Elvira returned a moment later. 'Follow me, please, Miss Hester.'

Bunny had already seen Dani's home once before, at a cocktail party, but it looked even lovelier by day. She would have liked nothing more than to wander through the rooms at a leisurely pace, stopping to look at and touch all the beautiful pieces. But Elvira walked briskly, and Bunny, clutching the ad under her arm, had to hurry to keep up with her.

'In here, please.' Elvira motioned Bunny into Dani's office.

Bunny ignored Monika's glower and bent over to kiss Dani's pale cheek. 'I'm so sorry, Dani,' she said softly.

'Hello, Barbara. Thank you for those beautiful flowers,' said Dani.

'What's the big emergency?' Monika interrupted, sure that Barbara had just been looking for a good excuse to tell people she'd been up to visit Dani.

'Saks needs you or Dani to sign off on these boards right away. It seemed too important to wait until you got back to the office,' Bunny explained. She set the boards down on the table and pointed out the changes to Monika, all the while watching Dani out of the corner of her eye.

'Dani, do you want to look at these?' Monika asked.

'No, no, if you think it's all right, I'm sure it is,' Dani said listlessly. 'Barbara, I'm sorry you had to go to all this trouble. I'm just having a very hard time these days and – '

'Please, it's my pleasure,' Bunny assured her. 'Dani, it makes perfect sense to me that you need to take time off. Don't you worry about a thing and don't worry about rushing back, either. We have everything under control.'

'I appreciate that, Barbara.'

Monika was seething at Barbara's effrontery. She stood up abruptly and said, 'Don't ring for Elvira. I'll show Barbara out myself.'

She grabbed Bunny by the elbow and steered her to the front door. Once they had reached the foyer of the apartment, Monika turned, her eyes blazing. 'How dare you encourage her to stay home! You know nothing about her needs, you presumptuous little upstart. What she needs is to keep her mind focused, to forget about what happened. The sooner she gets back to work, the better off she'll be. Which reminds me, isn't it time *you* got back to work?'

'It's lunchtime,' Bunny said airily. 'This is a company, you know, not a Nazi forced-labor camp.'

Monika stared, aghast, furious beyond words. When she recovered her composure, she spat out, 'You bitch.'

Bunny smiled as she rang for the elevator. 'You just *bet* I am, *Fräulein*.'

Despite all of Monika's and Maurice's efforts to persuade her, Dani didn't go back to work the next day or the day after that. Just when she thought she'd conquered her sorrow, fresh nightmares about Nino would plunge her into blackest despair. Two months had passed since his death, and she had still not recovered. Roberto's angry words haunted her day and night. Over and over again she asked herself whether she could have prevented Nino's death if she'd spent less time at the office. Some days the guilt was so overwhelming that she couldn't get out of bed.

Nothing seemed important to her anymore. What good was success if she had no one to share it with? More than anything in the world, she wanted Nino back. But he was gone forever, and she couldn't seem to face that fact.

She took minimal interest in the business, attending only to the most essential details. The ad copy that she'd once written herself she now barely skimmed before scribbling her initials on the bottom of the page. She listlessly approved the merchandising plans and licensing renewals. Swatches of fabrics lay on the worktable in her office, gathering dust.

Monika continued to shuttle back and forth between the office and the Dakota, trying to nurse her friend through her terrible depression. After one visit she called Dani's doctor and poured out her fears to him.

'She's probably mourning not just her husband but her mother as well,' the doctor explained. 'His death may

346

have triggered the pain she felt when her mother died. Give her time. She'll be all right.'

Still, Monika was unnerved to find Dani curled up in an armchair in her bedroom, staring out the window at Central Park, looking only half alive herself.

One evening she turned to Monika and said, 'I've had my will revised. If anything happens to me, you get all of Countess Dani and fifty percent of my personal assets. The other half goes to Maurice.'

Monika shuddered. '*Ach, liebchen*, don't talk stupid. What could happen to you? And why on earth would I want the headaches of owning Countess Dani?'

Frightened by Dani's morbid tone, she quickly changed the subject. It hurt her to see Dani in this terrible condition. She was worried for her and for the company as well. Dani was the creative force, and her prolonged absence was hurting the business.

Monika knew all too well how these things worked. As each day passed, the business would suffer just a little more. Word would get out. And eventually, the fuse of gossip would reach the barrel of explosives.

Reggie walked into Bogart's, a gay bar on East Fifty-ninth Street, for a happy-hour drink. Bogart's was a fashionable, understated place with walls covered in green felt and fox-hunting prints. Gay businessmen in pinstriped suits were standing three deep at the bar, while at the piano a singer torched out Sondheim's 'Send in the Clowns.'

'That's appropriate,' Reggie said under his breath, appraising the crowd.

He was buying himself a Stoli on the rocks when Mitchell Barton walked up to the bar. How perfectly delightful. A little dish with his drink. Reggie sidled up next to him and pecked him on the cheek. 'Mitchell

347

darling, you look wonderful. Thank God you're here. I needed a familiar face.'

'What's new?' Mitchell wanted to know.

Reggie smiled. The perfect question from a Seventh Avenue columnist, especially one listened to by the outside press and Wall Street. He'd have to play this right. Mitchell was too smart to buy unsubstantiated vitriol.

'Have you heard the rumors about Countess Dani?' Reggie asked casually.

'Some of them,' Mitchell nodded, waiting for Reggie to open up.

'Darling, let me give you the *facts*.'

The picture Reggie painted wasn't a pretty one. Dani wasn't showing up at the office. Monika was having her problems. There'd been defections among the assistant designers, problems with the signature stores in New York and Beverly Hills. Several key sales reps had quit, and business from the retail side was falling off as confidence in Dani waned.

Reggie discharged his final salvo: 'She's drinking heavily. I hear she's having a nervous breakdown. She may even be suicidal.'

'Because of her husband's death?'

Reggie nodded solemnly. 'And mark my words, the company will be finished.'

Mitchell mulled this over. He knew that Dani and Reggie were long-standing sworn enemies. But he, more than anyone, loved the dish and dirt. And he'd already heard some of what Reggie was telling him. Most of it probably wasn't true, but as in any tightly knit industry the farther rumors spread, the more valid and credible they became. Probably there was at least a morsel of truth in Reggie's assertions.

Reggie's hand squeezed his shoulder. How better to

seal the countess's fate than with a kiss? Correction – a cock. 'Anything interesting on the agenda tonight, lover boy?'

Mitchell considered the proposition. It certainly beat jerking off while he watched a porno flick on his VCR. 'Rah Rah not home tonight?' he asked.

Reggie sniffed his annoyance. 'Acting lessons. I humor him. What do I care?'

As they left the bar together, Reggie licked his lips at the prospect of Mitchell's next column. One way or another, he was going to bury that bitch.

Mitchell didn't care how much damage was done to his victims, only whether or not he could get sued for libel. He had perfected a wonderful way of playing with words so that even an idiot could read between the lines, but he made sure to do his homework and check his facts. Thus, the next day he phoned Countess Dani, Inc., for confirmation of Reggie's story.

Bunny was passing by the receptionist's desk when she heard the receptionist say, 'I'm sorry, Mr Barton, but the countess isn't available. No, Ms von Reich isn't in yet either. Would you like to leave a message?'

Mr Barton . . . Bunny stopped dead in her tracks. She'd always wanted to talk to the infamous Mitchell Barton. 'Tell Mr Barton I'll take the call,' she ordered the receptionist. 'Transfer it to my office.'

Bunny closed her door and picked up the phone. 'Mr Barton? I'm Barbara Hester, Dani's fashion coordinator. What can I do for you?'

Mitchell explained that he was in the midst of writing a column about rumors floating around the avenue concerning Countess Dani. 'Any of it true?'

Bunny smiled, relishing the thought of being a 'Deep Throat' for an important columnist like Barton. Here at last was her chance to dump on Monika. 'Well, completely off the record, of course, Ms von Reich *is* having some problems . . .'

She ticked off with great certainty the internal problems Monika had been facing ever since Nino's death.

'That's *very* interesting, Barbara. And what about Dani? How's she holding up?' he asked.

Flattered by his warmth and interest, Bunny replied, 'As well as can be expected. She's taking it very hard.'

'They say she's been drinking more than she should. They're also saying she's suicidal.'

Suicidal? Bunny couldn't connect that notion with the Dani she'd seen just recently. Then again, Monika was really the only one who saw Dani regularly, though it seemed to Bunny that she, too, had a right to know exactly what was going on. She chose her words carefully. 'All I can say, and you can read into this what you like, is that it's been *very* difficult. They were so . . . close. It's been hard on me, too. We were all such good friends.'

She could hear Barton clicking away at his word processor at the other end of the line. 'This is all off the record?' she asked nervously.

'Of course,' he assured her, delighted to have a new source. 'Barbara, we should have lunch sometime.'

'Should we set up a date now?' Bunny flipped excitedly through her date book. Visions filled her head of being a trusted confidante to the industry power brokers.

'I'm booked for a couple of months. I'll call you when my schedule opens up. But thanks so much. You've been very helpful.'

'Of course,' Bunny said, trying to hide her disappointment. 'Good talking to you.'

After she hung up she realized he hadn't told her when the column would appear. Then she began to worry about being fingered as his source. Better cover her tracks, she decided.

She waltzed back out to the reception area. 'Listen,' she scolded the receptionist, 'that *wasn't* Mitchell Barton. It was Michael Blewston, a buyer from Duluth. Next time be sure you get your names straight so I don't waste my time. Got it?'

The receptionist nodded wearily. She was used to Barbara Hester's ways.

The column created an immediate sensation. The New York *Post* picked up the story and ran it on page one, with the shrill headline, 'Dani Suicide Watch.'

'What the hell are they talking about?' Dani raged to Monika. 'I'm in mourning, not cutting my wrists!'

Unnamed sources? Ha! The story had Reggie's signature written all over it. How like him to go after her when she was most vulnerable. That son of a bitch. And Mitchell Barton – she'd sue the bastard for everything he was worth. She'd haul his ass into court so fast he'd have dizzy spells for the rest of his life!

Certainly nobody would believe the story . . . it was preposterous.

But within the week, two of Dani's bankers phoned and insisted on speaking to Dani personally. 'Just to check in,' they said soothingly.

But Monika knew they wanted to see for themselves whether it was true that Dani was on the verge of mental collapse. Dani's lawyer brought her the bad news that her case against Mitchell was weak at best. Attorneys specializing in bankruptcy proceedings called to offer their services. Competitors wanted to discuss the possibility of a buy-out. Several placement agencies sent letters to her employees, offering to help relocate any who were laid off.

Dani's phone at the Dakota rang constantly.

A producer from '60 Minutes' called. They wanted to interview her for a feature on the rise and fall of a great American designer.

'What do you mean "fall"?' she screamed into the phone.

Finally shaken out of her mourning stupor, Dani realized it was time to emerge from the protective cocoon of her apartment and rejoin the living. She would have to move quickly to regain lost ground. Yes, she had been having a hard time, and yes, she missed Nino terribly, but it was time to pick herself up. Get on with life. She had a company to run.

Her first priority was to take care of Mitchell Barton. She made a few phone calls, a few inquiries, then called a number in California. A price and travel expenses were agreed upon.

During the next few days, she put together a list of key industry analysts and CEOs of major department store chains. And then she started dialing their numbers, asking questions, and taking notes.

They'd all heard about Nino's death, and they were all delighted to speak to her. Of course she was still a contender, she assured them. In fact, she had an idea in mind, but she first wanted to check with them.

Even before she crossed off the last name on her list, she had formulated her plan. The only way to show Seventh Avenue that she was alive and kicking was to shake things up a little bit.

Suicide? Ha! Mitchell – along with Reggie and all the rest of them – could shove it up his ass.

Part Three

Chapter Thirteen

New York

Mitchell Barton stepped out of the shower in his Green-wich Village apartment, threw on his green velour robe, and arranged himself on his bed with the latest issue of *Blueboy*. He was just reaching for the baby oil when his doorbell buzzed. Christ Almighty, who the hell could that be? He really ought to be living in a doorman building. Couldn't a guy jack off in peace?

He peered through the peephole and gasped at the vision that stood at the other side of the door.

'Y-yes?' Mitchell stammered.

'Mitchell Barton?'

Mitchell swallowed hard and bravely opened the door. 'That's me. What can I do for you?'

'I'm a present from Dani diPortanova,' said the vision, a dark-haired blue-eyed young man who looked like a cross between Mel Gibson and James Dean.

'I – I don't understand,' said Mitchell, trying not to stare at the young man's bulging crotch. 'There must be some mistake.'

The vision smiled. 'No mistake. Can I come in?'

'I – I don't think – '

Without waiting for permission, the young man stepped past Mitchell and closed the door. Looking around the apartment, he said, 'I told you, Dani diPortanova sent me.'

Dani diPortanova, whom he'd so recently trashed in his column? Mitchell backed nervously toward the telephone, ready to call the cops on this hunk of mouth-watering flesh whom Dani had apparently hired to bash his brains into dog meat.

'Please,' he said, reaching for the phone, 'I didn't mean to – '

The young man covered Mitchell's hand with his own. 'You don't have to call anyone. This party's just for the two of us.'

'I'll give you money, whatever you want, but please don't hurt me,' Mitchell pleaded.

The man took off his leather jacket, revealing a well-developed set of pecs beneath his form-fitting T-shirt. 'You don't have to pay me,' he said, laughing. 'I told you, Dani diPortanova's picking up the tab. And I won't hurt you unless you want me to. I mean, whatever turns you on.' He glanced at Mitchell's wet hair. 'Did I get you out of the shower?'

Mitchell gulped. 'No . . . I mean, yes.'

'Good. Then you're all nice and clean and ready to eat.'

Slowly it was dawning on Mitchell that perhaps this guy really was telling the truth. Torn between fear and lust, he circled around toward the fireplace and felt behind his back for the poker . . . just in case.

'I don't understand. Why did Dani send you here?' he asked warily.

The vision fell to his knees in front of Mitchell and groped beneath his robe until he found what he was looking for. His fingers closed around Mitchell's penis, which hardened on contact.

'Ooh,' Mitchell said in ecstasy.

'Feel good?' The hustler gazed up at him. 'Dani wanted me to tell you that, contrary to rumor, she's not going under. But' he said, rubbing the tip of Mitchell's penis against his soft lips, '*I'm* going down – on you.'

His tongue flickered up and down the shaft of Mitchell's penis, sending sharp quivers of warm, pleasurable sensation through his groin and up into his chest.

'Ah, good,' whispered Mitchell, surrendering to the young man's ministrations. 'Very good.'

On second thought, maybe Dani diPortanova deserved a major reassessment.

The morning after the hustler had paid a visit to Mitchell Barton, Dani got to work early, before anyone else had arrived. She had to dig in her purse to find the key that unlocked the twin glass doors. That was just as well, because she had lots to do before the others arrived. And, oh, it was good to be back, she realized, glancing around her office. Even the stack of bulging color-coded file folders piled neatly in the middle of her desk looked good.

Lance, bless his soul, had sorted through all the past weeks' incoming correspondence and made careful notes as to which matters were still pending and which had already been taken care of. One folder contained a long list of all her telephone calls – who'd called, what the caller wanted, and who had returned the call on her behalf. Many of the messages were from acquaintances and admirers in the business who'd phoned to express their condolences.

She was touched by the number of people who'd said 'Let me know if there's anything I can do.'

She made herself a pot of coffee, then dived into the top folder and didn't come up for air until she heard a noise just outside her door.

'Lance, is that you?' she called.

Barbara appeared in her doorway, looking startled. 'Dani! I . . . It's so great to see you! I didn't know you were coming in today.'

357

'I thought I'd surprise everyone. But what an early bird you are. Did you want something?'

Barbara stared at her blankly. 'Want something?'

'I heard you at Lance's desk.'

'Oh! No, no . . . I was just returning the stapler I borrowed from him yesterday. Listen, I'm sure you're busy, so I'll let you get back to your work. Dani, it's great to see you in here again.'

By the time Lance arrived at nine on the dot, Dani had separated out the most urgent matters and was ready for him.

Lance wasn't one to stand on ceremony. For a kid just out of FIT, he had more than his share of savvy and sophistication. 'Aren't you a sight for sore eyes!' he exclaimed.

'Likewise.' Dani smiled. 'Lance, before you do anything else, make sure everyone knows we have a ten o'clock staff meeting. Let them know this is important.'

Lance nodded. 'Yes, ma'am,' he said. 'I guess Mitchell Barton had it all wrong.'

'*All* wrong,' Dani agreed. 'But I already took care of him.'

She closed her door and worked right up until ten, then hurried into the conference room, where she was greeted with loud cheers and a standing ovation.

'It's good to be back, and I appreciate all you've done to keep this business running smoothly while I was recovering from Nino's death,' she told her staff. 'Now I've got some news for you. I know you've heard all the rumors about me. Well, forget 'em. They were bullshit from day one. I may have been in mourning, but my brain hasn't atrophied. And, starting today, we're going to launch the most aggressive new line this town has ever seen.'

358

She winked at Monika, the one person to whom she'd revealed her plan.

'Sheets,' she announced. 'We're going into sheets. And that's only the beginning. We're going to do everything from sheets, shams, and comforters to towels, shower curtains, you name it. A complete line of bed and bath accessories. Martex gave me the verbal go-ahead yesterday. I've spent the last three days on the phone, and every top industry analyst in the country agrees that the time to strike is now. Bedding sales have gone through the roof in the past six months. People, especially young professionals, are killing themselves at the office during the day and sleeping horribly at night. Besides stereos and televisions, they're buying better beds and luxury linens. They've got the money and they want comfort. They're our buyers.'

Every eye in the room was riveted on her. They were smiling. Dani was on a roll. They'd seen it happen before. She had yet to disappoint them.

'Granted, we're not the first in the market. As you well know, we're going up against the biggies. But with one important difference. *We* have a better handle. A theme that's going to make the Hot Flash campaign sound like a fairy tale.'

She had been selling America subliminal and not-so-subliminal sex for years now. What better place to do it from than a bed? And what better product to sell from a bed than sheets?

Heads were nodding. They could almost hear the cash registers ringing. If anyone could do it, Dani could.

'The ads, which will feature me in bed with a gorgeous man, will be so hot and sultry the camera lenses are going to get all steamed up. And' – she paused dramatically – 'I have the perfect ad line: "*Nothing* feels better than sleeping with royalty – Countess Dani Sheets."'

The Costa Brava, Spain

For the last half hour, Karola had been playing with Roberto's flaccid penis. She'd sucked it, greased it with lubricant, manipulated it until her hand was tired, and Roberto still wasn't rising to the occasion. Karola was bored. She hadn't flown all the way from Austria to her villa on the Costa Brava to play with a limp dick.

'Roberto,' she sighed, 'you need to get the blood flowing.'

Roberto rolled over, sat up, and pulled on his silk pajama bottoms. Without bothering to respond, he walked over to the balcony and stared with moody resignation at the sea below. What was there to say, except that he wasn't in the mood for sex? Or for food, or conversation, or anything else that once had given him pleasure.

He had been like this ever since Nino's horrible senseless death. He went through his daily routines, kept his business running, and tried to console Benedetta. But inside he was numb. Utterly numb. This rendezvous with Karola, their first since the funeral, was his attempt to revive his appetite. He'd hoped that the sight of Karola naked would restoke his fire. But the spark was gone . . . dead and buried with his son.

From where he stood, he could see two medieval lookout towers rising from the neighboring property. Karola's villa was over three hundred years old, and its walls were covered with ivy and bougainvillea. Old by some standards, but not as old as the ancient and honorable diPortanova name, which after all these centuries would die with him.

He sighed mournfully and said, 'Let's get some air.'

Karola grunted with impatience. 'Look, Roberto,

what's wrong? This isn't like you. I didn't come here for the scenery. I came to have sex with you.'

Roberto turned, his lip curled in a sneer. 'Is sex all you have on your mind? Is that all I am to you, a stud to trot out every now and then? All you liberated women are alike. You never consider what a man needs or desires. You only know how to take, take, take. You're destroyers, that's what you are.'

Karola glared at him coldly. 'I think you have me confused with your former daughter-in-law.'

'You're *all* alike.'

She laughed spitefully. 'It's still tearing you up that Nino left her his money, isn't it?'

'Money!' he raged, pacing the room like a caged animal. 'It has nothing to do with that money. I piss on that pittance he left her! I piss on *her*!'

What a wasted trip. When Roberto called to suggest they get together, she'd assumed he had recovered from his loss and was ready for action. Obviously he wasn't. That was his bad luck. She didn't have the time or the temperament to play nursemaid. 'Then what's the problem?' she taunted him. 'Because you obviously have one.'

Roberto clenched his fists and glared at his mistress. 'That was my *son*, you bitch. My only son. My heir. My name will die. Six hundred years of the diPortanova name *gone* because of that fucking woman.'

Karola yawned. Roberto was turning into a crybaby. The game was no longer amusing. She sat up and dangled her long legs over the edge of the bed. 'You're a fool, Roberto. And you're lying to yourself. Nino would never have given you an heir. Everyone knew he was a homosexual.'

Roberto covered the distance between himself and Karola with a swiftness that stunned her.

'Roberto – '

But he didn't give her a chance to finish. Breathing heavily, his eyes bulging with fury, he backhanded her jaw with such force that she was knocked off the bed and onto the floor.

Karola stared up at him, dazed with pain and shock.

'You cunt! You've seen the last of me,' Roberto shouted and stormed out of the room.

Karola gingerly touched her bruised jaw. Her fingers came away with blood on them. *Oh, my God*, she thought. *He's gone mad.*

New York

All through the summer, when she'd had to run Countess Dani almost single-handedly, Monika had only rarely managed to find time to stop in at Lucky's. On the few evenings when she had dropped by, she'd been too distracted by her worries about Dani and all the extra problems at work to keep her mind on the game. She'd played poorly and lost money – enough that she was feeling twinges of anxiety about how to recoup her losses.

But tonight . . . tonight she was going to win. She could feel it as she stood in the entryway to Bonne Chance, the French restaurant located behind the playing room on Lucky's first floor. She scanned the dimly lit room, looking for her date. She didn't find him, but she did spot Hollis Worthington, the young man who'd brought Barbara Hester to the club. Monika had overheard a couple of the secretaries at work saying that Barbara had been in a foul mood after Hollis dumped her. Tonight he was with another woman. And thank God for that. She didn't need Barbara Hester poking her sharp little nose into her private life.

'Right this way, Ms von Reich,' murmured the maître d'.

Monika followed him to her favorite corner table and nodded at the other diners, most of whom she knew.

'Are you dining alone this evening, Ms von Reich?' asked her waiter.

'No, I'm expecting Mr Standish. But in the meantime you can bring me a bottle of Cristal.'

She studied her menu. The food at Bonne Chance was excellent, and she was starving. Tonight she would have the chateaubriand, with oysters to start. She needed energy for the evening ahead.

When she looked up again, Scott Devane was standing over her. 'So nice to see you, Monika. It's been a while,' he said, slithering into the banquette beside her. 'I know you're expecting a guest, so I won't stay long. But I did want to chat with you briefly.'

'Certainly. What's on your mind?' Monika asked in as pleasant a voice as she could muster. As if she didn't know.

'You've had a run of bad luck recently,' Devane reminded her.

Monika shrugged, feigning insouciance. 'So? It happens to all of us eventually.' She forced a smile. 'You know as well as I do that in one night I could win back everything I've lost.'

'True,' the manager agreed. 'You could. But what if you don't? You've already exceeded your line of credit.'

'So extend it,' Monika declared in her best imitation of Karola.

But the manager was impervious to her authoritative tone. 'I'm afraid we can't do that, Monika,' he told her, running a hand across the side of his slicked-back hair. 'Not unless you can offer us some collateral as a guarantee

363

against the loan. Your brownstone, or your Jaguar, perhaps?'

It frightened her more than a little that Devane not only knew she owned a car but knew the make as well. What else did he know about her, she wondered? Determined not to show any emotion, she pointed to the diamond choker around her neck and said, 'This necklace is worth almost one hundred fifty thousand dollars. Isn't that collateral enough for you?'

The manager shook his head. 'That's quite all right, Monika. You don't have to give up your jewelry. We're far more civilized than that. I have a better solution. We offer a special service for our most valued customers when they find themselves in this predicament.'

'Service?'

Devane leaned forward and lowered his voice. 'Let me tell you how it works . . .'

Banff, Canada

As an attractive and wealthy young widow, Dani soon discovered that she was a valuable commodity, as sought after as a two-bedroom, rent-controlled apartment in a pre-war building. Her friends seemed to have an endless stream of single men they wanted her to meet, and in the six months after Nino's death, she had her pick of New York's bachelors. But though she appreciated their attempts to play matchmaker, she discovered that she simply couldn't work up any enthusiasm for the oh-so-eligible men to whom she was being introduced. They were all sweet and charming, but compared to Nino (and she couldn't help but compare them to Nino) they all struck her as rather . . . dull. Or perhaps, she confided to Monika, she just wasn't ready to get involved again.

So she threw herself into her work. She'd always flirted with being a workaholic; now she embraced the concept with open arms. She worked around the clock, from early morning until late at night, seven days a week. Her company became her husband, lover, paramour. And she traveled, logging as many miles that fall and winter as any traveling salesman . . . Los Angeles, the Orient, Paris, London, a whirlwind ten-city tour doing personal appearances across the United States, and a weekend in Barbados.

Monika insisted that she go away with her for Christmas, and the two of them spent the week skiing in the Canadian Rockies. Sitting down to Christmas dinner at the house they'd rented near Banff, Dani couldn't help but think about how optimistic Nino had sounded the previous Christmas. But the combination of Monika's irreverent sense of humor and brisk exercise in the bracing winter air finally managed to perk up her spirits.

Curled up on pillows in front of the fireplace in their living room, she and Monika talked for endless hours about men. Monika had long since written off Rick Flood. She'd always known he wasn't right for her, she told her friend, but Dani kept remembering Nino's take on the situation – and when it came to women and affairs of the heart, Nino was seldom wrong.

'Describe your ideal man,' she said to Monika.

Monika took a long time answering. Finally, staring deep into the glow of the fire, she said, 'A kind man. Unpretentious. Someone who understands that I need to do my own thing . . . who accepts me just as I am, no matter what.'

Dani had to hold her tongue to keep from blurting out, *You mean someone just like Rick.* Instead she asked, 'But until you find him, don't you get lonely?'

'Lonely? Don't be silly. You know I'm never home.'

'That's for damned sure.' Dani laughed. Time after time she had called Monika late at night and been answered by her machine. Monika was always so vague about where she'd been that Dani was reluctant to press her. But now she said, 'Where *do* you go, anyway?'

'Oh, here and there. Sometimes I go dancing at one of the clubs. You should come with me. When's the last time you had fun? I mean, real fun?'

Dani shrugged. 'Can't even remember.'

'You need to get laid,' Monika teased.

'But Nino's only been dead six months . . .'

'*Six months!* Dani, aren't you horny?'

Yes, of course she was horny. She ached for a man to touch her. The men she'd dated were all terribly respectful. A chaste kiss on the cheek, a quick peck on the lips if they were really daring. 'When you're ready,' they'd murmur as they pressed her hands between theirs. But she would never be ready for the likes of them.

'Dani, do you know what happens if you don't get yourself serviced on a regular basis? The gears get jammed, the parts get rusty, and you have a broken-down car on your hands. *Liebchen*, you need a good strong pair of jumper cables to get you started again.'

'I'd settle for just one good strong jumper cable,' Dani said, giggling.

'Good, because I have a great idea. When we get back to New York, we'll go out together one night and hit the clubs. It will be good for both of us. *Ja?*'

New York

Area was New York's hottest club of the moment. Every night hordes of would-be club-goers made their way through the cobblestoned streets of the meatpacking district to the nondescript building on Hudson Street where they would vie to be among the chosen few to be allowed entry.

Dani and Monika were recognized as soon as they stepped out of Dani's limo. One of the doormen whisked them inside, past the play windows, which changed from week to week. This week's offering included a homage to plastics – everything from Bakelite to vibrators.

He escorted them past the unisex bathroom to the crowded VIP room. Dani looked around the high-tech-style room, which was mobbed with club regulars wearing everything from tuxedos and evening gowns to downtown punk regalia complete with work boots, multicolored hair, and safety pins through the nose.

'Like old times,' she told Monika. 'Only the faces and some of the costumes are different.'

'*Plus ça change.*' Monika shrugged.

But there was one other difference. In the olden days, if a club was hot, chances were good that Nino would be there drinking and snorting coke and dancing with the prettiest girls – and boys.

Well, the pretty young things were still around, eyeing everyone who walked through the door, and Dani was suddenly hit with waves of insecurity. It was one thing to go out on arranged dates with men whose interests were served by being seen with Dani diPortanova. But this scene was an altogether different matter. Everyone here looked so young. She felt as if she'd aged decades since she'd retired from the club circuit. And she'd never played the dating game. She didn't even know the rules.

She should never have agreed to come. She felt as if she'd been hurled back in time to when she was seven-teen. She was sure that if she looked at herself in a mirror, she would not see a beautiful, self-assured countess, but dumpy Dani Lieberman, the perennial wallflower who stayed home on Saturday nights and pigged out on Helene's rich, buttery cakes and cookies. The girl all the boys called 'thunder thighs,' 'porker,' 'watermelon tits.'

Panic-stricken, she grabbed Monika's arm and whispered, 'What if nobody asks me to dance?'

'*Ach*, so what?' Monika scoffed. 'We ask them!'

But what if they all say no? wailed a voice deep inside her. What if the joke was on her? Nervously, she licked her lips and patted back her hair.

'How do I look?' she asked Monika.

'Fantastic, of course.'

'Excuse me, ladies?' The bartender tapped Dani on the shoulder.

'Oh, yes, I'd like a drink – '

'Actually, that gentleman over there' – the bartender pointed to a man standing at the far end of the bar – 'asked me to open a bottle of champagne for you. With his compliments.'

Dani peered through the mob, trying to catch a glimpse of their admirer. Perhaps this evening wouldn't be a total loss. 'Ask him to join us, will you?' she told the bartender.

It took her a minute to recognize him. 'Monika, look who's here.'

'Small world,' Monika said dryly. 'That's Rick's former room-mate, the model who came on to you, *ja*?'

'The very one. What was his name . . . Jack something?'

His dark, wavy hair was shorter, his tan less pronounced. His clothes were Armani instead of California casual. But otherwise it was the same Jack Andrews they'd met in Los Angeles, and he was grinning from ear to ear as he kissed them both on each cheek.

'I can't believe it!' he exclaimed. 'I was hoping I'd run into someone I knew. I looked over and saw the two of you . . .'

'How are you, Jack?' Dani asked, looking into his gray eyes.

'Great, I'm really great. You even remember my name! Hey, I kept hoping I'd bump into you, Dani . . . and you, too, Monika, of course.'

Monika smiled. This couldn't have turned out better if she'd planned it herself. Now it was up to Dani to carry the ball. 'Would you two excuse me? I think it's time to go powder my nose.'

'Hey, don't leave on my account,' Jack protested.

'As you Americans say, "three's a crowd." I'll see you both later.'

'She's subtle, isn't she?' Dani laughed.

'She's right on the money. Hey, Dani, I was sorry to hear about your husband – '

'Thank you, but please, not now. I would love to dance . . . I mean, if you'd like to . . .'

If he'd like to! Was she kidding? Did a bear shit in the woods? Who wouldn't want to be seen in the company of Dani diPortanova? She was only the most beautiful woman in the world. He'd been hot to trot for her ever since that night in LA, but he'd never dreamed – not even after he'd read about her husband's death – that he'd see her again. He'd sent her a condolence card and gotten back from her a printed card thanking him for his kind words. When he spotted her across the room and sent over the champagne, he wondered if she'd even remember who he was. Evidently, she did.

'Sure, I'd love to dance.'

And after that . . .? He prayed that this night would go on forever.

If only his mother could see him now . . .

Jack had been only six when his mother sued his father for divorce after she caught him in bed with another woman.

Selma Andrews not only won an excellent financial settlement but also got custody of Jack and the court's permission to leave San Francisco and move south to Los Angeles.

Shy little Jack had a hard time making friends in his new neighborhood. He clung to his mother's side, which made Selma very happy. 'You're my little man, aren't you?' she often reminded him. 'You'll never betray me the way your father did.'

Jack tried his best to make up for his father's sins, but it seemed he could rarely please his mother. If he didn't obey her immediately, if he brought home a less than straight-A report card, if he asked her too often whether he could play at a friend's house, she would berate him mercilessly for being stupid, lazy, inconsiderate, selfish.

Matters only worsened as Jack got older and became interested in sex. Selma wouldn't speak to him for a week after she caught him reading a copy of Playboy.

'You want to see breasts?' she raged, pulling up her blouse and bra. 'I'll show you breasts, Jack! I'll show you breasts you'll never forget!'

Jack never did forget the sight of his mother's dark brown nipples protruding from her large blue-veined breasts.

She would pound on the bathroom door and shout, 'Why is this door locked? Let me in! I know you're up to something nasty!'

But all he wanted was to take a shower in private, without Selma barging in and offering to wash his back.

By the time Jack got to high school, the girls were lining up to go out with him. He had muscles, a slim waist, and broad shoulders. High, androgynous cheekbones. Long, curly lashes that framed his big gray eyes.

'As handsome as a model,' the girls would murmur as they drew hearts around his name and theirs.

Selma forbade him to go on dates, so Jack began lying to her about where he went on Saturday nights. And, inevitably, she found out. Their fights grew increasingly bitter.

One Saturday night he arrived home after midnight to find the front door chained and bolted.

'Come on, Mom, let me in,' he yelled, ringing the bell and knocking loudly.

Lights went on in his mother's bedroom. Her window flew open and her voice rang out loud and clear in the still night air. 'I love you, Jack, but I hate the sin!'

Jack spent a sleepless night in the backseat of his car, wondering what sin he'd committed by taking a girl to the movies. Toward dawn he fell asleep and had lurid, angry nightmares about his mother. When he woke up, the front door was unlocked and she'd already left for church. Neither of them ever mentioned the incident again, but after that Selma seemed much less concerned with his comings and goings. Jack was both relieved and surprised when she stopped asking personal questions and trying to persuade him to come out with her to dinner, the movies, or the theater.

Surprise turned to hurt and shock, however, the day she introduced him to a hearty-looking red-faced man named Bill who called Selma 'hon' and laughed loudly at his own bad jokes.

'Bill's going to be your new daddy, Jack. Congratulate me, I'm getting married again,' Selma said with a smirk.

He had never suspected that she was dating anyone. He hated Bill on sight. He refused to call him 'Dad,' refused to sit down with them when Bill came for dinner, and refused to give the bride away when Selma and Bill were married.

'Very well,' Selma declared. 'If you can't find it in your heart to make friends with my husband, there's no longer

371

a place for you in this house. I've enrolled you in a very fine boarding school in Seattle. Perhaps you'll be happier there.'

He liked his new school. The guys were okay, and the girls all fell madly in love with him. But he only had eyes for pretty, vivacious Anne Clayton, the junior class vice president. When he invited her to the prom and she said yes, he was sure this was the happiest day of his life.

The blackest day came the following fall when Anne invited a boy from a rival prep school to be her date at the Thanksgiving Turkey Trot. Afterward Jack swore to the principal that the other guy had started the fight. And the punch he'd thrown was meant for the boy, but Anne had suddenly gotten in the way. Because certainly he'd never meant to break her nose.

Unconvinced by Jack's explanations and apologies, the principal expelled him. Jack tried not to think about what his mother would say when she found out. Then he decided, the hell with her. She didn't give a shit about him. He knew he could make it without her. He had something to sell – his face and body.

He hitchhiked back to Los Angeles, made the rounds of the modeling agencies, and before too long he was getting steady bookings. Through the classified ads, he found an apartment in West Hollywood and a roommate, Rick Flood. But when Rick's career took off and Jack's languished in LA, he decided to take his chances in the big-time world of New York modeling.

He'd been in New York for almost a year now, and he was fast becoming one of the more sought-after male models in town. But he had less luck with women, and though he looked for her everywhere, he hadn't yet found the girl of his dreams.

Until tonight.

* * *

As much fun as she had dancing the night away with Jack, Dani didn't invite him to come home with her. 'Call me crazy, but I just wasn't ready,' she told Monika the next day.

'Well, *get* ready,' Monika ordered her. 'Because that boy was breathing fire at you. And you know what they say about men in their early twenties – they can get it up and keep it up for as long as you want it. Check it out.'

'Maybe I will.' Dani winked, then got serious. 'But what if he doesn't call?'

'Then you call *him*,' Monika said practically. 'But he'll call. Trust me.'

He not only called but also sent flowers. A dozen long-stemmed roses arrived before lunch, with a note that said, 'Dinner tonight?'

Five minutes later, Lance poked his head in her office. 'Do you know a Jack Andrews? He says it's personal.'

'I'll take it.'

'Want the door shut?'

'Please.' Dani nodded, picking up the phone. 'Hi, Jack. These flowers are beautiful. Thank you. But you shouldn't have.'

'I wanted to. So? How about it?'

'How about what?'

'Dinner. Tonight. I'll pick you up at eight.'

'Tonight?' Dani looked at her calendar. She was having dinner with Ian McAdam, part business, part social. 'Well, I really – '

'Please say yes.' His voice was warm and coaxing.

She remembered how sweetly he'd kissed her when she dropped him off at his apartment. Ian would understand if she rescheduled. 'Okay,' she said. 'You're on. Eight o'clock.' She gave him her address.

'I can't wait to see you again, Dani,' Jack told her.

Well, he certainly wasn't shy. She stared thoughtfully

at the roses, which Lance had arranged in a crystal vase on the side table, and suddenly found herself wondering what Jack would be like in bed.

That evening, by the time they finished dinner, she had decided she was not going to wait much longer before she found out. She was dying to sleep with Jack – and Jack was obviously on the same wavelength. Their hands were all over each other even before they were inside her apartment, and Dani left a trail of clothes and underwear all the way down the hall and up the stairs to her bedroom.

Their first round in bed was an explosion of hormones. The second time around, it was all fun and giggles as Dani began to relax. Jack grinned at her through a haze of postcoital intimacy and went for round three. He reached over and nudged her legs apart.

'More?' she groaned.

'No?'

'Oh, yes, yes, yes,' she whispered as his tongue traveled south. 'Definitely more.'

Publicly, Reggie professed to be all in favor of Rah Rah's acting lessons. 'Keeps the boy off the streets,' he'd say, and chuckle generously when the subject came up with his friends. 'Of course he doesn't have a lick of talent, but far be it from me to point that out to him. Just as long as he's happy. Because if *he's* happy, he keeps *me* happy.'

Privately, Reggie whistled an altogether different tune. Ever fearful that his lover-for-hire was meeting new faces, younger and prettier than his own, Reggie had nagged, bullied, and pleaded with Rah Rah to give up the classes. But Rah Rah wouldn't yield. Acting had become his lifeline to sanity, his road back to self-respect.

Week after week his acting teacher demanded that he bare his soul for the sake of his art. But Rah Rah had sold his soul to Reggie, in return for more money than he could possibly make doing anything respectable. One day soon, he'd buy back his life. In the meantime, not yet ready to sever the tie, he and Reggie maintained an uneasy truce.

Reggie's patience, however, was wearing thin.

Yet another day had passed without so much as a phone call from the money-grubbing little bastard to check when Reggie would be coming home. Obviously Rah Rah couldn't care less whether Reggie had made plans to be out for the evening. Probably he'd be just as happy to stay home alone, memorizing his monologues or dialogues or whatever the hell he so tiresomely insisted upon rehearsing. Of all the phony pretensions . . . Well, he'd give John Barrymore exactly one more hour, and if he didn't call by then –

His private phone rang. Reggie reached for it, then jerked back his hand. He didn't want Rah Rah to think that he was just sitting here waiting to hear from him. Dammit! The boy had it all wrong. Reggie was the one who was shelling out the money. He was supposed to be the one who was calling the shots. Well, no more Mr Nice Guy. He would have a little chat with Rah Rah and set things straight. Tonight. Over dinner.

He counted four rings, then picked up the phone and affected boredom. 'Yes?'

'Are you in the middle of something?' asked Rah Rah.

Though he'd spent the better part of the afternoon getting a manicure and pedicure, he couldn't resist the opening. 'Yes, I am, as a matter of fact. *Some* of us have to work for a living,' he jabbed.

Rah Rah ignored the taunt. 'Do you want to call me back?'

His equanimity infuriated Reggie. 'No, I don't want to call you back,' he snarled. 'I have better things to do with my time. All I want to know is what we're doing about dinner. Lydia's off, so I suppose we'll have to go out.'

'How about ordering in Chinese?'

'How many times do I have to tell you that Chinese gives me gas,' Reggie said peevishly. 'Besides, I'm in the mood for ambience this evening.'

'I'm sorry, Reggie, but I can't do it tonight. I finally got a callback for a show. They want me to come in tomorrow to do a second reading. I really need to work to get the part down.'

Reggie couldn't believe what he was hearing. Some idiot actually thought Rah Rah had talent? More likely he'd been seduced by Rah Rah's looks. Or had it gone further than looking? 'Whose cock did you have to suck to get that callback?' he asked.

'Nice talk, man,' Rah Rah replied, telling himself to ignore Reggie's bitchiness.

Reggie rolled his eyes at the phone. 'Oh, can't you take a joke? I'm just wondering why they would want you when there are so many other actors with more experience who – '

'You know, Reggie, a simple "congratulations" would more than suffice,' Rah Rah broke in. 'Or is that word missing from your vocabulary?'

'Jesus! When did you get to be so fucking sensitive?' Reggie demanded, his voice thick with sarcasm. 'But all right, if it makes you happy, congratulations.'

'Thanks,' Rah Rah said shortly.

'Now that we're updated on your incipient stardom, can you please tell me what we're supposed to have for dinner if you can't go out? *You* may be too busy to eat, but I, for one, would like a decent meal.'

Rah Rah tried to sound conciliatory. 'Let's just scramble some eggs, or I could make you an omelette, okay?'

Scrambled eggs? Screw that! 'That may be fine for you,

376

but I'm not going to eat breakfast for dinner. I'll make other plans,' Reggie snapped, slamming down the phone.

He hadn't come this far to sit at home night after night while Rah Rah mumbled over one of his scripts. He wanted to go out and be seen with Rah Rah by his side. Because what the hell good was having a pretty boyfriend if people didn't know that Rah Rah belonged to him?

His intercom buzzed. 'Yes? What do you want?'

His secretary sighed. All she ever got from Mr Reggie was abuse. She promised herself that this Sunday she'd definitely check the classified ads for a new job. 'Excuse me, Mr Reggie. Mitchell Barton on line two.'

'Oh, all right. I'll take it.' He picked up the phone and gushed, 'Darling, I was just thinking about you. It's been too long.'

'Ages,' Mitchell agreed. 'But I happen to have two tickets to the ballet burning a hole in my wallet. Are you free? We could have an early dinner at Joe Allen and – '

'I'd love to,' said Reggie, cheered by the thought that at least someone cared if he lived or died. 'See you there at six.' He hung up, wondering whether the tickets were freebies and whether Mitchell meant for him to pay for dinner. Well, if Mitchell was amusing enough, maybe this time he would pick up the tab. And the hell with Rah Rah.

The hell with all of them, most especially those bastards at Megacorp who seemed intent on cheapening his image with each new product they licensed. The fragrance line was the exception, and Reggie was delighted to see that the sales for the line were continuing to rise. If those idiots would only read his memos, they'd understand it was because the line was sold in only the most exclusive department stores – where he belonged.

But no. They thought they knew better. They could sell his lines where they pleased. They could license as they saw fit. They could stick a label bearing his name on budgetwear, if they desired. They didn't know diddly-squat about designing, but he was tired of complaining about the quality of the lines that bore his name. When they let him know they were tired of his complaints, he had taken his case to his lawyer. The idiot lawyer had informed him that he was tied to Megacorp by an ironclad agreement that couldn't be broken.

'Oh, yes it can,' Reggie had shot back. Because contracts, like promises, were made to be broken. 'And you'd better get your boys busy figuring out a way. You got me into this; now you can find a way to get me out.'

Just in case his lawyer hadn't gotten the point, Reggie spent what was left of the afternoon dictating a letter to that effect. He wanted his name back, he wanted an end to his name appearing on less talented people's designs, and he wanted O-U-T of this mess.

He handed the tape to his secretary on his way out to meet Mitchell. 'I want this typed and on my desk in the morning.'

The secretary had a date and was hoping to leave as soon as Reggie did. Now she would have to stay late to get the letter done. She cursed the day she'd ever taken the job at Mr Reggie, Inc. 'Of course. And here's the mail from the pouch,' she said, knowing how much he hated the endless stream of memos that arrived each afternoon by messenger from corporate headquarters at Rockefeller Center.

Probably more of those goddam awful sketches, Reggie thought with a pained sigh as he left the building and settled into his limo. Or maybe they'd sent him yet another batch of licensing agreements. He supposed he shouldn't complain. After all, the more licenses, the greater the royalties. His net worth was growing by leaps and bounds.

He took a sip of the vodka martini his driver had mixed for him and tore open the manila envelope, marked 'Personal and Confidential.' Inside was a memo from Frank Gladstone. Quickly Reggie scanned the contents. He almost choked on his martini when he got to the key paragraph.

Megacorp's market research people, wrote Gladstone, had determined that it was time to expand into bath accessories – towels, bath mats, shower curtains, toilet seat covers. And the greatest indignity of all – Mr Reggie toilet paper. A graphic design studio was already working on the logo that would be imprinted on the rolls.

Toilet paper? So that people could wipe their asses with *his* name? No way! No fucking way! Tears of rage and indignation sprang to his eyes. He gulped back the rest of the martini and poured himself another. Megacorp had betrayed him, and Gladstone hadn't even given him the courtesy of a phone call before proceeding. He would be the laughingstock of Seventh Avenue.

How long before Mitchell got wind of this hideous new development? What if he decided to run it in his column? Reggie shuddered. He could only hope and pray that their long-standing relationship would count for something.

The next few hours loomed ahead like a bad dream. He would have to put on a happy face, pretend all was well, and trade gossip as usual. What a farce. Tonight he had no stomach for dinner and the theater. What he wanted . . . craved . . . was a tranquilizer and the comfort of his bed.

Toilet paper?

That was really too much.

'I think I've finally come to understand the meaning of the word "stud,"' Dani announced to Monika several weeks into her affair with Jack.

'Sort of like an American Express Gold Card, *ja*? No woman should be without one.'

'That's one way of looking at it. Put it this way – I used to drink coffee and read the *Times* in the morning before I went to work. Now I make love. Monika, I know he's too young and not at all right for me, but my God, I haven't had this much fun in years!'

Monika felt a twinge of jealousy. That was how it had been between her and Rick. Nowadays she bounced from one man to the next. None of them meant anything more to her than dinner and a quick fuck. Just as well, since she really didn't have the energy or the time for anyone as attentive as Jack.

Occasionally she wondered what might have been had she made more of an effort to stay in touch with Rick. Again and again he'd asked her to visit him in Los Angeles, and always she'd said no. And then they'd had that stupid fight because she'd been so sure he was sleeping with Katie Quinn. He still sent Monika postcards from Japan or Australia or wherever he was touring, and whenever he put out a new record, a copy would arrive in the mail with a note, 'Compliments of Rick Flood.' Probably a secretary had gone through his address book and put her on his comp list.

She shook off her melancholy and tried to focus on her friend's happiness. 'So, have you thought about using Jack for the sheet ads? Talk about hot! What could be more authentic than the two of you in bed together?'

'We do seem to spend rather a lot of time there,' Dani admitted. 'And Lord knows he's dying for the job, but I don't think I want to use him for the ads.'

'Why not? He's certainly handsome enough.'

'But he's not quite right . . . too pretty, too young. Besides, I don't need people to accuse me of being a cradle robber.'

Monika was surprised. 'After everything else you've been called, I shouldn't think you'd mind.'

'It's more than that. We need a man who screams sex. Who lets you know he's going to be one hot fuck without even saying a word.'

'Ooh, sounds delicious. You'll find him sooner or later – and when you do, send him my way, *ja*?'

'Sure, sweetie. Only it had better be sooner rather than later. We don't have all the time in the world on this. And speaking of time,' she said as she checked her watch, 'I'd better get going. I'm taking Jack to dinner at Le Cirque.'

Monika raised an eyebrow. Usually Dani preferred someplace where she was less likely to be recognized by many people. 'Le Cirque? Better watch out not to spoil the boy.'

'It's Jack's birthday, and I told him he could choose the restaurant. I don't dare ask him how old he is,' Dani said with a laugh. 'Would you like to join us?'

'Thanks, but I already have plans,' Monika said. 'Besides, I wouldn't want to ruin Jack's birthday celebration. And from what you've been telling me, it sounds as if he wants you all to himself.'

'Unfortunately, yes. That's okay in bed, of course. But he has some funny ideas about us. He's even mentioned marriage a couple of times.'

'Marriage? You hardly know each other!'

'I know. I also know I don't *ever* want to be married to him. I've tried not to lead him on, Monika, honestly I have. But when I try to tell him this is just for kicks, he always changes the subject. Do you think I'm making a terrible mistake?'

'Sounds like he's the one making the mistake. Don't worry, *liebchen*. He's very young, probably not very experienced. Say no to him a few times, and he'll get the idea. Now, go have a romantic evening.'

Their evening was almost ruined because the usually elegant, serene atmosphere of Le Cirque was disturbed by loud conversation punctuated by gales of laughter coming from the table next to theirs. One man in particular caught Dani's attention. When Jack excused himself to go to the men's room, she glanced over and took a longer look. The man was certainly the life of the party, gesturing broadly, speaking with an accent she couldn't quite place, making sure everyone was having a good time.

Who could he be, she wondered, that he'd been allowed into Le Cirque dressed like a cowboy, in blue jeans, boots, and a leather bomber jacket?

The man looked up, caught her staring, and grinned. 'To you, pretty girl,' he called out, raising his glass.

Dani blushed and quickly turned away.

Jack came back to the table, frowning and shaking his head. 'What a jerk,' he said.

'Who?' she asked.

'That Aussie loudmouth at the next table. If he doesn't know how to behave, he oughta go back to where he came from instead of causing a ruckus here.'

'Do you know who he is?'

'Yeah, sure I do. Kyle Lord. I used to see him in LA all the time. The girls were always falling all over him 'cause they thought he was real hot shit. The next Mel Gibson, that sort of thing.'

'He's an actor?'

'Hey, how come you're so interested in him?' Jack asked sourly. 'Let's talk about something interesting, not that dumb Australian asshole.'

It annoyed Dani that Jack got jealous so easily. More

of his immaturity. She'd told him over and over again that she wasn't his girlfriend, that she was seeing other men. 'I hope you're not sleeping with anyone else,' he'd muttered. In point of fact, she wasn't, but he didn't have to know that. Far better for him to think he didn't have exclusive rights to her – which he most certainly did not.

But it *was*, after all, his birthday, so she obligingly changed the subject and tried to concentrate on what Jack was telling her about his latest modeling assignment.

'Excuse me, mate,' came a voice over Jack's shoulder. Kyle Lord, all six-feet-plus of him, peered down at them. 'Hope you don't mind,' he said, 'but I've been staring at this lovely lady here, and I just wanted to give her this rose to stick in her hair.'

Jack bristled. 'Who the hell – '

'Jack, please,' Dani said, embarrassed by the commotion. 'Mr Lord, I really don't think – '

Kyle Lord looked pleased. 'Oh, you know who I am, then?'

'Well, yes, I mean, not really, but – '

'But you'd like to *get* to know me?' Kyle grinned, and dimples formed on either side of his mouth.

She mentally groaned at his gauche come-on but found herself falling for the dimples. For all his crudeness, he had something . . . an animal magnetism . . . that caught her by surprise. But she didn't want him to think she was in the same class as the LA girls who'd obviously puffed up his ego. She wouldn't play his game, not with Jack looking as if he might haul off and deck the guy.

'Excuse me, Mr Lord, is it common practice in Australia for men to approach women who are obviously otherwise engaged?' she said.

'Engaged, are you? To this pup?'

Well-heeled diners at nearby tables began to watch the exchange.

'Listen, you son of a bitch,' Jack growled, 'why don't you go back down under? My girlfriend and I are just trying to have – '

'Your girlfriend?' Kyle Lord began to roar with laughter, causing heads to turn all over the restaurant. 'I thought she was your mum – or your big sister, anyway. You don't even look old enough to drink.' He picked up Jack's wineglass and took a swig. 'Hmm, nice. You've got good taste in wine, I'll say that much.'

Dani flushed bright red. What a waste that such an attractive man should behave like such a boor.

'Why don't you just take the bottle, Mr Lord,' she said icily. 'And now, if you'll excuse us, this is a private party – and you're not invited.'

'Right-o, I get the hint. Some other time, maybe,' Lord said jauntily, not in the least intimidated by her sarcasm.

His arrogance astonished her. Where did he get off talking to her like that? Stifling an impulse to slap his grinning face, she said stiffly, 'Don't hold your breath, Mr Lord. You'd have to put a gun to my head first.'

384

Chapter Fourteen

New York

A week later Monika walked into Dani's office, dropped a press packet on her desk, and announced, 'I've found the perfect man for you.'

'You sound just like my father,' Dani said, laughing.

'Really,' she insisted. 'He's tall, dark, handsome . . .'

'Don't tell me he's Jewish, too.'

'Dani, I'm serious. I'm not talking about getting married. I mean for the sheets campaign. I was invited to a screening last night of a movie called *Lost Survivor*. Dani, I swear to you, every time this man looked through the camera at me, I got wet. Here – take a look for yourself, though you have to see him in action to get the true effect.' She thumbed through the press kit and picked out an eight-by-ten glossy of the male lead.

Dani glanced at the picture and almost choked on her coffee. Kyle Lord stared back at her. 'I've seen him in action, thank you very much, and he's got the manners of a Neanderthal man. I'd rather walk on hot coals than get into bed with him.'

'Who gives a damn about his manners? We're talking about sex appeal. If you want to sell sheets, this is the guy. Just go see the movie.'

Dani stuck the photo in her desk and forgot all about it until the movie opened the following Friday, and she read a review of it in the *Times*. The reviewer called it a 'passably good romantic adventure,' then went on to say, 'Rising star Kyle Lord plays the part to perfection. He is rugged but gentle, gruff but honest, determined but not so ruthless that we don't fall absolutely madly in love with his character every time he struts across the screen.'

'Struts' is right, Dani thought as she sat alone in the darkened movie theater, munching on popcorn. Kyle Lord was cocky beyond all endurance. But cocky was good, she reminded herself. And Monika was right on the money. She and Kyle would make a great-looking couple. He was taller than she, probably over six feet with muscles that she could tell had developed naturally, not in a gym. His sandy hair looked as if even mousse couldn't tame it. He had deep brown eyes, not quite the color of Nino's but close, and a mischievous grin. And, oh, yes, those dimples – she remembered those dimples.

Kyle Lord had the star quality they'd been searching for. They could be an unbeatable combination. Of all the men in the world . . . No! Life was too short, she decided. She just wasn't that desperate.

Monika thought differently. Normally she didn't second-guess Dani's creative decisions, but this time she was so convinced Dani was wrong that she mounted a one-woman campaign on behalf of Kyle Lord. She tracked down the name of his agent, Samantha Martin, and sent Dani a memo: 'Don't you know her? How about calling her before you go out to LA next week? Perhaps she could set you two up for drinks or dinner. Dani, at least talk to the guy! P.S. Have you noticed that *Lost Survivor* has been number two in box office receipts for the past month?'

Yes, she had noticed, but she probably would have ignored Monika's plea if Ian McAdam hadn't called an hour later to remind her that they were about to run into scheduling problems. 'I'll be happy to send over more head shots, but keep in mind that we have to make a decision soon,' he said.

Dani had just one question for him. 'Tell me the truth – did Monika put you up to this?'

'What are you talking about?' Ian asked, all wide-eyed innocence. 'Monika who?'

'All right, I get the message,' she said, faintly irritated. She hung up, searched through her drawer for the picture of Kyle Lord, and propped it up against the lamp on her desk. Okay, she decided after a long look, she owed it to her company to check him out. Sighing, she picked up the phone and called Samantha, a fast-talking, gum-cracking transplanted New Yorker whom everyone called Sam.

'Dani,' said Sam, 'I'd love to help you out, but our boy Kyle's between a different pair of sheets every night. It's a miracle he hasn't caught the clap yet – or worse. Just kidding, of course. Listen, if the money's right, it's fine with me, but the final decision is his. Tell you what, next time you're in town, let me know. I'll arrange a meeting.'

'How about next week? Tell him I'm looking forward to it,' Dani said, trying to sound enthusiastic.

Los Angeles

Dani felt even less enthusiastic when she pulled up in front of Spago, late as usual after a day spent talking to her customers at the shop. The last thing in the world she was in the mood for was a second-round sparring match with the man who obviously thought he was God's gift to womankind.

The first words out of his mouth when he rose to greet her did nothing to reassure her. 'You! Well, fancy that, love. Guess you decided to invite me to your party after all.'

'Small world, isn't it, Mr Lord?' she said, shaking his hand.

'Please, call me Kyle. Can't stand on formalities if we're going to be tumbling around together between the sheets.'

Was he being a wise guy? She couldn't help wondering about his choice of words but decided to ignore the double meaning. 'Oh, so you've made up your mind to do the ads?' she asked, smiling brightly and mentally crossing her fingers. Maybe this would be easier than she'd anticipated.

'Now, I didn't say that, did I?' Kyle grinned. 'It kind of depends on how the . . . chemistry feels between us. Know what I mean?'

'Yes, I think I do,' she said stiffly.

Kyle looked at her. Did she have a stick up her ass or what? He had no use for this snooty rich-bitch shit. Sam had given him a quick take on Dani diPortanova: she'd started her own design company; she'd been married to an Italian fellow who had died the year before in a car wreck; she was very rich and a tough negotiator.

As far as he could tell, what all that added up to was that she was a spoiled girl who'd got lucky playing designer with her rich husband's money. She was also a hot broad with nice tits and a great pair of legs. He liked the idea of jerking her chain a bit. He said, 'I've got some questions for you. First off, why'd you pick this place to eat? Look at everyone staring at us. We'll be in all the trades tomorrow, you can count on it. Tinsel Town gossip.'

'I'm sure you're used to that by now. Doesn't it come with the territory of being a star? The way I see it, gossip sells clothes. And I can live with whatever increases my sales.'

'Including me?'

She almost laughed aloud at his bluntness. 'Well, yes, now that you mention it.'

'So where's your boyfriend tonight?'

She was saved from having to reply by the appearance of a waiter who offered them menus and a wine list. 'How's white?' she asked.

He shrugged. 'Sounds fine.'

'Good. We'll have a bottle of your best California Chardonnay,' she told the waiter. 'And we'll need a few more minutes to decide what we want to eat.'

As Kyle studied his menu, Dani surreptitiously studied him. He was dressed much the same way he'd been dressed in New York, but he looked less out of place here than he had in the more formal atmosphere of Le Cirque. And though Sam had made a point of telling her Kyle was the current Hollywood darling, there was something distinctly un-Hollywood about him.

She discovered during dinner that behind his brusque, macho exterior lurked a much more complicated man than she might have guessed. He was surprisingly well read and probably one of the most unpretentious people she'd ever met.

'Tell me more about yourself,' she said, and to her surprise, he did, describing what it had been like to grow up in the Australian outback.

His father, he told her, a third-generation Aussie, was the general manager of the Newcastle Waters cattle station in northern Australia, a vast and untamed territory. His mother, who had died when Kyle was six, was English – a wild, rebellious girl who'd come out to visit her sister and stayed to marry Kyle's father. It was from her that Kyle inherited his love of reading. Whenever he could sneak away from his chores, he would hole up with one of the books she'd had sent over from England, and lose himself for an hour or two.

For the most part, however, he and his two older

brothers had grown up outdoors on horseback, helping their dad run the 4,000-square-mile cattle station. Surrounded by men, except for Emma who kept the house and cooked their meals, he concluded early on that women were either stout and motherly like Emma or fun-loving 'Sheilas,' as his big brothers called the girls from town who liked to be bought a drink and shown who was the boss.

He might never have left home had he not been discovered by an Australian director who was shooting a film at Newcastle Waters and hired him as an extra. When a bit player took ill, the director gave the tiny speaking part to Kyle. He was instantly hooked on the movies, drunk on visions of Sheilas falling all over him, dreams of life in Hollywood. When the director casually suggested that he think about taking a shot as an actor, Kyle decided that the two-day trip to Sydney by bus and train was worth the gamble. It sure beat spending the rest of his life on a cattle station.

He rented a flat at Bondi Beach and soon made friends with the surfers who threw him into the water and taught him how to ride the waves. 'No harder than riding a horse,' he wrote his father and brothers. 'So far, no complaints about this place.'

He looked up the director, who tossed a few small parts his way and sent him around to some of his friends. In between films, when the money was short, he earned his rent laying bricks. His evenings were spent with his mates at the Hotel Cecil in Cronulla, playing snooker and getting drunk on Castlemain beer. After midnight when the crowds got rough and the bottles began to fly, he would duck over to the more sedate Cronulla Leagues Club where one of his pals played sax with a band he'd put together called Men at Work.

By the time his fourth movie, Royal Decree, was released in the United States, he was ready to move on. He blew into Hollywood like a tornado, and his irreverent Aussie attitude drove the studio execs crazy. They tried to refine him, tried to teach him better table manners, and tried to give him pointers on how to handle the press.

Kyle wasn't interested. 'Stuff it,' he told them. He wasn't about to make himself over – not for all the fame and money in Hollywood. The execs shrugged their shoulders and backed off. Kyle Lord's rugged looks, undeniable sex appeal, and native intelligence added up to a very marketable package. None of them wanted to jeopardize their piece of the pie by antagonizing him.

Kyle's first couple of years in America were a blur of wild parties, silver trays piled with coke, and plenty of women with big soft tits, hard nipples, and wet pussy. Before long he had developed a reputation as Hollywood's hottest and baddest boy – the stud from Down Under who could always get it up. And in a town where one's status was based on momentary notoriety rather than lasting achievement, Kyle moved almost overnight from a nobody to an A list regular.

The cognoscenti told him he was fantastic, fabulous, incredible, too fucking much. Privately, Kyle thought they were full of shit, but he enjoyed the perks that came with his celebrity rating. He could show up at Spago or Ma Maison dressed in his usual jeans, boots, and faded white shirt and be guaranteed the best available table. The kid from the outback was hot stuff. Almost overnight he had lots of money and lots of girls who wanted to help him spend it.

A writer for Rolling Stone *magazine paid a visit to his house in Malibu and remarked on the large collection of unopened cologne bottles stashed away in a bathroom cabinet. 'Christmas gifts,' Kyle said carelessly, from women who'd slept with him once or twice and hoped to be invited back. 'But what would I want with that bloody perfume? If you have to slap that crap on you, you probably don't have the goods.'*

Obviously he did have the goods, because women never said no to him. Nor did his manager, his press agent, or the studio VIPs. They recognized that Kyle Lord had that oh-so-rare star quality, and they weren't about to piss him off and risk losing him.

Because none of them took the time to dig beneath the surface, none of them understood that Kyle Lord would never walk away from a friend or a deal. He saw the glitz for what it was – all flash and trash that could fade as quickly as the smog in the noonday LA sun. He loved getting paid for acting, because nothing else he'd ever done was even half as much fun. But he also knew that the day they stopped sending the good parts his way, he could happily catch a flight back home and never mind a bit. And that was the real secret of Kyle Lord's success . . .

'Sorry,' he said to Dani as he waited for his espresso to cool, 'I didn't mean to go on like that. You must be bored silly.'

'No, not at all,' Dani assured him. 'I'm glad we had this chance to talk, Kyle. I hope we can work together. I think it could be mutually satisfying.'

The smirk on his face made her regret her words the instant they were out of her mouth. *Shit!* He would think she was coming on to him, which couldn't be further from the truth. Unlike all those other women who threw themselves at Kyle Lord's feet, Dani found that he didn't do a thing for her. Not a goddam thing. Blushing violently, she signaled the waiter for their check. The sooner they brought this evening to a close, the better.

'So, about the ad campaign . . .'

'Talk to my agent,' Kyle said, bored with the subject. For a while, she'd had him fooled. Now he saw she really was no different from the rest of the women he'd balled lately.

'I have,' Dani said, trying not to lose her temper. For a smart man, Kyle Lord certainly could act dumb. 'She told me to talk to you. That's why we're here tonight.'

'Is that right? And here I thought you wanted to see more of my pretty face.' He grinned. 'All right, talk to Sam again. I never mix business with pleasure.'

Dani tapped her foot angrily beneath the table. 'Mr Lord,' she began. She stopped mid-sentence as the waiter appeared with the check.

Kyle grabbed for it before she had a chance to say a word.

Did this cowboy think she couldn't afford to pick up the tab? Or did he expect to be repaid for his generosity? She hesitated a moment, trying to decide whether it was worth arguing over. 'Mr Lord,' she said again.

'Kyle . . .'

'Kyle, *I* invited you to dinner. I'd love for you to be my guest.'

'Sure thing, Dani, but where I come from ladies don't pay for themselves, no matter how much money they have. I would love to be your guest, though. Just name the time and place.'

Again, there was that exasperating grin and those two damn dimples. Did he practice smiling like that? Sam hadn't told her Kyle Lord was such a wise guy. But two could play the same game, if necessary. 'Fine,' she conceded. 'If you insist. And thank you for dinner.'

'Thank *you*.'

Exasperated, she leaned across the table and demanded, 'Do we have a deal or not?'

'Why don't we discuss it at my place?' Kyle said, figuring she'd hem and haw but finally say yes. The electricity buzzing between them was unmistakable.

Dani stood up abruptly. She'd had about as much as she could take of this clown. Barely controlling her anger, she said crisply, 'Get this straight, Mr Lord. I'm not one of your bimbo starlets. I'm here to make a deal with you. If you're still interested in working with me, you can reach me in the morning at the Beverly Hills Hotel.'

She was still fuming when she got back to the hotel. Maybe she was making a big mistake. Maybe she should call Samantha Martin and tell her to forget it, she'd changed her mind about Kyle Lord. Instead, to blow off steam, she dialed Monika's number. To her surprise she got Monika, not her machine. 'You're home,' she said. 'Thank God. I needed a friendly voice.'

Monika got straight to the point. 'Well? How was Mr. Aussie Stud?'

'Monika, he's the most infuriating, barbaric, insulting man I've ever met,' she snapped, as if she held Monika personally responsible for Kyle Lord's behavior.

'*Liebchen*, you didn't have a good time,' Monika said sympathetically. 'And here my imagination was going wild.'

'The hell with your imagination! That man is impossible. He's a crude egomaniac who has only one thing on his brain – sex!'

'How thrilling! Too bad you didn't get a chance to check out the equipment. So? Do we have a deal?'

'He hasn't said yes yet, but I think he was just jerking me around. I have the feeling he'll come around. And God help us if he does.'

'*Ach*, don't be such a pessimist,' Monika scolded. 'I'm sure he's not as bad as you say. He could grow on you if you get to know him better.'

'Fat chance of that,' Dani huffed. 'I'd rather snuggle up with a rattlesnake.'

'*Ja*, sure you would, Dani. Whatever you say,' Monika agreed.

They both knew she was lying.

Monika wished Dani pleasant dreams, replaced the receiver, and broke down in tears. How much longer, she wondered, could she keep up the facade of cheerfulness and enthusiasm when her life was verging on disaster? There were times when she truly loathed herself for all the lies she told to hide the truth from her best friend. How could this have happened? How could she possibly admit to Dani that she owed the management of Lucky's close to a million dollars?

At first they'd been polite. And why not, for as Scott Devane had made a point of reminding her, she'd been a loyal customer for quite some time. They would hate to lose her as a player. Monika had shuddered. His words sounded more like a threat than reassurance.

Devane had proposed a payment plan for a new line of credit. The only catch was the semiannual 50 percent interest rate. '*Ja*, certainly,' Monika had said, as if the money meant nothing to her. What choice did she have?

Much as she hated to do it, she had sold her Jaguar to make the first payment of $40,000. Now the second payment was coming due, and she was half mad with worry about how to find the money to meet it. Piece by piece she'd already stripped her once beautifully furnished brownstone of the most valuable antiques. Her jewelry collection was now down to a few pieces she'd held on to in order to keep up appearances. The only valuable items she had left were a few furs, including the sable she'd brought with her years ago from England.

She'd paid almost $200,000 for it back then. Now? She had no idea how much the coat would fetch, but she soon might have to find out. Christ! This was too humiliating, having to sell the very clothes off her back.

In her head she composed a letter to Karola: 'Dear Mother, I'm terribly sorry for all the shame I caused the family. Won't you please forgive me? Love, Monika. P.S. Could you also please restore my inheritance and send a check for $1 million . . . no, make that $1.5 million . . . posthaste?'

To quote Dani, she'd rather snuggle up with a rattle-snake. Karola was at least as cold-blooded as any reptile and far more calculating.

That was one letter that would never get written, much less mailed. She would have to come up with some other solution. All she needed was a little time.

Lake Garda, Italy

The diPortanova family photo albums were neatly lined up on a corner shelf of Roberto's library. The albums, covered in silver and embossed with the family coat of arms, contained a carefully documented pictorial history that spanned several generations of diPortanovas. Engagements, weddings, births, christenings, anniversaries, funerals, and the other less momentous but equally noteworthy moments that make up the life of a family – all were chronicled within these albums, carefully tended to by Benedetta.

Roberto hadn't so much as glanced at the albums in years. But on this second day of April, 1982, on what would have been his son's thirty-fourth birthday, he locked the library door and pulled out the volume Benedetta had marked with the date of Nino's birth.

Here was a picture of Nino cradled in his adoring mother's arms.

Nino taking his first steps.

Nino all dressed up for his first day of school.

Nino, age nine, behind the wheel of Roberto's Alfa Romeo, pretending to drive.

Roberto turned the pages slowly, seeing his son again through the eye of the camera. So much joy and life. So many promises of a bright, shining future. Promises destined to remain unkept.

The album ended with several pages of informal pictures taken on the eve of Nino's wedding. Nino, his parents, his sisters, his aunts and uncles and cousins.

Pain and anger gnawed at Roberto's heart as he stared at a shot of Nino surrounded by his nieces and nephews. One of the little girls had flung her arm around his shoulder; another had her tiny fist buried in his dark curls. A chubby baby, smiling good-naturedly, dangled from his lap.

If there was any justice in the universe, another album should have been dedicated to Nino's growing family – pages of photos of Nino surrounded by his *own* children. But, of course, no such album existed. Would never exist, thanks to the cruel and ugly twist of fate that had wiped out his son's life and forever destroyed, along with all Roberto's hopes and dreams for Nino, the ancient house of diPortanova.

'My son, you must find forgiveness in your heart,' the priest had counseled Roberto when he had poured out his anguish in the privacy of the confessional booth. 'You must reach out to the living. Remember our Holy Father's lessons on forgiveness from the book of Matthew: "Your heavenly Father will forgive you if you forgive those who sin against you, but if you refuse to forgive them, He will not forgive you."'

But hadn't the Bible also taught him about 'an eye for

an eye, a tooth for a tooth . . . Vengeance is mine, thus sayeth the Lord'?

Could Roberto permit himself the luxury of ignoring that lesson? Could he truly allow his son's death to go unavenged? Did he not owe it to the memory of his beloved Gianni to reach out and smite the whore in their midst?

Los Angeles and New York

To no one's great surprise, Kyle agreed to do the sheet ads. Sam asked for a lot of money, Dani offered a little more than she'd planned to, and they quickly agreed on a compromise figure. 'Dynamite!' Sam exclaimed, cracking her gum. 'You'll see, Dani. He's worth every penny.'

'He just better behave himself. No prima donna bullshit,' Dani warned her. She was more pleased with his decision than she'd admit to being. He *was* perfect for the ads, even if he was an arrogant jerk.

'I can't guarantee what he'll do at night, but you can depend on him to show up on time and follow orders like a dream,' Sam promised.

Her business in LA successfully completed, Dani flew back to New York. Her limo was waiting at the airport to take her straight to the office. 'Good trip?' her driver asked as he picked up her bags and stashed them in the front seat.

'Great, Joe,' she said. When she'd left New York two days ago, the air had smelled as soft and sweet as spring. Now it suddenly felt like winter again, but she didn't mind a bit. She was glad to be home, even if the early-morning skies were brooding and gray with the threat of April showers and the temperature was a good fifteen degrees lower than in Los Angeles.

She settled back against the seat, quickly scanned the *Times* and *WWD*, which Joe had picked up on his way out to La Guardia, and didn't look up again until the car emerged from the Queens-Midtown Tunnel. 'Is it supposed to stay cold like this all day?'

'All day, continuing into the night,' Joe said.

A good night to cuddle up in bed and catch up on her phone calls and reading. Ugh, that sounded virtuous but terribly dull. How about a good night to cuddle up in bed with Jack? She had decided in Los Angeles that she would see him less often, so as to discourage his fantasies about their relationship. But didn't she owe it to him to let him down easy?

Bullshit. She was horny. She wanted to get laid. With any luck, Jack would be free to play with her.

'Joe,' she said, 'I'll need you to pick me up at seven and drive me home. After that, you've got yourself a night off.'

At her office, Dani bounced past the receptionist, made a beeline for her office, and waved gaily at Lance. 'What's new?' she sang out.

Lance grimaced. 'Please, you know how I feel about a cheerful face first thing in the morning. What did *you* drink for breakfast? Or was it something you ate in LA?' He handed her a stack of messages. 'You'll notice that Jack has already called four times, and it's not even ten o'clock. I beg of you, Countess D., call the boy back. He's getting paranoid . . . accused me of hiding his messages from you.'

If she hadn't trusted Lance to keep her deepest secrets, she would have been furious with Jack for being so indiscreet. As it was, she was mortified. 'Lance, I'm sorry. I'll talk to him.'

That night she tried, as she and Jack sat in her living

room. First, she broke the news to him that they would be using Kyle in the ads instead of him.

'You're making a big mistake, Dani,' he said, throwing back a long gulp of scotch. 'But it's none of my business, right?'

Right. But she didn't answer him out loud.

'So tell me, when and where are you filming the commercials?'

Dani steeled herself for what was likely to be a tense few moments. She had a feeling she knew what Jack was leading up to – and she had already decided the answer would have to be no. 'We'll be shooting in the Caribbean. Ian hasn't decided exactly where yet, but the shoot will probably be in mid-May. It sounds exhausting – two days of work and all that traveling.'

Jack got up and walked over to the bar to pour himself more scotch. 'Feel like company? I could arrange to come down with you. It'd be fun. Maybe we could take an extra day down there and – '

'Jack,' Dani said gently, 'that sounds lovely, but I don't think so. Our schedule will be very tight. You'd be bored.'

And if he bought that . . . The truth was that she would have felt uncomfortable with Jack watching her in bed – even if it was just for the cameras – with Kyle Lord.

'Another time, maybe, all right?' she murmured, ashamed of herself for lying.

'Yeah, sure, another time,' Jack muttered. 'So, uh . . . I really missed you, Dani. I've been thinking about making love to you ever since you called this morning.'

'Me, too.' She smiled, relieved that he was letting her off the hook so easily. But she felt guilty, too, because what was for her a fling – a way to let off steam – was obviously something very important to Jack. *Monika, help!* she thought.

'Well, what are we waiting for?' Jack said, coming over

and taking her hand. 'Last one into the bedroom has to give a full body massage.'

After her first climax, when she was well on her way to a second, Jack rolled away from her and said, 'I have a surprise for you.'

'Mmmmm,' she purred, and stretched. 'What are you going to do to me now?'

'Something different tonight. You're going to love it. Close your eyes and relax.'

She heard him rustling around in the pile of clothes on the floor.

'What are you doing, Jack?' she asked.

'Hey, no peeking,' he said. He rubbed his finger along the outer lips of her vagina and whispered, 'Time to go skiing, honey.'

'Jack, what's that?' she murmured. 'Ooh, it tingles.'

Then she realized what he was doing to her.

'Goddammit!' She sat up and grabbed for a tissue. 'Get that shit off me! How dare you?'

'Hey, baby, just a little coke down there. What's the big deal?'

She glared at him. 'Are you nuts? That's dangerous. Besides, my husband was addicted to cocaine, among several other substances. Coke almost killed him. Don't you ever bring drugs into my house again, do you understand?'

'Yeah, sure, babe, sorry,' he stammered, furious with himself for being so dumb. 'Do you want me to get you a towel or something to – '

'Forget it. I'm going to take a shower.' She jumped up, stalked into the bathroom, and slammed the door.

Shit. He'd heard all the stories about Nino, but he never thought she'd . . . Suddenly his mother's voice echoed in his head: *That's right, Jack. You never think.*

Dear God, now he'd gone and totally fucked everything up.

As usual, Jack. Because you can never do anything right, came his mother's voice again.

Tears of frustration and anger welled up in his eyes. He slammed his fist into the pillow and bit down hard on his lip, trying to hold back the sobs. Dani meant so much to him . . . she was his whole life. He'd never met a girl like her before. He buried his face in the pillow so she wouldn't hear him crying. He would never want her to know how much it hurt that he'd made her mad.

But he could make it up to her. She still loved him and needed him. He could see it in her eyes when she looked at him. He could feel it in her lips when they kissed.

He would apologize to her. Make love to her in the shower. It would be as if nothing had happened. Wiping his eyes, he picked up the vial of coke, fished a tiny mirror out of his pants pocket, and sprinkled a line across the surface of the glass. Just one little toot of nose candy was all it took for him to feel okay again.

Checking himself in the mirror to make sure there were no telltale flakes clinging to his nose, he knocked on the bathroom door. 'Dani,' he called, trying to be heard above the running water. 'Dani, I'm sorry. Please say you'll forgive me, Dani. Please . . .'

Chapter Fifteen

New York

Bunny, standing by her assistant's desk, tapped her foot impatiently and snapped, 'Messages?'

She wasn't in any particular hurry, but sometimes she enjoyed hassling her assistant, just to remind the girl that Bunny was the boss. 'C'mon,' she snapped again, 'I don't have all day to stand here and wait till you get your act together.'

The assistant, whose name was Carter and who came from Texas, smiled sweetly. 'They're already on your desk, Barbara,' she drawled in an accent that was thicker than barbecue sauce. 'Did y'all have a good lunch?'

Bunny ignored the question and hurried into her office, her heels tapping smartly against the tiles. Hiring Carter had been a huge mistake. The girl, it turned out, was from one of Texas's first and best families. Remember the Alamo, and all that shit. When Bunny had told her she was from North Carolina, Carter's face had lit up. 'I've got relatives there, too,' she had said. 'Maybe we're related.'

Not real likely, unless Carter's granddaddy had a love-child hidden away in Moccasin Bottom. But of course Bunny couldn't tell her that, and now she lived with the fear that somehow Carter could damage the fiction she'd carefully woven about her family.

Maybe if she made life miserable enough for her, the girl would quit. Too bad she was so damn efficient. Bunny's phone messages were stacked on the spindle. She plopped herself down and thumbed through them, pleased to note that her new beau had called. If he wanted to have dinner, she'd say yes.

Barry Weintraub was kind of dull, always babbling on about trade regulation and interlocking directorates and how many miles he'd run that week. But he was totally loaded and a whole lot more generous than all those tight-assed preppies she'd been dating. He was a partner at a *very* hotsy-totsy law firm, drove a gorgeous BMW, and owned a co-op on Park Avenue and a house on Shelter Island. Best of all, unlike old Irving, he didn't mind a bit that she was a *shiksa*. In fact, she suspected that only added to her charm as far as he was concerned.

Hell, she was tired of flitting around from man to man. Maybe she'd even marry this one if he asked. She could do a whole lot worse. He could certainly afford the life-style to which she'd like to become accustomed. Plus he was hardly ever home, always rushing off to Dallas or Washington or Chicago on business, which added to his charm as far as *she* was concerned.

The last message was from a Stan Moore with a 213 area code. Bunny knew that 213 was Los Angeles, but who was Stan Moore? She drummed her fingernails on her desk as she searched through her mental data base of names and faces. Moore . . . Moore . . . Then it came back to her. The sleazy TV producer with the awful gold chains who'd been seated next to her at that dinner party on Central Park South. The one who'd squeezed her ass under the table.

Well, well. That must have been at least nine or ten months ago. Either Stan Moore had a good memory, or she must have made quite an impression on him, because she'd only mentioned once in passing that she worked for Countess Dani. What on earth could he want from her, besides the obvious? Now *that* was a revolting thought.

Did he take the gold chains off before he got into bed? she wondered. Or did he make his girlfriends work around them? Well, thank God she would never know the answer to that.

She crumbled up the message slip and tossed it into the wastebasket. Stan Moore could go slime up some other girl's legs. She didn't need him, certainly not with Barry Weintraub, Esquire, practically tucked away in her back pocket.

She buzzed Carter. 'If Stan Moore calls again, tell him I'm unavailable. Tell him I'll get back to him when I have the time.'

Which would be never.

Mustique

On Mustique, the Caribbean island playground of the elite, Dani had arranged for the film crew to take over several cottages at the island's only hotel, the Cotton House. For Ian and herself she rented one of the private mansions that came complete with a French chef and a five-person staff – and separate bedrooms, of course.

'At five thousand dollars a week, thank you very much,' Monika grumbled. 'Couldn't you have found a less expensive island on which to shoot these damn commercials?'

'It's a write-off,' Dani scoffed. Besides, why was Monika suddenly worried about money? That wasn't like her.

To make a dramatic ad, Dani was willing to spend more for the perfect sandy beaches, the cloudless azure sky, and the sparkling blue water lapping gently at the shore. Mustique would be the ideal spot for a honeymoon or a romantic adventure with the man of Dani's dreams, whoever that man might be. He certainly wasn't Kyle Lord.

Dani hadn't expected to see Kyle until they started shooting the commercials. But the night before she left for Mustique, as she walked out of her store at the Plaza, she had spotted him across the hotel lobby. A busty blonde, her tits falling out of her low-cut silk shirt, was hanging on his arm and giggling madly. Earlier, Dani had almost called Sam Martin to find out where Kyle was staying so she could invite him to dinner with his number one fan, Monika. Now she was glad she hadn't bothered. She should have known he'd find his own entertainment.

Well, he'd better not be planning to bring his entertainment along with him to Mustique, she had thought when she saw him in the Plaza. The schedule Ian had set up didn't allow any room for fucking around. Speaking of which, the blonde was now running her hand up and down Kyle's back, her fingers lingering suggestively on his butt. How tacky. Why didn't they just go upstairs to his room and screw their brains out if that's what they wanted to do?

All of a sudden she was in no mood to chitchat with Kyle Lord and his latest conquest. She turned around and hurried back into the store to wait until the coast was clear. She wondered as she waited whether she'd made a big mistake by choosing him to do the ads with her. Something about that man set her teeth on edge. She only hoped they could both be professional enough to give the kind of performance their respective audiences had come to expect.

She shouldn't have worried. Once they were settled in Mustique, she discovered that in front of a camera Kyle was as professional as anyone she'd ever worked with. Most of the first day was spent setting up for the three spots that Ian had written. Dani and Kyle hardly had time to say hello before their director, Bud Nelson, had them rehearsing the first ad, which was to be shot late in the afternoon with the glorious Caribbean sunset as their backdrop. The pressure-cooker atmosphere suited Dani just fine because it left little or no time for conversation with Kyle.

She spent most of their lunch break huddled with Ian. Then Bud clapped his hands and said, 'Okay, boys and girls, let's do it. Take one!'

Dani and Kyle climbed into the queen-sized bed that stood alone on the deserted beach. She was wearing a flesh-colored body stocking. He was wearing only briefs. The Hot Flash Pink sheets were artfully arranged so that the top sheet crept midway up Dani's cleavage.

'Okay,' Bud said, 'you both know what you have to do?'

They nodded.

'Roll 'em,' he shouted.

The cameras came in for a close-up of Kyle leaning on one elbow, staring soulfully at Dani, who was pretending to be asleep. She opened her eyes and flashed a carefully rehearsed smile, wordlessly beckoning him to take her in his arms.

'Oh, shit,' he whispered.

'What? What's wrong?' she whispered back, trying to maintain her sexy, romantic expression.

A hint of a smile tugged at his lips.

'You're supposed to move closer now,' she whispered.

'Right-o,' he said quietly, following the instructions Bud had given them earlier.

Something hard pressed up against her thigh.

The look on Kyle's face told her what it was.

'Dammit!' she hollered.

'Cut!' screamed Bud. 'Dani, what's the problem? I had a great shot going there!'

She gritted her teeth with anger. 'Sorry. A small problem.'

Kyle struggled to hold in his laughter. 'I'd say a big problem. Scream at me, Bud. That was my fault.'

'Come on, you two, get serious,' Bud shouted. 'We're not here for fun and games, you know.'

Fun and games? Dani was ready to punch Kyle Lord in his big grinning mouth. She must have been stark raving mad to have thought this would work. 'Can't you control yourself?' she hissed as the art director rearranged the top sheet.

'Remains to be seen, doesn't it?' Kyle quipped, unfazed by her fury. 'I should think you'd be flattered to know that you get me hard. Perhaps you'd like a closer look?'

'In your wet dreams,' Dani assured him. 'That's as close as *I'll* ever get.'

Later that afternoon, between takes, she threw a long shirt around her shoulders and set herself up under a beach umbrella with a folder of paperwork. In the middle of dictating a memo to her division heads, she suddenly felt herself being showered with a spray of warm water. A thin sad-faced dog, his fur matted with sand and mud, was shaking drops from his dripping wet body.

'Hey, get away from here, you ugly mutt. I'm going to kick your butt,' yelled a production assistant.

Kyle hurried over. 'You keep away from that dog,' he shouted indignantly. 'No need to abuse a dumb animal.'

He picked up the forlorn-looking dog and brushed off the sand. 'Who do you belong to, mate?' he asked, stroking the poor creature's quivering belly.

'Just a stray dog, man,' said one of the locals. 'I'll get rid of him for you.'

Kyle ignored the offer. 'Hey, hon,' he told the gofer assigned to him by the ad agency. 'Do me a favor, will you? Take this dog up to my cottage and give him some food and a bowl of water.'

'What are you going to do with him?' Dani asked.

Kyle stared at her for a long moment. 'Take him home and show him some love.' He flashed his grin. 'You already had *your* chance.'

Whatever they were thinking or feeling when Bud went for the final take, the chemistry between them crackled like an electromagnetic charge. 'Whew, that's *hot*!' he whistled. 'Boys and girls, that's a wrap!'

Dani called, 'Thanks, Bud,' then threw back the sheets and jumped out of bed without a word to Kyle. She hurried over to Ian. 'I need a swim, a run on the beach, and a shower. After that, a relaxing dinner – with you, if you're free.'

'Why do I get the feeling you're avoiding someone?' Ian gave her a broad wink.

Dani laughed. Ian could read her like a book. 'I suppose you think we should ask Kyle, too.'

'Did I say that?' Ian asked innocently.

'Look, I know I'm being rude, but please humor me.'

'You're the boss.' He shrugged. 'Besides, maybe Lord has already made his own plans for dinner.'

Dani didn't ask Ian what excuses or explanations he made to Kyle, but apparently Kyle got the hint. The next day he behaved like a perfect gentleman. Not a single bad joke. Not one tasteless crack or comment.

She was vaguely disappointed.

The rest of the shoot went like clockwork. Dani and Kyle parted at the airport with only the briefest good-bye. She put out her hand and said briskly, 'It's been a pleasure, Kyle. I'll be in touch.'

Kyle threw her a glance she couldn't read and shook her hand. He said, 'Yeah, sure you will, love. In my wet dreams, isn't that right? G'bye, then, Countess.'

'Good-bye, cowboy,' she retorted, and immediately wished she could take it back. The words had come out sounding like a putdown. The look on Kyle's face as he turned away made her realize she'd hit him in a vulnerable spot. Part of her wanted to grab his arm and explain that she hadn't meant to sound nasty.

As he strolled off in the direction of his gate, she couldn't help wondering why it was that she acted the role of society grande dame around him. As soon as she came within three feet of him, her guard went up and she started sounding like uptight Eunice.

But what the hell did she care what Kyle Lord thought of her?

New York

The show was called 'The Seducers.' It was a heavily backed steamy new prime-time television series – NBC's answer to 'Dynasty' and 'Dallas'.

The producer called Dani the day after she returned from the Caribbean to tell her she was one of three people being considered as exclusive designer for all the costumes worn on the show. The other contenders were Bob Mackie and Reggie Bolt. Was she interested?

How could she not be? It would be a once-in-a-lifetime opportunity. The clothes would be seen and ogled over each week by forty million glamour-hungry Americans, more than half of whom were women. That kind of exposure, along with her signature stores and licensing operations, could hurl her into the stratospheric heights inhabited by the likes of Ralph Lauren and Calvin Klein. She would be able to name her price in the industry for future licensing deals. She could increase her clothing price points by at least 50 percent, which would mean millions in additional profits. She would beat Reggie Bolt at his own game. She would be the most successful woman designer in America. Victory would be so sweet.

'I am *absolutely* interested, Mr Moore,' she assured him.

'Call me Stan,' he said, 'seeing as how we may be working together. So here's the deal. I'm in New York next week. Let's get together and talk about the concepts. Then you got a good three, four weeks to come back to me with your sample designs.'

Considering the number of characters involved, he wasn't giving her very much time. She pointed that out to him.

'That's television, baby. If you don't think you can hack it, say so now and let's stop wasting each other's time,' he retorted.

She hadn't even met the guy, and he was already getting on her nerves. But the lure of the potential contract was too strong. 'No problem, Stan,' she said sweetly. 'I'm used to working under pressure. I look forward to meeting you.'

'Yeah, me too,' the producer grunted, and hung up without saying good-bye.

Too excited to sit still, Dani jumped up from her desk and paced the office. She wished she had thought to ask Stan Moore what the show was about and where it was set. It would be glamorous, of that she was sure, with lots of room to play with the various characters. A couple of times she'd watched 'Dynasty' specifically to see the much-talked-about Nolan Miller creations. Now she might have a chance to design a series wardrobe herself.

Correction. Think positive. She would *definitely* have the chance. That contract was hers.

Suddenly she was starving. No wonder, it was almost one o'clock. She couldn't wait to break the news to

Monika who was hopefully free for lunch. Grabbing her bag and coat, she called to Lance, 'Be back in about an hour and a half,' and hurried down to Monika's office.

The door was half closed. She could hear Monika's muffled voice, talking to someone on the phone.

'Knock-knock,' she said, poking her head inside.

Monika hung up abruptly and shoved a batch of papers into the top drawer of her desk. 'Yes?'

'Sorry, did I interrupt something personal?'

'No, no. I just . . . You startled me.' Monika sounded strained. 'What did you want?'

Dani was taken aback by her cold tone of voice. 'I . . . I was wondering if you wanted to grab a sandwich or something. I just got some news that could mean big, big bucks for Countess Dani and I'm dying to tell you all about it.'

Monika gestured to the papers piled up on her desk. 'I don't really have time to – '

'Well, can't you make the time, Monika?' Dani said. 'I told you, this is important. Jesus! What's wrong with you lately? You walk around in a cloud. Is there a problem?'

'Nothing, there's no problem,' Monika said nervously. 'I have a lot of work to do.'

'So we'll hire you another assistant – or we can divvy up the responsibility and give some of it to Barbara. Would that help?'

'No!' Monika looked agonized. 'No, please, don't do that. I can handle it.'

Something was definitely wrong. Monika, the least emotional of women, looked as if she might burst into tears. Dani said softly, 'Honey, this is me, remember? Your oldest and best friend. Please – whatever's wrong, you can share it with me.'

Monika shook her head violently. 'Nothing. Nothing is

wrong. You're imagining things. Well, let's go have lunch, and you can tell me your big news. I'm fine, I swear it.'

Dani gave up badgering her – for now. 'If you say so,' she conceded, totally unconvinced.

Reggie waltzed into Le Cirque and was immediately escorted to his customary banquette. Before he could even unfold his napkin and order a drink, which he suspected he would sorely need for this command lunch with Frank Gladstone, the ladies came flitting over, blowing kisses and cooing compliments.

The ladies . . . those pencil-thin, expensively lifted, expensively outfitted, and totally plastic women whose husbands made their fortunes taking over and dismantling other companies, thereby depriving thousands of workers of their jobs.

Nice people. Wonderful people. The sort of people Reggie loved to have kiss his ass. And kissing it was precisely what they were doing today. Evidently the word was already out on the street, not to mention in the trades, in Liz Smith, Suzy, and everywhere else, that Reggie was up for the 'Seducers' contract.

'The Seducers.' A trashy-sounding title if ever he'd heard one, but who gave a royal fuck? He certainly didn't. They could have called it 'The Sodomites,' and he would still want to do the show. Because he, more than anyone else, *deserved* that contract in recognition of the fact that he was America's foremost fashion visionary.

And then there was the other reason Reggie so desperately craved to be named exclusive designer for 'The Seducers.' The reason he didn't dare share with anyone but Magee, his most trusted confidante. God forbid anyone else should know that he, Reggie Bolt, was a prisoner of his own success, kept under careful lock and key by the almighty Megacorp.

But now word had come from Hollywood that Mr Reggie was among the three top contenders for the privilege of designing the wardrobe for 'The Seducers.' The timing couldn't have been more perfect. It had been months since those scumbags at Megacorp had accepted any of his personal designs. If there was any justice in this world, Reggie would once again experience the special thrill of satisfaction that came of seeing his stamp of genius transformed from sketch to outfit.

The only problem was that, according to the contract he'd so foolishly signed, the Mr Reggie label was the exclusive property of Megacorp. They had total approval over its use – approval *and* full participation in the profits accrued therefrom, as his attorney was so quick to point out. The name Reggie Bolt, however, was another matter entirely. Technically, Megacorp had to give its okay, but legally there should be no reason why he couldn't use his own full name in any way he saw fit. Megacorp would not be entitled to a penny of the money he earned designing for the Reggie Bolt label. Not that money was the issue, of course. Reggie was fighting for creative freedom.

How fortuitous that Frank Gladstone had agreed to have lunch with him today. Time was of the essence. Reggie had already set up an appointment for next week with the show's producer. Now all he had to do was get Gladstone's permission.

He ordered a Martini and held court for a bevy of his admiring 'girls,' as he called them, until Gladstone finally showed up twenty minutes late. He didn't bother with an apology. Reggie got the hint. Well, fuck 'em. Maybe all of five men on Wall Street knew who Frank Gladstone was. Reggie's name was famous across America.

Over pasta primavera, Reggie made his pitch. As he spoke, he glanced anxiously at Gladstone's face, trying to read his reaction. Nothing. The man showed about as much expression as a dead fish. Reggie's leg jiggled nervously under the table. He had to have this contract. It was a matter of life and death.

Their plates were cleared away. The waiter asked, 'Dessert for you gentlemen today?'

Gladstone shook his head. 'No. Just the check.'

In another two minutes, Gladstone would be gone. 'Please, Frank,' he wheedled, hating himself for sounding so pathetic, 'I need an answer on this.'

Gladstone shrugged his shoulders and said, 'Okay, sure, do the goddam show.'

Reggie couldn't believe he'd heard correctly. Could it really be that simple? "The Seducers" will be all mine, no creative interference from the corporation? And I can keep the fees?'

Gladstone nodded. Why not throw the fruit a bone and let him do the dresses for a television show? If that's what it took to keep him happy, then it was well worth the potential lost revenue. Anything to stop his infernal yammering.

Just when she was feeling on top of things, Bunny overheard Lance tell Monika's secretary that Dani had already left for her meeting with Stan Moore. As in Mr Area Code 213 Gold Chains? *Her* Stan Moore? What kind of business could he have going with Dani?

She had to have some answers to her questions. Luckily she knew just where to get them.

She bided her time until lunch. Then she tracked Lance down in the kitchenette. 'Hi, honey,' she said cheerily. 'Gosh, I'm glad I ran into you. It's been forever since we've had a chance to visit.'

She'd been stroking him with words and gifts ever since he'd started working at Countess Dani, Inc. For his last birthday she'd given him a fifty-five-dollar bottle of Santos de Cartier cologne. That was a ridiculous sum of money to spend on fragrance, especially for someone else, but she had reminded herself that the gift was an investment in her future at Countess Dani.

Now she was about to make that investment pay off.

She poured herself a cup of coffee and said, 'I love that blue on you, Lance. It does such wonderful things for your eyes.' She'd always treated him nicely. She knew just how to pull his strings so he'd go on like a Chatty Cathy doll. 'So how did Dani's meeting go with Stan Moore? She started telling me about it, but we got interrupted.'

Within a few minutes she had the whole story from Lance. Only one question was left unanswered. Why was Barbara Hester, the fashion coordinator, the last to know?

She brooded in her office all afternoon, mentally kicking herself for having forgotten her first business rule of thumb: Follow up on every connection. One never knew where it could lead. She should have returned Stan Moore's call right away. She'd lost ground, and she had no one to blame but herself.

The knowledge of her failure hurt. She had such plans for the future. First, the title she badly coveted: Barbara Hester, vice president, director of design. That would do nicely for starters. Then her own line, just like Donna Karan for Anne Klein or Karl Lagerfeld for Chanel. Barbara Hester for Countess Dani.

Already people were urging her to leave Countess Dani and go off on her own. She was flattered that they recognized her abilities, but none of them had offered to be her benefactor. And without backing, she was nothing. During that long bus ride from North Carolina, she'd promised herself she would never again have to struggle. When she left Countess Dani, Inc., she would go in style, with loads of money in the bank and the kind of recognition that would gain her instant access to the pages of *Vogue, Harper's Bazaar*, and *WWD*.

And she had just figured out how she was going to make that happen.

Step number one, swallow her pride and get in touch with Stan Moore. Hope that he was still interested. If he wasn't, she'd go to step number two: *Get him interested*.

She phoned his office and was informed that Mr Moore was in New York. He could be reached at the Hotel Pierre.

Quickly she dialed the Pierre and was put through to his suite. Someone in heaven must have been watching out for her, because Stan himself picked up the phone.

'Mr Moore?' she drawled.

'Yeah, that's right. Who's this?'

'It's Barbara Hester. I don't know if y'all remember who I am, but I sure do remember you.'

'Sure, sure I remember you. How come you're calling me back all of a sudden?' Stan growled. 'I don't suppose this has something to do with my meeting today with your boss, huh?'

'Why, Mr Moore,' Bunny replied tremulously, 'I've been trying to work up my nerve to call you for weeks.'

'Aw, cut the crap, Barbara. I don't really give a fuck,' Stan said jovially. 'Let's stop farting around and get to the point.'

Bunny almost lost her nerve. Stan Moore was still every bit as vile as she remembered. But a lot was at stake, she reminded herself. This was not the time to get finicky. 'I just broke my engagement,' she lied. 'That's why I couldn't see you before. But now I'm hoping you might still want to get together . . . for dinner or whatever.'

'Yeah, let's celebrate your freedom. How'd you like to paint the town?'

'Well, I'm not much of an artist, but I think we could have fun.'

Stan howled with laughter. 'What a fuckin' joker. Hey, as long as you don't look like a Rubens under those pretty clothes of yours . . . I'll see you at the Pierre, eight o'clock.'

Bunny giggled and hung up. What a creep. She felt like spraying the phone with disinfectant. Still, she was prepared to do whatever she had to, even screw Stan Moore, to make sure that Countess Dani won the design contract for 'The Seducers.'

After Jeremiah and Irving Blatt, how bad could Stan Moore be?

With that consoling thought in mind, she marched down the hall to Dani's office. She'd hoped to find Dani alone, but unfortunately, Monika was settled comfortably on the couch, jabbering away. Bunny knocked on the door and smiled as if she'd just won the lottery.

'I hope I'm not interrupting, but my good friend Stan Moore just told me the exciting news about "The Seducers,"' she trilled. 'I can't wait to hear more when I have dinner with him tonight. Dani, honey, I just know we're going to get that series.'

Monika glared at her. 'You certainly have a lot of confidence in yourself, don't you?'

'Why, yes, I do have confidence – in *us*,' Bunny simpered. 'After all, I'm just like you, Monika . . . I love a good gamble.'

Monika could hardly contain her rage. How dare that bitch throw gambling up in her face? One of these days, Barbara would push her too far, and then Monika would sting her but good.

Dani sighed. Both women were so capable. Why was there all this tension between them? They could hardly spend five minutes together in the same room. Frustrated, she said, 'Would you two stop bickering? We do have a company to run.'

Monika looked hurt and shocked.

Barbara looked stricken.

Dani felt guilty. 'I'm sorry,' she apologized. 'It's the pressure. We have a lot riding on this deal. But we're a great team, so please, let's pull together. All three of us will be winners if we get that contract.'

Chapter Sixteen

New York

Between gearing up to launch the new sheets division and plotting to keep up the payments on her debt, Monika was beginning to feel that she might lose her sanity. When she hallucinated a vision of Rick Flood in front of the office on Seventh Avenue, of all places, she *knew* she'd lost it. But, oh, he was such a mouth-watering sight, this man who looked so much like Rick, that it was all she could do not to fall into his arms. Remembering how warm and safe she'd felt cuddled next to him in bed, she shivered with the sudden longing to re-create that time. Life had been so simple back then. Rick was just getting started as a singer, and financial problems were the furthest thing from her mind.

Such a long time ago . . . She'd always said they weren't meant to be anything more than friends. Now they weren't even that. Sad. But so many other changes had taken place over the years that she hardly cared. She hardly had time to care.

Still, this man striding toward her as she turned to step into a waiting cab could have been Rick's brother, the resemblance was that striking. And then she realized, at the same moment that he reached out to grab her arm, that this *was* Rick, standing right here in front of her with a fourteen-carat smile that had to mean he was as happy to see her as she was to see him!

She barely had a chance to choke out his name before he grabbed her in a bone-crushing bear hug and swung her up off the ground. 'How the hell are you, Monika von Reich?' he whooped.

She was laughing so hard she could hardly speak. 'I'll be fine as soon as you put me down. What a surprise to see you. How did you know where I worked?' she gasped.

'I didn't,' Rick said, releasing her. He removed his sunglasses and stood back to get a better look. 'But now that you mention it, of course I should have realized . . .'

From his tone she knew he'd read her mind. What a fool he must think her. Of course he wasn't here to see her. There was sure to be some other reason why he happened to be taking a stroll down Seventh Avenue through the garment district.

'I was joking,' she said quickly, embarrassed by her slip. She wondered whether he was currently involved with someone. For a while she had followed his romances via the gossip columns, which always had him madly in love with one pretty girl or another. The last she'd read of him in *People*, he'd just broken up with a young actress who'd been quoted as saying that she was interested in a serious relationship, but 'I had to face the fact that Rick Flood just isn't the marrying type.'

He was looking better than ever. Same muscular body, same tousled dark brown hair, same jeans and T-shirt. She said, 'You look great. I'm glad success hasn't changed that.'

'You look good, too,' Rick said, still smiling. 'You're thinner, though. And your hair's different.'

'Shorter. So, what does bring you to this neighborhood?'

'I'm headed for the Garden. I'm doing a concert there Thursday. I guess you didn't read about it.'

There was a time when she had known about every concert he gave in the New York area. He'd never have believed how closely she'd followed his career. But now

421

she was too preoccupied with the complications of her life to pay attention to what was happening to anyone else – especially former lovers.

'I thought rock stars only traveled in limos,' she joked. 'Where's your entourage?'

Rick grinned sheepishly. 'Aw, forget it. You know it's not my style. Only thing different is I always have to hide behind these damn sunglasses now. Other than that, same old me. Damn, I wish I wasn't so late already, but I have to be there five minutes ago. How about I give you a call later? Maybe we could have a drink or – '

'No, no,' Monika broke in. 'Impossible. My schedule, you know . . .' She waved her hand, as if to indicate the multiple commitments on her calendar. 'You know how it is.'

'Sure, yeah.' Rick nodded. 'Sure I do. I'm real busy these days, too.'

'*Ja*, of course you are.'

Instantly she regretted having dismissed his invitation as if it meant nothing to her. If only she could press the rewind button and play the moment differently. But what would be the point, after all? What they had shared had been lovely. It had ended. Certainly she didn't believe it could ever be recaptured or even reinvented. Still, a drink . . . even dinner. What would be the harm?

Plenty. She felt too confused and vulnerable to become Rick Flood's next girl of the moment. Not fair, she told herself. She was too important to Rick. He would never toy with her.

'Do you want a couple of tickets to the concert?' Rick asked earnestly.

'No. I'm busy. But thank you, Rick,' she said stiffly. Why was she being such a pain in the ass? It was as if a nay-saying demon had taken possession of her tongue. For no reason she could understand, she wanted to shut the door tightly on Rick Flood and any feelings from the past that might have tried to force their way to the surface.

'Busy. As usual. That's why I stopped sending you the comps. You never were able to make it to LA.'

'Good-bye, Rick. Nice to see you again,' she said, her voice trembling. 'I must go. I'm late, too.' She could feel herself losing control. In another moment she would burst into tears. She reached over and awkwardly patted his cheek. And laughed. 'Same old Rick. You need a shave.'

'Same old Monika.' He smiled sadly.

Their eyes locked, and she knew they were sharing a memory: all the nights she'd made him get out of bed and shave because his scratchy beard hurt her fair skin.

'Monika – '

'Take good care, Rick,' she mumbled and quickly sought refuge in the taxi. She ducked her head and wiped away the tears that were falling down her cheeks. And because she couldn't allow him to see her crying, she missed the look of stark longing and disappointment that Rick didn't take the trouble to hide.

The Countess Dani linens line was launched during the third week in July, 1983. Controversy followed her advertising campaign like streams of smoke from a rocket. Up and down Madison Avenue people talked about the lead copy line: '*Nothing* feels better than sleeping with royalty – Countess Dani Sheets.'

Once again the Moral Majority screamed.

At the diPortanova's summer villa in Asolo, Roberto called the ads 'a disgusting disgrace.'

Some newspapers and magazines refused to run the ads, while local television stations were forced to decide on yet another of Dani diPortanova's 'hot spots.'

Naturally, the controversy worked to Dani's advantage.

Sales in every division climbed to an all-time high. Bloomingdale's, Saks, Neiman's, and Bergdorf's were soon reporting Countess Dani linens as their number one seller, surpassing Halston, Perry Ellis, and Diane Von Furstenberg.

The same bankers who'd phoned after Nino's death to request a review of her financial records were now calling with offers from corporations interested in buying the company. Their bids were astronomical. Dani refused even to consider selling. If she didn't need those jerks when she was down and almost out, why the hell would she want them now that she was back on top again?

'Tell them,' she said sweetly to her favorite bank president, 'they can shove their offers up their ass.'

'Of course, Countess.' The man coughed. 'Whatever you wish.'

Dani hung up and laughed out loud. Whatever she wished . . .

She shut her eyes and wished for the contract for 'The Seducers.' Weeks had passed since she'd submitted her portfolio of sketches – four changes of costume for each of the five main characters, all members of a very wealthy newspaper family that had lived in Atlanta since before the Civil War. The story was juicy, full of complicated twists and turns, and the glamorous larger-than-life characters were forever getting themselves and their loved ones into no end of mischief.

A designer's dream come true, she'd thought, opening up her sketch pad. And the designs, which normally might have taken weeks to conceive and perfect, had flowed from her pencil as easily as if they'd been stored in her brain, waiting to be born.

She'd asked Monika, Barbara, and her two top assistant designers to read the show's 'bible,' the detailed plot summary and character descriptions, then look at her designs and give their opinions and suggestions. Except for a few minor quibbles, they'd been unanimously wild about the outfits. Now all she could do was hope and pray that she would outshine the competition.

She wished that she could just as easily design a man to walk into her life. People assumed that wealth and fame brought the men out in droves. How wrong they were. More often than not, the men she met were so intimidated by her success and independence that they went running in the other direction. The men who didn't run all too often turned out to be most interested in using her to enhance their own position in society or business. And then there was Jack, who had made no secret of his willingness to do anything to make her happy. If only life were that simple.

Bunny knew that if she was instrumental in getting the 'Seducers' contract for Countess Dani, Inc., there would be no limit to what Dani would do for her. The sketches they'd submitted were wonderful, but she also knew that sometimes a girl had to go the extra mile to make sure her work was properly appreciated. Dani sure as hell wasn't going to put out for Stan Moore. She didn't need to. If they lost the contract, she would have other fish to fry. But Bunny didn't want to wait for other fish. She wanted to catch the big one now, even if she had to use her own body as bait to hook Stan Moore.

Of all the men she'd ever slept with, he was by far the most repulsive. But he held the key to her future success and happiness. So even if she had to endure his constant use of words like 'fuck' and 'suck,' even if she had to blow him until her throat ached and her lips were chapped, she'd do whatever it took. Just as long as she got something in return for her investment.

Think 'dividends,' she told herself when Stan invited her to join him in Acapulco for a long weekend.

'Oh, but Stan . . .' She hesitated, knowing full well she would go. She'd wanted to visit Acapulco ever since she'd read in *Town & Country* that many of the rich and famous kept vacation homes there. Maybe she'd even get to meet some of them. Stan certainly seemed to know everyone.

'Don't "but-Stan" me, hot lips,' Stan chortled. 'I've already made all the arrangements. The ticket'll be delivered to your office.'

'Well, gosh, if you've already got the tickets . . . Oh, Stan, we'll have so much fun!' she gushed.

'We'd better,' Stan snorted, and hung up.

Four days at the Princess Hotel was a far cry from the Grapefruit Tree in Saint Croix. The Princess, Stan bragged, was where Howard Hughes had holed up in his suite, watching movies all day, letting his hair and nails grow long, walking around on tissues so his feet wouldn't get dirty. A fuckin' weirdo, Stan called him. His life had turned into one of those grade-B horror flicks Stan had made early in his career.

Bunny nodded, but she was hardly listening. She was too busy watching out for famous people, though Stan had bluntly assured her that by now most of the celebs were well on their way to their summer watering holes. But she wasn't to worry, he'd said, pinching her ass. He'd keep her plenty busy.

He lived up to his promise. After breakfast, when Bunny wanted to catch some rays or parasail, Stan wanted to screw. After lunch, when she wanted to read a book by the swimming pool, Stan wanted to screw. After dinner, when Bunny wanted to watch a movie in the hotel's theater or go into town, Stan wanted to screw.

She would rather have kicked his fat ass over their sixteenth-floor bedroom balcony railing than have him pinch her breasts again. But she reminded herself that her future was at stake, so she endured the creep's demands.

On their last night in Acapulco, they had a late dinner and then stopped for a nightcap in the bar across from the pyramid-shaped open-air lobby. The place looked like an ancient Mayan temple. *How appropriate*, Bunny thought. *And I'm the sacrifice*. Then Stan leered at her. 'Time for more suck-and-fuck, babe.'

They took the elevator back up to their suite.

Luckily he was too tired for anything more than a quickie. He was done in five minutes flat, then rolled off her and lit up a cigar. 'Fabulous, baby, fabulous,' he said. 'What a great weekend. Hey, listen, any time you need a favor, baby, just ask Stan the Man.'

Finally, this was the moment she had been waiting for. 'Well . . .'

Fluttering her eyelashes delicately, she explained how much it would mean for her career if Countess Dani won the contract for 'The Seducers.' The simple truth was that they deserved it.

Stan smiled. So this was what the bitch was after. Good for her. He liked a calculating cunt. It turned him on. He'd already made his decision about the contract, but he sure as hell wasn't about to let her know that. 'The design contract? Well, babe, we do have a couple of other real talented contenders. Guys with real fuckin' class, you know what I mean? But then again, your boss is a pretty classy dame, so it's gonna be tough decidin', know what I mean?'

Bunny gently caressed Stan's limp penis. 'I . . . er . . . we *really* need to get this contract,' she murmured. 'We're on the brink of becoming as big as Ralph Lauren or Calvin Klein. This exposure could help put us over the top.' *Not to mention me, but that goes without saying*.

Stan put down the cigar and squeezed her breast. 'Well,

if it means that much to you, you got it, babe. Now, how about a little more head?' he asked, straddling her face.

Bunny almost gagged as Stan shoved his flaccid penis in her mouth. But as she worked on getting him hard one more time, she smugly consoled herself with the thought that she had just scored the biggest coup of her career. Dani would not be able to thank her enough.

Jack had been getting weird vibes from Dani. Nine times out of ten when he called, she was busy or too tired or she had some other half-assed excuse why she couldn't see him. Okay, maybe she really was too busy. The head of a multimillion-dollar corporation naturally would be. He just had to learn some patience, learn how to handle things better, if he was at all serious about keeping her.

Hell, he was dead serious. They were meant for each other.

Trouble was, if he hadn't known her better he'd have thought she was messing with his head. But she wasn't like that. She was different from the other girls. She didn't play games . . . or maybe she did. Shit, who was he kidding? He oughta be smarter than that. Women were all alike, even Dani diPortanova.

Maybe it was time for him to start playing some games himself. *GQ* sent him to Bermuda for a week to do a shoot for their cruisewear issue. He left without telling her he was going away. That would teach her, he decided. She'd figure out soon enough how much she needed and missed him. For sure there would be a message from her on his machine when he got home. 'Jack, where are you?' she'd say. 'Jack, I'm sorry. Call me as soon as you can. I miss you. I love you.'

Imagining the pleasure he would get from hearing her message, he performed for the camera as he never had before. The ad agency account executive couldn't believe her luck. Every time he smiled, her heart melted. Jack Andrews was something special. Her top fragrance account was looking for a new face to be its exclusive rep. It looked as if she'd just found their boy.

But Jack wasn't smiling when he got back to his apartment at the end of the week and checked his machine. Lots of messages, but not one of them was from Dani.

Bitch!

He'd worked his ass off, smiling and strutting his stuff so she'd be proud of him, and she hadn't so much as picked up the phone to call him.

Who the *fuck* did she think she was?

Didn't she realize he could have any girl he wanted? Hadn't she figured out he wasn't exactly sitting home nights dicking off just because she couldn't see him?

Apparently not.

He called her office number and was put through to her assistant, who said, 'I'm sorry, Mr Andrews. The countess is out of town.'

Jack felt like telling him, *'Don't give me this "countess" shit. You're talking about my girlfriend, you goddam fag.'* But he managed to curb his anger so he could squeeze some information out of the cocksucker. 'Right, I forgot she was going away. I just got back myself,' he said chattily. 'So . . . uh . . . Lance, where'd you say she was?'

'I didn't say,' Lance replied curtly. 'But since you asked, she's in Los Angeles.'

Probably screwing her brains out with that son of a bitch Aussie, Jack fumed.

'Did you want to leave a message, Mr Andrews?'

'No, forget I even called,' Jack snapped, and slammed down the phone. Instantly he regretted his rudeness. Not because he gave a shit about Lance what's-his-face. The guy dripped attitude. The way he mouthed off to Jack, he deserved whatever happened to come his way. But what if Lance went crying to Dani that her boyfriend had been mean to him?

She wouldn't like that one damn bit.

Nice going, Jack, he thought bitterly, sinking down on his couch. His mother's taunts rang in his ears. Stupid, she'd called him. Pig-headed. Fool.

Wrong! They were all wrong if they thought *he* was the fool.

Los Angeles

Dani was in California all right, but not in bed with Kyle Lord. Thanks to her much-talked-about commercials, she'd been asked to appear on the 'Tonight' show. Unfortunately, she wasn't informed until she was seated in the green room that Kyle Lord was also scheduled to appear.

Just what I need, she thought, hoping Kyle would cancel his appearance at the last minute. She'd about had her fill of him in Mustique.

Joan Rivers was the guest host. First she talked to Dani, touching on everything from Dani's nail polish ('Hot Flash Puke . . . I mean Puce') to how Dani managed to stay so thin.

She didn't ask about the linen ads, which should have warned Dani.

Then Joan introduced Kyle, who had just arrived at the studio.

Dani's mouth went dry with nervousness when he smiled at her.

'Oh, please, *please*!' Joan crowed to Dani. 'Is this Kyle a *huge* star or what? I hear he needs an extra pocket in the front of his bathing suit – just like a kangaroo!'

The audience howled. The censors sweated. Kyle grinned.

Dani blushed the exact shade of Hot Flash Red. 'Joan,' she said, 'I honestly don't know. It never came up.'

'Oh, please, *please*! You expect us to believe that? After *those* ads?'

Kyle leaned forward and grinned. 'It sure felt up to me.'

Cut to commercial.

The rest of Joan's interview was devoted to Kyle's movie career. Dani seethed in silence, for once grateful to be able to keep her mouth shut. As soon as the show was over, Kyle said, 'How about a drink or dinner? For old times' sake?'

She was astonished by his gall. 'How *dare* you humiliate me like that after the fortune we shelled out for you!' she said. 'When are you going to learn some manners, you pig?'

Kyle looked sheepish. He said, 'Hell, I'm sorry. I didn't mean – '

Dani stalked away. She'd heard enough of *his* apologies.

New York

Monika had set her VCR to tape Dani on 'Tonight,' just in case she was late getting home from her date – dinner at Lutèce with an exceedingly rich publisher whose personality was every bit as ugly as his physical appearance. As usual the médaillons of veal and raspberry soufflé were superb, but Monika felt as if she were choking on every mouthful.

How could she even have considered marrying this pockmarked, foul-breathed gargoyle who habitually

431

spouted venomous racist bile such as she hadn't heard since she'd said good-bye to Karola? She was desperate, *ja*, but not desperate enough to tie herself to this excuse for a human being.

As he signed for the check, Monika considered the facts. Even after selling her sable coat and the Jag, she still owed Lucky's $900,000, thanks to all the accumulating interest. The week before, Scott Devane had summoned her into his office and frightened her with barely veiled threats of violence. All she needed was one good night at baccarat or blackjack and she'd be back on top, but she didn't dare show her face at Lucky's.

If only she could take a trip down the New Jersey Turnpike to Atlantic City, as tacky as it was, and try her luck at Harrah's. The only problem was she didn't have any money, and the gargoyle didn't approve of gambling.

Terrific. A match made in heaven.

They stepped outside onto East Fiftieth Street. 'Well, what's next?' The gargoyle leered, rubbing his hands with eager anticipation. He pointed to his limo, waiting down the block. 'A romantic drive through Central Park?'

Ach, she couldn't. Not for all the money in the world. 'It's such a lovely night,' she said, thinking quickly. 'So balmy. The perfect night for a stroll, don't you think?' Without waiting for his answer, she set off uptown at a brisk pace. Her escort, who was several inches shorter than she, panted as he struggled to keep up with her. His limo crawled behind them. By the time they'd covered the eleven-block distance to her house, he was gasping for breath.

'Such good exercise, walking,' Monika said pitilessly. 'I wish I could ask you in, but I must walk my poor doggie. Unless you'd like to join us?'

'No, no,' the publisher hastily declined. 'It's late. Maybe another time.' He leaned up and pecked her on the cheek. Then he waddled over to his limo, mopping the sweat off his forehead.

Monika was still laughing as she unlocked the door and stepped inside. 'Coco? Coco, Mama is home. Come, baby, let's have our walk,' she called, expecting the spaniel to come rushing out to greet her as usual. The dog had been a gift from Dani for her last birthday after Dani had heard Monika pine for her old German shepherd, Heinzie, once too often.

Monika switched on the lamp on the foyer table. 'Coco? Where are you? No games, you silly girl. I'm exhausted. Coco!' she called again, more sharply this time.

Strong fingers of tension tugged at the back of her neck. Something terrible must have happened. Maybe the dog had taken ill or hurt herself. She hurried upstairs, calling Coco's name over and over again.

Perhaps she'd fallen asleep on the bed. *Ja*, that must be it, Monika told herself as she hurried into her bedroom.

'*Mein Gott!*' she gasped.

A beefy, ruddy-faced man lounged on her bed. A second man, dark and skinny, stood in front of her dresser, combing his curly hair.

From the ransacked state of the room, she could see that they'd been there awhile.

'Good evening, Miss von Reich,' the man on her bed said, waving a gun.

Monika clutched at her throat. 'My dog,' she said faintly. 'Where's my dog?'

'She's okay, just taking a little nap. She's real cute, your dog. Isn't she, Sal?' the bigger man asked his friend.

Sal nodded agreeably. He gestured to her collection of perfumes, then picked one up and sniffed it. 'Expensive stuff, huh?' he commented, as if he were a connoisseur of fine fragrances.

Speechless with horror, Monika watched as he hurled

the dozen or so bottles against the far wall. One by one, they cracked open. Moments later, the room reeked of the overpowering mix of scents.

'Please,' she pleaded, her voice cracking. Then her stomach rebelled, and she doubled over, struggling not to vomit.

'Stay with us, baby, the evening's young,' the man on the bed told her, picking his teeth with the pin of her antique emerald brooch. 'Show her what you found in her top drawer,' he instructed Sal.

Sal grinned and held up her dildo.

'Maybe later you'll show us how you fucky-wucky with your rubber dick, Monika,' chortled the ruddy-faced man, heaving himself off the bed.

'Please, I beg you,' Monika rasped, 'don't hurt me. I'll give you money, whatever you want . . .'

'Cut the crap, baby. You don't *have* any money. That's your whole problem, isn't it?'

So. Now she knew who'd sent the hoods. She prayed they wouldn't rape or kill her, that they were only here to scare her, to warn her.

The ruddy-faced man opened the door to her closet. 'Nice clothes,' he said. 'My wife don't got such nice clothes.'

'Take them.' She sobbed hoarsely. 'Take anything.'

The man swept a billowing armful of her dresses and evening gowns off their hangers and tossed them at Sal. 'Here you go, take care of 'em,' he said.

Sal picked up a pair of pinking shears and brandished them at Monika. 'Convenient.' He grinned as he sliced into the first gown, a Givenchy she'd bought in Paris. She bit her lips to hold back her cries of protest as he systematically shredded and destroyed thousands of dollars' worth of clothes.

'What about the dress she got on?' Sal suggested, holding up the shears.

'Oh, yeah, good thinkin'.' The ruddy-faced man nodded. 'Take it off, Monika.'

She stood paralyzed, her heart pounding a staccato message of terror.

'Maybe she needs help,' said Sal. He beckoned to her. 'C'mere.'

'No,' she whispered, clutching her arms across her chest. 'No – '

The ruddy-faced man took a step toward her and smacked her hard across the cheek. 'I said, *take it off*!'

Her fingers were slick with sweat, and her hands were shaking so badly she could hardly undo the buttons on her sweat-stained blouse.

'The skirt, too,' he said. When she dropped her skirt to the floor, he breathed a deep, happy sigh. 'Nice. I like black garter belts.'

'Hey, boss,' said Sal, moving closer, 'let's see what she got underneath.'

'You heard him, Monika, hurry it up. Sal wants to see your tits and twat.'

She was past thinking. Past caring. They would do as they pleased with her. Some instinct told her it would be worse if she resisted or disobeyed. Numbly she stripped off her bra and panties and clumsily unhooked her garter belt.

When she stood naked before them, trembling with terror and cold, they moved in on her. They called her the filthiest, foulest names she'd ever heard. They poked and pinched and fondled every inch of her body as if she were a slab of meat offered up for their inspection and approval. And then they made her show them how she used her dildo.

435

They didn't stop until she fell to her knees and groveled before them, crying and begging for mercy.

'Pay up, Monika,' said the ruddy-faced man. 'Or we'll be back. Understand?' He tilted her head up with the toe of his shoe.

She nodded. Yes, she understood.

She could hear them laughing as they walked down the stairs. She heard them slamming around in the kitchen, opening drawers and cupboards. Then they were in the foyer. She held her breath, terrified they'd changed their minds and were coming back upstairs. She heard more loud laughter, then a hammering noise.

Then came the sound of them opening and shutting the front door. And finally . . . silence. Blessed, merciful, welcome silence.

When she was sure they were gone, she grabbed a robe and crept downstairs.

There was a large, acrid-smelling puddle at the bottom of the steps, spreading across the surface of her Aubusson carpet where one of them must have urinated.

Animals. Pigs. Scum.

But they were far worse than that, she discovered a moment later when she glanced across the foyer.

They had left her a souvenir.

Coco, her cocker spaniel, nailed by her ears to the inside of the front door.

They'd stuffed a handkerchief in her mouth to keep her from barking, but they needn't have bothered. Coco was dead.

Monika screamed until her throat was raw.

Lance had dropped by Uncle Charlie's Downtown, the city's most popular gay bar, to grab a couple of beers and watch his boss's Carson appearance on one of the large-screen TVs above the bar. He shook his head ruefully,

436

watching Dani squirm as Joan Rivers gave her and Kyle Lord a hard time.

Afterward he said good night to his friends and walked across Greenwich to Charles Street, thinking about how good Dani and Kyle looked together. Based on looks alone, they'd make a great couple, though Dani rolled her eyes in horror whenever Lance suggested the possibility.

Kyle was *such* a hunk. Too bad he was straight. But by all accounts he was strictly a ladies' man, so Lance figured that Dani ought to have him in her life. God knew she needed someone who had more going for him than Jack Andrews, whose whining pathetic calls were beginning to drive Lance crazy.

This tiny one-block section of Charles Street was one of Lance's favorite New York City streets. It felt so typically Greenwich Village, with its pretty, well-preserved red-brick row houses, many of them decorated with neat, colorful window boxes. He stopped a moment to savor the fragrance of the summer blossoms.

Closing his eyes, he imagined that he could smell the breeze wafting off the Hudson and got lost in a fantasy that had him wrapped in the arms of a man who resembled Kyle Lord. He didn't hear the footsteps coming up behind him until it was too late. An arm grabbed him around the neck. A hand was clamped tightly over his mouth before he had a chance to cry out for help. Lance struggled to free himself as the attacker dragged him into the shadows of one of the town houses, but the man was too strong.

He never saw the fist that came down across the bridge of his nose. The next blow caught him square on the forehead. After a third punch, to his windpipe, Lance passed out cold.

* * *

Rah Rah plopped himself down on his brand-new navy blue corduroy couch, just delivered from Macy's. *His* couch, in *his* apartment, where he'd slept last night for the very first time. The third-floor brownstone walk-up, which the rental agent had described as 'a real find, a charming, sun-drenched one-bedroom for only nine hundred fifty dollars' – was the first and only place he'd looked at. The minute he stepped inside, he had known he was meant to live there.

He loved the window seat under the arched window that faced West Sixty-ninth Street. He loved being only a block away from Central Park. Best of all, he loved the idea of living by himself.

Reggie had jeered at Rah Rah's announcement that he wanted to terminate their financial agreement because he was planning to move out. 'You won't last two weeks alone. You'll come running back to Papa with your tail between your legs, and see if I'll ever take you back,' he'd said, his lip curling with scorn.

He smirked when Rah Rah broke the news that he'd actually rented an apartment. 'On the *West Side*? Oh, I suppose you think you'll have a lot of fun over there on Columbus Avenue. Well, I always did think you were rather tacky.'

He'd carefully scrutinized each and every item that Rah Rah packed, as if he'd been keeping a mental checklist of his possessions and wanted to make sure Rah Rah didn't rip him off.

'Not that I haven't been ripped off anyway,' he whined, stalking out of their bedroom.

But two nights ago, when they sat down for the last time to one of Lydia's special dinners, Reggie had picked at the food on his plate and gulped martinis as if they were water. And then he'd burst into tears.

'If I've done anything to hurt you, I'm sorry,' he said,

sobbing. 'Forgive me, but please . . . please don't leave me.'

Rah Rah was stunned by the improbable sight of Reggie crying and filled with remorse. For a fleeting instant, pitying this lonely middle-aged man, he was tempted to stay. He could tear up the lease he'd signed and ask for a refund on his deposit.

But then he remembered all the days and nights when Reggie had treated him like a piece of property. Ordered him around like a dumb animal. Called him a hustler, a whore, a cocksucker. He recalled how Reggie had snickered when he'd first mentioned acting lessons. But Reggie wasn't snickering now that Rah Rah had a six-month contract to play a new character on a leading nighttime soap. No wonder Reggie was so miserable. He was mired in the notion that beautiful clothes, priceless furniture, and endless amounts of money could bring him happiness and love.

But happiness wasn't a commodity to be bought and sold. Thank heaven, thought Rah Rah, he'd figured that out before it was too late. Selling his soul had been the biggest mistake of his life, but now he was determined to make a fresh start – begin a new life in his new apartment.

Not that he hadn't brought plenty of stuff with him. Stacked all over the apartment were cartons crammed full of the possessions he'd accumulated through the years. He'd had to rent a van to cart over the twelve suitcases of clothes, eight boxes of hardcover and paperback books, his stereo, TV, and VCR, a rowing machine, a ten-speed bike, a Soloflex machine, plus all his record albums, cassettes, and videotapes.

Okay, so he hadn't exactly taken a vow of poverty. But as some of his friends were quick to point out, he'd given up his meal ticket and the keys to a luxurious, antique-filled penthouse with its panoramic views of Manhattan for an uncertain career as an actor and a nice but modest apartment. A couple of them had come right out and said they thought he was crazy.

Crazy? Maybe. He shrugged, getting up to order himself Chinese food. But the apartment was his, to do with as he wished. He had plenty of money in the bank to fall back on if his acting hit a dry spell. And no one would ever again have the right to call him a dumb blond hustler.

Dani tiptoed into Lance's room at Saint Vincent's Hospital, just a couple of blocks away from where he'd been attacked, carrying a shopping bag full of books, a box of Godiva chocolates, and a stack of tapes for his Walkman.

'I'm awake,' he said, waving at her to come in and sit down.

'I brought you some goodies.' She smiled, holding up the shopping bag.

'Is there anything good to read in there? I swear I'll die if I watch one more hour of television,' Lance said, clicking off the set. 'There's nothing like a week-long stay in the hospital to make a guy appreciate his humdrum office routine. Speaking of which, what's new?'

Dani was glad Lance was sounding more like himself today. She still couldn't believe the beating he'd taken. He'd suffered a mild concussion, a broken nose and jaw, a lacerated eye, and a couple of broken ribs. A passerby had found him lying unconscious on the sidewalk.

Beyond the physical injuries, however, were the emotional wounds that the doctors couldn't clean and dress as easily. Lance still shook whenever he spoke of the incident, as if he feared that his assailant was still lying in wait for him. It didn't look as though the police were ever going to find the attacker, and they didn't seem to care.

When they'd questioned him in his hospital room,

they'd sounded as if they were interrogating *him*. One of them had even implied that the assailant was a disgruntled trick. When Lance had insisted he didn't have any ex-lovers gunning for him, they'd accused him of lying.

'They're assholes,' he'd complained to Dani.

'I know,' she'd agreed sympathetically. She herself had gotten a call from one of the cops working on the case. The cop had asked if she could tell him anything about Lance – problems at the office, personal life, friends – that might give them a lead.

'Nothing that I can think of. But what makes you think Lance was mugged by someone he knew?' she'd asked.

'Who says he was mugged?' the cop replied. 'He had seventy-five bucks and a couple of credit cards in his wallet. No mugger would have walked away from that. I'll tell you one thing, though. Whoever jumped him sure meant business.'

'What are you saying?'

The cop hesitated momentarily, as if wondering whether he'd told her too much. Then he said, 'It was like the guy was fixing to kill him.'

She remembered the cop's words now as she fussed with the top of the gold Godiva box. 'Has the doctor said how much longer you'll have to be here?' she asked, offering up the box for Lance's inspection.

He shook his head and said in a low voice, 'Dani, I'm afraid to leave.'

She reached for his hand, which was surprisingly cold. 'You've been through a bad time,' she soothed. 'But this is New York. You can't let your fear imprison you.'

'Dani, it's not that. I've been mugged before. There's something else . . . something I didn't tell the cops.'

'What?' she asked, almost afraid to hear the answer.

'The attacker whispered something in my ear just

before I fainted. It was horrible. I keep hearing it over and over again.'

'What did he say?'

Lance turned his head away. 'It . . . it doesn't matter, Dani. I can't tell you.'

'Lance, please. I don't shock easily,' she coaxed, wondering what filthy homophobic epithet the attacker had used.

Lance picked at the edge of his blanket. 'Whoever it was said, "Your boss's days are numbered".'

Dani's mouth went dry.

Don't be ridiculous, she told herself. *The bastard must have mistaken Lance for somebody else.* Why on earth would anyone want to harm her?

The temp who was filling in for Lance buzzed Dani's intercom. The poor woman still didn't understand how the machine worked. She thought she had to keep her finger planted on the buzzer, so the noise seemed to go on forever.

Dani reminded herself to be patient. 'Yes?'

'There's a Mr Stan, uh . . . Moore, I think it is, on the phone – '

'Yes, I'll talk to him,' she said quickly, crossing her fingers under the desk for luck. They must have made their decision. Finally! She'd been waiting weeks for this call. *Please let it be yes*, she prayed silently.

'Stan? How are you?' She wondered whether her voice betrayed her nervousness.

'Great! But let's skip the bullshit. I'm calling to say you're our man . . . I mean our woman. Heh, heh, heh. Congratulations. It's a fabulous opportunity. I know you're very pleased.'

She was more than pleased. She was thrilled. But she had to laugh at Stan Moore's self-serving good wishes.

'I'm delighted,' she assured him. 'And *I* know how much we'll *both* benefit from your decision.'

'Hey, I'm glad I made ya so happy, Countess,' said Stan, ignoring her comeback. 'My lawyer'll be in touch.'

The line went dead. He'd hung up.

Evidently Stan didn't have time for chitchat. He would take some getting used to, but she was sure they could work out a mutually satisfactory relationship. She would learn his ways, and he'd learn hers.

Welcome to Hollywood, Dani diPortanova!

Bunny was so wildly angry she could hardly see straight. After all the god-awful, disgusting times Bunny had gone down on Stan, after she had made *sure* to let Dani know Stan was her beau, after she'd done more than anyone else at the company to make sure they won the television contract, how had Dani rewarded Bunny's extraordinary efforts?

A raise. Period.

No new title.

No exclusive line with her name on it.

'Is there anything more?' she'd asked Dani expectantly.

Dani, still smiling, genuinely happy that she could give Barbara a raise, asked, 'No, Barbara, why?'

'I was just thinking . . . wondering about . . .'

'Oh, of course, when the raise becomes effective, right? I'll tell payroll to make it immediate.'

That was all. End of discussion.

Damn that bitch and her stinking company. And now Stan was holding on line three, probably on his way in from LA and hoping to score. She'd nip that in the bud real fast.

She picked up the phone and yawned. 'Yes?'

'Babe, it's me. Get ready, I'm at La Guardia. I wanna be between those juicy legs of yours ASAP.'

'Sorry, *babe*. I've got other plans,' Bunny said coldly.

'Break 'em.'

'Can't.'

'Listen, doll. I arranged this deal, and it wouldn't kill you to show a little gratitude. Nobody's signed on the dotted line yet. I could still change my mind, you know.'

She was tempted to say, *Go ahead, fuckface*, but didn't. For the time being, she still needed her job. Instead, she faked enthusiasm. 'Oh, Stan, why is it I can never say no to you? I'll see you in an hour. My place.'

It got worse every time Bunny saw Stan. Within seconds of saying hello, he would tear off her clothes and squeeze her breasts so hard they'd hurt for days. And when she protested, he seemed to get off even more.

Now she was completely nude, on her knees in her living room in front of the television. Stan stood in front of her, inches away from her face, jerking himself off as he watched a tape of one of his game shows on her Betamax.

The show was almost over.

The companies who supplied the prizes were thanked; then the credits rolled. Stan was getting more excited. His hand picked up speed. His breathing quickened. His dick reddened as the director's name rolled by. Then the sound engineers, lighting, wardrobe, makeup, hairstylist.

Quickly he grabbed the remote control and hit the Still button, freezing the image.

The final credit – 'A Stanley Moore Production' – filled the screen.

He spurted semen all over Bunny's face.

Bunny went straight into the shower, turned the water on scalding hot, and frantically scrubbed her face. Now he *really* had gone too far. She'd done her duty, scored that fucking contract for that no-talent bitch, all for a puny little raise. Well, she was going to dump Stan, and

444

if he didn't sign the contract, too bad. She could always get another job.

She turned off the water. The phone was ringing.

'Stan!' she yelled. 'Get the damn phone!'

Stan lay spent on Bunny's bed, flipping the remote control, trying to catch another one of his shows. He grabbed the phone. 'Yeah?'

'Bunny?' a woman asked in a heavy southern accent.

'Who?'

The woman gave the number she was trying to reach. Yeah, it was Barbara's, all right.

'Bunny's her nickname. Ah'm her mother, Irma Rae Hester. Is Bunny around?'

He cocked his head. The shower was still running. He said, 'She's at the grocery store. I'll get her to call you back.'

'Ah'm callin' long distance and ah ain't gonna be at this number long. This here's my neighbor's party line. We ain't got no phone.'

Was she joking? Everyone had a phone. Christ, he had nineteen in his Beverly Hills house alone.

'Ah'll jest have to try her again tomorra. But mah lawyer says it's real important that she come down here.'

Who was this country bumpkin who was obviously tanked to the gills? Barbara had told him her parents were well off and lived in Chapel Hill. The southerners he knew certainly didn't sound like this. 'Oh, yeah, Mrs Hester. Bunny's mentioned you. I'm a friend of hers. I'm Stan Moore, the producer.'

'Oh, mah!'

'So, where'd you say you were calling from?'

'Why, Henderson, of course. You ever been to North Carolina, Mr – '

'Moore. No, I haven't.'

'Well, life wasn't never easy for me and Bunny and her

445

sister. 'Course, then she walked away from the best thing ever coulda happened to a girl from Moccasin Bottom, and ah been worryin' about her ever since. How is mah little girl, Mr Moore?'

The shower noises had stopped. Stan waited until he heard the whirring sound that meant Barbara was drying her hair. 'She's doing just fine. But, hey, I'd love to hear about this great thing she walked away from.'

Irma Rae obligingly told Stan all about Jeremiah Blair. When Stan encouraged her to keep talking, she explained about the Heinz pickle plant and Bunny's daddy.

Stan sputtered with excitement. 'You're telling me that Bunny's father is also her grandfather, Mrs Hester? You mean you and your own father – '

'Well, yes, Mr Moore. Ah'm ashamed to say that's so,' Irma Rae interrupted him, as if she couldn't bear to hear the words spoken aloud.

Fabulous! He thought this kind of thing happened only on television shows.

'He beat me all the time, and after mah mama died he made me live with him like ah was his wife. An' ah always thought, long as he never lays a hand on mah daughters . . . But then mah little girl, Verna, she tole me he had . . . you know, gotten her to do things . . .' Mrs Hester began to sob.

'One night last week ah walked in and found them doin' it. Ah got so upset ah just kilt him. An' ah'm glad ah did. Though mah lawyer says ah could spend the rest of mah life in jail if Bunny don' come down to speak up for me. Ah' unnerstan why she don't want to do that, honest, ah do. But, Mr Moore, mah lawyer, he says ah should ask her again. Otherwise, we ain't got no supportin' testimony.'

Stan and Irma Rae talked for another ten minutes. Stan hung up just as Bunny was coming out of the bathroom.

She didn't notice the look of triumph on his face as she walked over and picked up the clothes he'd dropped on the floor earlier in the evening. Tossing his pants and shirt in his face, she announced, 'I want you out. Now. We're through.'

'Not quite, *Bunny*. We've only just begun.'

Bunny? She stared at him, wondering how in the world he'd found out about that horrible nickname.

Chapter Seventeen

New York

A few days after Dani won the contract for 'The Seducers,' Reggie Bolt plucked off his black sleep-mask and gingerly patted the soft, sensitive skin under his eyes, testing for puffiness. The damage seemed minimal. It was the morning after too many cognacs. Struggling to an upright position, he leaned back against his floral-patterned quilted headboard and squinted at the clock.

Eleven o'clock. Jesus! Why hadn't Lydia made sure he was up?

He switched on the intercom on the wall next to his bed.

'Lydia!' For what he paid the woman she could at *least* make sure he had lived through the night. He could be dead and rotting up here for all she cared.

He jabbed the buzzer connected to the intercom in the kitchen.

'Lydia!' he wailed again.

No response. Where was she? What was he supposed to do, get up and make his own breakfast? He thrust his lower lip out in a pout and bit his knuckle.

He was about to yell for her again when Lydia pushed open his bedroom door. How many times did he have to tell her to knock?

'*Buenos días*, Señor Reggie,' she greeted him. Then she shook a finger at him. 'So, you are finally up. You are late for a meeting with your accountant.'

'Why didn't you wake me?' he whined. 'And where's my breakfast? I'm staarrvving!'

Lydia didn't bother to remind him he had told her never to disturb his sleep for anything short of a fire raging through his house.

'Breakfast?' she asked, unruffled as always by his petulance. 'With what you've been eating lately, it doesn't matter whether you eat or not. But I will bring the tray in five minutes.'

Reggie glared at her as she left the room. 'And hurry up, for once,' he snapped as soon as she was out of earshot. He waited until he knew she was in the kitchen, then buzzed sharply.

'*Si*, Señor Reggie?'

He hated her patient, long-suffering tone.

'Don't forget –'

'Two codeine tablets and the paper.'

Reggie hissed into the speaker, then turned it off without another word. She was a good housekeeper, and she did keep the place immaculate, but how much insolence was he supposed to tolerate from the hired help? That she took care of him as if he were her son was utterly beside the point. Loyalty was not one of the character traits Reggie most admired.

Sighing, he eased himself out of bed and put on the white terry-cloth robe he so loved, stolen years ago from the Hotel George V. Ah, what fun he'd had with that hot Algerian boy he'd picked up in the lobby . . .

He dragged himself into the mirrored dressing room to assess the damage. The ravages of the night before – every wrinkle and blemish – jumped out at him from the well-lighted mirrored walls. His eyes were as bloodshot as a basset hound's.

Time for some cellular repair. He eyed the selection of mud packs and scrub creams. Yes, this was definitely a

449

Terme di Montecatini mud pack morning. He slapped on a thick layer of the brown lightly scented gunk and crawled back into bed.

Lydia reappeared, carrying his breakfast tray. It held his favorite Royal Doulton china cup filled with chamomile tea, a tall glass of freshly squeezed grapefruit juice, three celery sticks, two codeine aspirins, and *The New York Times*.

'Finally,' he huffed, settling himself among the Porthault pillows. He took a long sip of tea. Ugh. Vile stuff.

'Yes?' Why didn't the woman leave him to his misery?

Lydia was holding a cream-colored envelope between her fingers as if it were a dog turd. 'Señor Reggie,' she said, 'a messenger bring this to you.'

'Fine,' he said airily. 'Leave it on my desk.'

'Señor Reggie, I *know* what is in this envelope. I told you this is very bad business.'

'Lydia,' he wheedled, 'pul-lease let me eat my breakfast in peace without sermonizing. I'm under such pressure lately.'

She shook her head and sulked out of the room.

Screw it, he would *definitely* need the coke to get through *this* day. He gulped down the grapefruit juice. He was sick of this diet. In the past few years, he had already tried Dr Fishbein's Biblical diet, the Beverly Hills diet, the Southampton diet, and the Palm Beach diet. He had personally consulted Dr Robert Haas and Dr Stuart Berger. And he still had love handles and a belly that made him look like a stuffed Gund bear.

'A Pooh belly!' Rah Rah used to say to taunt him.

It was easy for him to laugh with his washboard-flat belly that came of all the hours he spent at the gym, thanks to the membership Reggie's money paid for. Well, screw Rah Rah. Reggie was thrilled to have the apartment all to himself again, and how lovely not to have to share his big comfy bed with anyone. And no more of those horrendous bills to pay!

Yes, life was going to be absolutely wonderful now that he'd seen the last of that ungrateful little hustler.

At least that's what he kept telling himself.

He unfolded the *Times* and turned first, as always, to the obits. Nobody he knew. Too bad. Next a quick glance at the stock listings. In a boom market, he was losing a fortune. It was enough to put him off his feed. Then he read the Style page to see whether those idiots had mentioned him in one of their pissy columns. All too often they wasted the space on asinine articles about how divorced parents coped with the holidays or about couples who couldn't make babies. Who *cared*?

Today it was a story about how to help children adjust to nursery school. And worse, much worse, on the facing page was a full-page ad with Dani diPortanova's face staring out at him. Beneath her picture the text read: 'Countess Dani diPortanova and Countess Dani, Inc., are pleased and proud to be associated with NBC Television and Stanley J. Moore Productions for the forthcoming fall series, "The Seducers".'

He'd seen the exact same ad in *Women's Wear Daily*, *Variety*, and the *Hollywood Reporter*. 'That bitch,' he hissed, cracking his mud pack. Chunks of thick mud fell into his chamomile tea.

'Lydia!' he wailed, shoving the tray away so quickly he spilled tea all over his lavender silk duvet cover. 'Lydia, come here. I need you!'

'*Si*, Señor Reggie? Oh, no, you spill your tea.' She clucked sympathetically.

'Get rid of this shit!' he raged. 'I can't deal with bird food this morning. I need a *real* breakfast.' He stared at her defiantly as he ticked off his order. 'Get me a real cup of coffee, strong – and none of that half-and-half shit in it. I want heavy cream. Two poached eggs. Exactly two minutes. Don't ruin them. A couple of slices of Orwasher's rye. Toasted. And a fresh croissant with damson preserves.'

Lydia grinned. She loved to cook and hated his diets. '*Bueno*, Señor Reggie. But I have no fresh croissant, just frozen.'

'Then get some!' he said stubbornly, crossing his arms.

'*Si*, Señor Reggie.' She removed the tray and left without another word.

Reggie threw back the stained quilt and glared again at the offending page. Another chunk of mud fell off, landing precisely between Dani's well-defined breasts, like a great green brooch.

He shook his head, furious that that titled cunt was flaunting his loss for all the world to see. Cursing loudly, he ripped the ad to shreds. Dani diPortanova's announcement littered the room like confetti at a returning hero's parade – except that this was no celebration. It might well be his swan song as a designer.

'Those morons at Megacorp buy me out and then destroy my reputation bit by bit,' he had railed at Mitchell in a weak moment when he'd had too much to drink. 'It's the most sadistic ownership I could ever have imagined. Why, why did I ever agree to ally myself with them? I might as well be owned by Woolworth's, for all the respect they show me.' And then, remembering Mitchell's column, he had quickly shut up.

He padded into the bathroom, turned on the malachite water faucet, and scrubbed off the mud pack so furiously that it spattered all over his white robe.

The mirror told him he needed another face-lift. Dani diPortanova had created road maps on his face. *He*, Reggie Bolt, should be outfitting 'The Seducers.' *He* was the one whose designs everyone on Seventh Avenue copied year after year. He was the only one who ever displayed one ounce of creativity or imagination. And what did he have to show for it? *Nada*, as Lydia would say. Nothing but headaches and memos from those assholes at Megacorp.

'The Seducers' had been his best shot for a creative comeback.

A fast, steaming hot shower cleaned out his porcs but not his anger. As the steam rose in the shower stall, so did his fury.

Lydia arrived with his carbo-loaded breakfast. She set the tray on the Louis XVI table by the bay window and drew open the floor-length chintz drapes.

Bright sunlight hit him right between his still aching eyes.

'Pul-lease, Lydia, how many times must I tell you? No sun on an empty stomach.'

Lydia paid no attention. This was an ongoing battle between them.

His private phone rang. Only his very closest friends had the number, and he had instructed Lydia not to answer that line.

'That will be all,' he said pointedly.

Lydia stood quietly, hands folded in front of her.

The phone shrilled again.

'*Thank you*, Lydia.'

Alone at last, he picked up the antique French phone and said, 'Yes?'

'Reggie?' singsonged Mitchell.

'Yes, darling, what do you want? I'm really busy.'

'I called your office, and they said you weren't there. It's past eleven – '

'Mitchell, I'm in a meeting and I don't have time for chitchat.'

'Well, I just called to give you some sympathy,' Mitchell explained. 'Isn't that a *wonderful* ad in today's *Times*?'

Turning the screw, Reggie thought. All because of Dani diPortanova. She had ruined it. She had taken it all away from him and now she was flaunting it. He smeared a glob of damson preserves on his croissant.

'Poor Reggie,' Mitchell continued, 'whatever will you do about the countess?'

Reggie picked up the knife, dripping with bright purple preserves. 'I'll bury that bitch.'

Ever since the night the goons had invaded her home, Monika slept poorly. More than once she was awakened by her own screams in the middle of a hideous nightmare about men fondling her. A security expert she consulted recommended a brand-new state-of-the-art security system. 'It's expensive, but it's worth it,' he assured her.

'*Ja*, but is it guaranteed?' she pressed him.

'You know what they say, ma'am. Nothing's guaranteed but death and taxes,' the security man replied.

She would have to think about it, she told him. In the meantime, she carefully checked her doors and windows each night before she went to bed.

Still she couldn't sleep. Finally she called her doctor, who gave her a prescription for sleeping pills. She slept soundly for the first time in weeks . . . so soundly that she missed hearing the glass shatter in the attic window, missed hearing the creaking of the attic steps.

She didn't wake up until the intruder had found his way to her bedroom and shaken her to consciousness. Her eyes widened when she saw him standing there above her, his face masked.

'No, please, don't hurt me . . .' she begged, her voice cracking with terror.

The man leaned closer, jerked back the sheet and

blanket, and ripped away her camisole. She saw the blade, felt it press against her breast.

'Pay up, or you're *dead*,' he whispered as he cut her just below the nipple. 'Same goes if you call the cops.'

She knew better than to do that. The police could tell her how the intruder had broken into her house, and they might even be able to come up with a couple of finger-prints. *So what?* she thought as her blood spattered across the sheets. That wouldn't bring her any closer to repaying her debt. What she needed was one very good night at the tables. Or to find out that a rich relative had died and left her a lot of money.

She thought about what Dani had told her after Nino died: *'I've had my will revised. If anything ever happens to me, you get all of Countess Dani, Inc., and fifty percent of my personal assets.'*

If anything happened to Dani . . .

Los Angeles

The late, great Dani di Portanova. Why am I forever late? Seated in the backseat of the limo, Dani remembered Nino, who was himself rarely on time, scolding her because she'd missed the curtain at the Met and had to spend the first act in the late-arrivals room to the right of the orchestra.

She'd particularly wanted to arrive on time for the press conference that NBC and Stanley J. Moore Productions had arranged to introduce the stars of 'The Seducers.' But she had gotten hung up at the store. Her manager blamed the recently shrinking profit margin on shoplifters. She had urged Dani to hire more security guards or to install a more sophisticated security system. Dani suspected that the manager was embezzling money, but she hadn't yet figured out what her system was. She would have to discuss the problem with Monika as soon as she got back to New York.

She probably should have stuck around the store a while longer, but she'd worried that if she didn't show up, Stan might 'forget' to mention Countess Dani, Inc. He'd invited her to the press party with his typical charm. 'Come on out here, pretty lady, and take a bow. You certainly deserve it more than some of these other broa – women.'

Pretty lady? She supposed that was a compliment, but it wasn't much of a step up from 'honey,' 'babes,' 'cookie,' and some of his other terms of endearment.

'Are we almost there?' she asked her driver. It was four years since she'd opened the store on Rodeo Drive, and she still didn't know how to get around in this town. Geographically speaking, of course.

'Yes, ma'am,' the driver answered, flashing her a blinding smile in the rearview mirror.

Dani had him pegged as an out-of-work actor, just like every chauffeur, waiter, and secretary in Hollywood. But this one wasn't the typical pretty boy. He was knockdown gorgeous – dark-haired and well muscled, with a physique that exploded through his chauffeur's uniform.

They had given each other the once-over when she strolled out of the Beverly Hills Hotel where he stood by the limo, ready to open the back door for her. She had read appreciation and approval in his dark brown eyes. Why not? She looked terrific, and she knew it. Her double-breasted red silk shirt fell away to reveal just a hint of cleavage. The padded shoulders emphasized her own broad shoulders and underscored her full breasts. The matching red silk crepe pants rode saucily on her slim hips, then flared gently below. A loose-fitting black alligator belt completed the ensemble. The outfit was from

456

the Countess Dani resort collection and perfect for the balmy end-of-the-summer Los Angeles weather.

They were heading down Santa Monica Boulevard. She liked the way he drove. Fast, smooth, and sure of himself. And in bed . . .?

'What's your name?' she asked, knowing she shouldn't.

'Gene, ma'am.' He gave her another smile through the rearview mirror. Boyish charm edged with ambition.

Gene.

Didn't anybody in Hollywood have real names? They were all one-syllabled, like Rob or Mel or Sean or Kyle.

'Is that your real name?'

'A nickname,' he replied, his voice warm and sweet.

Of course. Probably short for Eugene. Could he get a job in television with a name like Eugene?

'What's it short for?' asked Dani.

He laughed. 'Gianni. My parents are Italian. I grew up in Little Italy, New York.'

Dani's heart missed a beat. *Gianni*. Not a single day went by that she didn't think about Nino. She missed him at the oddest moments – while speeding down the country roads near the Roxbury house, in the middle of the night when she was worried about the business and needed someone to make her laugh, whenever she heard Marvin Gaye singing 'Let's Get It On,' their song from that first summer in Cannes so long ago. If he had lived, she wasn't sure they would still be married, but she did know they would still be the best of friends.

'Are you Italian, Countess?'

Dani played with her long gold necklace, tracing the pattern of the multicolored sapphires embedded in the heavy links. 'No. My husband was.' She changed the subject. 'Don't you get bored, always waiting for people?'

'Sure, sometimes. Not today, though. I'm up for a good part in a prime-time soap. I've had my head in the script

457

all morning.' He took his hand off the steering wheel and waved a script at her.

'How long have you been out here?'

'Three years. Three *long* years.' He laughed. 'I shouldn't complain. My luck has been pretty good. I had a couple of lines in "Cheers," and I played a cop once on "Hill Street Blues." Too bad I got killed off in the first few minutes of the show.'

Dani smiled. He had a nice way about him. They stopped at a red light, and Gene glanced back to make sure she was still interested.

The ride was turning out to be a good break between her problems at the store and the Hollywood zoo scene that awaited her. 'Do you think you'll make it?'

His answer came right away. 'Oh, yeah. I'm a tough kid from New York. Not much scares me. And I'm good. I can't lose with that combination. You know what I mean?'

'Yes.' Dani smiled. 'I do.' She knew exactly what he meant. It was the same sort of drive and determination that had made her a success. She admired anyone who rose up and fought the odds.

'Do you have an agent?'

'Oh, yeah. I hustle and all, but it's who you know . . . that's the name of the game.'

'Okay, Gene. Now you know me. Give me your agent's name and number. I'll pass your name along to a couple of people I know.'

'Wow, that would be great. I really appreciate it.'

'Don't worry about it. I like people who believe in themselves.'

'Well, thanks, really. Here we are, Countess,' he said, turning off Santa Monica Boulevard. 'The Century Plaza Hotel.'

* * *

458

Stan had insisted that the press party be held in the Presidential Suite at the Century Plaza. NBC complained about the expense, but they weren't about to buck one of La La Land's most successful producers. Besides, in an unusual *grand geste*, Stan agreed to pick up most of the tab. He could afford to. He had gotten four of his five stars below market, and this show was going to make him yet another fortune. He could feel it in his kishkes.

First came the press conference, held in one of the downstairs conference rooms. An enormous NBC peacock loomed in living color on a backdrop behind the dais. Giant bold black letters spelled out 'Stanley J. Moore Productions, Inc.' across the front of the stage. NBC had objected, but Stan said, 'Hey, equal time – a sign for you, a sign for me.' He had wanted his logo, a picture of a huge man who roughly resembled Mr Clean with a tall television tower resting in his outstretched palm.

'No,' said NBC, shuddering at the phallic-shaped tower. 'Absolutely not.'

Stan the Man backed off.

The ten chairs on the dais faced six rows of chairs filled by the Hollywood press corp regulars, as well as correspondents from *Women's Wear Daily*, the *National Enquirer*, and a couple of feature writers from the newspapers in Atlanta where 'The Seducers' was set. Stan had paid their way out to make sure he got good local coverage.

A pretty young NBC spokeswoman welcomed the press and was about to introduce the stars of 'The Seducers.' Stan bounded up beside her.

Stan was in his element. Introducing the cast was his big moment. No way was he going to let some dumb broad in pearls steal his glory. Not after all the pre-production shit he'd gone through.

'Don't worry 'bout it, babes,' he said. 'Stan the Man'll handle this.' He jabbed her aside with an elbow move perfected as a kid playing basketball in East New York. He positioned himself behind the lectern, sucked in his belly, and threw back his Bijan-suited shoulders.

Got to get to the gym, he reminded himself. He tipped his cigar at the girl from the *Hollywood Reporter* who was smirking at him from the front row. She was as ugly as a used tire, but he had *shtupped* her last month in a weak moment. He hoped the broad would give him good press. She sure hadn't given good head.

Half an hour later he finished introducing the last of the five stars, Ginger Lee, a buxom brunette. Ginger had the role of a sweet young thing whose secret ambition was to marry into the seducers' family so she could take control of their newspaper empire. Ginger wasn't the most talented starlet in Hollywood, but hell, her tits were big as watermelons – and Stan had gotten her for *bupkes*.

He fiddled with his gold cuff links in the shape of a fat Havana cigar – a birthday present from his wife. Charged, of course, on his Visa card. 'I'm sure,' he said, winding up his spiel, 'that you can all appreciate why we are expecting such *big things* from "The Seducers".' He all but pointed to Ginger Lee's bosom with his cigar and leered at the reporters.

The men roared. The women rolled their eyes and looked disgusted. Hollywood macho humor. Stan the Man was notorious for it . . .

New York

Bunny had been expecting an invitation to Stan's party up until the moment Dani swept out of the office the previous day. The invitation never came. Stan was too much of a

460

pig to think of inviting her, but she had expected Dani to realize that if anyone deserved the trip to LA, it was she, Barbara Hester.

Hollywood parties were the pits, Dani had said, but Bunny knew she was lying. Dani didn't want her there. Who did they think she was, the hired help? She had style. She had class. Besides, it was only because of her and all those disgusting blow jobs she had given Stan that Countess Dani had landed the contract for 'The Seducers.'

On Thursday night her sleep was ruined by a nightmare that her father and Jeremiah Blair had traded her to Stan for a chance to appear on one of his game shows. In her dream they packed her carefully in a shipping crate and sent her off to LA.

'Bye-bye, Bunny babes,' her father and Jeremiah shouted just before they nailed the crate shut.

She had seethed silently all through her breakfast meeting at the Helmsley Palace with the young woman from the Color Institute whose friendship she had carefully cultivated. It didn't hurt to have the inside track about which colors the experts at the institute were touting for the upcoming season, and she had picked up more than a few good tips in return for some expense-account meals and a pretense of caring.

Breakfast meetings were Bunny's secret weapon. She was a morning person, always had been. She was at her best when every other yo-yo was yawning and just waking up. But today, although she was smiling her sweet Barbara Hester smile, she was wound up tighter than an eight-day clock. Waves of paranoia washed over her like the ocean pounding at the shoreline in the middle of a hurricane.

What if Dani and Stan had a cozy post-party tête-à-tête? What if Stan opened his foul, fat mouth and told

461

Dani the *real* story of Barbara Hester? What if he blew apart her carefully constructed biography?

No. No way was she about to let that happen. She had fought too hard to pull herself out of the slime of Moccasin Bottom.

By the time the waiter handed her the check, Bunny had made up her mind. To hell with not getting an invitation. She would go to Stan's party whether or not he and Dani diPortanova wanted her there.

She fretted all during the cab ride to the office and picked nervously at her fingernails as the elevator took what seemed like ages to reach their floor. So much to do . . . She had to clear up a couple of problems here at the office, then rush home to pack. She knew exactly what she was going to wear, but what about accessories?

The elevator stopped at every floor. Bunny felt as if she might faint. She had to calm down. Everything would be fine. She took a deep breath and reminded herself that she was no longer the country bumpkin from Moccasin Bottom. She would get a manicure and a facial. Could she afford it? She didn't care. For once she wouldn't stop to count her pennies.

She hurried to her office, stopping at Carter's desk to pick up her messages.

'Get me a flight to Los Angeles for this afternoon. I need to be there by seven o'clock. And book a room for one night at' – Dani always stayed at the Beverly Hills Hotel, so that was out of the question – 'the Beverly Wilshire. And reserve a car for me at the airport.'

Carter was thrilled. The bitch would be out of her hair for the rest of the day. 'Do you want to go first class?'

'Are you going to pay for it?' Bunny snapped. 'Listen, when it's my money you're playing with, book coach!'

Quickly checking her appointment book, she saw that she had no meetings today. Good. She owed Monika a progress report on the household furnishings designs by Monday. If she was late, Monika wouldn't forget it. She'd write the report on her way to LA. She imagined herself sitting on the plane, busily scribbling away with her gold Mark Cross pen (a gift, of course), being recognized for the influential and powerful executive that she was. One never knew what a chance encounter – or a calculated one – could lead to.

She buzzed Carter. 'What about those reservations? I'm waiting!'

Carter sighed. 'I'm working on it. Pan Am has me on hold.'

'Either get them on the line or get another airline. And get me an appointment at Georgette Klinger for a facial and a manicure at eleven or twelve.'

Carter couldn't believe her ears. Barbara was finally flipping out. Did she really think she could get a same-day appointment on a Friday morning? She couldn't wait to tell the other assistants.

Bunny was sorting through her notes, deciding what she needed to take, when Monika suddenly appeared in her doorway.

Now what? Monika rarely stepped foot in her office, always communicating via memos.

'Good morning, Monika,' said Bunny. 'Hot, isn't it?'

'You're finally in. *Gut*.'

'I had a breakfast meeting. Whatever can I do for you?' Occassionally she liked to bug Monika by being sweet as molasses. She knew it drove her crazy.

'Who was your meeting with?'

Now she was prying? 'A friend from the Color Institute,' she replied, shuffling her papers to indicate she was busy. Monika looked like shit. That red she was wearing washed all the color out of her face. And why did she keep touching the left side of her chest? Bunny hoped

Monika wasn't about to have a heart attack. She was in no mood to play Florence Nightingale to Brunhilde.

'Look, Barbara,' Monika said, 'I have to leave early today. Mr Chen, the manager of our Hong Kong factory, is in town. I would like you to take him to dinner. You can take him wherever you like.' Monika smiled as pleasantly as she could. She knew Barbara loved eating out on the company. She all but listed her laundry on the expense account vouchers.

Dammit to hell, Bunny thought. She'd been wanting to meet Mr Chen for a long time. She would stroke anyone if she thought he could help her. Today, however, she had much bigger fish to fry.

'I'm sorry, Monika, honey. I sure wish I could help you out. But I already have plans.'

Monika opened her mouth, was about to say something, then shrugged her shoulders and turned to go.

'Barbara!' Carter yelled from her desk. 'I've got you booked on Pan Am, flight eight-eleven out of Kennedy at four today. You'll get into Los Angeles at six-fifty, their time. You're also booked into the Beverly Wilshire.'

Dammit. How many times had she told Carter to buzz her on the intercom instead of advertising her business through the halls?

'Going to Los Angeles?' Monika asked, hand on her chest.

'Yes, indeed, I am,' Bunny answered sweetly, ready to drop the bomb. 'I'm going to the "Seducers" party. Weren't you invited?'

Monika refused to acknowledge the hit. 'Have a pleasant time,' she said. She tugged at her oversized linen jacket, pulling it more closely around her, as if to protect herself against Bunny's next attack. Her jaw tightened, and she retreated to her office.

Monika kept her face blank, carefully masking the

464

feelings of hurt and rage, until she had quietly shut the door of her office. Then she sank into her chair and twirled around to the window, looking out at but not seeing the bustle of Times Square five blocks north.

She placed her hand over her breast. Beneath the silk blouse, the wound ached, reminding her with each throb of the horror of the other night. She had to find a solution – a way to come up with all that money. Their latest visit had been the second warning. She couldn't count on Lucky's to give her a third.

How had she let her debts pile up like this? Why didn't she have the share of the von Reich fortune she had been born to, was entitled to? Damn her mother.

And God damn Dani. Since when had she gotten so cozy with Barbara? Had she been so preoccupied with her problems that she had missed noticing that Dani was shutting her out? Dani always made fun of Hollywood because, she said, it was all 'honey, baby, cookie, darling.'

Ach. Better 'cookie, baby' than somebody calling you 'bitch' and holding a knife to your breast.

We are very lucky, ja?

Nein, Dani. Nein.

Lighting a cigarette, Monika picked up the phone and called the Woodstock Inn in Vermont to confirm reservations she'd made for the weekend. She needed some time away from New York to think. To consider her options. To pull herself together and find the strength to face the nightmare that haunted her every waking hour.

How was she going to raise the money?

Dani had caught the last few words of Stan's crack about Ginger Lee's bosom as she came into the conference room. She didn't so much as flicker an eyelash. She had learned long ago in the garment district that the best way to deal with dumb-broad jokes and male put-downs was to ignore them. And if that didn't work, she had learned to give the joker a verbal jab in the balls.

She waved at the *Women's Wear Daily* reporter – they had known each other for years – and walked swiftly to the front of the stage, tossing back her thick black waves.

Stan was about to suggest that the reporters save their questions for upstairs, where they could talk with a drink in their hands. But he took a look at Dani and changed his mind. He figured he better introduce her. From what he'd been told, the broad always demanded what she had been promised.

Stan tipped his cigar to her. 'Ladies and gentlemen, I'd like to introduce the show's costume designer, Countess Dani diPortanova. This little lady is going to make Nolan Miller look like a has-been.'

Dani smiled graciously, but inside she was furious. She didn't need to be compared to Nolan Miller or anyone else. How dare he! As for this 'little lady' bullshit . . . She deliberately moved closer to Stan. In her two-inch heels, Dani towered above him by several inches.

'Thank you for your kind words, Stan. I'll admit to being talented, but I don't think anyone has called me little before.'

Everyone laughed except Stan.

'Any questions?'

Stan's face turned purple. Who the fuck did this broad think she was, opening up the floor for questions? She was upstaging the *real* stars.

One of the reporters raised a hand. 'Countess,' she said, 'will the costumes for "The Seducers" work only for the series, or will they translate to clothes for the rest of America?'

Dani flashed her famous smile. 'Absolutely. I started my business because I felt American women weren't being offered clothes that were fun, glamorous, and comfortable. My customers have been very valuable to me. I am not about to desert them for television. I will make television work for them, not the reverse.'

Stan coughed nervously.

Dani's friend from *WWD* stood up. 'Dani, what colors are you using this year?'

'Bright, bold colors, Claire. This is the year for reds, golds, green, purple . . . everything bold and strong. At Countess Dani we call this color' – she pointed to her outfit – 'Fabulous Fuchsia.'

Stan chewed furiously on his cigar. These jokers were supposed to be talking about his show, for chrissake, not about colors. Who gave a shit about what American women were wearing?

'Food and booze upstairs in the Presidential Suite,' he announced. 'Take a look in the bedroom while you're up there. President Reagan and Nancy sleep there when they come to town. Although I doubt if they ever *come* here,' he guffawed.

The reporters stood up and headed for the elevators.

Stan turned to Dani. 'Great entrance, honey,' he said, patting her on the cheek. 'Joan couldn't have done it better.'

'Joan?' Dani asked, feeling as though she should disinfect her cheek.

'Collins, baby, Collins.'

Dani barely managed a smile. Why did she always want to take a shower after she talked to Stan?

'Listen, Stan,' she said, looking around to make sure nobody was within hearing distance. 'I think we better settle something.'

'Yeah, babes? What's on your mind?' What was on *his* mind was screwing her silly.

'You can call me Countess or Dani, but you are not to address me as babes, baby, little lady, pretty lady, or any other of your pet names. Got it?'

Stan looked hurt. 'Sure, okay, bab – I mean, Dani. Hey, I didn't mean any harm, you know. It's just my way of being friendly.'

'I understand that, Stan. But let's try it my way.'

A tough broad. Stan respected that even if it pissed him off. He followed her to the elevators, never taking his eyes off her ass. Stan the Man ached to stick it to her.

The members of the press were milling about the suite, wolfing down overstuffed corned beef and pastrami sandwiches with pickles and cole slaw, drinking beer, hard liquor, and diet colas. Stan ordered his usual vodka martini, 'very dry, with just a twist,' and a Perrier for Dani. 'Nothing stronger than that?' he asked, sounding disappointed.

'No, thanks.' She hadn't eaten anything yet, and it was going to be a long day.

'Here's to us, ba – Dani,' Stan toasted, raising his glass and downing the martini in two gulps before Dani had a chance to respond. He belched. 'Not a bad turnout, huh?' He surveyed the room. 'But the party tonight at my place is the *fun* one. You're coming, aren't you?'

'I'm planning on it,' Dani said as politely as she could. That was noncommittal enough. Just in case she changed her mind at the last minute. Like hell Stan's party would be fun.

Hollywood parties were all the same. There was either

468

a lot of coke or a lot of bullshit, and often both. People talked deals over caviar and mushrooms stuffed with clams, and everyone hoped to impress the man of the moment by comparing the party to the one they had just left. There were conversations about who had shown up and who hadn't and whether the caterer and the florist were 'in' or 'out.' She wondered how Kyle Lord could stand the scene . . . he seemed at home in it. The only reason she had gotten involved with this circus was for the publicity.

'Will you excuse me, Stan? I have to call my office.'

'Sure. If you really want privacy, you can use the phone in the bathroom. Take care of all your business at the same time,' he chortled.

'Thanks, Stan.'

She closed the bathroom door to block out the party noise.

Lance answered the phone. 'Countess diPortanova's office.'

'Hi, Lance. What's doing?'

'Dani! How's life in Hollywood?'

'Fabu, baby, just fabu.'

'At least you haven't lost your sense of humor.'

'Well, it helps to hear your cheery voice.' She meant it. Thank God he seemed to be recovering from that horrible mugging. 'Anything new?'

'No, you know what Friday afternoons in August are like. Hot as hell and quiet as my sex life. The agency sent over some new ad layouts for your approval, and Dawn Mello called. She wants to have lunch. Ditto Gerrie Stutz. Have you seen Kyle Lord yet?'

She ignored his question. 'Would you put me through to Monika?'

'She left right after lunch for the weekend.'

'You have the number?'

'No, she just left.'

How strange. Dani wondered for the umpteenth time what was going on with her. 'Okay, what about Barbara? She still around?'

'No, she took off early, too.'

Dani was annoyed. She realized Fridays were slow, but one of them should have stuck around. 'Well, I'm glad you stayed to guard the fort.'

'Oh, yeah, I forgot to tell you.' Lance sounded bored. 'Jack called about fifteen times.'

Dani's heart sank. Somehow she was going to have to disentangle herself from him once and for all. The relationship had gone completely beyond the boundaries of whatever she had originally intended. She felt sorry for him, but they were going nowhere, and she couldn't see continuing it. In fact, he had proposed to her again just before she'd left for LA. 'No, really, how many times did he call?'

'At least five or six.'

'Thanks, Lance. If Monika calls, please have her call me right away. There's a problem with the Rodeo store I need to talk to her about. You have a good weekend. *Ciao*.'

She sat down on the side of the bathtub and rested her chin on her palm. Damn, she was tired. Where was the balance in her life? The money, power, and fame were wonderful, but more and more lately she felt as if she were juggling too many balls at once. And with so little help.

Monika was acting a little schizoid, but she was such a private person that Dani hesitated to ask questions even if she was her best friend. But this wasn't simply a question of Monika's personal life. Whatever was bugging her was affecting her professionally as well. And that was definitely Dani's business.

470

She checked her hair in the mirror and washed her face, then patted on some moisturizer. She had planned to fly back to New York tomorrow afternoon, but maybe she should take another day and drive up to Carmel and relax. She needed a day of doing absolutely nothing.

The party was still in full swing. The five 'Seducers' stars, flanked by NBC publicists, were talking about how excited they were to be a part of the Stanley J. Moore – NBC family, how sure they were that this show would be a big, big hit. Somebody asked Ginger Lee how she had landed the role of Roxanne. She blushed, darted her eyes at Stan, then giggled, cracking her gum and flashing a capped-tooth smile. 'Through my agent, of course.'

Laine Clark, another 'Seducers' star, hurried over and thrust herself in front of Dani. 'Countess, I had to say hello,' she gushed. Her eyes were riveted on Dani's necklace. 'I'm thrilled to death to be wearing your designs. I hope you're planning something sexy and sophisticated for me.'

Laine Clark was playing a tight-assed society matron who leaned towards frills and flounces. Sexy and sophisticated? Not according to the show's bible.

'I adore your outfit,' Laine went on, rubbing the fabric of Dani's sleeve between her thumb and forefinger. 'Silk is so incredible, don't you think?'

'Yes, I do. You can buy one just like this at my store on Rodeo.' *Because you're not going to get one free from the show*.

Her friend Claire walked over, along with four or five other reporters. They had plenty of questions for Dani, so she settled into her familiar one-leg-up-on-a-chair pose and started enjoying herself. She was doing what she loved – telling the world why Countess Dani, Inc., was number one.

Chapter Eighteen

Los Angeles

Dani rolled over in bed and checked her watch. Seventen. The party was supposed to start at eight, which meant she didn't have to be there until nine. Plenty of time to take a nice long bath and get dressed.

The nap had helped. What a day she'd had. After the press conference she had gone back to the store, then wandered up and down Rodeo Drive, checking out the competition. After that, she'd had a quick drink at the Polo Lounge with a young designer who'd been recommended to her by several people.

Jumping out of bed, she stretched and touched her toes. Her mirrored reflection told her that she might be feeling her age, but she sure wasn't looking it. Her body was as shapely and well proportioned as ever. She turned and took a look at her ass. Nice.

The bungalow refrigerator was stocked with diet sodas and orange juice, as well as a bottle of Roederer Cristal with a tag around the neck that said, 'Compliments of the Beverly Hills Hotel.' She eyed the bottle of champagne. Should she open it just for herself? What the hell . . . she didn't have anybody to share it with.

She carried the bottle and an ice bucket into the bathroom and turned on the water. After she had opened her store and begun staying at the Beverly Hills when she was in LA, the management had agreed to replace the generic package of bath giveaways in each room with a set of Countess Dani Royal Bath products. Dani added

472

the bubble bath to the water and unwrapped the lavender soap bearing her name.

Popping the champagne cork, she poured herself a glass, then stuck the bottle into the bucket resting on the side of the oversized tub. Mmmm, the hot water felt wonderful. She twirled her fingers through the lavender-scented bubbles and sipped champagne. Icy cold Cristal trickled down her throat as the steamy bathwater enveloped her. Her nipples showed above the surface of the water. Dani touched them lightly. They sprang erect. If only all of life happened so easily and naturally.

Another sip of champagne. She shut her eyes and leaned back, sinking slowly deeper into the water. She could feel herself relaxing, the tension flowing out of her. The problems of the real world faded.

Random thoughts . . . of her mother. How she had loved to sit cross-legged on the floor of the bathroom and watch her mother bathe.

Sophie had made bathing into a ritual: carefully testing the water with her finger to make sure it was exactly the right temperature. Adding a cupful of the Kneipp's Meadow Blossom bath salts her cousin used to send her from Switzerland. Finally getting into the tub but sitting up so straight, never relaxing. Her Viennese upbringing wouldn't permit her to sink into the water and luxuriate.

But she would allow Dani to scrub her back with the loofah. 'Please, Mama,' Dani would ask each time, although she knew the answer in advance, 'please let me do the loofah.'

And then it would be Dani's turn to bathe. While Sophie washed her hair, carefully rinsing all the shampoo out of her thick black curls, she listened to Dani's stories and complaints about school. She would sympathize and console, reminding Dani how lucky she was to have been born with so much talent and so much beauty.

Dani laughed aloud in the steamy room. What would Sophie say if she could see her now, stretched out like an Oriental princess, drinking champagne that sold for seventy-five dollars a bottle? Born rich in talent, married richer. Feted and celebrated and recognized wherever she went.

And now, with the 'Seducers' contract and the launching of her first couture collection, she would be the undisputed number one designer in America.

So why was this tiny worm of dissatisfaction gnawing at her? Because she wished someone else were here with her, watching her bathe, sharing the champagne with her, admiring her firm breasts, her flat stomach, her long, slim legs.

Dani could almost feel the hands and lips traveling down the length of her body, stopping to fondle and kiss, finding at last the perfect spot to explore.

Ahh . . .

More champagne? Yes, of course. She giggled again. What a waste of a horny broad. Trouble was, she didn't know whose lips and hands she longed for.

Like hell she didn't.

The champagne felt wonderful. Oops, mustn't drop the glass.

She knew exactly whose tongue she wanted to lick her into a frenzy of orgasms.

Another long sip. She should slow down.

She sat up, turned on the faucet to replenish the hot water, then leaned back again. As the steam rose and swirled around her head, Dani savored the thought of the man she longed for.

Kyle Lord shifted into second, then into third as his Land-Rover convertible picked up speed. Heading down Santa

474

Monica Boulevard toward Stan Moore's house on Doheny, Kyle wasn't happy, and it showed in his driving.

Piss on having to go to Stan Moore's party. He was all partied out. This one didn't promise to be any different from the hundreds – or was it thousands? – he had been to since he had landed in LA. All those white teeth, lifted asses, siliconed boobs. He'd kissed, patted, and pawed so many he was beginning to recognize which plastic surgeon had been there first. But his agent had made him promise to put in a brief appearance tonight. Stan, she swore, had a movie that had Kyle Lord stamped all over it.

The bimbo starlet sitting next to him was a girlfriend of his best mate's fiancée. 'Do me a favor and take her,' the bloke had begged. 'She's lots of fun and has a big heart.'

She was a big mistake. He had realized that as soon as he pulled up in front of her West Hollywood apartment. She had taken one look at the Land-Rover and yelped like a high-strung poodle being given a rectal thermometer.

'We're going in that? Where's the stretch?'

Stretch? This gal was just like all the rest of them. Stacked, blond, and about as bright as a twenty-watt bulb.

'Honey,' wailed the bimbo starlet, 'the wind is ruining my hair.'

Kyle pushed his lizard-skin cowboy boot down on the accelerator. The starlet wailed even louder, clutching at her meticulously waved and moussed blond hair. A hundred bucks and two hours of Allen Edward's painstaking styling destroyed before she'd even had a chance to make her entrance.

Kyle shouted an apology as he took a sharp corner at fifty miles an hour. The bimbo swerved, too, landing with her head between his legs. She grinned up at him like a Cheshire cat.

Bloody hell, he thought, shifting down at a red light

475

and wishing he were at home watching an Eastwood flick on his VCR. He drummed his fingers on the steering wheel. He was tired of all the star-fuckers, tired of having to think of excuses to get them out of his Malibu house. Tired of all the goddam cologne they sent him as remembrances.

He wouldn't have admitted the truth even to his best mate, but Kyle Lord hadn't been laid in weeks. The *National Enquirer* would have loved that. 'Stud Movie Star Losing His Touch,' the headline would scream. The problem was he hadn't even met a *real* woman in ages. Not since Dani diPortanova. And of course she needed him about as much as a 'roo needed another pouch.

'Terrific,' he announced, depressed and not caring if the bimbo knew it.

'Thanks, hon.'

Thanks for what? If it was true that human beings used only one-tenth of their brains, where did that leave this one?

'Hey, want anything?' the girl asked brightly, running her tongue over her high-glossed lips.

'Yeah,' he said, shifting again as the light changed. 'But you don't have it.'

'Bet I do. Coke? Ecstasy? Poppers? 'Ludes?'

'No, thanks,' Kyle said, wondering whether he could hook her up with someone at the party and take off.

Bloody hell, he thought again. Everything was going so right for him. *Lost Survivor* had grossed $150 million to date, making it one of the biggest movies of the year, and *Smash* was in the can and would be released in a few months. He had just seen the final cut, and it looked great. Principal photography on *Tough Enough* was set to start next week in New York. He was getting three million plus a piece of the gross. MCA/Universal was talking to

476

his agent about a $15 million multi-picture play-or-pay contract. So why did he feel so bloody rotten?

He had come so far so fast. But who did he have to share all this success with? It wasn't that he didn't *want* a long-term relationship. He just hadn't met anyone he wanted to be with for more than a couple of screws.

Until Dani.

Fat chance he would ever get anything going with her.

'Countess, I can't tell you how happy I am that you could make it,' Mrs Stan Moore trilled. 'My husband has told me so much about you.'

Describing Dani, Stan had said she was 'tougher than Fonda and hotter than Kathleen Turner. She's got balls bigger than most of the men in this town.'

It wasn't often that Stan had such kind words to say about a woman. His wife had been aching to meet the countess. In photographs she looked gorgeous. In person, spectacular.

'Welcome to what my designer calls a "dreamscape"', she gushed. 'I'd show you around myself if I weren't so busy playing hostess. You know,' she said as she leaned closer to Dani and breathed scotch fumes in her face, 'when I was growing up in Bakersfield, I dreamed of a house like this. It lets me look at the world through peach-tinted glasses. You know, I drive my Corniche to the Beverly Hills city limits and I just freeze up! I shudder to think what lies beyond.'

Dani smiled politely, recognizing Mrs Moore's Andre Van Pier gold lamé pants and matching gold brocade jacket, and quickly helped herself to a glass of champagne from the tray of a passing waiter.

'Countess, please feel free to take a tour of the house. I'm dying for you to see everything.' She deftly propelled

477

Dani into the crowd and turned to greet another newly arrived guest. 'Hello! Don't you look wonderful!'

Dani walked through the foyer and into the crowded living room, hoping to find somebody she knew. The room glimmered, shimmered, sparkled, and glowed. It looked like a Turkish sultan's midnight fantasy.

Ostrich-patterned leather wall paneling. Copper-colored patterned velvet sofas that snaked around the living room. Carved lacquered wooden arm chairs with leopard-skin upholstery and clawed feet. An enormous silk pouf done in two shades of orange with tassels dangling from the four corners like fringed anchors.

There were crushed glass-topped tables; travertine floors; shiny brass overhead beams and wall light fixtures; ficus trees strung with tiny lights that glittered like Christmas trees; African and Balinese wood sculptures with pointed breasts and erect phalluses; and an extravagant collage in orange and yellow. The rest of the house was decorated in variations on the same theme.

Dani thought she was seeing double until she realized that the entire ceiling and one whole wall were covered with gleaming mirrors. Among the guests, she spotted a Galanos, a Dior, a Herrera, and a Jacqueline De Ribes. Her own gown, one of her favorites from her soon to be launched couture collection, had a clingy, long-sleeved black silk halter top with a finely sculpted cerise skirt. The cerise sash was wrapped asymmetrically around her waist, falling in a graceful bow down one side of the dress. Her only accessory was an antique Spanish mantilla comb that Nino had brought back from one of his trips to Argentina. Artfully arranged so that it held in place a luxuriant sweep of black waves, the priceless ruby-studded comb threw sparkles of blazing color against the highly polished surfaces in the room.

478

From every direction, even in the midst of a star-studded collection of guests, people turned to take her in.

Surrendering her empty glass and grabbing another, she circled the room, eyeing the outfits and saying hello and how are you to the people she recognized. All around her the Hollywood cognoscenti sniped away at their best friends and worst enemies.

'. . . Can't you tell she's had a lift?'

'Yeah, and the crane broke.'

'. . . They call him Mr Vienna Sausage.'

'You mean it's that small?'

'Smaller.'

'. . . She thinks it's glamorous and stunning. *I* think it looks like a Castro convertible showroom.'

'. . . Well, he's the only one in town who isn't buying a studio.'

'. . . I just this minute got back from my eighteenth Club Med.'

'Really? I *am* sorry.'

Dani had heard it all before. Hollywood parties were like fashion industry parties, only worse.

Ginger Lee came over and pecked her on the cheek. She was sucking on a maraschino cherry, the waxed stem protruding from between her puckered bloodred lips.

'Hiya, Contessa. Remember me? Ginger Lee?' She giggled loudly. 'Isn't this a *fantastic* party? Isn't this the most *incredible* home?'

Dani nodded. '"Incredible" is certainly the right word.'

Ginger clutched her arm. 'Aren't you excited to be working with Stan? Don't you think he's a genius? Isn't he the most?'

'He is definitely the most.'

'Have you ever seen so many cute men in one room before?'

Dani looked around the room and nodded. The men

479

were wearing the best that the boutiques of Beverly Hills had to offer – Armani, Bijan, Perry Ellis, Gucci, and Valentino. They sported tans that looked as though they'd been perfected in a Toastmaster. Their teeth, perfectly white and straight, were the result of thousands of dollars' worth of caps or, for the less affluent, years of chemical bleaching. Their eyes were rich shades of blue, green, and brown, thanks to tinted contact lenses. Their eyes darted and winked as they assessed themselves and one another in the mirrors.

With the flick of a wrist, the lick of their lips, the shift of a skirt, a change in stance, actresses and Hollywood wives vied for their attention. And so did some of the other men.

Dani sighed as Ginger Lee rattled on. Not one of the men appealed to her. She thought of Kyle. She hadn't seen him since the last time she was out here when they appeared together on the 'Tonight' show and he totally humiliated her in front of Joan Rivers.

She had snagged Kyle for the Countess Dani sheets commercials just in time. *Lost Survivor* was a blockbuster, and Sam Martin had told her to forget about any future spots. 'Kyle's getting three mil per flick, Dani. Who needs commercials?'

Kyle had moved from heartthrob star to superstar. She wondered if he ever thought about her. Probably not, with all those worshipful blondes offering him every pleasure under the sun. He reminded her of the boy in a candy store who had never grown up. Still, she had hoped he might be here. The A list people always showed up at the same parties. But Kyle probably couldn't be bothered.

Well, screw him. Arrogant son of a bitch. Who needed him, anyway?

She did.

'Shouldn't we get another round, Contessa?' Ginger Lee shrilled, pulling the cherry stem out of her mouth.

Dani downed what was left in her glass. 'No, thanks. Actually, I need to get something to eat.'

Just then a tall black man dressed as if he'd stepped off the set of *Gone With the Wind* walked into the noisy living room and hit a steel triangle with a silver rod.

'Dinner is now being served on the back lawn.'

In keeping with the Atlanta setting of 'The Seducers,' the caterer had convinced Mrs Stan Moore to outdo herself in southern style. Set out on long tables with pink and green tablecloths were platters of herb-fried chicken, barbecued baby spareribs, duck grilled with muscadine jelly, fried catfish, fresh hot crabmeat in a mayonnaise and sherry sauce, pan-fried country ham with redeye gravy, corn on the cob, collard greens, oven baked beans, a huge basket of corn bread, hush puppies, and buttered biscuits. And, of course, mountains of mashed potatoes.

The waitresses were ladling out more than generous portions.

'What's that?' asked the ultra-skinny Beverly Hills lady who was standing in line in front of Dani.

'White cream gravy, ma'am,' the server replied, about to pour a hefty ladleful over the woman's mashed potatoes.

'Stop!' screeched the woman. 'I'm on a diet. Don't you people serve salad?'

Dani spotted the head of NBC Entertainment cooling his heels in the gazebo to the right of the pool. On her way to chat with him, she stopped at the bar. For the time being, she would stick to Dom Pérignon.

Bunny got directions to Stan's house from the front desk clerk at the Beverly Wilshire. She was paying $150 for one night's sleep here, but how often did Barbara Hester

481

get to stay in a place that looked like something out of *Town & Country*? From the minute she drove through the Louis XV bronze and iron gates that guarded the cobblestone driveway and gazed upon the elegant Louis XVI chandeliers and winding stairways, Bunny was in hog heaven.

But her heart sank when she drove up Doheny Drive and saw the long line of stretch limos, Rolls-Royces, Mercedes, BMWs, and Jaguars waiting to be parked by the attendants the Moores had hired for the evening. *Dammit to hell.* She should have rented a limo.

Pulling out her Hot Flash compact, she applied a fresh coat of Burning Sienna lipstick and adjusted her diamond hoop earrings.

Well, maybe her car was déclassé, but she looked expensive in her Countess Dani green silk dress with the padded shoulders, two-tiered sleeves, and deeply plunging V-neck. The bodice covered her breasts but left a narrow strip of skin exposed from neck to waist. The instant she had seen Dani's sketch she had known this gown would be stunning on her.

She stepped from the Thunderbird and fluffed out the ends of her hair. Five or six men with cameras were lounging near the front door. Paparazzi! Great! Maybe they would take her for a celebrity.

'Good evening,' she called out airily. She was *made* for Hollywood.

No response. One man lit up a cigarette. Another started changing the film in his camera.

How *dare* they ignore her! She looked famous. She knew she did! And of course she looked as beautiful as any television actress. One day soon they would be clamoring for her picture.

'Yes?' asked the security guard at the Moores' front door. In his hand was a list of invitees.

482

'Barbara Hester of New York,' announced Bunny. 'I'm not sure whether Mr Moore was expecting me, but I'm a *very* close friend of his.'

Suddenly there was Mrs Stan Moore. 'I don't believe we've met,' she said graciously.

Bunny appraised her coldly. Who was this in all that gold lamé?

'Miss Hester isn't on the guest list, but she says she's a very close friend of your husband,' explained the guard.

Bunny stiffened. She had always wondered what kind of creature would have married Stan the Man.

Mrs Stan Moore looked Bunny up and down and immediately grasped the situation. She and Stan had an understanding. He never paraded his indiscretions in front of her and vice versa. But here was one of his girls in the flesh. And what flesh!

Naturally Stan hadn't mentioned she was coming. Not that he ever told her anything. She didn't care. So long as her bills at Lina Lee and Van Cleef & Arpels got paid, and so long as his Nielsen ratings stayed high, he could screw his brains out. Nevertheless, this *was* her party. Fortified by two Chivas on the rocks and a Quaalude, she decided to call this party-crasher's bluff.

'Is my husband expecting you?' she demanded.

Bunny bridled. 'I'm with Dani diPortanova.' She quickly flashed her business card under Mrs Moore's nose.

Mrs Stan Moore reappraised the woman. Perhaps she had made a mistake.

'Do come in. The buffet is out by the pool. You can pick up a drink in the living room or on the terrace. Stan's around here somewhere. If you don't see him, I'm *sure* you'll hear him.' She roared at her own wit.

Bunny headed toward the pool. She couldn't believe it. *She was at a real Hollywood party!*

She spotted a famous actress talking to the handsome

star of a half-dozen miniseries. Robin Leach walked by. *Oh, my Lord*, she thought. *Mr Lifestyles of the Rich and Famous himself!* Now there was a man she would like to get to know better.

One of Stan's game-show hosts was holding court with a couple of models from 'The Price is Right.' Bunny's mother would have died to be here. She used to love to watch the host French-kissing all the contestants.

She walked up to the bar, wondering what to order. Nobody paid attention to her as she eavesdropped on their conversations.

'*I* should have gotten *Rambo*, but my agent said it would hurt my career. Ha! It hurt hers. I fired the dumb twat.'

'. . . and he only does it with rubber gloves on.'

'Oh, likes to play gynecologist, huh? Sweetie, it's better than wearing fishnet stockings. I told you about . . .'

'. . . I think she should write one of her own and dispute what her daughter says.'

'Yeah, she could call it *You Ungrateful Little Bitch*.'

Bunny decided to break her strict no-liquor rule. Tonight she needed something, for when she bumped into Stan and Dani. She deserved to be here, she kept telling herself, but butterflies were dancing in the pit of her stomach.

'Yes?' asked the bartender, who was dressed in a Confederate Army uniform. 'What can I get you?'

'Ummm . . .' She stared at him helplessly.

Aspiring actress, thought the bartender. He could see them coming a mile away. New in town. A real looker. He ought to keep an eye on her. Maybe he'd take her home.

'Mint julep?' he suggested.

Bunny nodded. 'Thanks,' she said. 'That would be lovely.'

* * *

'So I said, not only did Sly turn it down, but so did Clint. So then I said, forget it, take it to Zanuck-Brown.'

'Really? How interesting.' Dani had no idea what this man was talking about. And why should she care? And who was this man who had hurried over to tell the head of NBC he had a phone call, then cornered her with his endless babbling?

Dani was drunk. She felt like reaching over, removing the man's toupee, and flinging it into the pool. Instead she said, 'Excuse me, I really have to get something to eat.' And fast.

The line at the buffet was shorter now. Only the most dedicated eaters were coming back for seconds. She was about to step in line when she slipped on a discarded corncob, fell against the arm of the man next to her, and almost crashed into the spareribs.

'I'm so sorry,' she said. Oh, dear. She was behaving like Nino.

The man was too fascinated by his companion to notice. 'He says he's working on something big, big, big,' Dani heard him say.

'Ha!' hooted his red-haired date. 'Then how come his wee-wee is so small, small, small? Careful,' she warned. 'Don't let that barbecue sauce drip.'

The man snickered. 'I *never* drip.'

'That's not what I heard!' Stan Moore boomed, slapping his guest on the back so hard that the sauce spattered all over the man's white linen jacket. Stan turned to Dani and noticed that she didn't have a plate.

'Don't tell me you're dieting. You oughta put some meat on those bones.' He was about to squeeze her arm to prove his point, then thought better of it. Not this broad. She was too uptight.

Dani forced herself to focus on Stan. He had appeared out of nowhere, like a nasty, fat genie popping out of a champagne bottle. 'I'm sorry. I don't have much of an appetite tonight.' And she was losing what was left of it with each passing moment.

'Well, help yourself,' Stan said expansively, waving his hand and sloshing his martini. 'After all, it's only money. 'Scuse me, there's Lee Majors. I gotta talk to him. He's after me for a new show.'

Dani looked at her empty glass. She really shouldn't have any more champagne . . . but against her better judgment, she did.

'Countess diPortanova? I'd recognize you in the middle of a darkened movie theater. I've had a crush on you ever since your Hot Flash ads. My ex-wife almost bankrupted me buying your dresses. I can't believe it's you in the flesh. Or should I say, in the "flash"?'

Dani looked through a bubbly alcohol haze at a man dressed like a Wall Street investment banker who had landed at the wrong party. She had to be polite. She was here only for public relations. But the way she was feeling, she wasn't going to impress anyone. She had to make a fast exit.

'You're too kind. Would you excuse me for a moment? I'll be right back,' she said, carefully pronouncing each word.

She made it halfway to the house before she had to stop and lean against a statue. She looked up. Was she drunk or was this really a reproduction of Michelangelo's David with painted-on pubic hair?

Getting to a bathroom wasn't any problem. But getting past the interior designer's 'dreamscape' of mirrors and apricot-colored furniture without getting sick would take some doing. Why was she here? There was nobody she really wanted to talk to. Nobody she cared about meeting. And the one person she had hoped to see hadn't bothered to come.

She hiccuped and leaned her head against David's marble leg. She should have swallowed her pride and called him. Maybe he would have agreed to have dinner with her. Then they could have gone out somewhere wonderful, quiet, intimate. Instead, she was here . . . drunk and unhappy. And where was he?

Kyle was itching to go walkabout. He had been at the party an hour and had finished what Sam was always calling 'the obligatory rounds.' He had made sure he was friendly to the head of Paramount, who was rumored to be leaving that studio to head up Fox. He had run into Universal's head, who had initiated the big-money talks with his agent. He had been cornered by the bloke who had directed *Tootsie* and who was keen to talk to him about a new film project. His duty done, he had tucked into a plate of ribs and fried chicken, while Miss Bimbo, glued to his side and lapping it all up, opted for mint juleps, explaining with a titter that she was on a liquid diet.

Now they were making their way back through the house on the round of post-dinner chatter. Suddenly Miss Bimbo grabbed his arm and jerked him past Bob Newhart.

'Hi!' she said to a short bald-headed man. 'You're Squeaky Lazar, aren't you?'

Irving Lazar glanced at her through his thick glasses, then shook Kyle's hand. 'Hello, Kyle,' Lazar said, ignoring Miss Bimbo, and continuing to scope out the room. 'I hear your movie's doing great. When you gonna do one for Mary? I can get you a terrific deal with Tri-Star.'

'Talk to my agent, but somebody already has an offer on the table.'

Lazar straightened his necktie. 'Okay, kid. I'll call her

487

first thing tomorrow. We'll have lunch. There's Richard Chamberlain. If you'll excuse me . . .'

'Kyle,' Miss Bimbo wailed, 'why didn't you introduce me to Squeaky?'

'It's *Swifty*, and he doesn't like the nickname.'

'Oh, pooh,' she said. Then, after another infusion of mint julep, she whispered in his ear, 'Hey, stud, why don't we go into a bathroom? I want to give you something special.'

Kyle weighed the offer. She hadn't stopped eye-fucking him all evening. He didn't much feel like it, but maybe he was daft to turn her down. He hadn't had any action in days, and his balls were crying for relief.

'Okay, darl',' he said, taking her hand and treating her to the smile that had been his ticket to America. 'Let's have a go at it, then.'

Miss Bimbo stroked the palm of his hand with her index finger, a promise of things to come. She had played this scene in her head every night for the past week.

The powder room off the library was empty. 'Bugger,' said Kyle. 'What's this, a tease?' Somebody had left a coke spoon on the vanity next to the gold-plated Sherle Wagner sink.

Miss Bimbo dropped to her knees and licked her lips, noting in the overhead and facing mirrors how fantastic she looked against the cocaine-white walls and marble surfaces.

Kyle unzipped his jeans and out popped the stuff legends are made of.

'Wow!' gasped Miss Bimbo, her eyelashes fluttering. Was she supposed to fit that in her mouth? It would probably poke her tonsils out. 'You really are a big star!'

She cupped his balls and slowly began licking him . . .

* * *

488

Stan the Man threw a hearty 'How's it goin'?' to Charlton Heston and his wife, then stepped into the hallway that led to the guest bathrooms. He slipped around the corner, neatly out of sight, and pressed a panel hidden by the simulated-mica wallpaper. The panel slid open, revealing the best-kept secret in Hollywood – a room no larger than a walk-in closet, which looked like a command center.

Stan stepped quickly inside, and the door slid shut. This was his sanctuary and secret playroom. In the completely ventilated and soundproofed room, Stanley J. Moore played out his fantasy of being a director. One wall was covered with an elaborate bank of television monitors, offering him a panoramic view of each of the eight bathrooms in his house. The cameras, concealed behind the bathrooms' wall-to-wall, floor-to-ceiling mirrors, allowed Stan a wide range of possible shots.

Martini in hand, he settled himself in his canvas-back director's chair and toyed with the buttons on the console in front of him. Time for a close-up of room number one, where the wife of an independent producer was hiking her skirt up to pee. Stan did a double-take. Holy shit . . . the woman had no hair on her pussy.

On monitor number two, a Hollywood legend was picking his nose.

'That gross son of a bitch,' Stan muttered as the legend wiped his pickings on a Pratesi guest towel. Then the legend, who billed himself as a born-again Christian, pulled out a vial of coke and inhaled a couple of spoonfuls before leaving the room.

On monitor seven, Stan was surprised to see the supposedly straight chairman of a major studio passionately making out with a notoriously closeted television executive.

'Ha!' Stan bellowed. 'I always knew that prick was a queer.'

He picked up the martini shaker he'd brought in with him, let out a fart, and poured himself another drink. Let his wife handle the party. This was better than the movies.

When was she going to run into Stan and Dani? Bunny circled the pool to check out the action on the tennis courts, hoping somebody would ask her who she was. This party wasn't so different from the parties she had been to in New York, except that most of the faces were instantly recognizable and everyone was tanned. The women's gowns were expensive, but there was nothing she hadn't seen before.

Eyeing a sequined Geoffrey Beene she had priced in Bergdorf's at $3,200, she bumped into a perpetually tanned sometime movie star, and spilled her third mint julep down the front of her dress and his shirt. She couldn't even find the words to apologize.

Leaving the star's date to mop up the damage, she dashed past the buffet table, almost running over Mrs Stan Moore, who grabbed her arm.

'Having fun?' Mrs Moore slurred, flashing a sloppy smile. She was on her fourth Chivas, second Quaalude.

Bunny tried to compose herself. 'I just spilled my drink,' she said, dabbing at her wet bosom with a napkin.

'Oh, poor sweetie. All over your titties. You ought to wash that out right away before it stains that gorgeous outfit. Here, honey, lemme take you to the little girls' room.'

Bunny was ever so grateful. At least Stan's wife was a human being, not a pig like her husband.

Mrs Moore shut the bathroom door and grabbed a white hand towel off a rack. Teetering over the sink on three-inch heels, she wet the towel and turned to Bunny. 'Now, now, honey, let me take care of that awful mess.'

Bunny smiled her sweet Barbara Hester smile and unzipped her dress.

'Oh, my,' said Mrs Stan Moore. 'Don't you have pretty breasts.'

Watching monitor number two, Stan was impressed by the size of Kyle's prick. With that piece of meat, the guy could have been a porno star. And the broad seemed to be doing a good job of sucking him off. He'd like to have those luscious lips around his tool sometime. He whipped out his tiny tape recorder and said, 'Get the name and number of the broad who blew Kyle Lord.'

His eyes shifted to monitor four. He almost swallowed his cigar.

It was Barbara. With his wife!

Stan leaned forward in the director's chair. What was that cunt doing here? And why was his wife wiping Barbara's tit?

With a quick jab at the control board, Stan cut to a different camera angle.

What were they doing together?

He switched to a close-up.

He couldn't fucking believe it. His wife was nuzzling Barbara's neck and rubbing her tits. The tits he had squeezed so often. What was this, Dykesville?

He knew his wife was a dyke. He didn't care what she did, so long as he didn't see or hear about it. But who did she think she was, making a pass at his girlfriend? And who the hell did Barbara think she was, showing up at his house and shoving her tits in his wife's face?

He'd crucify the both of them.

Dani hiccuped a hello to one of her favorite Motown singers, who was looking gorgeous in a Calvin Klein purple silk pants outfit. She thought, *Have to remember*

491

to send her one of my new gowns . . . Thought I saw one here . . . the plunging V-neck in green . . . No . . . impossible. Not available yet. God, I'm sooo drunk.

She weaved past the screening room, the dining room, the library. Oh, there were too many people.

'Dani, are you all right?' asked a familiar-looking woman.

'This is a bathroom?'

'Yes, but – '

Dani opened the door. A woman in a silver sequined jumpsuit was on her knees, her blond hair falling forward as she . . . gave someone a blow job.

'Oops,' Dani said, giggling. *Well, I wouldn't mind doing that to . . .*

Kyle.

Who was spurting all over the blond's face and hair.

'Kyle!' the blond cried. 'I told you in my mouth. You'll ruin my makeup!'

'Oh, God,' Dani moaned, backing out of the bathroom.

Kyle opened his eyes and looked up into Dani's white, stricken face.

Bugger it to bloody hell. The one woman who rattled his brain had caught him with his dick hanging out for some girl he couldn't care less about.

Kyle shoved Miss Bimbo roughly aside and quickly zipped his jeans.

'Where the hell are you going?' Miss Bimbo shrieked, running out of the bathroom behind him. 'You think you can just get your rocks off and leave?'

Dani fled down the crowded hallway, almost shoving people out of the way in her urgency to put space between herself and the sight of Kyle with that woman. She negotiated the living room and hurried across the lawn to the far end of the pool, past the row of pink cabanas, sobbing and gasping for breath.

Kyle found her leaning against the high stucco wall that separated the Moores' property from that of their neighbors. 'Dani . . .' he said awkwardly.

Dani took one look at him and threw up all over the wall. *Dear God*, she thought. *Let me die right here and now.*

He put his arm around her shoulders and held her forehead until she stopped shaking. 'Hell,' he said, 'I don't have a handkerchief.'

Dani nodded weakly toward her purse. 'In there.'

He fidgeted with the clasp, finally unsnapped it, and pulled out a lace handkerchief. Then he gently wiped her mouth and tear-soaked face. Still holding her around the shoulders, he smoothed back her hair and discreetly led her past the house to the front driveway. Dani leaned against him, not saying a word.

'Dani diPortanova's car, please,' he told the valet. He would have to arrange to get his Land-Rover in the morning.

The valet summoned Gene, who immediately realized the countess had had a few too many. He helped Kyle settle Dani into the back of the limo.

'Where's she staying?' asked Kyle.

'The Beverly Hills.'

'Right, then. I'm coming, too. Take it as softly as you can, eh, mate?'

'Yes, sir,' said Gene, nearly saluting Kyle, one of the men he most admired in Hollywood.

Huddled against the velvet upholstery, Dani rested her head on Kyle's chest and whispered over and over again, 'Haven't been this drunk in . . . long time . . . sorry . . . so sorry.'

'Hush, now,' Kyle said, taking her hand and resting his lips lightly against the top of her head.

He had to shake her awake when they reached the

hotel. 'I'm fine,' she said, giving him a phony smile. Then suddenly she couldn't stand up straight.

'Where to?' asked Kyle, gently picking her up in his arms.

'Bungalow five.' She almost managed a laugh. 'I didn't quite plan for it to be like this.'

How many times had he wanted to carry her into the bedroom and make love to her? Kyle thought as he pulled back the coverlet of her bed and propped Dani up against the headboard. Now all he wanted to do was make her feel better.

'Easy does it,' he said, unzipping the back of her gown and pulling the top down over her hips. *Silk against silk*, he thought.

He tucked her under the sheet and arranged the pillows. Then he brought her two aspirins, a glass of water, and a wet hand towel to wipe her face. He had never forgotten, in all the years since his mother died, how she used to wash his face with a cool towel whenever he was sick. No one else had ever done that for him. Now it seemed terribly right that he wipe Dani's face and forehead.

Dani opened her eyes for an instant and looked at the towel.

'It's one of mine,' she whispered.

'You silly bitch.' Kyle smiled, his hand brushing her cheek. 'Always thinking of business. Go to sleep.'

She already had.

The next morning Dani found Kyle sitting in the living room, reading the *Los Angeles Times*. He was unshaved, and his clothes were rumpled, but to her he looked terrific. She was so embarrassed. She had acted like a high school kid who couldn't hold her liquor.

'I'm so sorry – ' she began.

'Don't be. I'm Mr Party Boy, remember? It's happened to me more bloody times than I care to think about.' He wasn't going to mention the blow job if she didn't.

'But you didn't have to stay the night.'

Kyle grinned. 'Somebody had to be here to look after you. And I just helped myself to a bed. It wasn't the first time, believe me.'

'I do,' she said with a laugh, suddenly aware that he must have undressed her.

She reached over and placed her hand on his. 'Thank you, Kyle.'

He held her hand for a moment, then brought it up to his mouth and brushed her fingers across his lips.

'Kyle,' she said, her voice catching, her mouth gone dry with lust, 'I want you.'

'I'm yours,' he said, standing up to undo the button on her nightshirt.

Dani felt almost paralyzed by her hunger for him. She trembled as he slid the cotton shirt over her shoulders and down her arms so that she stood utterly exposed. His hands, surprisingly gentle, sculpted her body, mastering the shape of her neck and throat, her shoulders and breasts.

She cried out her pent-up desire as he let his fingers linger on her nipples, stroking them between his thumbs and forefingers. His callused skin caught against her softness so that she felt as if she were suspended from his fingertips like a drop of rainwater quivering on the edge of a leaf.

As his eyes told her how often he had thought of her, how badly he wanted her, he stroked her stomach, her hips, her curved behind, moving his fingers slowly forward across the fronts of her thighs to trace the delicate skin hidden beneath the wispy, dark pubic hair. More slowly still, his fingers trailed across her mound, stopping to stroke the swollen, already moist lips, pressing farther into her wetness. She ached to reach out and touch him, but her limbs were numb with pleasure. His fingers carefully parted the lips of her vagina and slid deeper inside her.

Then, with the sound of an animal too long without its mate, she tore frantically at his jeans, resenting the fabric that lay between her hands and his skin. Kyle was breathing hard, groaning as she grasped his penis, full and heavy in her hand, needing to stroke and kiss it.

'No, wait,' he said as she knelt to take him in her mouth. And he pressed her so tightly to him that they might have been one body, one person.

She could feel his heat throbbing against her, could not postpone for another instant her yearning to feel him deep within her.

It was as if she were making love for the very first time.

For the first time since she left North Carolina, Bunny Hester wished she were back in Henderson. Seated next to Stan in the first-class section of the plane – Stan had made her upgrade her seat at her own expense – she tried to tell herself there was nothing he could do to harm her.

But she couldn't rid her mind of the image of Stan, his face purple with rage, bursting in on her and his wife, screaming words like 'cunt' and 'dyke' until Bunny had almost fainted from fear. He had grabbed her by the back of her neck and all but thrown her out the front door, shouting at her that she should be ready for his call first thing in the morning.

She didn't even want to think, not that she gave a damn, what he might have said or done to his wife.

Her head ached from a killer hangover and the memory of that nightmarish scene. Stan had hardly said one word upon meeting her at the Pan Am ticket counter, just growled an abrupt greeting and hustled her through the security check and onto the plane.

'You saw me slap her hand away,' Bunny said for what seemed like the fiftieth time.

'You're missing the point, Bunny babes. Who the hell do you think you are, flying out here without asking me and waltzing into my house like you belonged there?'

Bunny wished he would stop using that awful nickname. 'Listen,' she hissed, 'I *deserved* to be at that party. How was I supposed to know that the hostess – your wife! – would try to make me in the bathroom? How was I supposed to know she was into women? But wouldn't the gossip columnists just love to know that Stan Moore's wife is a lesbian?' she said, cheered by the weapon she held.

'Old news, baby, old news. Tell whoever you want. I don't give a fuck. You better worry about yourself, Bunny babes. Don't forget, I can make you and I can break you. I can give you everything you want or I can take it all away. One phone call and *your* story is all over the columns. Got it, Bunny?'

She got it. She took a sip of her club soda, hoping it would calm her stomach. 'Well, I'm tired of always getting the tail end of things,' she pouted.

Stan just laughed.

He was silent in the back of the limo for most of the ride from Kennedy to Manhattan. That was a bad sign. The quieter he got, the more demanding he was in bed later on. He was probably thinking about her blowing him or about jerking off between her breasts or whatever disgusting thing he was in the mood for tonight.

'Get into the bedroom,' he ordered as soon as they walked into her apartment.

'Stan,' she began, willing to plead with him just this one time.

'Get in there,' he said, not bothering to look up as he fingered the television remote control switch. 'Get your clothes off. I gotta catch the end of one of my shows.'

Not daring to disobey, Bunny undressed and settled herself primly beneath the sheet, pretending to read *Vogue*. Her heart was pounding. Why was she so scared? He was a pig and a bastard, but at this point there was nothing more he could do to humiliate or hurt her. She could hear the closing theme song of Stan's top-rated sitcom, and then the television went silent.

'Great episode,' he pronounced, coming into the bedroom.

Maybe she should try to placate him by offering to perform his favorite – her most hated – service.

'Do you want a blow job, Stan?'

'Nope. I got something else scheduled for us tonight, Bunny.'

He quickly stripped, took another puff of his cigar, walked over to the bed, and threw back the sheet. From the drawer of her night table he pulled out the K-Y jelly Bunny needed for lubrication.

So tonight he just wanted to screw her, plain and simple. Okay, she could deal with that. Except that he wasn't telling her to 'grease up the cunt,' as he so crudely put it. He was slathering the K-Y all over his penis.

'Get rid of the magazine and get on your hands and knees,' he told her, wiping his greasy hands on his balls.

From behind? Like she was some dog or a horse? Well, at least she wouldn't have to look at his ugly face.

He smacked her ass a couple of times. Hard. What a sadist. She hated him so much when he did that. And then he was fingering her between the cheeks of her ass, cramming his fingers deeper and deeper inside her.

'No!' she protested. 'Don't touch me there, Stan.'

He grabbed her hips and suddenly, incredibly, he was

shoving his prick in there, pushing harder and harder against her tight, resistant muscles.

'No, please, no!' she screamed. 'No!' He couldn't be doing this to her! Searing pain tore through her body as he penetrated and began thrusting within her.

'Loosen up, Bunny babes. It'll be better for both of us,' Stan grunted.

'Oh, my God, Stan, stop it! Please, stop!' She couldn't take it. 'You're . . . hurting . . . me!'

He was ripping her apart, raping her.

Tears streamed down her cheeks as he pulled her against him, pounding to the tempo of her anguished sobs. He thrust again and again, harder and harder. The bastard was killing her!

Her cries of protest seemed to belong to someone else, so alien did they sound to her ears. Bunny clenched her fists and pounded at the pillows as Stan gave one last thrust and filled her with his hot burning fluid.

If only she could faint, block out all the torment and rage. But one thought kept her from losing consciousness . . .

She wanted to kill Dani diPortanova.

Chapter Nineteen

Los Angeles

Dani and Kyle strolled out of the lobby of the Beverly Hills Hotel. The press was waiting for them. A hotel employee had spotted Kyle stepping out of Dani's limo the night before and called his friend at UPI. Word had spread quickly.

'Rehearsing for the next sheets ad?' called out one of the photographers, snapping pictures.

'Combining pleasure with business?' asked the UPI man.

Looking radiant in black-and-white striped linen Bermuda shorts cut very full above the knee and a bright gold linen scoop-neck shirt, Dani smiled and waved, but had nothing to say. She would let them draw their own conclusions.

For once she didn't want to think about public relations or photo opportunities. Today she was not the public Countess Dani diPortanova, ready at the flash of a bulb or the presence of a microphone to promote her company. Today she was Dani Lieberman diPortanova, a woman very much in love with the wonderful man who stood by her side. The man with whom she wanted to spend the rest of her life.

Earlier that morning, Kyle had arranged to have his Land-Rover dropped off at the hotel. Now he threw Dani's bag onto the backseat and opened the door for her. 'See ya, mates,' he said, grinning at the reporters, and off they sped.

The weather was in perfect sync with Dani's mood: hot and sunny, without a cloud in the bright blue sky. Dani leaned back against the seat, feeling completely relaxed, enjoying the warm wind that kept her long hair dancing about her face.

'Where are we going?' she had asked Kyle as they were leaving her bungalow.

'Trust me' had been his reply. 'I want to take you to a very special place.'

He already had. He had taken her to a place deep within herself where she had found the peace and contentment she had been searching for. And afterward, after they had made love, there was still the promise of much, much more for them to discover together. She knew she could trust him. Knew that although he wanted her totally, he didn't need to own her. Their excitement and passion had erupted out of the meeting and merging of two equals.

'Do you have jeans and sneakers with you?' Kyle asked, slowing down to turn onto Route One.

Dani smiled, nodding. 'I feel as if I'm being kidnapped.'

'Bloody right.' Kyle laughed. 'And what a price I could get for you, love. But since I don't need the money, I'm going to gallop off into the sunset with you. Do you know how to ride?'

Of course she did. She'd had all those lessons at the Claremont Stables, trotting the bridle paths of Central Park. For a while she had even kept a couple of horses at her country house in Connecticut, but she hadn't ridden much in the last several years. Too busy, she had told herself. The truth was that it hadn't been much fun to go out alone.

Now they were driving up the coast past Malibu and Oxnard. To the right were the Santa Monica Mountains. On her left lay the Pacific, as blue as the cloudless sky.

Gulls soared and wheeled in the distance, touching down briefly on the waves to search for fish beneath the surf.

Wherever Kyle was taking her, she already felt they were halfway to paradise. New York was a universe away. Her problems could wait until Monday. This weekend was just for the two of them.

'Not too much farther,' he shouted above the noise of the wind and the tape he had stuck in the tape deck.

Stevie Wonder's hit, 'I Just Called to Say I Love You,' began to play.

'No, you didn't,' Dani yelled.

'Would you have listened if I had?'

She shook her head and reached over to touch his tanned cheek. She hadn't felt this way since her schoolgirl crush on Nino thirteen years earlier. But what she shared with Kyle was so much more. Nino was a boy. Adorable, impulsive, reckless, extravagant.

Kyle was a man – a man worth waiting for. What a fascinating blend of intellect and action he was. She had sensed, almost from their first meeting, that his Aussie outback act masked a sensitivity and intelligence that accounted in part for his star quality. That was what had drawn her to him – that and his restless curiosity.

Despite the obvious differences in their backgrounds and upbringing, she and Kyle were cut from the same cloth: independent, prepared to take risks, ready to explore new ideas and places, eager to embrace life fully.

Kyle brought her hand up to his mouth so that her fingers were caressing his lips.

'Now look what you've done,' he shouted, showing her the bulge in his jeans. 'Lucky for you, we're almost there.' He pointed to the sign for Montecito and swung into the left-turn lane.

Dani couldn't stop smiling, couldn't contain the happiness that bubbled up from her stomach and overflowed so

502

that she had to throw back her head and giggle as if she were breathing in pure laughing gas. She remembered how she used to feel as a child, those early evenings in Massachusetts, south of Stockbridge, at the house her parents rented every August.

Restless after an afternoon of sitting quietly on a blanket, listening to the Boston Symphony Orchestra concerts at Tanglewood, she and her friends would spend their pent-up energy playing breathless games of hide-and-seek. Running madly across the sloping green lawn to jump over the stream that bordered the woods, Dani would conceal herself among the trees, holding her breath so that all she could hear was the chirping of crickets, signaling the end of summer. Then, the moment made sweeter with the exquisite tension of never knowing whether this time she would get tagged by whoever was 'it', she would take a chance and bolt out of the woods, shrieking and gasping with laughter.

Dani recalled the pleasure of those endless games. It was so scary to crouch in the deepening shadows of the trees, so exhilarating to risk exposing herself so that she could reach the safety and security of 'home,' the evergreen that towered above her parents' cottage. And when she had made it to the tree, she would leap with joy. 'Home free, home free,' she would scream triumphantly. 'I knew you could never catch me.'

But now, this time, she had been caught. And she was glad of it. For so very long, even before Nino died, she had protected herself from hurt and disappointment by not getting involved. She had been an attentive pupil to her parents' lesson that she trust no one but herself and her family. That was how they had survived, they had told her again and again.

Their lesson had been borne out by Reggie's theft of her designs, by Roberto diPortanova's betrayal of her, by

503

Nino's behavior as their marriage deteriorated. Dani had wrapped herself up in a thick, protective jacket, working, playing, winning – but not loving.

Certainly not loving Jack. Holding tight to Kyle's hand, Dani allowed herself to think, for one brief second, about Jack. He was sweet, and they had had incredible sex together, but that was all the relationship had been. Sex and letting off steam. Nothing to do with adult emotions and needs. As soon as she got back to New York, she would tell him, once and for all, that it was over. She wanted him as a buddy, not a lover.

She was ready to love and be loved as an adult, as a woman who had proved to herself and to the world that she could have her own life. Now she was choosing to share that life with Kyle.

They had turned off the main highway and were driving down a secondary road paved with asphalt. 'The Santa Ynez range,' Kyle said, gesturing to the mountains that rose above them. 'Have you ever come up this way?'

Dani shook her head. They had traveled only an hour and a half from Los Angeles, but this part of southern California wore a face that was very different from what they had left behind. The Land-Rover was the only vehicle on the narrow road that hugged the wall of the canyon. It was as if, magically, they had been set down in an exotic wilderness, far away from civilization, populated only by themselves and the birds that flitted among the riot of brilliant yellow, gold, and green wildflowers in the canyon meadows.

Kyle braked in front of a padlocked gate. A large sign hung from it. 'Private property. Guarded by attack dogs. Keep out.' Except for the birds twittering overhead, the silence was absolute.

'Here we are,' he announced.

Was he teasing her? Or were they really going riding?

'Do you keep horses here?' Dani asked, watching him undo the padlock and push open the gate.

'Yeah, I do. And goats and sheep and dogs and a couple of cats. And up there in the hills you can find bobcats and coyotes and wild boar. Last year a mountain lion came down and killed one of my sheep.' He drove through the gate, then jumped out and relocked it.

'Welcome to the best-kept secret in Hollywood,' he said proudly. 'The Lord ranch. It's what keeps me sane, and one of these days it may even turn a profit.'

'You own all this?'

'All six hundred acres. And I work it, too, whenever I have the time. Just like the ranch I grew up on – but better,' he said, pointing to the ocean that swept the beach at the foot of the canyon. 'I herd sheep in the morning with the crew, then surf in the afternoon. Do you surf?'

'No . . .'

'Well, then, I'll have to teach you.'

The winding gravel road was bordered by tall eucalyptus trees. Two or three dogs barked a welcome from the front porch of his two-story redwood house. 'Hope you like animals,' Kyle said, hugging the dogs who leapt with excitement. 'This is Irish. She's an Irish setter. And these two mutts were strays. The big one's Syd – short for Sydney – and you remember the little one from the beach at Mustique. I named him Cujo.'

'Cujo?' Dani asked.

'After the dog that turns into a killer in that Stephen King novel. This little guy is so shy, I thought the name might give him some courage.'

'Are these your attack dogs?'

'Yup. My golden retriever and sheepdog could knock you down, they're so friendly.'

Inside, Kyle's house was comfortable and informal.

Two walls of his living room were lined with bookcases. A grand piano dominated one corner, and a fireplace with logs stacked at the side took up a third wall. The fourth wall was one long picture window, fronting on the terraced back lawn and the ocean below. Plants and intricately patterned Oriental rugs splashed color about the otherwise simply furnished room.

Kyle slid open the glass door, and they walked outside and down several steps. Dani suddenly found herself surrounded by apricot-colored marigolds, purple and red poppies, violet bluebells, pink and blue delphiniums, deep blue and creamy yellow lupins, and roses in every shade of pink and red. Roses clustered on bushes that clung to and climbed the brick wall extending from the sun porch.

'Kyle, this is absolutely exquisite.'

'I think I told you my mum was English,' Kyle said. 'And there's never been an Englishwoman who didn't love to garden. After she married my dad and moved to the cattle station, she planted a garden back of the house. Of course, Dad wanted her to grow veggies, but she was a stubborn girl and had to have her way. Guess I take after her, eh?'

'Guess you do,' Dani said, shielding her eyes with one hand so she could watch the expression on his face.

'When I was a nipper, I used to help her garden. You can imagine how much help I was, but she never let on that I might be in the way. I suppose I learned a thing or two, small though I was.' He paused, as if remembering that little boy, watering the flowers with his tiny watering can, collecting the petals and leaves that had fallen to the ground.

'That summer she was dying, when I was six, I had the idea that as long as we took care of her garden, she wouldn't die. Afterward, I'd throw a bloody fit if they forgot to water the flowers or cut back the branches.' His

voice trailed off. 'These Sarabandes remind me of you.'
He pointed to a low bed of brilliant scarlet roses.

'Of me?'

'Their color is so bright and clear. And they never fade,
rain or shine.' He guided her fingers over the soft petals.
'Feel how delicate they are. Though it's hard to tell
because they are protected by so many thorns.'

Dani wondered whether her heart would ever again
feel as full as it did at this moment when her eyes feasted
on the explosion of colorful blossoms.

Kyle picked one of the Sarabandes and tucked it into
her tangled hair just behind her ear. She stepped closer
and kissed the dimple in his cheek, then moved her lips
across his.

'More?' he murmured.

'Mmmm . . . much, much more.'

She buried her head against his throat and took a long,
deep breath, inhaling his sweaty male aroma and the
fragrance of the flowers, of the rich earth beneath their
feet, and of the ocean far below them.

'Now show me your bedroom,' she whispered, and Kyle
led her back to the house, his arm locked tightly around
her waist.

New York

Jack Andrews stared at the front page of the New York
Post. He couldn't believe it. There was a picture of *his*
girlfriend, *his* fiancée, with that Australian prick. The
caption beneath the photo announced in large bold type,
'The Aussie and the Countess Keep Company.'

Dani had told him that the trip was strictly for business.
A couple of parties for 'The Seducers.'

Yeah, he bet the seducers had a party all right. All night long.

He loved her, and she had betrayed him. But love meant forgiving. He *had* to forgive her. Dani was his whole life. He couldn't wait to marry her, to show them all, his bitch mother and that stupid shit, Anne, that he didn't need them. He had everything he wanted.

Gulping down his Diet Coke, Jack tried to figure it out. Why was Dani playing games with him, teasing him like this? Here he was, stuck in the city on this shitty summer weekend. He could have gone out to East Hampton with that model who was so hot to get into his pants. But he'd stuck around, in case Dani got back from LA.

He turned on the radio. 'Hazy, hot, and humid,' the deejay said. 'Temperatures going up into the nineties this afternoon. A perfect day to take your girl out to the beach . . .'

Not his girl. She was too busy two-timing him.

Bitch.

Slut.

Just like his mother.

'So pack up a lunch, take along a blanket, and keep that dial on Z-one hundred, your power station playing all the hits for a summer of romance.'

'Go fuck yourself and your romance,' Jack screamed at the deejay, picking up the radio and hurling it at the breakfront that separated his kitchen from the dining room.

The radio crashed into his makeshift bar. His liquor supply went flying. 'Fuck all of you!' he screamed again above the noise of the scotch, bourbon, gin, and vodka bottles shattering against the hardwood floor into hundreds of tiny wet shards.

508

Rome

Jack Andrews was not the only person to be deeply affected by the photographs of Dani diPortanova walking arm in arm with Kyle Lord. Roberto, in Rome on business and staying as he usually did at the Hotel Hassler, was resting in his room before dinner when he turned on the evening news program. The media, which had breathlessly chronicled Dani and Nino's every move from the moment Dani had married into one of Europe's most famous families, were still devoting generous amounts of ink and film footage to 'the widow diPortanova.' On this particular night Roberto was treated to a detailed account, via satellite from America, of Dani's supposed tryst at the Beverly Hills Hotel with movie star Kyle Lord.

Roberto glowered at the picture of his former daughter-in-law, looking, in the words of the Los Angeles correspondent, 'as happy and radiant as we've seen her since the death of her beloved husband.' Where was that slut's sense of decency? Where was the heavy black veil, the traditional symbol of her grief? He should have known she wouldn't mourn Nino's death properly. She certainly hadn't comported herself properly during their excuse for a marriage.

She was showing no respect whatsoever for her dead husband, just as she had shown him no respect in life. She had driven him out of his home and onto the racetrack, where he had tried, as best he could, to recapture the masculinity she had stripped from him. She had killed him, pure and simple. Danielle Lieberman diPortanova had killed Roberto's son as surely as if she had been behind the wheel herself. She had robbed Nino of his manhood and his life. She had robbed Roberto of his namesake.

Regardless of what the church told him, Roberto could not . . . could *never* forgive her for those sins.

He buried his face in his hands, remembering how his confessor had urged him to forgive this woman. He had searched his soul, tried not to hate her, tried to grant her forgiveness. But she made it impossible. She was a wicked woman, far more wicked than Karola (ah, Karola!) could ever be. At least one could anticipate Karola's maneuvers, but with this murdering bitch, one never knew. She would continue to humiliate him, his family, and the memory of his beloved son for as long as she lived. Which could be . . . what? Another thirty years? Another forty?

Unacceptable. He could not bear to contemplate four more decades of humiliation at the hands of this woman who had already wreaked so much damage.

An eye for an eye, a tooth for a tooth . . .

With this latest scandal, this latest affront to his family's honor, he realized that she must be made to pay. Benumbed by his pain, he had only been postponing the inevitable.

There was still time to make plans before he had to leave for dinner. He made several phone calls, then left word for his secretary to cancel all his appointments for the rest of the week. He would not be staying on in Rome. No, he had other urgent business to take care of.

He was flying to New York.

Chapter Twenty

New York

Returning to New York aboard the Lear jet, Dani listened to Mozart and sketched fanciful, extravagant designs of bridal gowns. She'd been wondering how to close her first couture showing, which was scheduled for next spring. Now she thought, *Why not with a Countess Dani original wedding gown?* Perhaps the very gown she would wear if she married again. At her first wedding, she'd worn a Givenchy original, especially commissioned for her by Nino. Oh, the trouble she'd had with that twenty-five-foot train. Just like Nino – so wonderfully extravagant, so gloriously larger than life.

So different from Kyle. Kyle was real life. He had his feet planted firmly on the ground, so that even when he dreamed his dreams, he didn't lose touch with reality.

They had said good-bye not two hours ago, and already she missed him. How could she not, after the three idyllic days they'd spent together at his ranch – talking, laughing, making love, swimming, riding, walking the mountain trails, even (she could hardly believe it) surfing. And waking up early, the sunrise painting Kyle's east bedroom the palest peach pink, and finding him already awake and quietly watching her.

'I love how you look when you're asleep,' he'd whispered. Then they'd made love, so sweetly and gently that afterward she wondered if she had only dreamed his kisses and caresses.

The Jupiter Symphony filled the aft cabin, drowning

out the hum of the Lear's twin engines. The flight attendants were in the galley kitchen, preparing to serve dinner to her and the flight crew. How she wished Kyle had been able to come along. They could have made love in the bedroom, climaxing at twenty-five thousand feet somewhere above the Midwest.

Soon enough, she reminded herself. He'd be flying east in a few days to start filming his new movie on location in SoHo. She had always loved fall in New York, and this fall would be especially wonderful with Kyle in town. She hoped his shooting schedule would allow them to steal a couple of three-day weekends so she could kidnap him to *her* country hideaway. Though for all she cared, they could spend every free minute holed up at the Dakota if they had to. As long as they were together.

She wasn't going to get much work done if she spent the rest of the flight staring out the oval windows of the jet at the endless horizon, lost in her fantasies. Nor did she have the time to sketch wedding gowns, she reminded herself, standing up to stretch her legs – not with everything else she had to think about.

The Coty Fashion Critics Awards were being held next week. She'd already won three Cotys, but on this occasion she would be inducted into the Hall of Fame, one of the youngest designers ever to be so honored.

But now that the media were on to her and Kyle, she could be sure the awards ceremony would be a circus. She could write the script, since she'd been through the scene so often. The media coverage had worked wonders for her company, but for once she regretted being Dani diPortanova, media darling. And what with Kyle's celebrity status, they were in for the Taylor-Burton treatment.

First, though, she had to deal with Jack, who had left messages with Elvira and at the office, insisting he *had* to see her. One of the papers – the *Post*, probably – must have run a picture of her and Kyle. She didn't blame Jack if he was furious, though she'd tried repeatedly to tell him that she wasn't his 'girlfriend' and that she had no intention of marrying him. She'd wanted to tell him herself about Kyle, but obviously it was too late for that.

Sighing, she picked up the phone and called Jack to suggest they have dinner that night or whenever he was free. At the very least she needed to tell him face to face that she was sorry if he'd misunderstood her intentions. She hadn't meant to hurt him. She was sure he would find a woman who loved him as much as he deserved to be loved.

She only hoped they could stay friends.

Vermont

The Woodstock Inn was situated in one of the oldest and quaintest villages in New England. But Monika managed to see very little of the town or the surrounding lush countryside. She'd planned to take a drive or a hike into the nearby Green Mountains. But a chill, steady rain fell all weekend, so she spent most of her time drinking in the bar just off the lobby.

Though she wasn't a drinker by habit, she became one during the weekend. There was, after all, only so much a person could bear. The wound on her breast still ached, but it was her fear and panic that kept her ordering 'another one, please.' When one of the other customers tried to get friendly, she fled to the safety of her room. Too tense to sleep or eat, she spent most of Sunday curled up in bed, the quilt pulled over her head, trying to figure out how the hell to extricate herself from the mess she was in.

Suicide, she thought glumly. She supposed she could

save the mobsters some trouble by slitting her own wrists or hanging herself or committing some other equally gruesome act of self-destruction. She rejected the options with a heartfelt shudder. Depressed though she was about returning to New York to face the nightmare, she still wasn't prepared to kill herself.

But she *could* run away, she thought, turning over in bed to block out the view through her window of the gray, rain-soaked landscape. Simply pack a bag and escape . . . to where? California? Europe? Asia? No, eight hundred thousand dollars meant that no matter how carefully she tried to cover her trail, those goons would track her down.

Besides, New York was home.

New York was also work, and as much as she might want to, she couldn't simply disappear off the face of the earth, unless she wanted to leave Dani high and dry. Too much was going on at the office – some of which, she bitterly realized, she wasn't privy to, like Barbara's sudden ascent.

And then there was Dani's induction into the Coty Hall of Fame on Wednesday evening. She wished she could find it within herself to be happy for Dani. But in the context of her problems, the award ceremony was a ridiculously absurd and shallow event. Of course she was expected to be present, and Dani would never forgive her if she didn't show up.

Well, screw Dani. Monika had more important things to worry about than a goddam award. The last thing she needed was for her face to be plastered all over the television screen with Dani's while those bastards at Lucky's drummed their fingers, waiting for her to repay them by Thursday midnight.

Thursday . . . or else.

She summoned up all of the steely reserve she had

inherited from Karola and brooded about the alternatives. She was damned if she would die to pay off a gambling debt. Her life was worth a great deal more than eight hundred thousand dollars.

Monika lay awake most of Sunday night, staring into the darkness. She wept, knowing with fatal certainly what she must do. In the morning, she wearily dragged herself out of bed and downstairs to the dining room to fortify herself with coffee for the long drive back to New York.

She had many plans and arrangements, all of them painful, to take care of before the week was even half finished. Never had she imagined she would arrive at such a point in her life. Dear Lord, how would she ever find the strength? She despised herself for choosing this solution. But really, was there any other choice?

Was dying better? she wondered.

No, not for her. Not for a von Reich.

Dani arranged to meet Jack at Café Un Deux Trois, a cheerful, high-ceilinged restaurant that specialized in hearty Parisian bistro fare and waiters who looked like out-of-work actors. She chose the place because it was close to her office and because the atmosphere was suitably casual and unromantic.

When she'd spoken to Jack from the plane, he'd sounded curt and cold. 'We have to talk,' he'd said.

'Yes, we do,' she agreed.

She hadn't thought about him again until she was getting ready to leave the office. The day – what had been left of it by the time she'd arrived from the airport – had been hectic. Barbara had called in sick. Monika was moping in her office, looking as angry and forbidding as Dani had ever seen her. Dani had hoped to talk to her before she went to meet Jack, but Monika had already left when Dani stopped by to visit.

'A doctor's appointment,' Monika's secretary explained.

Was Monika ill? Maybe that was why she seemed to be in a perpetual bad mood lately. To hell with her privacy. Dani made up her mind there and then to find out what was wrong and what she could do to help. Screw-up number one was having allowed this thing with Jack to go on for as long as it had. Screw-up number two was worse – having become so wrapped up in her own life that she had missed the boat with her best friend. She had a lot of housecleaning to do, starting tonight.

Jack was already seated at a leather banquette in a corner when she arrived, breathless and apologizing for being late. On her way over she'd debated whether to have it out with Jack *before* dinner or to keep things light until after dessert.

Jack made the decision for her. 'I saw your picture in the *Post*,' he greeted her before she'd even sat down. 'Whatever you have to tell me, I want you to save it for later. We have lots of time. You don't have to ruin dinner with your explanations.'

His tone sounded friendly, but a flicker of tension curled around the edges of his words and rang a warning bell in her head. Or perhaps it was the way she caught him staring at her while they ate dinner and he described his trip to Bermuda.

Finally she couldn't pretend any longer. She put down her fork and tried to explain as gently as possible that Kyle Lord had nothing to do with their breaking up. They weren't right for each other, she said. She was too old for him. He wanted too much without knowing what he really wanted. He was ready to jump the marital gun. But she wouldn't be jumping with him.

Jack wouldn't meet her gaze. Picking up one of the

crayons conveniently provided at each table by the management in case patrons wanted to leave their mark on the butcher-paper tablecloths, he concentrated on his drawing. She wasn't even sure he was listening.

'Do you have anything you want to ask me? Or is there anything you want to tell me?' she said, reaching across the table to touch his hand.

That was a mistake, she realized immediately.

Jack laced his fingers around hers. He brought her hand up to his lips to kiss it. 'Look,' he said, and pointed to his drawing.

It was a heart, pierced by an arrow. Inside the heart he'd written, 'J. A. loves D. dP.'

She groaned silently. 'Jack – '

'Can I get you two some coffee or dessert?' asked the waiter, a Tom Cruise look-alike.

'No . . . thanks,' Dani said.

Jack smiled at the waiter. 'I'd like coffee. And . . . do you have chocolate mousse cake?'

'We sure do.'

'Great. One for me. Sure you don't want any, Dani?'

'I'm sure.'

When the waiter was gone, she tried again. 'Look, Jack, I hope we can stay friends. But I want you to know it's over between us.'

'It *is* because of that Australian, isn't it?'

'Jack, we're not talking about anyone else, just us. I want to see other people. And you should, too,' Dani urged, feeling more than a little guilty that she wasn't being completely straight with him about Kyle.

The check arrived along with coffee and dessert. Jack took one bite of his mousse cake, pushed away the plate, and said, 'Let's get out of here.' He grabbed for the check.

'No, please . . . let me,' offered Dani.

'I've got it,' he said sullenly. 'I can afford to pay for my girl's dinner.'

Dani's limo was waiting in front of the restaurant. 'Can I give you a lift home?' she said, hoping he understood he wasn't coming home with her.

Jack grabbed her hand. 'Let's go dancing, okay? I'm not in the mood to go home yet.'

Dani studied his face, wondering whether he had heard a word she'd said. His gray eyes burned through her, making her feel like a prisoner of his desire. 'Jack,' she said gently, 'I really meant what I said.'

'Okay, okay, if you say so. But please, do this for me? Just one last time?'

She'd slept only fitfully the night before aboard her plane and wanted nothing more than to go straight home, take a hot bath, and fall into bed. But because she felt sorry for him, she agreed. 'All right, dancing it is.'

He slipped his arm through hers as they walked to the limo. 'Let's go to Area,' he said, looking like a little boy who had just been told he could have a second helping of ice cream. 'It'll be like old times. After all, we did hook up there.'

A raucous private party was in full swing in the VIP Room. Dani was immediately recognized and ushered inside.

'Great scene, isn't it?' Jack shouted above the clamor.

Dani nodded, trying to summon up the proper enthusiasm.

The crowd was young and very glitzy. The faces were equal parts Hollywood, Eurotrash, and New York. The bodies were thin, lithe, and beautifully tanned.

'Want a drink?' yelled Jack.

'Sure. I'll wait for you right here,' Dani mouthed.

Somebody grabbed her elbow. She turned around and gasped. 'Kyle!'

'Fancy meeting you here, love,' he shouted into her ear.

Standing next to Kyle was Rick Flood.

Before she had a chance to say a word, Kyle had enveloped her in a hug that made her feel as if she were flying far above the earth. Cameras were flashing all around them as Kyle kissed her. For once, Dani paid them no attention. He must have flown in early . . . but why hadn't he called?

Never mind; her questions could wait. There were more pressing things to take care of now.

'You two know each other?' Rick asked, eyebrows raised in mock surprise.

'Rick, I need to talk to you,' she told him. 'Tomorrow, all right? Call me, please! Promise?'

Rick nodded. 'Cross my heart.'

'Let's get out of here, then,' urged Kyle, his arm around her shoulders as if he never wanted to let go of her.

'Wait, I came with someone . . . I need to find him.' She turned to look for Jack, craning her neck to see if she could spot him at the bar. Then she saw him, standing several feet away, staring daggers at her and Kyle. The look on his face told her how badly he was hurting.

'Jack!' she yelled, motioning to him. 'Jack, please!'

His mouth crumpled as if he was about to burst into tears. He held his clenched fist up to his lips, and then he disappeared into the crowd. By the time she and Kyle got outside, he was nowhere to be found.

'Can't you call him tomorrow and apologize?' asked Kyle.

'It's not that simple.' She sighed, signaling to her driver. 'Now tell me, what are you *doing* here?'

'I couldn't wait to see you,' Kyle said, helping her into the car. 'So I flew in early to surprise you. But you'd already left the office, and your housekeeper said you were out for dinner.'

'What were you doing here?'

'I bumped into Rick on the plane. He said there was a birthday party tonight at Area for some friend of his, and why didn't I drop by if I had nothing better to do. You can imagine how I felt when I looked up and saw you.'

What was harder to imagine was how Jack had felt when he saw Kyle hugging her. But she pushed that unpleasant thought to the back of her mind and snuggled closer to Kyle. Never in her whole life had she felt so safe and loved.

Jack stormed out of Area and started walking uptown, oblivious of everything but the anguish of seeing Dani with Kyle Lord. He hit the first bar he passed and ordered a double scotch. And then another. His pain dulled, and he glanced around and realized that he'd stumbled into a gay leather bar.

All around him, dressed from head to toe in leather, were men with cropped hair, well-developed muscles, and tiny tight asses. Some of them were wearing cop uniforms. A few were even dressed up as Nazi storm troopers. In the darkened corners, men were groping and fondling each other. *Fucking pervert clones*, he thought contemptuously. He'd gotten used to being cruised when he went on shoots, but he hated the men's appraising stares, their inviting smiles.

He threw down some bills, made a quick exit, and headed uptown to the Hellfire, New York's most notorious S & M club, located in a hard-to-find seedy building in the meatpacking district, down by the Hudson River piers. Jack had no trouble finding his way to the unmarked entrance, for the Hellfire Club had become one of his favorite late-night haunts, his own special secret. His regular attendance there was a part of his life that Dani and his other friends knew nothing about.

He ambled downstairs, stripped to his briefs, and checked his clothes with the girl behind the counter, then wandered through the dimly lit, smoky room to the bar, where he ordered another double scotch. A woman he'd seen there before held up her nasal inhaler and offered him a couple of snorts of coke. He helped himself, but declined her offer of a three-way with one of her girlfriends.

Tonight he had something else in mind.

Fortified by the coke and scotch, he prowled the dark recesses of the crowded, musty-smelling rooms where every manner of sexual variation and perversion was offered for the taking. His eyes were caught by a young woman spread-eagled and handcuffed against a wall. She was naked, and her dark hair fell just to her shoulders, which were crisscrossed with lash marks. Jack moved closer to get a better look.

'Is she yours?' he asked the man who stood before her, a horsewhip in his hand. The man nodded. 'Want to take a turn?'

Jack usually preferred to indulge himself with older women – women with droopy breasts and blond pubic hair, such as he imagined his mother had. But in the room's dim light, he could almost imagine the woman to be Dani diPortanova. Dani was much prettier, of course, but if he half closed his eyes . . . there she was, standing before him. Chained and shackled and all his.

He stepped closer and whispered, 'You want it from me, don't you, Dani?'

Her drug-dulled eyes flickered as he raised the leather whip and took aim . . .

* * *

521

Bunny lay on her bed amid her cotton Countess Dani sheets, shams, and down comforter, aimlessly switching the TV channels. For three days she had done nothing but watch television and take sitz baths to heal the wounds Stan had inflicted on her. She had called the office and told her secretary she had the flu. She was sure they couldn't have cared less. It was quite clear to her now that nobody at Countess Dani cared about Bunny Hester except Bunny. Especially not Dani. Sure, she'd phoned this afternoon to ask how Bunny was feeling.

'Better,' Bunny had replied, barely containing her rage. 'But not well enough to make it to the Coty Awards, I'm afraid.'

'Oh, don't worry about that. Just take care of yourself,' Dani said soothingly.

'Thanks, I will,' Bunny replied. As if there was a chance in hell she'd go to that bitch's award presentation tonight. She'd already done more than enough for Dani. The throbbing pain in her rectum was a vivid reminder of just how much she'd done. And what had she received in return? Nothing but pain and degradation.

As long as she lived, she would never forget the humiliation of lying bare-assed and exposed on her doctor's examining table, trying to explain her injuries. The shame she'd felt had been worse, almost, than the rape itself.

She held Dani responsible. Dani, who'd wanted the 'Seducers' contract so badly.

Bunny threw down the remote control and picked up the latest issue of *Vogue*, which she'd had her secretary send her by messenger, along with the rest of her mail. Maybe reading would take her mind off her troubles. But she hadn't flipped past three pages when Dani's face smirked up at her from a sheet ad. That bitch. That ungrateful bitch. Bunny had worked so hard for her – and for what? So that Dani diPortanova could once again bask in the limelight of success, collecting all the kudos and compliments.

Her fury blazed anew.

She threw down the magazine and checked her watch. Six-thirty. In a couple of hours, Dani would walk to the middle of the stage at the FIT auditorium to accept her award. And she, Bunny, would be conveniently left out of the picture. Just as she'd been left out on so many other occasions. She'd had to find out secondhand about the 'Seducers' competition. She hadn't been invited to Stan's party in California. The list went on and on. She was nothing to Dani, nothing but a source of talent to be mined for gold.

But not anymore.

Wincing with pain, she gingerly got up from the bed, plodded into the bathroom, and turned on the shower. Too bad for Dani that she underestimated what she was up against in Barbara Hester. How unfortunate that she didn't understand just how far Barbara Hester was prepared to go in order to take her place at the top, where she belonged. It was time Dani learned that she couldn't keep Barbara Hester down.

Bunny couldn't wait to see the look on her face.

Dani's stretch limousine headed down Seventh Avenue toward the Fashion Institute of Technology. Shaking her head from side to side to loosen the waves that hung down her back, Dani adjusted the top of her strapless red silk evening gown, the pride of her soon to be launched couturier collection.

Earlier she'd considered wearing the Van Cleef diamond necklace that Nino had given her on their fifth anniversary, but then she'd changed her mind. Though she owned hundreds of thousands of dollars' worth of diamonds and emeralds and rubies, once she got over the thrill of being able to afford such jewelry, she'd decided they weren't her style. She preferred rhinestones, Art Deco gold and silver, and one-of-a-kind pieces, set with semiprecious stones, which she could find in small, out-of-the-way stores in out-of-the-way places.

Tonight, however, she didn't want her accessories to distract from the drama of her gown, which covered barely enough to be in good taste. A sexy statement just this side of obscene.

'All set, Dani?' asked her driver as FIT came into view.

'All set, Joe.'

'For what it's worth, you look more beautiful than ever tonight.'

'Thanks, Joe. I'm happy. I guess it shows.' She grinned and thought, *Happy because of Kyle*. He couldn't be with her at the awards ceremony because this was the first night of shooting for his new movie. But they were hoping to wrap around ten o'clock, and he'd promised to be back at the Dakota by the time she got home.

Life couldn't possibly get much better than it was right at this very moment.

Roberto diPortanova pushed his chair forward and snapped the buckle of his seat belt as his private Lockheed jet prepared to land at New York's Kennedy Airport. On his lap was a specially constructed brown leather briefcase. As Roberto stared out the window at the twinkling lights of the city miles below, he absentmindedly stroked the soft-as-butter brown leather. Inside the case was a disassembled rifle, the very rifle Karola von Reich had presented to him years ago during their first fateful meeting.

He sighed, remembering how alluring Karola had looked that day in his Rome office. So beautiful. So sexy.

So tough. He had never met a woman that tough. She'd aroused him as no other woman ever had before or since.

He hadn't spoken to Karola since that day in Spain when he'd left her lying on the floor of her villa, her face bearing the mark of his hand. For what she'd said to him about Nino, she deserved the beating he'd given her – and more. He'd sworn that it was finished between them. He would never see her again. He wanted nothing further to do with her, not even if she came crawling on her knees to apologize.

Just let her try to contact him . . .

The weeks had passed without a word from Karola.

It was just as well, thought Roberto. He'd had his fill of her nasty tricks.

A month went by. Then another month. Still no communiqué, not even so much as a note, expressing her remorse.

And then, to his great shock, he realized that he actually *missed* her. Hard as it was for him to accept, he had almost come to love Karola. He knew he had to see her again. She would have to apologize, of course. But he was sure that if he made it clear he was prepared to accept her apology, she'd be overjoyed to be back in his good graces.

He was even prepared, if need be, to pave the way to a reconciliation by reaching out to her via the telephone. So call her he did, only to be told repeatedly by her staff that she was not in, or that she was unavailable, or that her whereabouts were unknown.

All lies, he was convinced of it. He saw right through the deception. What he did not see was why she refused to be in touch with him.

Perhaps she needed some written reassurance that he was prepared to resume their relationship. But what he'd intended to be a friendly though restrained note became, in a weak moment during the flight across the Atlantic, a passionate love letter, in which Roberto poured out his heart to Karola and begged her to be with him again.

It was the closest Roberto diPortanova had ever come to apologizing to anyone. He closed with a passionate, heartfelt quotation from Dante and telexed the letter from the plane to her home in Salzburg.

Now all he had to do was wait for her response.

But first he had to deal with the matter of his daughter-in-law.

As a former recipient of the Coty Hall of Fame Award, Reggie had naturally been invited to the ceremony. But as soon as he learned that Dani diPortanova was among the honorees, he had declined with a scathing indictment of those responsible for bestowing the award.

It was an insult to all its previous recipients, himself included, he'd raved. It was preposterous to think that she was worthy of the award! Obviously the committee had decided to cheapen the currency of the honor. Frankly, he'd huffed, he was seriously considering sending his back.

Unfortunately, he had no other plans for the evening.

In the days before Megacorp, his calendar would have been solidly booked. Mr Reggie had reigned as the toast of the town, *the* guest to snare for cocktails or dinner. Now those who had once pursued him so relentlessly for their own social gains saw him as a businessman, a creative genius who'd sold out for money. And as much as New Yorkers worshiped money, they worshiped artistic integrity and creativity even more. The invitations still came, but only a trickle of what once had been.

The ladies who had rushed to lunch him now waved politely and kept their distance. The phone didn't ring as it used to. Gone were the days when people vied to be included at his *intime* dinner parties. When Reggie poked his head out and looked around, he noticed other, prettier, talented young men on Seventh Avenue making their ascent. He was terrified by the thought that soon he would be nothing but a has-been, a relic to trot out for industry functions.

Contemplating that hideous thought, Reggie poured himself a Stoli and switched on the TV, only to be treated to a commercial for Mr Reggie toilet paper. A perky young housewife was explaining to her adoring husband that Mr Reggie toilet paper really was much softer and more absorbent than any other leading brand. 'Feel it, honey,' she said, rubbing the roll up and down across her husband's cheek. 'Soft,' admitted hubby. 'Just like you.' Cut to a shot of the couple in the clinches.

Reggie almost wept with frustration. Frank Gladstone hadn't even bothered to show him the storyboards for the ad. And the commercial, as insipid as it was, reminded him how terribly alone he was, now that Rah Rah was gone. They spoke only rarely, and Reggie preferred it that way. He found it too painful to be reminded of all the money he had invested in the boy, only to be abandoned by the ungrateful wretch. Still, he longed for him, hoped he would come back.

He stared listlessly at the screen, oblivious to what was being shown. Towels and toilet paper? How had it come to this? He'd been such a bright, shining star. Now even Mitchell Barton hardly bothered to take his calls.

Life could be terribly cruel, he thought. He hauled himself off the sofa and went to pee. Walking back down the hall to the sitting room, he was sure he heard Rah Rah's voice. His heart jumped. Could it be? But how . . .? He rearranged his face and casually sauntered into the room, prepared to accuse Rah Rah of entering his home without his permission.

'You can't do this to me. I'll tell Mother!' Rah Rah shouted with rage at the man who played his older brother on 'Upper East,' NBC's new series about a group of wealthy and would-be-wealthy Wall Streeters.

Reggie sagged down in a chair and stared disconsolately at the screen. He'd forgotten Rah Rah's show was on this evening. Now the older brother was accusing Rah Rah of being an ungrateful hustler who thought of no one but himself.

Talk about typecasting, Reggie thought bitterly. *That must have been the easiest audition he ever had.*

In a preview of next week's program, Rah Rah was about to make love to his brother's girlfriend. Reggie's chest constricted with pain. He flipped to the ten o'clock news, where a reporter was gushing about the Coty Awards.

'. . . and tonight's star, of course, is Countess Dani diPortanova,' the reporter proclaimed, cutting to a shot of Dani, emerging barefoot from her limousine.

The pain worsened. Reggie wondered whether he was having a heart attack. Perversely, he forced himself to listen as the reporter droned on about how the countess had made believers out of even the most cynical followers of fashion . . . had overcome personal tragedy after the death of her handsome young husband . . . had just scored yet another triumph by being chosen as the exclusive designer for 'The Seducers.' And then a quick interview with Dani herself, babbling about how deeply honored she was to join the exalted ranks of designers she'd admired for so long.

'Fuck you, bitch!' Reggie screamed. He silenced the TV with a click of the remote button. He clutched at his chest. The woman was poison. She was killing him. With all his heart he wished he could finally, once and for all, silence the Countess of Seventh Avenue.

* * *

528

The Coty ceremonies drew to a close in a flourish of ardent tributes and applause. Dani accepted the congratulations of her friends and admirers, and smiled one last time for the television cameras. She scanned the audience again, looking for Monika, then hurried out to her limo. She wanted to get home as quickly as possible. Home to Kyle.

Within minutes, they were uptown and coming out of the park onto Central Park West when Dani said, 'Joe, would you take a right and head over to Columbus and Seventy-fifth?'

'A Häagen-Dazs run, huh?'

'How well you know me.' She laughed. As eager as she was to get home, it would take only a couple of minutes to pick up some ice cream . . . for afterward.

The limo pulled up in front of the red and white Häagen-Dazs store, and Dani, as usual, jumped out before Joe came to a full stop.

In the last few years the Upper West Side, and Columbus Avenue in particular, had undergone a transformation. Elegantly dressed people in fancy limos were not an uncommon sight. Nevertheless, more than a few passersby stared in astonishment as one of the city's best-known women strode into the ice-cream store.

'Hi,' Dani said to the high school kid behind the counter.

The boy stared nervously at the beautiful woman standing in front of him. 'Can I help you?' he asked, his voice cracking.

'Yeah, just a second.' She scrutinized the flavors listed on the board on the back wall. Chocolate chip or vanilla Swiss almond? Rum raisin or maple walnut? Boysenberry or peach?

She tried to remember what Kyle liked. In California they'd been watching a movie and eating strawberry ice cream in bed when he'd all of a sudden spooned some of the rich, creamy ice cream over her breasts and licked it off as it melted around her nipples.

Not that they needed sexual stimulants to ignite the electricity that flowed between them. Kyle . . . he had reached across the chasm of their cultural and emotional differences and touched her heart.

Just thinking about his smile and the touch of his hands made her almost go limp with love and longing. How lucky she was that they had found each other.

'Ma'am . . .'

She blushed. 'Uh . . . I'll take a pint each of strawberry and vanilla Swiss almond, please.'

She paid the boy, smiled her thanks, and hurried back to the limo.

Five minutes later they pulled up in front of the Dakota.

'Good night. I won't need you tomorrow till about eleven,' Dani told Joe.

The Dakota guard opened the car door. He looked almost startled to see her. She asked whether Mr Lord had come in yet.

No, he told her.

Disappointed, she passed through the courtyard and took the elevator up to her apartment. The ice cream went in the freezer. She was glad the servants were off tonight. She and Kyle would have the whole place to themselves. She hoped he wouldn't be much longer. She debated whether to take a bath now or wait until Kyle arrived. A shower, she decided. Then, later, she and Kyle could drink champagne in the Jacuzzi.

As she undressed, she thought of Kyle. She stared at herself in the mirror and saw, behind the reflection of her naked body, a figure standing in the shadowy darkness behind her. The figure took a step forward . . .

And then she saw the gun.

A burglary . . . she'd walked in on a burglary. She had to stay calm, had to stay in control.

The intruder took another step into the dim light cast by the lamp on her night table.

It was a woman, wearing one of the dresses that had made Dani a millionaire.

'I have to kill you, Dani, I'm sorry,' the woman said in a strange, hoarse whisper. 'So terribly, terribly sorry.'

'Do you want money?' Dani asked, her voice betraying her fear. Her eyes were fixed on the gun in the woman's hand. *Don't shoot me*, she pleaded silently. *Please don't kill me*.

Willing herself to stop shaking, she turned around and took a step closer to the woman. 'What do you want from me? How did you get in here?'

The intruder backed away from the light, still pointing the gun directly at Dani. 'I walked right in. The guard thought I was you.'

'I can give you anything you want, just don't hurt me,' Dani pleaded. She peered through the shadows, trying to see the intruder's face. 'I know you, don't I? Who *are* you?'

The woman raised the gun and pointed.

Not stopping to think, Dani grabbed her gown from her bed and flung it in her attacker's face. She sprang, smashing up against her, trying to grab for the gun, which went skidding across the highly polished hardwood floor.

Both women lunged for it.

Kyle's shoot dragged on longer than he'd expected. But he jumped in his car and was on his way the instant the director, who would have worked all night had Kyle's contract allowed it, yelled, 'That's a wrap for today.'

He was uptown in no time flat. He gave his name to the

guard, who said, 'She's expecting you,' and whisked him through the electronically locked inner gate.

He waited impatiently for the elevator to open on five, then fished in his pocket for the set of keys Dani had given him. He had just inserted the first key in the top lock when he heard a crash from somewhere inside the apartment.

Both women were rolling on the floor, flailing their arms, kicking at each other. The intruder grabbed Dani by her hair, but Dani lunged forward on her hands and knees and finally . . . her fingers closed around the gun.

She turned on the woman whose face was just inches away from her own, whose eyes gleamed with madness as she tried to knock the gun away.

Panting for breath, Dani jerked away as the intruder lunged forward.

'Please don't make me do this.' Dani sobbed convulsively.

The woman lunged closer.

'Please don't!' Dani begged, taking uncertain aim . . .

Kyle heard the gunshot and yelled Dani's name as he raced down the hall toward the master bedroom. He found her, crouched naked in the doorway of her bedroom, sobbing over a woman's body. A gun lay on the floor next to them. Blood was spreading down the front of the woman's dress. Her gray eyes were wide open, and a strand of her long hair obscured the lower half of her face.

Dani wept as she brushed away the hair.

'Dani,' the woman whispered weakly, coughing blood.

Dani bent closer to hear.

'Dani, I loved you so much.'

'I'm sorry.' Dani sobbed. 'I never meant – ' She gently pulled the wig away and stroked Jack Andrews's forehead.

'Too late, Dani. But you were going . . . to leave me.' He took a shallow breath. 'If I couldn't have you, then no one would,' he rasped.

He coughed again and more blood trickled out of his mouth.

And then his eyes grew vacant as he stared into the afterlife.

Epilogue

New York, 1984

Three days had passed since that terrible night when Dani shot and killed Jack Andrews in self-defense. Three days of talking to the police, answering questions, trying to piece together the puzzle of why Jack had tried to kill her.

Dani was racked with guilt, remembering Jack's last words: 'If I couldn't have you, then no one would.' She had misled him. Now he was dead – and she had only herself to blame for his death. She should have foreseen the misunderstanding and prevented it.

'No,' Kyle reassured her again and again, never letting go of her hand.

The police echoed his assurances. Slowly a picture had begun to emerge of a deeply troubled young man. There had been problems with his mother and stepfather. He'd been expelled from his prep school in Seattle for punching a girl in the nose.

More recently, a woman, a customer at the Hellfire Club, had filed an assault charge against Jack because he'd so brutally whipped her that she'd had to spend the night in the hospital. Apparently Jack was a regular at the club, the police told Dani. She was shocked by the revelation. But more shocking still was their theory that Jack might have been Lance's assailant. They had no hard evidence to tie him to the attack, just bits and pieces of information that pointed in his direction, including Lance's memory of what the assailant had whispered to him: 'Your boss's days are numbered.'

The press arrived at the Dakota just minutes after the police. Through Kyle, Dani issued a statement: 'I am deeply saddened by the terrible tragedy of Jack Andrews's death.'

'That's it?' screamed the reporters. 'But when do we get to talk to Dani in person?'

For once, Dani wasn't giving any interviews. This was one story they would have to write all on their own.

Rick Flood called as soon as he heard the story on the morning news. He came rushing over to the apartment and talked to the cops, who wanted to hear any information he might have about his former roommate. But it had been years since he'd spoken to Jack, and they'd never been more than casual friends, even when they were living together.

'He was an okay kind of guy,' Rick told the detective who interviewed him. 'Not someone you could ever really get to know. Kind of kept things in, you know what I mean?'

Rick volunteered to stay with Dani while Kyle went downtown for a couple of hours after lunch to pacify his director. He was trying to distract her with tales of his life on the road when Monika came rushing into the living room.

'I got here as soon as I could,' she said, her normally pale face ashen. 'Are you all right? Omigod, Dani, I was so frightened for you . . .'

She burst into tears of relief and stared numbly at Dani, who was holding her hand and saying, 'It's okay, I'm fine. Don't worry.' Rick was holding her other hand, but Monika was too tired and confused to ask how he happened to be here.

The events of the past twenty-four hours were just now catching up with Monika.

Faced with the mob's ultimatum, she'd flown yesterday

afternoon – was it just yesterday? – to Zurich, then on to Salzburg, to beg Karola to lend her the money to repay her debt. Pride had given way to terror and desperation. Certainly not even Karola would turn her back on her own daughter, when it was truly a matter of life and death. Monika had chewed her nails to the quick, wondering how best to approach Karola, with whom she hadn't spoken in ten years.

When the taxi pulled up in front of the house where she'd spent so many unhappy years, her hands were icy cold with tension. 'I shouldn't be too long,' she told the driver. 'Please wait for me.'

The butler who opened the door stared at her in shock. 'Fräulein Monika!' he exclaimed.

'Shh,' Monika said. 'I want to surprise my mother. Is she here?'

'Upstairs,' the butler told her. 'In her bedroom.'

Her heart thumping so loudly she was sure Karola could hear her coming, Monika marched upstairs, feeling as if she were about to face a firing squad. She stopped short in the doorway of her mother's room.

Karola was standing on a low stool in front of a mirror, modeling an elegant pale ivory silk suit. Her seamstress knelt on the floor beside her, pinning up the hem.

'Mother?' Monika said uncertainly.

Karola glanced her way, then immediately returned her gaze to the mirror. 'I don't know why you're here, but I want you out. Immediately!'

'Mother, please, I must talk to you,' Monika said, coming into the room. 'Please, won't you listen to me for just a minute?'

Still refusing to look her way, Karola grimly replied, 'I suppose you heard about the wedding and now you think that – '

Monika was totally bewildered. She hadn't the slightest

idea what Karola was talking about. 'Wedding? What wedding?'

Karola snorted. 'Don't play innocent! My wedding, of course.' She gestured at her silk suit, as if that should explain everything.

Her legs trembling, Monika sank down on Karola's bed. 'You're getting married? But what about my . . . my father? Did he . . . is he – '

'Get off the bed!' Karola snapped. 'What about your father? Did you think I had him shot, you stupid girl? We're divorced. Finally, after all these years, the lawyers arranged it for us. And I'm getting married again next week to Salim Abu-Faud. Perhaps you've heard of him?'

Monika vaguely remembered reading about the wealthy Salim Abu-Faud. Whatever attraction he held for Karola, Monika was sure it had more to do with money than love or companionship.

'Mother,' she began again, but Karola cut her off.

'Don't you *dare* call me that! You disgraced me. Disgraced us all. I can never forgive you. Now get out of my sight this instant before I have my bodyguards throw you out!' With that, Karola turned on her seamstress. 'Hurry up, I don't have all day.'

The audience was over.

Monika leadenly retraced her steps down the long marble stairway, nodded to the butler, and whispered, 'When you see my brother, please give him my love.'

'Certainly, Fräulein Monika,' the butler said pityingly, wondering whether he should tell her that Herr Dieter was at this very moment only a few feet away in the library. He struggled with his conscience – but his decades-old fear of Karola won out over his compassion for her poor daughter.

'Good-bye, then,' she said softly, knowing she would never again set foot in her mother's home.

She was halfway to the taxi when she heard Dieter calling her name.

'Monika! Monika, wait!' He came running after her. 'I saw you through the window . . . you came for the money, didn't you? I knew you wouldn't let her get away with it!' he exclaimed excitedly.

'Dieter.' She gave him a quick hug. 'I didn't realize you were here. Otherwise I would have waited to see you. But Karola was quite insistent that I leave immediately.' She stared curiously at her brother. 'But how did you know I'd come to ask her for money?'

Dieter glanced nervously toward the house. 'I thought one of the lawyers had contacted you,' he stammered. 'I told her she was wrong not to let you know. I fought for you, Monika. Truly I did.'

'Dieter! What are you talking about? You *must* tell me!' she cried, pulling him away from the house.

And so he did tell her . . . about how their father – whom they hadn't seen in so many years that neither could remember what he looked like – had agreed to the divorce on one condition: that Karola deposit ten million dollars in each of two separate Swiss bank accounts in the names of their two children.

'It probably doesn't seem like very much,' he said apologetically, 'but it seemed only fair you should have it. She wasn't going to tell you: she said you didn't deserve it. We had a terrible argument.'

Poor Dieter. Her heart ached for her brother, who had tried so hard to elude Karola's all-consuming control. He'd wandered the world for years, seeking peace. But inevitably he had returned to Salzburg to live his life as it suited his mother.

Monika quickly got from him the name of the bank in Zurich, and then she said, 'She didn't tell me. You did, Dieter, and that's even better. You've saved my life. You can be proud of that. I can only hope that someday you'll be free of Karola, too.'

He disappeared inside even before her taxi reached the end of the driveway. So that was what it meant to be a von Reich, Monika thought bitterly, gazing out the window of the cab at the familiar sights of her childhood. But she didn't have time to dwell on Karola's cruelty. She flew to Zurich, arranged to have the funds transferred to her account in New York, then immediately caught a flight to Kennedy.

She was en route from the airport to Manhattan, aching with weariness and half asleep in the backseat of the cab, when the driver turned on the radio and she heard the news about Dani: '. . . shot and killed a man, as yet unidentified, in her Upper West Side apartment last night as she – '

'The Dakota,' she ordered the cabbie. 'Hurry, please!'

Roberto found out about Karola's impending marriage at about the same time that Monika stood in her mother's bedroom, watching Karola being fitted for her wedding suit. He had quickly passed through US customs (on a diplomatic visa so that there would be no trouble about the rifle), and was heading for his waiting limousine when he stopped to grab a copy of the New York *Post*.

Crossing through Queens into Manhattan, he read the headlines, then scanned Suzy's column for incriminating items about his daughter-in-law. And read there, instead, the news of Karola von Reich's recent divorce and upcoming marriage to Salim Abu-Faud.

Sure that he had misread the item, he briefly closed his eyes to rest them, then looked again at the newspaper. A strangled sob escaped his lips. By now Karola would have received his telex.

He had bared his soul to her.

She had made a total mockery of his feelings. She hadn't even had the decency to tell him herself. She had kicked him in the balls and would probably laugh at him all the way to the altar.

He glanced listlessly at the briefcase on the seat next to him. What a fool he was to think he could barge into his daughter-in-law's home and frighten her with threats of Italian vengeance if she didn't conduct herself properly.

What difference did it make anyway? He had lost his son. Now he'd lost his mistress. He needed to go home to Benedetta.

'Driver,' he said into the speaker, 'turn around. I've changed my mind. I'm going back to Italy.'

Reggie had slept late and didn't hear the news about the attempt on Dani's life until Mitchell Barton called to get his reaction. To Mitchell's disappointment, Reggie was more horrified than gleeful about the incident. 'But you loathe Dani,' Mitchell reminded him. 'I've even heard you say you'd like to bury the bitch.'

'Please, Mitchell, what do you take me for?' Reggie sniffed. 'I was speaking metaphorically, of course. Tell me, what are the police saying? How did this person get into her apartment?' He hated hearing that even his worst enemy had been attacked in her own home, for fear that *he* might be the next victim. And if an intruder could get past the supposedly excellent security system at the Dakota, then who was to say his doorman and concierge couldn't be similarly outwitted?

'Supposedly she was fucking the guy. They think he must have stolen a set of keys out of her drawer.'

'Oh,' said Reggie, slightly mollified by the fact that Dani had known the intruder. Still, one couldn't be too careful. He wondered whether he should buy a guard dog, a big black Rottweiler that barked a lot and was trained to attack on command. He didn't much like dogs, but he could get Lydia to walk the animal. 'What else are they saying?'

'Read the papers, Reggie. The Countess diPortanova's story is all over the front pages.'

If he was looking to dish, Mitchell would have done better to call Bunny. Though publicly she professed to be deeply distressed on behalf of her good friend and employer, privately she wished Jack Andrews had accomplished what he'd set out to do. The poor dead soul deserved an A for effort. Imagine having the nerve to try to kill someone!

But how she wished Dani felt as miserable as she did. She was quite sure she hadn't helped her condition by dragging herself out of bed and over to FIT to watch Dani smilingly accept her award. After the ceremony, she had rushed over to where Dani stood talking to the press. She'd inched her way through the swirl of well-wishers, jockeying to get close enough to be included in some of the photographs. 'Hi,' she'd said as she waved. 'Hi, Dani, congratulations!'

But depend on Dani to hog all the limelight instead of acknowledging Bunny and the many contributions she'd made to Dani's singular success. She'd flashed Bunny a quick smile, waved, then turned back to the reporters. Not a word about Barbara Hester, her invaluable associate, without whose efforts . . .

Too agitated to sleep, Bunny had lain awake all night, asking herself how far she was prepared to go to achieve her goals. By morning she had the answer. She called the Pierre and asked for Mr Moore's room. Since the morning they returned together to New York, he had left dozens of messages on her machine. She hadn't bothered to return any of his calls.

'Yeah?' he answered the phone in his typically ungracious way.

'It's Barbara,' she said, hoping he would at least apologize for what he'd done to her.

'Hey, babes, hope you're not still mad at me for the other night. I guess I got a little carried away. So, how about what happened to your boss? Pretty wild, huh?'

Bunny pretended not to know what Stan was talking about. No, she hadn't heard what happened to Dani, nor did she care, she informed Stan. She was interested only in what happened to her. She wanted to leave Countess Dani. She wanted Stan to bankroll her so she could open up her own company.

'What's it gonna cost me?' Stan wanted to know.

Bunny gulped. 'A million dollars. But I swear, Stan, I'll make it worth your while.'

'Yeah, sure I'll lend you the money. And you know how you can thank me, Barbara?' Stan chuckled.

She was afraid to ask. She could hear him drawing on his cigar as he got ready to deliver the punch line.

'With a million-dollar fuck.'

The following spring, Countess Dani, Inc., presented its first couture collection, the Born Rich line. 'You don't have to be born rich to dress rich,' Dani suggested to her would-be customers in what struck many as an unusually demure (for Dani diPortanova) series of ads.

She and Kyle left for Australia a week after the spring show. They swam in the Indian Ocean at Perth, toured the Aboriginal Reserve in the Great Victoria Desert, rode camels through the Macdonnell Ranges, and got married on Kyle's father's cattle ranch. Determined to avoid a media circus at her second wedding, Dani didn't tell anyone but Monika and Maurice that she was getting married again.

To her surprise, Maurice insisted that he and Eunice be present. 'I missed your first wedding,' he ruefully reminded her. 'Thank goodness I'm getting a second chance.'

The wedding, very small and private, was held outdoors in the garden. Dani wore roses in her hair and a pale pink silk sheath studded with Mikimoto pearls down one side of the shirred bodice.

Maurice offered the first toast. 'To the health and happiness of my daughter and my new son-in-law. May I live long enough to see my first grandchild.'

Dani and Kyle exchanged secret smiles. She was already three months pregnant.

In Sydney, each of them received a telegram.

Kyle's said, 'Final cut of film just finished stop Studio going crazy stop They smell a hit stop Universal deal concluded for fifteen million for three pix stop Congratulations to both of you stop Love Sam.'

Dani's said, 'Great news stop Bergdorf's and Neiman's ordered $250,000 from couture collection stop We miss you stop Can't wait for you to get home and throw us a wedding stop We are very lucky *ja*? stop Love Monika and Rick.'

Ja, Monika. *Very* lucky.